FAULT LINES

FAULT LINES

Stories of Divorce

Collected and Edited by

Caitlin Shetterly

BERKLEY BOOKS, NEW YORK

A Berkley Book
Published by The Berkley Publishing Group
A division of Penguin Putnam Inc.
375 Hudson Street
New York, New York 10014

This book is an original publication of The Berkley Publishing Group.

PRINTING HISTORY
Berkley hardcover edition / September 2001

Visit our website at
www.penguinputnam.com

Library of Congress Cataloging-in-Publication Data

Fault lines : stories of divorce / collected and edited by Caitlin Shetterly.
p. cm.
ISBN 0-425-18161-8
1. Divorce—Fiction.   2. Short stories, American.   I. Shetterly, Caitlin.

PS648.D58   F38   2001
813'.0108355—dc21

2001035972

PRINTED IN THE UNITED STATES OF AMERICA

10   9   8   7   6   5   4   3   2   1

Thank you to all the people who made this possible:

David McCormick; John Updike; Richard Ford; Anthony Walton; Cressida Leyshon; Lisa Considine; Christine Zika; Amanda Margulies; Craig D. Burke; Fiona Capuano; Isaiah Sheffer and Katherine Minton; Ken and Cherie Mason; Mary, Marvin and Melorra Sochet; Stacey Tesseyman; Vanessa Wales; Victoria C. Rowan; and Hannah Pingree.

Thank you to the writers: Without your words, without your spirits, this book could never have been.

And thank you, David, my partner in life and love, for your unconditional support.

Contents

INTRODUCTION

Whether they are part of home or home is part of them is not a question children are prepared to answer.

—William Maxwell,
from *So Long, See You Tomorrow*

This book began in a dorm room one morning when I was in my first year of college. I sat huddled on my thin bed, the red quilt my mother had made for me when I was six draped around my shoulders. I was reading John Updike's story "Separating." As I read, I wept. I felt that I was finally understood—that the devastating anguish I felt from my parents' separation was not unique. For the next three years, as my parents divorced—disappeared into their own personal hells and then reappeared as strangely new people— I found myself drawn to stories of divorce. I discovered comfort and understanding in other lives, which have also been irrevocably altered by marital and familial heartbreak. As I read, my grief at the dissolution of my family began to feel, in the words of Walker Percy, "certified." Later, when I wrote my senior thesis on "Fathers and Children in Divorce in John Updike's Maples stories and Richard Ford's novels *The Sportswriter* and *Independence Day*," I began to define and name a genre of divorce literature.

As I was growing up, my mother told me that I would find my best friends in books. When I look back, I realize that literature in our household was probably the closest thing to religion. And, although I had many intense friendships with real people in my ado-

1

lescent and teenage years, I often stayed up all night reading novels. Sometimes, over breakfast the next morning, I would share plot summaries with my parents and even read aloud long passages that I believed were necessary for them to understand whatever book I was reading. When my parents' marriage finally came unglued, I realized that I could still find comfort in books; but it was not until I began to make a serious study of divorce literature that I discovered the characters and themes that I needed to help me understand who I was, despite my fractured family.

The architecture of a family—both real and symbolic—is a powerful and complicated thing. As a child, I used to think that if we lived in a different house, maybe we would be happier and maybe my parents wouldn't fight. I spent long afternoons in my room drawing plans on colored construction paper for the home I dreamed would keep us a family. Later, in college and briefly afterward, I studied architecture because I thought that if I could design a house that better accommodated a modern family, I might work against the divorce culture. This seems silly now. I was asking more of both myself and architecture than either could deliver. Instead, I began to build a house, a home, out of stories. I collected them, hoarded them, and recommended them.

This collection begins with John Cheever's story "The Season of Divorce." Although no one actually gets divorced in this story, I believe it is here that the experience of divorce takes its place as one of the central themes in American life and literature. Cheever's portrait of a marriage, which stays intact despite the fact that something has broken and cannot be repaired, is an unforgettable introduction into the profound territory of divorce literature.

Divorce is a personal journey, a disillusioning rite of passage for more than two million Americans each year. In these pages you will not necessarily find resolution—this, after all, is no self-help book—but instead, a fuller understanding of the human condition.

For this job, literature is uniquely qualified. The voices on these pages speak directly and unflinchingly to our changing cultural understanding of family. Richard Ford once wrote, "[G]reat books, like great friends, are to be shared." The stories in this collection are among the best friends I've ever had.

Caitlin Shetterly
New York City, August 2000

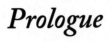

Prologue

John Cheever

———

The Season of Divorce

My wife has brown hair, dark eyes, and a gentle disposition. Because of her gentle disposition, I sometimes think that she spoils the children. She can't refuse them anything. They always get around her. Ethel and I have been married for ten years. We both come from Morristown, New Jersey, and I can't even remember when I first met her. Our marriage has always seemed happy and resourceful to me. We live in a walkup in the East Fifties. Our son, Carl, who is six, goes to a good private school, and our daughter, who is four, won't go to school until next year. We often find fault with the way we were educated, but we seem to be struggling to raise our children along the same lines, and when the time comes, I suppose they'll go to the same schools and colleges that we went to.

Ethel graduated from a woman's college in the East, and then went for a year to the University of Grenoble. She worked for a year in New York after returning from France, and then we were married. She once hung her diploma above the kitchen sink, but it was a short-lived joke and I don't know where the diploma is now. Ethel is cheerful and adaptable, as well as gentle, and we both come from that enormous stratum of the middle class that is distinguished by its ability to recall better times. Lost money is so much a part of our lives that I am sometimes reminded of expatriates, of a group who have adapted themselves energetically to some alien soil but who are reminded, now and then, of the escarpments of their native coast. Because our lives are confined by my modest salary, the surface of Ethel's life is easy to describe.

She gets up at seven and turns the radio on. After she is dressed, she rouses the children and cooks the breakfast. Our son has to be walked to the school bus at eight o'clock. When Ethel returns from this trip, Carol's hair has to be braided. I leave the house at eight-thirty, but I know that every move that Ethel makes for the rest of the day will be determined by the housework, the cooking, the shopping, and the demands of the children. I know that on Tuesdays and Thursdays she will be at the A&P between eleven and noon, that on every clear afternoon she will be on a certain bench in a playground from three until five, that she cleans the house on Mondays, Wednesdays, and Fridays, and polishes the silver when it rains. When I return at six, she is usually cleaning the vegetables or making some other preparation for dinner. Then when the children have been fed and bathed, when the dinner is ready, when the table in the living room is set with food and china, she stands in the middle of the room as if she has lost or forgotten something, and this moment of reflection is so deep that she will not hear me if I speak to her, or the children if they call. Then it is over. She lights the four white candles in their silver sticks, and we sit down to a supper of corned-beef hash or some other modest fare.

We go out once or twice a week and entertain about once a month. Because of practical considerations, most of the people we see live in our neighborhood. We often go around the corner to the parties given by a generous couple named Newsome. The Newsomes' parties are large and confusing, and the arbitrary impulses of friendship are given a free play.

We became attached at the Newsomes' one evening, for reasons that I've never understood, to a couple named Dr. and Mrs.

Trencher. I think that Mrs. Trencher was the aggressor in this friendship, and after our first meeting she telephoned Ethel three or four times. We went to their house for dinner, and they came to our house, and sometimes in the evening when Dr. Trencher was walking their old dachshund, he would come up for a short visit. He seemed like a pleasant man to have around. I've heard other doctors say that he's a good physician. The Trenchers are about thirty; at least he is. She is older.

I'd say that Mrs. Trencher is a plain woman, but her plainness is difficult to specify. She is small, she has a good figure and regular features, and I suppose that the impression of plainness arises from some inner modesty, some needlessly narrow view of her chances. Dr. Trencher doesn't smoke or drink, and I don't know whether there's any connection or not, but the coloring in his slender face is fresh—his cheeks are pink, and his blue eyes are clear and strong. He has the singular optimism of a well-adjusted physician—the feeling that death is a chance misfortune and that the physical world is merely a field for conquest. In the same way that his wife seems plain, he seems young.

The Trenchers live in a comfortable and unpretentious private house in our neighborhood. The house is old-fashioned; its living rooms are large, its halls are gloomy, and the Trenchers don't seem to generate enough human warmth to animate the place, so that you sometimes take away from them, at the end of an evening, an impression of many empty rooms. Mrs. Trencher is noticeably attached to her possessions—her clothes, her jewels, and the ornaments she's bought for the house—and to Fräulein, the old dachshund. She feeds Fräulein scraps from the table, furtively, as if she has been forbidden to do this, and after dinner Fräulein lies beside her on the sofa. With the play of green light from a television set on her drawn features and her thin hands stroking Fräulein, Mrs. Trencher looked to me one evening like a good-hearted and miserable soul.

Mrs. Trencher began to call Ethel in the mornings for a talk or to ask her for lunch or a matinée. Ethel can't go out in the day and she claims to dislike long telephone conversations. She complained that Mrs. Trencher was a tireless and aggressive gossip. Then late one afternoon Dr. Trencher appeared at the playground where Ethel takes our two children. He was walking by, and he saw her and sat with her until it was time to take the children home. He came again a few days later, and then his visits with Ethel in the playground, she told me, became a regular thing. Ethel thought that perhaps he didn't have many patients and that with nothing to do he was happy to talk with anyone. Then, when we were washing dishes one night, Ethel said thoughtfully that Trencher's attitude toward her seemed strange. "He stares at me," she said. "He sighs and stares at me." I know what my wife looks like in the playground. She wears an old tweed coat, overshoes, and Army gloves, and a scarf is tied under her chin. The playground is a fenced and paved lot between a slum and the river. The picture of the well-dressed, pink-cheeked doctor losing his heart to Ethel in this environment was hard to take seriously. She didn't mention him then for several days, and I guessed that he had stopped his visits. Ethel's birthday came at the end of the month, and I forgot about it, but when I came home that evening, there were a lot of roses in the living room. They were a birthday present from Trencher, she told me. I was cross at myself for having forgotten her birthday, and Trencher's roses made me angry. I asked her if she'd seen him recently.

"Oh, yes," she said, "he still comes to the playground nearly every afternoon. I haven't told you, have I? He's made his declaration. He loves me. He can't live without me. He'd walk through fire to hear the notes of my voice." She laughed. "That's what he said."

"When did he say this?"

"At the playground. And walking home. Yesterday."

"How long has he known?"

"That's the funny part about it," she said. "He knew before he met me at the Newsomes' that night. He saw me waiting for a crosstown bus about three weeks before that. He just saw me and he said that he knew then, the minute he saw me. Of course, he's crazy."

I was tired that night and worried about taxes and bills, and I could think of Trencher's declaration only as a comical mistake. I felt that he was a captive of financial and sentimental commitments, like every other man I know, and that he was no more free to fall in love with a strange woman he saw on a street corner than he was to take a walking trip through French Guiana or to recommence his life in Chicago under an assumed name. His declaration, the scene in the playground, seemed to me to be like those chance meetings that are a part of the life of any large city. A blind man asks you to help him across the street, and as you are about to leave him, he seizes your arm and regales you with a passionate account of his cruel and ungrateful children; or the elevator man who is taking you up to a party turns to you suddenly and says that his grandson has infantile paralysis. The city is full of accidental revelation, half-heard cries for help, and strangers who will tell you everything at the first suspicion of sympathy, and Trencher seemed to me like the blind man or the elevator operator. His declaration had no more bearing on the business of our lives than these interruptions.

Mrs. Trencher's telephone conversations had stopped, and we had stopped visiting the Trenchers, but sometimes I would see him in the morning on the crosstown bus when I was late going to work. He seemed understandably embarrassed whenever he saw me, but the bus was always crowded at that time of day, and it was no effort to avoid one another. Also, at about this time I made a mistake in business and lost several thousand dollars for the firm I work for. There was not much chance of my losing my job, but the possibility was always at the back of my mind, and under this and under the continuous urgency of making more money the memory of the eccentric Doctor was buried. Three weeks passed without Ethel's mentioning him, and then one evening, when I was reading, I noticed Ethel standing at the window looking down into the street.

"He's really there," she said.

"Who?"

"Trencher. Come here and see."

I went to the window. There were only three people on the sidewalk across the street. It was dark and it would have been difficult to recognize anyone, but because one of them, walking toward the corner, had a dachshund on a leash, it could have been Trencher.

"Well, what about it?" I said. "He's just walking the dog."

"But he wasn't walking the dog when I first looked out of the window. He was just standing there, staring up at this building. That's what he says he does. He says that he comes over here and stares up at our lighted windows."

"When did he say this?"

"At the playground."

"I thought you went to another playground."

"Oh, I do, I do, but he followed me. He's crazy, darling. I know he's crazy, but I feel so sorry for him. He says that he spends night after night looking up at our windows. He says that he sees me everywhere—the back of my head, my eyebrows—that he hears my voice. He says that he's never compromised in his life and that he isn't going to compromise about this. I feel so sorry for him, darling. I can't help but feel sorry for him."

For the first time then, the situation seemed serious to me, for in his helplessness I knew that he might have touched an inestimable and wayward passion that Ethel shares with some other women—an inability to refuse any cry for help, to refuse any voice that sounds pitiable. It is not a reasonable passion, and I would almost rather have had her desire him than pity him. When we were getting ready for bed that night, the telephone rang, and when I picked it up and said hello, no one answered. Fifteen minutes later, the telephone rang again, and when there was no answer this time,

I began to shout and swear at Trencher, but he didn't reply—there wasn't even the click of a closed circuit—and I felt like a fool. Because I felt like a fool, I accused Ethel of having led him on, of having encouraged him, but these accusations didn't affect her, and when I finished them, I felt worse, because I knew that she was innocent, and that she had to go out on the street to buy groceries and air the children, and that there was no force of law that could keep Trencher from waiting for her there, or from staring up at our lights.

We went to the Newsomes' one night the next week, and while we were taking off our coats, I heard Trencher's voice. He left a few minutes after we arrived, but his manner—the sad glance he gave Ethel, the way he sidestepped me, the sorrowful way that he refused the Newsomes when they asked him to stay longer, and the gallant attentions he showed his miserable wife—made me angry. Then I happened to notice Ethel and saw that her color was high, that her eyes were bright, and that while she was praising Mrs. Newsome's new shoes, her mind was not on what she was saying. When we came home that night, the baby-sitter told us crossly that neither of the children had slept. Ethel took their temperatures. Carol was all right, but the boy had a fever of a hundred and four. Neither of us got much sleep that night, and in the morning Ethel called me at the office to say that Carl had bronchitis. Three days later, his sister came down with it.

For the next two weeks, the sick children took up most of our time. They had to be given medicine at eleven in the evening and again at three in the morning, and we lost a lot of sleep. It was impossible to ventilate or clean the house, and when I came in, after walking through the cold from the bus stop, it stank of cough syrups and tobacco, fruit cores and sickbeds. There were blankets and pillows, ashtrays, and medicine glasses everywhere. We divided the work of sickness reasonably and took turns at getting up in the night, but I often fell asleep at my desk during the day, and after dinner Ethel would fall asleep in a chair in the living room. Fatigue seems to differ for adults and children only in that adults recognize it and so are not overwhelmed by something they can't name; but even with a name for it they are overwhelmed, and when we were tired, we were unreasonable, cross, and the victims of transcendent depressions. One evening after the worst of the sickness was over, I came home and found some roses in the living room. Ethel said that Trencher had brought them. She hadn't let him in. She had closed the door in his face. I took the roses and threw them out. We didn't quarrel. The children went to sleep at nine, and a few minutes after nine I went to bed. Some time later, something woke me.

A light was burning in the hall. I got up. The children's room and the living room were dark. I found Ethel in the kitchen sitting at the table, drinking coffee.

"I've made some fresh coffee," she said. "Carol felt croupy again, so I steamed her. They're both asleep now."

"How long have you been up?"

"Since half past twelve," she said. "What time is it?"

"Two."

I poured myself a cup of coffee and sat down. She got up from the table and rinsed her cup and looked at herself in a mirror that hangs above the sink. It was a windy night. A dog was wailing somewhere in an apartment below ours, and a loose radio antenna was brushing against the kitchen window.

"It sounds like a branch," she said.

In the bare kitchen light, meant for peeling potatoes and washing dishes, she looked very tired.

"Will the children be able to go out tomorrow?"

"Oh, I hope so," she said. "Do you realize that I haven't been out of this apartment in over two weeks?" She spoke bitterly and this startled me.

"It hasn't been quite two weeks."

"It's been over two weeks," she said.

"Well, let's figure it out," I said. "The children were taken sick on a Saturday night. That was the fourth. Today is the—"

"Stop it, stop it," she said. "I know how long it's been. I haven't had my shoes on in two weeks."

"You make it sound pretty bad."

"It is. I haven't had on a decent dress or fixed my hair."

"It could be worse."

"My mother's cooks had a better life."

"I doubt that."

"My mother's cooks had a better life," she said loudly.

"You'll wake the children."

"My mother's cooks had a better life. They had pleasant rooms. No one could come into the kitchen without their permission." She knocked the coffee grounds into the garbage and began to wash the pot.

"How long was Trencher here this afternoon?"

"A minute. I've told you."

"I don't believe it. He was in here."

"He was not. I didn't let him in. I didn't let him in because I looked so badly. I didn't want to discourage him."

"Why not?"

"I don't know. He may be a fool. He may be insane but the things he's told me have made me feel marvellously, he's made me feel marvellously."

"Do you want to go?"

"Go? Where would I go?" She reached for the purse that is kept in the kitchen to pay for groceries and counted out of it two dollars and thirty-five cents. "Ossining? Montclair?"

"I mean with Trencher."

"I don't know, I don't know," she said, "but who can say that I shouldn't? What harm would it do? What good would it do? Who knows. I love the children but that isn't enough, that isn't nearly enough. I wouldn't hurt them, but would I hurt them so much if I left you? Is divorce so dreadful and of all the things that hold a marriage together how many of them are good?" She sat down at the table.

"In Grenoble," she said, "I wrote a long paper on Charles Stuart in French. A professor at the University of Chicago wrote me a letter. I couldn't read a French newspaper without a dictionary today, I don't have the time to follow any newspaper, and I am ashamed of my incompetence, ashamed of the way I look. Oh, I guess I love you, I do love the children, but I love myself, I love my life, it has some value and some promise for me and Trencher's roses make me feel that I'm losing this, that I'm losing my self-respect. Do you know what I mean, do you understand what I mean?"

"He's crazy," I said.

"Do you know what I mean? Do you understand what I mean?"

"No," I said. "No."

Carl woke up then and called for his mother. I told Ethel to go to bed. I turned out the kitchen light and went into the children's room.

The children felt better the next day, and since it was Sunday, I took them for a walk. The afternoon sun was clement and pure, and only the colored shadows made me remember that it was midwinter, that the cruise ships were returning, and that in another week jonquils would be twenty-five cents a bunch. Walking down Lexington Avenue, we heard the drone bass of a church organ sound from the sky, and we and the others on the sidewalk looked up in piety and bewilderment, like a devout and stupid congregation, and saw a formation of heavy bombers heading for the sea. As it got late, it got cold and clear and still, and on the stillness the waste from the smokestacks along the East River seemed to articulate, as legibly as the Pepsi-Cola plane, whole words and sentences. Halcyon. Disaster. They were hard to make out. It seemed the ebb of the year—an evil day for gastritis, sinus, and respiratory disease—and remembering other winters, the markings of the light convinced me that it was the season of divorce. It was a long afternoon, and I brought the children in before dark.

I think that the seriousness of the day affected the children, and when they returned to the house, they were quiet. The seriousness of it kept coming to me with the feeling that this change, like a phenomenon of speed, was affecting our watches as well as our hearts. I tried to remember the willingness with which Ethel had followed my regiment during the war, from West Virginia to the Carolinas and Oklahoma, and the day coaches and rooms she had lived in, and the street in San Francisco where I said goodbye to her before I left the country, but I could not put any of this into words, and neither of us found anything to say. Some time after dark, the children were bathed and put to bed, and we sat down to our supper. At about nine o'clock, the doorbell rang, and when I answered it and recognized Trencher's voice on the speaking tube, I asked him to come up.

He seemed distraught and exhilarated when he appeared. He stumbled on the edge of the carpet. "I know that I'm not welcome here," he said in a hard voice, as if I were deaf. "I know that you don't like me here. I respect your feelings. This is your home. I respect a man's feelings about his home. I don't usually go to a man's home unless he asks me. I respect your home. I respect your marriage. I respect your children. I think everything ought to be aboveboard. I've come here to tell you that I love your wife."

"Get out," I said.

"You've got to listen to me," he said. "I love your wife. I can't live without her. I've tried and I can't. I've even thought of going away—of moving to the West Coast—but I know that it wouldn't make any difference. I want to marry her. I'm not romantic. I'm matter-of-fact. I'm very matter-of-fact. I know that you have two children and that you don't have much money. I know that there are problems of custody and property and things like that to be settled. I'm not romantic. I'm hard-headed. I've talked this all over with

Mrs. Trencher, and she's agreed to give me a divorce. I'm not un-derhanded. Your wife can tell you that. I realize all the practical as-pects that have to be considered—custody, property, and so forth. I have plenty of money. I can give Ethel everything she needs, but there are the children. You'll have to decide about them between yourselves. I have a check here. It's made out to Ethel. I want her to take it and go to Nevada. I'm a practical man and I realize that nothing can be decided until she gets her divorce."

"Get out of here!" I said. "Get the hell out of here!"

He started for the door. There was a potted geranium on the mantelpiece, and I threw this across the room at him. It got him in the small of the back and nearly knocked him down. The pot broke on the floor. Ethel screamed. Trencher was still on his way out. Fol-lowing him, I picked up a candlestick and aimed it at his head, but it missed and bounced off the wall. "Get the hell out of here!" I yelled, and he slammed the door. I went back into the living room. Ethel was pale but she wasn't crying. There was a loud rapping on the radiator, a signal from the people upstairs for decorum and si-lence—urgent and expressive, like the communications that pris-oners send to one another through the plumbing in a penitentiary. Then everything was still.

We went to bed, and I woke sometime during the night. I couldn't see the clock on the dresser, so I don't know what time it was. There was no sound from the children's room. The neighbor-hood was perfectly still. There were no lighted windows anywhere. Then I knew that Ethel had wakened me. She was lying on her side of the bed. She was crying.

"Why are you crying?" I asked.

"Why am I crying?" she said. "Why am I crying?" And to hear my voice and to speak set her off again, and she began to sob cru-elly. She sat up and slipped her arms into the sleeves of a wrapper and felt along the table for a package of cigarettes. I saw her wet face when she lighted a cigarette. I heard her moving around in the dark.

"Why do you cry?"

"Why do I cry? Why do I cry?" she asked impatiently. "I cry because I saw an old woman cuffing a little boy on Third Avenue. She was drunk. I can't get it out of my mind." She pulled the quilt off the foot of our bed and wandered with it toward the door. "I cry because my father died when I was twelve and because my mother married a man I detested or thought that I detested. I cry because I had to wear an ugly dress—a hand-me-down dress—to a party twenty years ago, and I didn't have a good time. I cry because of some unkindness that I can't remember. I cry because I'm tired—because I'm tired and I can't sleep." I heard her arrange herself on the sofa and then everything was quiet.

I like to think that the Trenchers have gone away, but I still see Trencher now and then on a crosstown bus when I'm late going to work. I've also seen his wife, going into the neighborhood lending library with Fräulein. She looks old. I'm not good at judging ages, but I wouldn't be surprised to find that Mrs. Trencher is fifteen years older than her husband. Now when I come home in the evenings, Ethel is still sitting on the stool by the sink cleaning vegetables. I go with her into the children's room. The light there is bright. The children have built something out of an orange crate, something preposterous and ascendant, and their sweetness, their compulsion to build, the brightness of the light are reflected perfectly and increased in Ethel's face. Then she feeds them, bathes them, and sets the table, and stands for a moment in the middle of the room, trying to make some connection between the evening and the day. Then it is over. She lights the four candles, and we sit down to our supper.

What Falls Apart

ANN BEATTIE

The Burning House

Freddy Fox is in the kitchen with me. He has just washed and dried an avocado seed I don't want, and he is leaning against the wall, rolling a joint. In five minutes, I will not be able to count on him. However: he started late in the day, and he has already brought in wood for the fire, gone to the store down the road for matches, and set the table. "You mean you'd know this stuff was Limoges even if you didn't turn the plate over?" he called from the dining room. He pretended to be about to throw one of the plates into the kitchen, like a Frisbee. Sam, the dog, believed him and shot up, kicking the rug out behind him and skidding forward before he realized his error; it was like the Road Runner tricking Wile E. Coyote into going over the cliff for the millionth time. His jowls sank in disappointment.

"I see there's a full moon," Freddy says. "There's just nothing that can hold a candle to nature. The moon and the stars, the tides and the sunshine—and we just don't stop for long enough to wonder at it all. We're so engrossed in ourselves." He takes a very long drag on the joint. "We stand and stir the sauce in the pot instead of going to the window and gazing at the moon."

"You don't mean anything personal by that, I assume."

"I love the way you pour cream in a pan. I like to come up behind you and watch the sauce bubble."

"No, thank you," I say. "You're starting late in the day."

"My responsibilities have ended. You don't trust me to help with the cooking, and I've already brought in firewood and run an errand, and this very morning I exhausted myself by taking Mr. Sam jogging with me, down at Putnam Park. You're sure you won't?"

"No, thanks," I say. "Not now, anyway."

"I love it when you stand over the steam coming out of a pan and the hairs around your forehead curl into damp little curls."

My husband, Frank Wayne, is Freddy's half brother. Frank is an accountant. Freddy is closer to me than to Frank. Since Frank talks to Freddy more than he talks to me, however, and since Freddy is totally loyal, Freddy always knows more than I know. It pleases me that he does not know how to stir sauce; he will start talking, his mind will drift, and when next you look the sauce will be lumpy, or boiling away.

Freddy's criticism of Frank is only implied. "What a gracious gesture to entertain his friends on the weekend," he says.

"Male friends," I say.

"I didn't mean that you're the sort of lady who doesn't draw the line. I most certainly did not mean that," Freddy says. "I would even have been surprised if you had taken a toke of this deadly stuff while you were at the stove."

"Okay," I say, and take the joint from him. Half of it is left when I take it. Half an inch is left after I've taken two drags and given it back.

"More surprised still if you'd shaken the ashes into the saucepan."

"You'd tell people I'd done it when they'd finished eating, and I'd be embarrassed. You can do it, though. I wouldn't be embarrassed if it was a story you told on yourself."

"You really understand me," Freddy says. "It's moon madness, but I have to shake just this little bit in the sauce. I have to do it."

He does it.

Frank and Tucker are in the living room. Just a few minutes ago, Frank returned from getting Tucker at the train. Tucker loves to visit. To him, Fairfield County is as mysterious as Alaska. He brought with him from New York a crock of mustard, a jeroboam of champagne, cocktail napkins with a picture of a plane flying over a building on them, twenty egret feathers ("You cannot get them anymore—strictly illegal," Tucker whispered to me), and, under his black cowboy hat with the rhinestone-studded chin strap, a toy frog that hopped when wound. Tucker owns a gallery in SoHo, and Frank keeps his books. Tucker is now stretched out in the living room, visiting with Frank, and Freddy and I are both listening.

". . . so everything I've been told indicates that he lives a purely Jekyll-and-Hyde existence. He's twenty years old, and I can see that since he's still living at home he might not want to flaunt his gayness. When he came into the gallery, he had his hair slicked back—just with water, I got close enough to sniff—and his mother was all but holding his hand. So fresh scrubbed. The stories I'd heard. Anyway, when I called, his father started looking for the number where he could be reached on the Vineyard—very irritated, because I didn't know James, and if I'd just phoned James I could have found him in a flash. He's talking to himself, looking for the number, and I say, 'Oh, did he go to visit friends or—' and his father interrupts and says, 'He was going to a gay pig roast. He's been gone since Monday.' *Just like that.*"

Freddy helps me carry the food out to the table. When we are all at the table, I mention the young artist Tucker was talking about. "Frank says his paintings are really incredible," I say to Tucker.

"Makes Estes look like an abstract expressionist," Tucker says. "I want that boy. I really want that boy."

"You'll get him," Frank says. "You get everybody you go after."

Tucker cuts a small piece of meat. He cuts it small so that he can talk while chewing. "Do I?" he says.

Freddy is smoking at the table, gazing dazedly at the moon centered in the window. "After dinner," he says, putting the back of his hand against his forehead when he sees that I am looking at him, "we must all go to the lighthouse."

"If only *you* painted," Tucker says. "I'd want you."

"You couldn't have me," Freddy snaps. He reconsiders. "That sounded halfhearted, didn't it? Anybody who wants me can have me. This is the only place I can be on Saturday night where somebody isn't hustling me."

"Wear looser pants," Frank says to Freddy.

"This is so much better than some bar that stinks of cigarette smoke and leather. Why do I do it?" Freddy says. "Seriously—do you think I'll ever stop?"

"Let's not be serious," Tucker says.

"I keep thinking of this table as a big boat, with dishes and glasses rocking on it," Freddy says.

He takes the bone from his plate and walks out to the kitchen, dripping sauce on the floor. He walks as though he's on the deck of a wave-tossed ship. "Mr. Sam!" he calls, and the dog springs up from the living-room floor, where he had been sleeping; his toenails on the bare wood floor sound like a wheel spinning in gravel. "You don't have to beg," Freddy says. "Jesus, Sammy—I'm just giving it to you."

"I hope there's a bone involved," Tucker says, rolling his eyes to Frank. He cuts another tiny piece of meat. "I hope your brother does understand why I couldn't keep him on. He was good at what he did, but he also might say just *anything* to a customer. You have to believe me that if I hadn't been extremely embarrassed more than once I never would have let him go."

"He should have finished school," Frank says, sopping up sauce on his bread. "He'll knock around a while longer, then get tired of it and settle down to something."

"You think I died out here?" Freddy calls. "You think I can't hear you?"

"I'm not saying anything I wouldn't say to your face," Frank says.

"I'll tell you what I wouldn't say to your face," Freddy says. "You've got a swell wife and kid and dog, and you're a snob, and you take it all for granted."

Frank puts down his fork, completely exasperated. He looks at me.

"He came to work once this stoned," Tucker says. *"Comprenez-vous?"*

"You like me because you feel sorry for me," Freddy says.

He is sitting on the concrete bench outdoors, in the area that's a garden in the springtime. It is early April now—not quite spring. It's very foggy out. It rained while we were eating, and now it has turned mild. I'm leaning against a tree, across from him, glad it's so dark and misty that I can't look down and see the damage the mud is doing to my boots.

"Who's his girlfriend?" Freddy says.

"If I told you her name, you'd tell him I told you."

"Slow down. What?"

"I won't tell you, because you'll tell him that I know."

"He knows you know."

"I don't think so."

"How did you find out?"

"He talked about her. I kept hearing her name for months, and then we went to a party at Garner's, and she was there, and when I said something about her later he said, 'Natalie who?' It was much too obvious. It gave the whole thing away."

He sighs. "I just did something very optimistic," he says. "I came out here with Mr. Sam and he dug up a rock and I put the avocado seed in the hole and packed dirt on top of it. Don't say it—I know: can't grow outside, we'll still have another snow, even if it grew, the next year's frost would kill it."

"He's embarrassed," I say. "When he's home, he avoids me. But it's rotten to avoid Mark, too. Six years old, and he calls up his friend Neal to hint that he wants to go over there. He doesn't do that when we're here alone."

Freddy picks up a stick and pokes around in the mud with it. "I'll bet Tucker's after that painter personally, not because he's the hottest thing since pancakes. That expression of his—it's always the same. Maybe Nixon really loved his mother, but with that expression who could believe him? It's a curse to have a face that won't express what you mean."

"Amy!" Tucker calls. "Telephone."

Freddy waves goodbye to me with the muddy stick. "'I am not a crook,'" Freddy says. "Jesus Christ."

Sam bounds halfway toward the house with me, then turns and goes back to Freddy.

It's Marilyn, Neal's mother, on the phone.

"Hi," Marilyn said. "He's afraid to spend the night."

"Oh, no," I say. "He said he wouldn't be."

She lowers her voice. "We can try it out, but I think he'll start crying."

"I'll come get him."

"I can bring him home. You're having a dinner party, aren't you?"

I lower my voice. "Some party. Tucker's here. J.D. never showed up."

"Well," she says. "I'm sure that what you cooked was good."

"It's so foggy out, Marilyn. I'll come get Mark."

"He can stay. I'll be a martyr," she says, and hangs up before I can object.

Freddy comes into the house, tracking in mud. Sam lies in the kitchen, waiting for his paws to be cleaned. "Come on," Freddy says, hitting his hand against his thigh, having no idea what Sam is doing. Sam gets up and runs after him. They go into the small downstairs bathroom together. Sam loves to watch people urinate. Sometimes he sings, to harmonize with the sound of the urine going into the water. There are footprints and pawprints everywhere.

Tucker is shrieking with laughter in the living room. ". . . he says, he says to the other one, 'Then, dearie, have you ever played *spin the bottle?*'" Frank's and Tucker's laughter drowns out the sound of Freddy peeing in the bathroom. I turn on the water in the kitchen sink, and it drowns out all the noise. I begin to scrape the dishes. Tucker is telling another story when I turn off the water: ". . . that it was Onassis in the Anvil, and nothing would talk him out of it. They told him Onassis was dead, and he thought they were trying to make him think he was crazy. There was nothing to do but go along with him, but, God—he was trying to goad this poor old fag into fighting about Stavros Niarchos. You know—Onassis's *enemy.* He thought it was *Onassis.* In the *Anvil.*" There is a sound of a glass breaking. Frank or Tucker puts *John Coltrane Live in Seattle* on the stereo and turns the volume down low. The bathroom door opens. Sam runs into the kitchen and begins to lap water from his dish. Freddy takes his little silver case and his rolling papers out of his shirt pocket. He puts a piece of paper on the kitchen table and is about to sprinkle grass on it, but realizes just in time that the paper has absorbed water from a puddle. He balls it up with his thumb, flicks it to the floor, puts a piece of rolling paper where the table's dry and shakes a line of grass down it. "You smoke this," he says to me. "I'll do the dishes."

"We'll both smoke it. I'll wash and you can wipe."

"I forgot to tell them I put ashes in the sauce," he says.

"I wouldn't interrupt."

"At least he pays Frank ten times what any other accountant for an art gallery would make," Freddy says.

Tucker is beating his hand on the arm of the sofa as he talks, stomping his feet. ". . . so he's trying to feel him out, to see if this old guy with the dyed hair knew *Maria Callas.* Jesus! And he's so out of it he's trying to think what opera singers are called, and instead of coming up with *'diva'* he comes up with *'duenna.'* At this point, Larry Betwell went up to him and tried to calm him down, and he breaks into song—some aria or something that Maria Callas was famous for. Larry told him he was going to lose his *teeth* if he didn't get it together, and . . ."

"He spends a lot of time in gay hangouts, for not being gay," Freddy says.

I scream and jump back from the sink, hitting the glass I'm rinsing against the faucet, shattering green glass everywhere.

"What?" Freddy says. "Jesus Christ, what is it?"

Too late, I realize what it must have been that I saw: J.D. in a goat mask, the puckered pink plastic lips against the window by the kitchen sink.

"I'm sorry," J.D. says, coming through the door and nearly colliding with Frank, who has rushed into the kitchen. Tucker is right behind him.

"Oooh," Tucker says, feigning disappointment, "I thought Freddy smooched her."

"I'm sorry," J.D. says again. "I thought you'd know it was me."

The rain must have started again, because J.D. is soaking wet. He has turned the mask around so that the goat's head stares out from the back of his head. "I got lost," J.D. says. He has a farmhouse upstate. "I missed the turn. I went miles. I missed the whole dinner, didn't I?"

"What did you do wrong?" Frank asks.

"I didn't turn left onto Fifty-eight. I don't know why I didn't realize my mistake, but I went *miles*. It was raining so hard I couldn't go over twenty-five miles an hour. Your driveway is all mud. You're going to have to push me out."

"There's some roast left over. And salad, if you want it," I say.

"Bring it in the living room," Frank says to J.D. Freddy is holding out a plate to him. J.D. reaches for the plate. Freddy pulls it back. J.D. reaches again, and Freddy is so stoned that he isn't quick enough this time—J.D. grabs it.

"I thought you'd know it was me," J.D. says. "I apologize." He dishes salad onto the plate. "You'll be rid of me for six months, in the morning."

"Where does your plane leave from?" Freddy says.

"Kennedy."

"Come in here!" Tucker calls. "I've got a story for you about Perry Dwyer down at the Anvil last week, when he thought he saw Aristotle Onassis."

"Who's Perry Dwyer?" J.D. says.

"That is not the point of the story, dear man. And when you're in Cassis, I want you to look up an American painter over there. Will you? He doesn't have a phone. Anyway—I've been tracking him, and I know where he is now, and I am *very* interested, if you would stress that with him, to do a show in June that will be *only* him. He doesn't answer my letters."

"Your hand is cut," J.D. says to me.

"Forget it," I say. "Go ahead."

"I'm sorry," he says. "Did I make you do that?"

"Yes, you did."

"Don't keep your finger under the water. Put pressure on it to stop the bleeding."

He puts the plate on the table. Freddy is leaning against the counter, staring at the blood swirling in the sink, and smoking the joint all by himself. I can feel the little curls on my forehead that Freddy was talking about. They feel heavy on my skin. I hate to see my own blood. I'm sweating. I let J.D. do what he does; he turns off the water and wraps his hand around my second finger, squeezing. Water runs down our wrists.

Freddy jumps to answer the phone when it rings, as though a siren just went off behind him. He calls me to the phone, but J.D. steps in front of me, shakes his head no, and takes the dish towel and wraps it around my hand before he lets me go.

"Well," Marilyn says. "I had the best of intentions, but my battery's dead."

J.D. is standing behind me, with his hand on my shoulder.

"I'll be right over," I say. "He's not upset now, is he?"

"No, but he's dropped enough hints that he doesn't think he can make it through the night."

"Okay," I say. "I'm sorry about all of this."

"Six years old," Marilyn says. "Wait till he grows up and gets that feeling."

I hang up.

"Let me see your hand," J.D. says.

"I don't want to look at it. Just go get me a Band-Aid, please."

He turns and goes upstairs. I unwrap the towel and look at it. It's pretty deep, but no glass is in my finger. I feel funny; the outlines of things are turning yellow. I sit in the chair by the phone. Sam comes and lies beside me, and I stare at his black-and-yellow tail, beating. I reach down with my good hand and pat him, breathing deeply in time with every second pat.

"*Rothko?*" Tucker says bitterly, in the living room. "Nothing is great that can appear on greeting cards. Wyeth is that way. Would *Christina's World* look bad on a cocktail napkin? You know it wouldn't."

I jump as the phone rings again. "Hello?" I say, wedging the phone against my shoulder with my ear, wrapping the dish towel tighter around my hand.

"Tell them it's a crank call. Tell them anything," Johnny says. "I miss you. How's Saturday night at your house?"

"All right," I say. I catch my breath.

"Everything's all right here, too. Yes indeed. Roast rack of lamb. Friend of Nicole's who's going to Key West tomorrow had too much to drink and got depressed because he thought it was raining in Key West, and I said I'd go in my study and call the National Weather Service. Hello, Weather Service. How are you?"

J.D. comes down from upstairs with two Band-Aids and stands beside me, unwrapping one. I want to say to Johnny, "I'm cut. I'm bleeding. It's no joke."

It's all right to talk in front of J.D., but I don't know who else might overhear me.

"I'd say they made the delivery about four this afternoon," I say.

"This is the church, this is the steeple. Open the door, and see all the people," Johnny says. "Take care of yourself. I'll hang up and find out if it's raining in Key West."

"Late in the afternoon," I say. "Everything is fine."

"Nothing is fine," Johnny says. "Take care of yourself."

He hangs up. I put the phone down, and realize that I'm still having trouble focusing, the sight of my cut finger made me so light-headed. I don't look at the finger again as J.D. undoes the towel and wraps the Band-Aids around my finger.

"What's going on in here?" Frank says, coming into the dining room.

"I cut my finger," I say. "It's okay."

"You did?" he says. He looks woozy—a little drunk. "Who keeps calling?"

"Marilyn. Mark changed his mind about staying all night. She was going to bring him home, but her battery's dead. You'll have to get him. Or I will."

"Who called the second time?" he says.

"The oil company. They wanted to know if we got our delivery today."

He nods. "I'll go get him, if you want," he says. He lowers his voice. "Tucker's probably going to whirl himself into a tornado for an encore," he says, nodding toward the living room. "I'll take him with me."

"Do you want me to go get him?" J.D. says.

"I don't mind getting some air," Frank says. "Thanks, though. Why don't you go in the living room and eat your dinner?"

"You forgive me?" J.D. says.

"Sure," I say. "It wasn't your fault. Where did you get that mask?"

"I found it on top of a Goodwill box in Manchester. There was also a beautiful old birdcage—solid brass."

The phone rings again. I pick it up. "Wouldn't I love to be in Key West with you," Johnny says. He makes a sound as though he's kissing me and hangs up.

"Wrong number," I say.

Frank feels in his pants pocket for the car keys.

J.D. knows about Johnny. He introduced me, in the faculty lounge, where J.D. and I had gone to get a cup of coffee after I registered for classes. After being gone for nearly two years, J.D. still gets mail at the department—he said he had to stop by for the mail anyway, so he'd drive me to campus and point me toward the registrar's. J.D. taught English; now he does nothing. J.D. is glad that I've gone back to college to study art again, now that Mark is in school. I'm six credits away from an M.A. in art history. He wants me to think about myself, instead of thinking about Mark all the time. He talks as though I could roll Mark out on a string and let him fly off, high above me. J.D.'s wife and son died in a car crash. His son was Mark's age. "I wasn't prepared," J.D. said when we were driving over that day. He always says this when he talks about it. "How could you be prepared for such a thing?" I asked him. "I am now," he said. Then, realizing he was acting very hard-boiled, made fun of himself. "Go on," he said, "punch me in the stomach. Hit me as hard as you can." We both knew he wasn't prepared for anything. When he couldn't find a parking place that day, his hands were wrapped around the wheel so tightly that his knuckles turned white.

Johnny came in as we were drinking coffee. J.D. was looking at his junk mail—publishers wanting him to order anthologies, ways to get free dictionaries.

"You are so lucky to be out of it," Johnny said, by way of greeting. "What do you do when you've spent two weeks on *Hamlet* and the student writes about Hamlet's good friend Horchow?"

He threw a blue book into J.D.'s lap. J.D. sailed it back.

"Johnny," he said, "this is Amy."

"Hi, Amy," Johnny said.

"You remember when Frank Wayne was in graduate school here? Amy's Frank's wife."

"Hi, Amy," Johnny said.

J.D. told me he knew it the instant Johnny walked into the room—he knew that second that he should introduce me as somebody's wife. He could have predicted it all from the way Johnny looked at me.

For a long time J.D. gloated that he had been prepared for what happened next—that Johnny and I were going to get together. It took me to disturb his pleasure in himself—me, crying hysterically on the phone last month, not knowing what to do, what move to make next.

"Don't do anything for a while. I guess that's my advice," J.D. said. "But you probably shouldn't listen to me. All I can do myself is run away, hide out. I'm not the learned professor. You know what I believe. I believe all that wicked fairy-tale crap: your heart will break, your house will burn."

Tonight, because he doesn't have a garage at his farm, J.D. has come to leave his car in the empty half of our two-car garage while he's in France. I look out the window and see his old Saab, glowing in the moonlight. J.D. has brought his favorite book, *A Vision*, to read on the plane. He says his suitcase contains only a spare pair of jeans, cigarettes, and underwear. He is going to buy a leather jacket in France, at a store where he almost bought a leather jacket two years ago.

In our bedroom there are about twenty small glass prisms hung with fishing line from one of the exposed beams; they catch the morning light, and we stare at them like a cat eyeing catnip held above its head. Just now, it is 2 a.m. At six-thirty, they will be filled with dazzling color. At four or five, Mark will come into the bedroom and get in bed with us. Sam will wake up, stretch, and shake, and the tags on his collar will clink, and he will yawn and shake again and go downstairs, where J.D. is asleep in his sleeping bag and Tucker is asleep on the sofa, and get a drink of water from his dish. Mark has been coming into our bedroom for about a year. He gets onto the bed by climbing up on a footstool that horrified me when I first saw it—a gift from Frank's mother: a footstool that says TODAY IS THE FIRST DAY OF THE REST OF YOUR LIFE in needlepoint. I kept it in a closet for years, but it occurred to me that it would help Mark get up onto the bed, so he would not have to make a little leap and possibly skin his shin again. Now Mark does not disturb us when he comes into the bedroom, except that it bothers me that he has reverted to sucking his thumb. Sometimes he lies in bed with his cold feet against my leg. Sometimes, small as he is, he snores.

Somebody is playing a record downstairs. It's the Velvet Underground—Lou Reed, in a dream or swoon, singing "Sunday Morning." I can barely hear the whispering and tinkling of the record. I can only follow it because I've heard it a hundred times.

I am lying in bed, waiting for Frank to get out of the bathroom. My cut finger throbs. Things are going on in the house even though I have gone to bed; water runs, the record plays. Sam is still downstairs, so there must be some action.

I have known everybody in the house for years, and as time goes by I know them all less and less. J.D. was Frank's adviser in college. Frank was his best student, and they started to see each other outside of class. They played handball. J.D. and his family came to dinner. We went there. That summer—the summer Frank decided to go to graduate school in business instead of English—J.D.'s wife and son deserted him in a more horrible way, in that car crash. J.D. has quit his job. He has been to Las Vegas, to Colorado, New Orleans, Los Angeles, Paris twice; he tapes postcards to the walls of his living room. A lot of the time, on the weekends, he shows up at our house with his sleeping bag. Sometimes he brings a girl. Lately, not. Years ago, Tucker was in Frank's therapy group in New York, and ended up hiring Frank to work as the accountant for his gallery. Tucker was in therapy at the time because he was obsessed with foreigners. Now he is also obsessed with homosexuals. He gives fashionable parties to which he invites many foreigners and homosexuals. Before the parties he does TM and yoga, and during the parties he does Seconals and isometrics. When I first met him, he was living for the summer in his sister's house in Vermont while she was in Europe, and he called us one night, in New York, in a real panic because there were wasps all over. They were "hatching," he said—big, sleepy wasps that were everywhere. We said we'd come; we drove all through the night to get to Brattleboro. It was true: there were wasps on the undersides of plates, in the plants, in the folds of curtains. Tucker was so upset that he was out behind the house, in the cold Vermont morning, wrapped like an Indian in a blanket, with only his pajamas on underneath. He was sitting in a lawn chair, hiding behind a bush, waiting for us to come.

And Freddy—"Reddy Fox," when Frank is feeling affectionate toward him. When we first met, I taught him to ice-skate and he taught me to waltz; in the summer, at Atlantic City, he'd go with me on a roller coaster that curved high over the waves. I was the one—not Frank—who would get out of bed in the middle of the night and meet him at an all-night deli and put my arm around his shoulders, the way he put his arm around my shoulders on the roller coaster, and talk quietly to him until he got over his latest anxiety attack. Now he tests me, and I retreat: this man he picked up, this man who picked him up, how it feels to have forgotten somebody's name when your hand is in the back pocket of his jeans and you're not even halfway to your apartment. Reddy Fox—admiring my new red silk blouse, stroking his fingertips down the front, and my eyes wide, because I could feel his fingers on my chest, even though I was holding the blouse in front of me on a hanger to be admired. All those moments, and all they meant was that I was fooled into thinking I knew these people because I knew the small things, the personal things.

Freddy will always be more stoned than I am, because he feels comfortable getting stoned with me, and I'll always be reminded that he's more lost. Tucker knows he can come to the house and be the center of attention; he can tell all the stories he knows, and we'll never tell the story we know about him hiding in the bushes like a frightened dog. J.D. comes back from his trips with boxes full of postcards, and I look at all of them as though they're photographs taken by him, and I know, and he knows, that what he likes about them is their flatness—the unreality of them, the unreality of what he does.

Last summer, I read "The Metamorphosis" and said to J.D., "Why did Gregor Samsa wake up a cockroach?" His answer (which he would have toyed over with his students forever) was "Because that's what people expected of him."

They make the illogical logical. I don't do anything, because I'm waiting, I'm on hold (J.D.); I stay stoned because I know it's better to be out of it (Freddy); I love art because I myself am a work of art (Tucker).

Frank is harder to understand. One night a week or so ago, I thought we were really attuned to each other, communicating by telepathic waves, and as I lay in bed about to speak I realized that the vibrations really existed: they were him, snoring.

Now he's coming into the bedroom, and I'm trying again to think what to say. Or ask. Or do.

"Be glad you're not in Key West," he says. He climbs into bed.

I raise myself up on one elbow and stare at him.

"There's a hurricane about to hit," he says.

"What?" I say. "Where did you hear that?"

"When Reddy Fox and I were putting the dishes away. We had the radio on." He doubles up his pillow, pushes it under his neck. "Boom goes everything," he says. "Bam. Crash. Poof." He looks at me. "You look shocked." He closes his eyes. Then, after a minute or two, he murmurs, "Hurricanes upset you? I'll try to think of something nice."

He is quiet for so long that I think he has fallen asleep. Then he says, "Cars that run on water. A field of flowers, none alike. A shooting star that goes slow enough for you to watch. Your life to do over again." He has been whispering in my ear, and when he takes his mouth away I shiver. He slides lower in the bed for sleep. "I'll tell you something really amazing," he says. "Tucker told me he went into a travel agency on Park Avenue last week and asked the travel agent where he should go to pan for gold, and she told him."

"Where did she tell him to go?"

"I think somewhere in Peru. The banks of some river in Peru."

"Did you decide what you're going to do after Mark's birthday?" I say.

He doesn't answer me. I touch him on the side, finally.

"It's two o'clock in the morning. Let's talk about it another time."

"You picked the house, Frank. They're your friends downstairs. I used to be what you wanted me to be."

"They're your friends, too," he says. "Don't be paranoid."

"I want to know if you're staying or going."

He takes a deep breath, lets it out, and continues to lie very still.

"Everything you've done is commendable," he says. "You did the right thing to go back to school. You tried to do the right thing by finding yourself a normal friend like Marilyn. But your whole life you've made one mistake—you've surrounded yourself with men. Let me tell you something. All men—if they're crazy, like Tucker, if they're gay as the Queen of the May, like Reddy Fox, even if they're just six years old—I'm going to tell you something about them. Men think they're Spider-Man and Buck Rogers and Superman. You know what we all feel inside that you don't feel? That we're going to the stars."

He takes my hand. "I'm looking down on all of this from space," he whispers. "I'm already gone."

JHUMPA LAHIRI

A Temporary Matter

The notice informed them that it was a temporary matter: for five days their electricity would be cut off for one hour, beginning at eight P.M. A line had gone down in the last snowstorm, and the repairmen were going to take advantage of the milder evenings to set it right. The work would affect only the houses on the quiet tree-lined street, within walking distance of a row of brick-faced stores and a trolley stop, where Shoba and Shukumar had lived for three years.

"It's good of them to warn us," Shoba conceded after reading the notice aloud, more for her own benefit than Shukumar's. She let the strap of her leather satchel, plump with files, slip from her shoulders, and left it in the hallway as she walked into the kitchen. She wore a navy blue poplin raincoat over gray sweatpants and white sneakers, looking, at thirty-three, like the type of woman she'd once claimed she would never resemble.

She'd come from the gym. Her cranberry lipstick was visible only on the outer reaches of her mouth, and her eyeliner had left charcoal patches beneath her lower lashes. She used to look this way sometimes, Shukumar thought, on mornings after a party or a night at a bar, when she'd been too lazy to wash her face, too eager to collapse into his arms. She dropped a sheaf of mail on the table without a glance. Her eyes were still fixed on the notice in her other hand. "But they should do this sort of thing during the day."

"When I'm here, you mean," Shukumar said. He put a glass lid on a pot of lamb, adjusting it so only the slightest bit of steam could escape. Since January he'd been working at home, trying to complete the final chapters of his dissertation on agrarian revolts in India. "When do the repairs start?"

"It says March nineteenth. Is today the nineteenth?" Shoba walked over to the framed corkboard that hung on the wall by the fridge, bare except for a calendar of William Morris wallpaper patterns. She looked at it as if for the first time, studying the wallpaper pattern carefully on the top half before allowing her eyes to fall to the numbered grid on the bottom. A friend had sent the calendar in the mail as a Christmas gift, even though Shoba and Shukumar hadn't celebrated Christmas that year.

"Today then," Shoba announced. "You have a dentist appointment next Friday, by the way."

He ran his tongue over the tops of his teeth; he'd forgotten to brush them that morning. It wasn't the first time. He hadn't left the house at all that day, or the day before. The more Shoba stayed out, the more she began putting in extra hours at work and taking on additional projects, the more he wanted to stay in, not even leaving to get the mail, or to buy fruit or wine at the stores by the trolley stop.

Six months ago, in September, Shukumar was at an academic conference in Baltimore when Shoba went into labor, three weeks before her due date. He hadn't wanted to go to the conference, but she had insisted; it was important to make contacts, and he would be entering the job market next year. She told him that she had his number at the hotel, and a copy of his schedule and flight numbers, and she had arranged with her friend Gillian for a ride to the hospital in the event of an emergency. When the cab pulled away that morning for the airport, Shoba stood waving good-bye in her robe, with one arm resting on the mound of her belly as if it were a perfectly natural part of her body.

Each time he thought of that moment, the last moment he saw Shoba pregnant, it was the cab he remembered most, a station wagon, painted red with blue lettering. It was cavernous compared to their own car. Although Shukumar was six feet tall, with hands too big ever to rest comfortably in the pockets of his jeans, he felt dwarfed in the backseat. As the cab sped down Beacon Street, he imagined a day when he and Shoba might need to buy a station wagon of their own, to cart their children back and forth from music lessons and dentist appointments. He imagined himself gripping the wheel, as Shoba turned around to hand the children juice boxes. Once, these images of parenthood had troubled Shukumar, adding to his anxiety that he was still a student at thirty-five. But that early autumn morning, the trees still heavy with bronze leaves, he welcomed the image for the first time.

A member of the staff had found him somehow among the identical convention rooms and handed him a stiff square of stationery. It was only a telephone number, but Shukumar knew it was the hospital. When he returned to Boston it was over. The baby had been born dead. Shoba was lying on a bed, asleep, in a private room so small there was barely enough space to stand beside her, in a wing of the hospital they hadn't been to on the tour for expectant parents. Her placenta had weakened and she'd had a cesarean, though not quickly enough. The doctor explained that these things happen. He smiled in the kindest way it was possible to smile at people known only professionally. Shoba would be back on her feet in a few weeks. There was nothing to indicate that she would not be able to have children in the future.

These days Shoba was always gone by the time Shukumar woke up. He would open his eyes and see the long black hairs she shed on her pillow and think of her, dressed, sipping her third cup of coffee already, in her office downtown, where she searched for typographical errors in textbooks and marked them, in a code she had once explained to him, with an assortment of colored pencils. She would do the same for his dissertation, she promised, when it was ready. He envied her the specificity of her task, so unlike the elusive nature of his. He was a mediocre student who had a facility for absorbing details without curiosity. Until September he had been diligent if not dedicated, summarizing chapters, outlining arguments on pads of yellow lined paper. But now he would lie in their bed until he grew bored, gazing at his side of the closet which Shoba always left partly open, at the row of the tweed jackets and corduroy trousers he would not have to choose from to teach his classes that semester. After the baby died it was too late to withdraw from his teaching duties. But his adviser had arranged things so that he had the spring semester to himself. Shukumar was in his sixth year of graduate school. "That and the summer should give you a good push," his adviser had said. "You should be able to wrap things up by next September."

But nothing was pushing Shukumar. Instead he thought of how he and Shoba had become experts at avoiding each other in their three-bedroom house, spending as much time on separate floors as possible. He thought of how he no longer looked forward to weekends, when she sat for hours on the sofa with her colored pencils and her files, so that he feared that putting on a record in his own house might be rude. He thought of how long it had been since she looked into his eyes and smiled, or whispered his name on those rare occasions they still reached for each other's bodies before sleeping.

In the beginning he had believed that it would pass, that he and Shoba would get through it all somehow. She was only thirty-three. She was strong, on her feet again. But it wasn't a consolation. It was often nearly lunchtime when Shukumar would finally pull himself out of bed and head downstairs to the coffeepot, pouring out the extra bit Shoba left for him, along with an empty mug, on the countertop.

————

Shukumar gathered onion skins in his hands and let them drop into the garbage pail, on top of the ribbons of fat he'd trimmed from the lamb. He ran the water in the sink, soaking the knife and the cutting board, and rubbed a lemon half along his fingertips to get rid of the garlic smell, a trick he'd learned from Shoba. It was seven-thirty. Through the window he saw the sky, like soft black pitch. Uneven banks of snow still lined the sidewalks, though it was warm enough for people to walk about without hats or gloves. Nearly three feet had fallen in the last storm, so that for a week people had to walk single file, in narrow trenches. For a week that was Shukumar's excuse for not leaving the house. But now the trenches were widening, and water drained steadily into grates in the pavement.

"The lamb won't be done by eight," Shukumar said. "We may have to eat in the dark."

"We can light candles," Shoba suggested. She unclipped her hair, coiled neatly at her nape during the days, and pried the sneakers from her feet without untying them. "I'm going to shower before the lights go," she said, heading for the staircase. "I'll be down."

Shukumar moved her satchel and her sneakers to the side of the fridge. She wasn't this way before. She used to put her coat on a hanger, her sneakers in the closet, and she paid bills as soon as they came. But now she treated the house as if it were a hotel. The fact that the yellow chintz armchair in the living room clashed with the blue-and-maroon Turkish carpet no longer bothered her. On the enclosed porch at the back of the house, a crisp white bag still sat on the wicker chaise, filled with lace she had once planned to turn into curtains.

While Shoba showered, Shukumar went into the downstairs bathroom and found a new toothbrush in its box beneath the sink. The cheap, stiff bristles hurt his gums, and he spit some blood into the basin. The spare brush was one of many stored on a shelf over the toilet. Shoba had bought the toothbrushes once when they were on sale, in the event that a visitor decided, at the last minute, to spend the night.

It was typical of her. She was the type to prepare for surprises, good and bad. If she found a skirt or a purse she liked she bought two. She kept the bonuses from her job in a separate bank account in her name. It hadn't bothered him. His own mother had fallen to pieces when his father died, abandoning the house he grew up in and moving back to Calcutta, leaving Shukumar to settle it all. He liked that Shoba was different. It astonished him, her capacity to think ahead. When she used to do the shopping, the pantry was always stocked with extra bottles of olive and corn oil, depending on whether they were cooking Italian or Indian. There were endless boxes of pasta in all shapes and colors, zippered sacks of basmati rice, whole sides of lambs and goats from the Muslim butchers at Haymarket, chopped up and frozen in endless plastic bags. Every other Saturday they wound through the maze of stalls Shukumar eventually knew by heart. He watched in disbelief as she bought more food, trailing behind her with canvas bags as she pushed through the crowd, arguing under the morning sun with boys too young to shave but already missing teeth, who twisted up brown paper bags of artichokes, plums, gingerroot, and yams, and dropped them on their scales, and tossed them to Shoba one by one. She didn't mind being jostled, even when she was pregnant. She was tall, and broad-shouldered, with hips that her obstetrician assured her were made for childbearing. During the drive back home, as the car curved along the Charles, they invariably marveled at how much food they'd bought.

It never went to waste. When friends dropped by, Shoba would throw together meals that appeared to have taken half a day to prepare, from things she had frozen and bottled, not cheap things in tins but peppers she had marinated herself with rosemary, and chutneys that she cooked on Sundays, stirring boiling pots of tomatoes and prunes. Her labeled mason jars lined the shelves of the kitchen, in endless sealed pyramids, enough, they'd agreed, to last for their grandchildren to taste. They'd eaten it all by now. Shukumar had been going through their supplies steadily, preparing meals for the two of them, measuring out cupfuls of rice, defrosting bags of meat day after day. He combed through her cookbooks every afternoon, following her penciled instructions to use two teaspoons of ground coriander seeds instead of one, or red lentils instead of yellow. Each of the recipes was dated, telling the first time they had eaten the dish together. April 2, cauliflower with fennel. January 14, chicken with almonds and sultanas. He had no memory of eating those meals, and yet there they were, recorded in her neat proofreader's hand. Shukumar enjoyed cooking now. It was the one thing that made him feel productive. If it weren't for him, he knew, Shoba would eat a bowl of cereal for her dinner.

Tonight, with no lights, they would have to eat together. For months now they'd served themselves from the stove, and he'd take his plate into his study, letting the meal grow cold on his desk before shoving it into his mouth without pause, while Shoba took her plate to the living room and watched game shows, or proofread files with her arsenal of colored pencils at hand.

At some point in the evening she visited him. When he heard her approach he would put away his novel and begin typing sentences. She would rest her hands on his shoulders and stare with him into the blue glow of the computer screen. "Don't work too hard," she would say after a minute or two, and head off to bed. It was the one time in the day she sought him out, and yet he'd come to dread it. He knew it was something she forced herself to do. She would look around the walls of the room, which they had decorated together last summer with a border of marching ducks and rabbits playing trumpets and drums. By the end of August there was a cherry crib under the window, a white changing table with mint-green knobs, and a rocking chair with checkered cushions. Shukumar had disassembled it all before bringing Shoba back from the hospital, scraping off the rabbits and ducks with a spatula. For some reason the room did not haunt him the way it haunted Shoba. In January, when he stopped working at his carrel in the library, he set up his desk there deliberately, partly because the room soothed him, and partly because it was a place Shoba avoided.

Shukumar returned to the kitchen and began to open drawers. He tried to locate a candle among the scissors, the eggbeaters and whisks, the mortar and pestle she'd bought in a bazaar in Calcutta, and used to pound garlic cloves and cardamom pods, back when she used to cook. He found a flashlight, but no batteries, and a half-empty box of birthday candles. Shoba had thrown him a surprise birthday party last May. One hundred and twenty people had crammed into the house—all the friends and the friends of friends they now systematically avoided. Bottles of vinho verde had nested in a bed of ice in the bathtub. Shoba was in her fifth month, drinking ginger ale from a martini glass. She had made a vanilla cream cake with custard and spun sugar. All night she kept Shukumar's long fingers linked with hers as they walked among the guests at the party.

Since September their only guest had been Shoba's mother. She came from Arizona and stayed with them for two months after Shoba returned from the hospital. She cooked dinner every night, drove herself to the supermarket, washed their clothes, put them away. She was a religious woman. She set up a small shrine, a framed picture of a lavender-faced goddess and a plate of marigold petals, on the bedside table in the guest room, and prayed twice a day for healthy grandchildren in the future. She was polite to Shukumar without being friendly. She folded his sweaters with an expertise she had learned from her job in a department store. She replaced a missing button on his winter coat and knit him a beige and brown scarf, presenting it to him without the least bit of ceremony, as if he had only dropped it and hadn't noticed. She never talked to him about Shoba; once, when he mentioned the baby's death, she looked up from her knitting, and said, "But you weren't even there."

It struck him as odd that there were no real candles in the house. That Shoba hadn't prepared for such an ordinary emergency. He looked now for something to put the birthday candles in and settled on the soil of a potted ivy that normally sat on the windowsill over the sink. Even though the plant was inches from the tap, the soil was so dry that he had to water it first before the candles would stand straight. He pushed aside the things on the kitchen table, the piles of mail, the unread library books. He remembered their first meals there, when they were so thrilled to be married, to be living together in the same house at last, that they would just reach for each other foolishly, more eager to make love than to eat. He put down two embroidered place mats, a wedding gift from an uncle in Lucknow, and set out the plates and wineglasses they usually saved for guests. He put the ivy in the middle, the white-edged, star-shaped leaves girded by ten little candles. He switched on the digital clock radio and tuned it to a jazz station.

"What's all this?" Shoba said when she came downstairs. Her hair was wrapped in a thick white towel. She undid the towel and draped it over a chair, allowing her hair, damp and dark, to fall across her back. As she walked absently toward the stove she took out a few tangles with her fingers. She wore a clean pair of sweatpants, a T-shirt, an old flannel robe. Her stomach was flat again, her waist narrow before the flare of her hips, the belt of the robe tied in a floppy knot.

It was nearly eight. Shukumar put the rice on the table and the lentils from the night before into the microwave oven, punching the numbers on the timer.

"You made *rogan josh*," Shoba observed, looking through the glass lid at the bright paprika stew.

Shukumar took out a piece of lamb, pinching it quickly between his fingers so as not to scald himself. He prodded a larger piece with a serving spoon to make sure the meat slipped easily from the bone. "It's ready," he announced.

The microwave had just beeped when the lights went out, and the music disappeared.

"Perfect timing," Shoba said.

"All I could find were birthday candles." He lit up the ivy, keeping the rest of the candles and a book of matches by his plate.

"It doesn't matter," she said, running a finger along the stem of her wineglass. "It looks lovely."

In the dimness, he knew how she sat, a bit forward in her chair, ankles crossed against the lower rung, left elbow on the table. During his search for the candles, Shukumar had found a bottle of wine in a crate he had thought was empty. He clamped the bottle between his knees while he turned in the corkscrew. He worried about spilling, and so he picked up the glasses and held them close to his lap while he filled them. They served themselves, stirring the rice with their forks, squinting as they extracted bay leaves and cloves from the stew. Every few minutes Shukumar lit a few more birthday candles and drove them into the soil of the pot.

"It's like India," Shoba said, watching him tend his makeshift candelabra. "Sometimes the current disappears for hours at a stretch. I once had to attend an entire rice ceremony in the dark. The baby just cried and cried. It must have been so hot."

Their baby had never cried, Shukumar considered. Their baby would never have a rice ceremony, even though Shoba had already made the guest list, and decided on which of her three brothers she was going to ask to feed the child its first taste of solid food, at six months if it was a boy, seven if it was a girl.

"Are you hot?" he asked her. He pushed the blazing ivy pot to the other end of the table, closer to the piles of books and mail, making it even more difficult for them to see each other. He was suddenly irritated that he couldn't go upstairs and sit in front of the computer.

"No. It's delicious," she said, tapping her plate with her fork. "It really is."

He refilled the wine in her glass. She thanked him.

They weren't like this before. Now he had to struggle to say something that interested her, something that made her look up from her plate, or from her proofreading files. Eventually he gave up trying to amuse her. He learned not to mind the silences.

"I remember during power failures at my grandmother's house, we all had to say something," Shoba continued. He could barely see her face, but from her tone he knew her eyes were narrowed, as if trying to focus on a distant object. It was a habit of hers.

"Like what?"

"I don't know. A little poem. A joke. A fact about the world. For some reason by relatives always wanted me to tell them the names of my friends in America. I don't know why the information was so interesting to them. The last time I saw my aunt she asked after four girls I went to elementary school with in Tucson. I barely remember them now."

Shukumar hadn't spent as much time in India as Shoba had. His parents, who settled in New Hampshire, used to go back without him. The first time he'd gone as an infant he'd nearly died of amoebic dysentery. His father, a nervous type, was afraid to take him again, in case something were to happen, and left him with his aunt and uncle in Concord. As a teenager he preferred sailing camp or scooping ice cream during the summers to going to Calcutta. It wasn't until after his father died, in his last year of college, that the country began to interest him, and he studied its history from course books as if it were any other subject. He wished now that he had his own childhood story of India.

"Let's do that," she said suddenly.

"Do what?"

"Say something to each other in the dark."

"Like what? I don't know any jokes."

"No, no jokes." She thought for a minute. "How about telling each other something we've never told before."

"I used to play this game in high school," Shukumar recalled. "When I got drunk."

"You're thinking of truth or dare. This is different. Okay, I'll start." She took a sip of wine. "The first time I was alone in your apartment, I looked in your address book to see if you'd written me in. I think we'd known each other two weeks."

"Where was I?"

"You went to answer the telephone in the other room. It was your mother, and I figured it would be a long call. I wanted to know if you'd promoted me from the margins of your newspaper."

"Had I?"

"No. But I didn't give up on you. Now it's your turn."

He couldn't think of anything, but Shoba was waiting for him to speak. She hadn't appeared so determined in months. What was there left to say to her? He thought back to their first meeting, four years earlier at a lecture hall in Cambridge, where a group of Bengali poets were giving a recital. They'd ended up side by side, on folding wooden chairs. Shukumar was soon bored; he was unable to decipher the literary diction, and couldn't join the rest of the audience as they sighed and nodded solemnly after certain phrases. Peering at the newspaper folded in his lap, he studied the temperatures of cities around the world. Ninety-one degrees in Singapore yesterday, fifty-one in Stockholm. When he turned his head to the left, he saw a woman next to him making a grocery list on the back of a folder, and was startled to find that she was beautiful.

"Okay," he said, remembering. "The first time we went out to dinner, to the Portuguese place, I forgot to tip the waiter. I went back the next morning, found out his name, left money with the manager."

"You went all the way back to Somerville just to tip a waiter?"

"I took a cab."

"Why did you forget to tip the waiter?"

The birthday candles had burned out, but he pictured her face clearly in the dark, the wide tilting eyes, the full grape-toned lips, the fall at age two from her high chair still visible as a comma on her chin. Each day, Shukumar noticed, her beauty, which had once overwhelmed him, seemed to fade. The cosmetics that had seemed superfluous were necessary now, not to improve her but to define her somehow.

"By the end of the meal I had a funny feeling I might marry you," he said, admitting it to himself as well as to her for the first time. "It must have distracted me."

The next night Shoba came home earlier than usual. There was lamb left over from the evening before, and Shukumar heated it up so that they were able to eat by seven. He'd gone out that day, through the melting snow, and bought a packet of taper candles from the corner store, and batteries to fit the flashlight. He had the candles ready on the countertop, standing in brass holders shaped like lotuses, but they ate under the glow of the copper-shaded ceiling lamp that hung over the table.

When they had finished eating, Shukumar was surprised to see that Shoba was stacking her plate on top of his, and then carrying them over to the sink. He had assumed she would retreat to the living room, behind her barricade of files.

"Don't worry about the dishes," he said, taking them from her hands.

"It seems silly not to," she replied, pouring a drop of detergent onto a sponge. "It's nearly eight o'clock."

His heart quickened. All day Shukumar had looked forward to the lights going out. He thought about what Shoba had said the night before, about looking in his address book. It felt good to remember her as she was then, how bold yet nervous she'd been when they first met, how hopeful. They stood side by side at the sink, their reflections fitting together in the frame of the window. It made him shy, the way he felt the first time they stood together in a mirror. He couldn't recall the last time they'd been photographed. They had stopped attending parties, went nowhere together. The film in his camera still contained pictures of Shoba, in the yard, when she was pregnant.

After finishing the dishes, they leaned against the counter, drying their hands on either end of a towel. At eight o'clock the house went black. Shukumar lit the wicks of the candles, impressed by their long, steady flames.

"Let's sit outside," Shoba said. "I think it's warm still."

They each took a candle and sat down on the steps. It seemed strange to be sitting outside with patches of snow still on the ground. But everyone was out of their houses tonight, the air fresh enough to make people restless. Screen doors opened and closed. A small parade of neighbors passed by with flashlights.

"We're going to the bookstore to browse," a silver-haired man called out. He was walking with his wife, a thin woman in a windbreaker, and holding a dog on a leash. They were the Bradfords, and they had tucked a sympathy card into Shoba and Shukumar's mailbox back in September. "I hear they've got their power."

"They'd better," Shukumar said. "Or you'll be browsing in the dark."

The woman laughed, slipping her arm through the crook of her husband's elbow. "Want to join us?"

"No thanks," Shoba and Shukumar called out together. It surprised Shukumar that his words matched hers.

He wondered what Shoba would tell him in the dark. The worst possibilities had already run through his head. That she'd had an affair. That she didn't respect him for being thirty-five and still a student. That she blamed him for being in Baltimore the way her mother did. But he knew those things weren't true. She'd been faithful, as had he. She believed in him. It was she who had insisted he go to Baltimore. What didn't they know about each other? He knew she curled her fingers tightly when she slept, that her body twitched during bad dreams. He knew it was honeydew she favored over cantaloupe. He knew that when they returned from the hospital the first thing she did when she walked into the house was pick out objects of theirs and toss them into a pile in the hallway: books from the shelves, plants from the windowsills, paintings from the walls, photos from tables, pots and pans that hung from the hooks over the stove. Shukumar had stepped out of her way, watching as she moved methodically from room to room. When she was satisfied, she stood there staring at the pile she'd made, her lips drawn back in such distaste that Shukumar had thought she would spit. Then she'd started to cry.

He began to feel cold as he sat there on the steps. He felt that he needed her to talk first, in order to reciprocate.

"That time when your mother came to visit us," she said finally. "When I said one night that I had to stay late at work, I went out with Gillian and had a martini."

He looked at her profile, the slender nose, the slightly masculine set of her jaw. He remembered that night well; eating with his mother, tired from teaching two classes back to back, wishing Shoba were there to say more of the right things because he came up with only the wrong ones. It had been twelve years since his father had died, and his mother had come to spend two weeks with him and Shoba, so they could honor his father's memory together. Each night his mother cooked something his father had liked, but she was too upset to eat the dishes herself, and her eyes would well up as Shoba stroked her hand. "It's so touching," Shoba had said to him at the time. Now he pictured Shoba with Gillian, in a bar with striped velvet sofas, the one they used to go to after the movies, making sure she got her extra olive, asking Gillian for a cigarette. He imagined her complaining, and Gillian sympathizing about visits from in-laws. It was Gillian who had driven Shoba to the hospital.

"Your turn," she said, stopping his thoughts.

At the end of their street Shukumar heard sounds of a drill and the electricians shouting over it. He looked at the darkened facades of the houses lining the street. Candles glowed in the windows of one. In spite of the warmth, smoke rose from the chimney.

"I cheated on my Oriental Civilization exam in college," he said. "It was my last semester, my last set of exams. My father had died a few months before. I could see the blue book of the guy next to me. He was an American guy, a maniac. He knew Urdu and Sanskrit. I couldn't remember if the verse we had to identify was an example of a *ghazal* or not. I looked at his answer and copied it down."

It had happened over fifteen years ago. He felt relief now, having told her.

She turned to him, looking not at his face, but at his shoes—old moccasins he wore as if they were slippers, the leather at the back permanently flattened. He wondered if it bothered her, what he'd said. She took his hand and pressed it. "You didn't have to tell me why you did it," she said, moving closer to him.

They sat together until nine o'clock, when the lights came on. They heard some people across the street clapping from their porch, and televisions being turned on. The Bradfords walked back down the street, eating ice-cream cones and waving. Shoba and Shukumar waved back. Then they stood up, his hand still in hers, and went inside.

Somehow, without saying anything, it had turned into this. Into an exchange of confessions—the little ways they'd hurt or disappointed each other, and themselves. The following day Shukumar thought for hours about what to say to her. He was torn between admitting that he once ripped out a photo of a woman in one of the fashion magazines she used to subscribe to and carried it in his books for a week, or saying that he really hadn't lost the sweater-vest she bought him for their third wedding anniversary but had exchanged it for cash at Filene's, and that he had gotten drunk alone in the middle of the day at a hotel bar. For their first anniversary, Shoba had cooked a ten-course dinner just for him. The vest depressed him. "My wife gave me a sweater-vest for our anniversary," he complained to the bartender, his head heavy with cognac. "What do you expect?" the bartender had replied. "You're married."

As for the picture of the woman, he didn't know why he'd ripped it out. She wasn't as pretty as Shoba. She wore a white sequined dress, and had a sullen face and lean, mannish legs. Her bare arms were raised, her fists around her head, as if she were about to punch herself in the ears. It was an advertisement for stockings. Shoba had been pregnant at the time, her stomach suddenly immense, to the point where Shukumar no longer wanted to touch her. The first time he saw the picture he was lying in bed next to her, watching her as she read. When he noticed the magazine in the recycling pile he found the woman and tore out the page as carefully as he could. For about a week he allowed himself a glimpse each day. He felt an intense desire for the woman, but it was a desire that turned to disgust after a minute or two. It was the closest he'd come to infidelity.

He told Shoba about the sweater on the third night, the picture on the fourth. She said nothing as he spoke, expressed no protest or reproach. She simply listened, and then she took his hand, pressing it as she had before. On the third night, she told him that once after a lecture they'd attended, she let him speak to the chairman of his department without telling him that he had a dab of pâté on his chin. She'd been irritated with him for some reason, and so she'd let him go on and on, about securing his fellowship for the following semester, without putting a finger to her own chin as a signal. The fourth night, she said that she never liked the one poem he'd ever published in his life, in a literary magazine in Utah. He'd written the poem after meeting Shoba. She added that she found the poem sentimental.

Something happened when the house was dark. They were able to talk to each other again. The third night after supper they'd sat together on the sofa, and once it was dark he began kissing her awkwardly on her forehead and her face, and though it was dark he closed his eyes, and knew that she did, too. The fourth night they walked carefully upstairs, to bed, feeling together for the final step with their feet before the landing, and making love with a desperation they had forgotten. She wept without sound, and whispered his name, and traced his eyebrows with her finger in the dark. As he made love to her he wondered what he would say to her the next night, and what she would say, the thought of it exciting him. "Hold me," he said, "hold me in your arms." By the time the lights came back on downstairs, they'd fallen asleep.

The morning of the fifth night Shukumar found another notice from the electric company in the mailbox. The line had been repaired ahead of schedule, it said. He was disappointed. He had planned on making shrimp malai for Shoba, but when he arrived at the store he didn't feel like cooking anymore. It wasn't the same, he thought, knowing that the lights wouldn't go out. In the store the shrimp looked gray and thin. The coconut milk tin was dusty and overpriced. Still, he bought them, along with a beeswax candle and two bottles of wine.

She came home at seven-thirty. "I suppose this is the end of our game," he said when he saw her reading the notice.

She looked at him. "You can still light candles if you want." She hadn't been to the gym tonight. She wore a suit beneath the raincoat. Her makeup had been retouched recently.

When she went upstairs to change, Shukumar poured himself some wine and put on a record, a Thelonius Monk album he knew she liked.

When she came downstairs they ate together. She didn't thank him or compliment him. They simply ate in a darkened room, in the glow of a beeswax candle. They had survived a difficult time. They finished off the shrimp. They finished off the first bottle of wine and moved on to the second. They sat together until the candle had nearly burned away. She shifted in her chair, and Shukumar thought that she was about to say something. But instead she blew out the candle, stood up, turned on the light switch, and sat down again.

"Shouldn't we keep the lights off?" Shukumar asked.

She set her plate aside and clasped her hands on the table. "I want you to see my face when I tell you this," she said gently.

His heart began to pound. The day she told him she was pregnant, she had used the very same words, saying them in the same gentle way, turning off the basketball game he'd been watching on television. He hadn't been prepared then. Now he was.

Only he didn't want her to be pregnant again. He didn't want to have to pretend to be happy.

"I've been looking for an apartment and I've found one," she said, narrowing her eyes on something, it seemed, behind his left shoulder. It was nobody's fault, she continued. They'd been through enough. She needed some time alone. She had money saved up for a security deposit. The apartment was on Beacon Hill, so she could walk to work. She had signed the lease that night before coming home.

She wouldn't look at him, but he stared at her. It was obvious that she'd rehearsed the lines. All this time she'd been looking for an apartment, testing the water pressure, asking a Realtor if heat and hot water were included in the rent. It sickened Shukumar, knowing that she had spent these past evenings preparing for a life without him. He was relieved and yet he was sickened. This was what she'd been trying to tell him for the past four evenings. This was the point of her game.

Now it was his turn to speak. There was something he'd sworn he would never tell her, and for six months he had done his best to block it from his mind. Before the ultrasound she had asked the doctor not to tell her the sex of their child, and Shukumar had agreed. She had wanted it to be a surprise.

Later, those few times they talked about what had happened, she said at least they'd been spared that knowledge. In a way she almost took pride in her decision, for it enabled her to seek refuge in a mystery. He knew that she assumed it was a mystery for him, too. He'd arrived too late from Baltimore—when it was all over and she was lying on the hospital bed. But he hadn't. He'd arrived early enough to see their baby, and to hold him before they cremated him. At first he had recoiled at the suggestion, but the doctor said holding the baby might help him with the process of grieving. Shoba was asleep. The baby had been cleaned off, his bulbous lids shut tight to the world.

"Our baby was a boy," he said. "His skin was more red than brown. He had black hair on his head. He weighed almost five pounds. His fingers were curled shut, just like yours in the night."

Shoba looked at him now, her face contorted with sorrow. He had cheated on a college exam, ripped a picture of a woman out of a magazine. He had returned a sweater and got drunk in the middle of the day instead. These were the things he had told her. He had held his son, who had known life only within her, against his chest in a darkened room in an unknown wing of the hospital. He had held him until a nurse knocked and took him away, and he promised himself that day that he would never tell Shoba, because he still loved her then, and it was the one thing in her life that she had wanted to be a surprise.

Shukumar stood up and stacked his plate on top of hers. He carried the plates to the sink, but instead of running the tap he looked out the window. Outside the evening was still warm, and the Bradfords were walking arm in arm. As he watched the couple the room went dark, and he spun around. Shoba had turned the lights off. She came back to the table and sat down, and after a moment Shukumar joined her. They wept together, for the things they now knew.

Separating

The day was fair. Brilliant. All that June the weather had mocked the Maples' internal misery with solid sunlight—golden shafts and cascades of green in which their conversations had wormed unseeing, their sad murmuring selves the only stain in Nature. Usually by this time of the year they had acquired tans; but when they met their elder daughter's plane on her return from a year in England they were almost as pale as she, though Judith was too dazzled by the sunny opulent jumble of her native land to notice. They did not spoil her homecoming by telling her immediately. Wait a few days, let her recover from jet lag, had been one of their formulations, in that string of gray dialogues—over coffee, over cocktails, over Cointreau—that had shaped the strategy of their dissolution, while the earth performed its annual stunt of renewal unnoticed beyond their closed windows. Richard had thought to leave at Easter; Joan had insisted they wait until the four children were at last assembled, with all exams passed and ceremonies attended, and the bauble of summer to console them. So he had drudged away, in love, in dread, repairing screens, getting the mowers sharpened, rolling and patching their new tennis court.

The court, clay, had come through its first winter pitted and windswept bare of redcoat. Years ago the Maples had observed how often, among their friends, divorce followed a dramatic home improvement, as if the marriage were making one last effort to live; their own worst crisis had come amid the plaster dust and exposed plumbing of a kitchen renovation. Yet, a summer ago, as canary-yellow bulldozers gaily churned a grassy, daisy-dotted knoll into a muddy plateau, and a crew of pigtailed young men raked and tamped clay into a plane, this transformation did not strike them as ominous, but festive in its impudence; their marriage could rend the earth for fun. The next spring, waking each day at dawn to a sliding sensation as if the bed were being tipped, Richard found the barren tennis court—its net and tapes still rolled in the barn—an environment congruous with his mood of purposeful desolation, and the crumbling of handfuls of clay into cracks and holes (dogs had frolicked on the court in a thaw; rivulets had eroded trenches) an activity suitably elemental and interminable. In his sealed heart he hoped the day would never come.

Now it was here. A Friday. Judith was re-acclimated; all four children were assembled, before jobs and camps and visits again scattered them. Joan thought they should be told one by one. Richard was for making an announcement at the table. She said, "I think just making an announcement is a cop-out. They'll start quarrelling and playing to each other instead of focusing. They're each individuals, you know, not just some corporate obstacle to your freedom."

"O.K., O.K. I agree." Joan's plan was exact. That evening, they were giving Judith a belated welcome-home dinner, of lobster and champagne. Then, the party over, they, the two of them, who nineteen years before would push her in a baby carriage along Fifth Avenue to Washington Square, were to walk her out of the house, to the bridge across the salt creek, and tell her, swearing her to secrecy. Then Richard Jr., who was going directly from work to a rock concert in Boston, would be told, either late when he returned on the train or early Saturday morning before he went off to his job; he was seventeen and employed as one of a golf-course maintenance crew. Then the two younger children, John and Margaret, could, as the morning wore on, be informed.

"Mopped up, as it were," Richard said.

"Do you have any better plan? That leaves you the rest of Saturday to answer any questions, pack, and make your wonderful departure."

"No," he said, meaning he had no better plan, and agreed to hers, though to him it showed an edge of false order, a hidden plea for control, like Joan's long chore lists and financial accountings and, in the days when he first knew her, her too-copious lecture notes. Her plan turned one hurdle for him into four—four knife-sharp walls, each with a sheer blind drop on the other side.

All spring he had moved through a world of insides and outsides, of barriers and partitions. He and Joan stood as a thin barrier between the children and the truth. Each moment was a partition, with the past on one side and the future on the other, a future containing this unthinkable *now*. Beyond four knifelike walls a new life for him waited vaguely. His skull cupped a secret, a white face, a face both frightened and soothing, both strange and known, that he wanted to shield from tears, which he felt all about him, solid as the sunlight. So haunted, he had become obsessed with battening down the house against his absence, replacing screens and sash cords, hinges and latches—a Houdini making things snug before his escape.

The lock. He had still to replace a lock on one of the doors of the screened porch. The task, like most such, proved more difficult than he had imagined. The old lock, aluminum frozen by corrosion, had been deliberately rendered obsolete by manufacturers. Three hardware stores had nothing that even approximately matched the mortised hole its removal (surprisingly easy) left. Another hole had to be gouged, with bits too small and saws too big, and the old hole fitted with a block of wood—the chisels dull, the saw rusty, his fingers thick with lack of sleep. The sun poured down, beyond the porch, on a world of neglect. The bushes already needed pruning, the windward side of the house was shedding flakes of paint, rain would get in when he was gone, insects, rot, death. His family, all those he would lose, filtered through the edges of his awareness as he struggled with screw holes, splinters, opaque instructions, minutiae of metal.

Judith sat on the porch, a princess returned from exile. She regaled them with stories of fuel shortages, of bomb scares in the Underground, of Pakistani workmen loudly lusting after her as she walked past on her way to dance school. Joan came and went, in and out of the house, calmer than she should have been, praising his struggles with the lock as if this were one more and not the last of their long succession of shared chores. The younger of his sons for a few minutes held the rickety screen door while his father clumsily hammered and chiseled, each blow a kind of sob in Richard's ears. His younger daughter, having been at a slumber party, slept on the porch hammock through all the noise—heavy and pink, trusting and forsaken. Time, like the sunlight, continued relentlessly; the sunlight slowly slanted. Today was one of the longest days. The lock clicked, worked. He was through. He had a drink; he drank it on the porch, listening to his daughter. "It was so sweet," she was saying, "during the worst of it, how all the butchers and bakery shops kept open by candlelight. They're all so plucky and cute. From the papers, things sounded so much worse here—people shooting people in gas lines, and everybody freezing."

Richard asked her, "Do you still want to live in England forever?" *Forever:* the concept, now a reality upon him, pressed and scratched at the back of his throat.

"No," Judith confessed, turning her oval face to him, its eyes still childishly far apart, but the lips set as over something succulent and satisfactory. "I was anxious to come home. I'm an American." She was a woman. They had raised her; he and Joan had endured together to raise her, alone of the four. The others had still some raising left in them. Yet it was the thought of telling Judith—the image of her, their first baby, walking between them arm in arm to the bridge—that broke him. The partition between his face and the tears broke. Richard sat down to the celebratory meal with the back of his throat aching; the champagne, the lobster seemed phases of sunshine; he saw them and tasted them through tears. He blinked, swallowed, croakily joked about hay fever. The tears would not stop leaking through; they came not through a hole that could be plugged but through a permeable spot in a membrane, steadily, purely, endlessly, fruitfully. They became, his tears, a shield for himself against these others—their faces, the fact of their assembly, a last time as innocents, at a table where he sat the last time as head. Tears dropped from his nose as he broke the lobster's back; salt flavored his champagne as he sipped it; the raw clench at the back of his throat was delicious. He could not help himself.

His children tried to ignore his tears. Judith, on his right, lit a cigarette, gazed upward in the direction of her too energetic, too sophisticated exhalation; on her other side, John earnestly bent his face to the extraction of the last morsels—legs, tail segments— from the scarlet corpse. Joan, at the opposite end of the table, glanced at him surprised, her reproach displaced by a quick grimace, of forgiveness, or of salute to his superior gift of strategy. Between them, Margaret, no longer called Bean, thirteen and large for her age, gazed from the other side of his pane of tears as if into a shopwindow at something she coveted—at her father, a crystalline heap of splinters and memories. It was not she, however, but John who, in the kitchen, as they cleared the plates and carapaces away, asked Joan the question: *"Why is Daddy crying?"*

Richard heard the question but not the murmured answer. Then he heard Bean cry, "Oh, no-oh!"—the faintly dramatized exclamation of one who had long expected it.

John returned to the table carrying a bowl of salad. He nodded tersely at his father and his lips shaped the conspiratorial words. "She told."

"Told what?" Richard asked aloud, insanely.

The boy sat down as if to rebuke his father's distraction with the example of his own good manners. He said quietly, "The separation."

Joan and Margaret returned; the child, in Richard's twisted vision, seemed diminished in size, and relieved, relieved to have had the bogieman at last proved real. He called out to her—the distances at the table had grown immense—"You knew, you always knew," but the clenching at the back of his throat prevented him from making sense of it. From afar he heard Joan talking, levelly, sensibly, reciting what they had prepared: it was a separation for the summer, an experiment. She and Daddy both agreed it would be good for them; they needed space and time to think; they liked each other but did not make each other happy enough, somehow.

Judith, imitating her mother's factual tone, but in her youth off-key, too cool, said, "I think it's silly. You should either live together or get divorced."

Richard's crying, like a wave that has crested and crashed, had become tumultuous; but it was overtopped by another tumult, for John, who had been so reserved, now grew larger and larger at the table. Perhaps his younger sister's being credited with knowing set him off. "Why didn't you *tell* us?" he asked, in a large round voice quite unlike his own. "You should have *told* us you weren't getting along."

Richard was startled into attempting to force words through his tears. "We *do* get along, that's the trouble, so it doesn't show even to us—" *That we do not love each other* was the rest of the sentence; he couldn't finish it.

Joan finished for him, in her style. "And we've always, *especially*, loved our children."

John was not mollified. "What do you care about *us*?" he boomed. "We're just little things you *had*." His sisters' laughing forced a laugh from him, which he turned hard and parodistic: "Ha ha *ha*." Richard and Joan realized simultaneously that the child was drunk, on Judith's homecoming champagne. Feeling bound to keep the center of the stage, John took a cigarette from Judith's pack, poked it into his mouth, let it hang from his lower lip, and squinted like a gangster.

"You're not little things we had," Richard called to him. "You're the whole point. But you're grown. Or almost."

The boy was lighting matches. Instead of holding them to his cigarette (for they had never seen him smoke; being "good" had been his way of setting himself apart), he held them to his mother's face, closer and closer, for her to blow out. Then he lit the whole folder—a hiss and then a torch, held against his mother's face. Prismed by tears, the flame filled Richard's vision; he didn't know how it was extinguished. He heard Margaret say, "Oh stop showing off," and saw John, in response, break the cigarette in two and put the halves entirely into his mouth and chew, sticking out his tongue to display the shreds to his sister.

Joan talked to him, reasoning—a fountain of reason, unintelligible. "Talked about it for years . . . our children must help us . . . Daddy and I both want . . ." As the boy listened, he carefully wadded a paper napkin into the leaves of his salad, fashioned a ball of paper and lettuce, and popped it into his mouth, looking around the table for the expected laughter. None came. Judith said, "Be mature," and dismissed a plume of smoke.

Richard got up from this stifling table and led the boy outside. Though the house was in twilight, the outdoors still brimmed with light, the lovely waste light of high summer. Both laughing, he supervised John's spitting out the lettuce and paper and tobacco into the pachysandra. He took him by the hand—a square gritty hand, but for its softness a man's. Yet, it held on. They ran together up into the field, past the tennis court. The raw banking left by the bulldozers was dotted with daisies. Past the court and a flat stretch where they used to play family baseball stood a soft green rise glorious in the sun, each weed and species of grass distinct as illumination on parchment. "I'm sorry, so sorry," Richard cried. "You were the only one who ever tried to help me with all the goddam jobs around this place."

Sobbing, safe within his tears and the champagne, John explained, "It's not just the separation, it's the whole crummy year, I *hate* that school, you can't make any friends, the history teacher's a scud."

They sat on the crest of the rise, shaking and warm from their tears but easier in their voices, and Richard tried to focus on the child's sad year—the weekdays long with homework, the weekends spent in his room with model airplanes, while his parents murmured down below, nursing their separation. How selfish, how blind, Richard thought; his eyes felt scoured. He told his son, "We'll think about getting you transferred. Life's too short to be miserable."

They had said what they could, but did not want the moment to heal, and talked on, about the school, about the tennis court, whether it would ever again be as good as it had been that first summer. They walked to inspect it and pressed a few more tapes more firmly down. A little stiltedly, perhaps trying now to make too much of the moment, Richard led the boy to the spot in the field where the view was best, of the metallic blue river, the emerald marsh, the scattered islands velvety with shadow in the low light, the white bits of beach far away. "See," he said. "It goes on being beautiful. It'll be here tomorrow."

"I know," John answered, impatiently. The moment had closed.

Back in the house, the others had opened some white wine, the champagne being drunk, and still sat at the table, the three females, gossiping. Where Joan sat had become the head. She turned, showing him a tearless face, and asked, "All right?"

"We're fine," he said, resenting it, though relieved, that the party went on without him.

In bed she explained, "I couldn't cry I guess because I cried so much all spring. It really wasn't fair. It's your idea, and you made it look as though I was kicking you out."

"I'm sorry," he said. "I couldn't stop. I wanted to but couldn't."

"You *didn't* want to. You loved it. You were having your way, making a general announcement."

"I love having it over," he admitted. "God, those kids were great. So brave and funny." John, returned to the house, had settled to a model airplane in his room, and kept shouting down to them, "I'm O.K. No sweat." "And the way," Richard went on, cozy in his relief, "they never questioned the reasons we gave. No thought of a third person. Not even Judith."

"That *was* touching," Joan said.

He gave her a hug. "You were great too. Very reassuring to everybody. Thank you." Guiltily, he realized he did not feel separated.

"You still have Dickie to do," she told him. These words set before him a black mountain in the darkness; its cold breath, its near weight affected his chest. Of the four children, his elder son was most nearly his conscience. Joan did not need to add, "That's one piece of your dirty work I won't do for you."

"I know. I'll do it. You go to sleep."

Within minutes, her breathing slowed, became oblivious and deep. It was quarter to midnight. Dickie's train from the concert would come in at one-fourteen. Richard set the alarm for one. He had slept atrociously for weeks. But whenever he closed his lids some glimpse of the last hours scorched them—Judith exhaling toward the ceiling in a kind of aversion, Bean's mute staring, the sunstruck growth in the field where he and John had rested. The mountain before him moved closer, moved within him; he was huge, momentous. The ache at the back of his throat felt stale. His wife slept as if slain beside him. When, exasperated by his hot lids, his crowded heart, he rose from bed and dressed, she awoke enough to turn over. He told her then, "Joan, if I could undo it all, I would."

"Where would you begin?" she asked. There was no place. Giving him courage, she was always giving him courage. He put on shoes without socks in the dark. The children were breathing in their rooms, the downstairs was hollow. In their confusion they had left lights burning. He turned off all but one, the kitchen overhead. The car started. He had hoped it wouldn't. He met only moonlight on the road; it seemed a diaphanous companion, flickering in the leaves along the roadside, haunting his rearview mirror like a pursuer, melting under his headlights. The center of town, not quite deserted, was eerie at this hour. A young cop in uniform kept company with a gang of T-shirted kids on the steps of the bank. Across from the railroad station, several bars kept open. Customers, mostly young, passed in and out of the warm night, savoring summer's novelty. Voices shouted from cars as they passed; an immense conversation seemed in progress. Richard parked and in his weariness put his head on the passenger seat, out of the commotion and wheeling lights. It was as when, in the movies, an assassin grimly carries his mission through the jostle of a carnival—except the movies cannot show the precipitous, palpable slope you cling to within. You cannot climb back down; you can only fall. The synthetic fabric of the car seat, warmed by his cheek, confided to him an ancient, distant scent of vanilla.

A train whistle caused him to lift his head. It was on time; he had hoped it would be late. The slender drawgates descended. The bell of approach tingled happily. The great metal body, horizontally fluted, rocked to a stop, and sleepy teen-agers disembarked, his son among them. Dickie did not show surprise that his father was meeting him at this terrible hour. He sauntered to the car with two friends, both taller than he. He said "Hi" to his father and took the passenger's seat with an exhausted promptness that expressed gratitude. The friends got in the back, and Richard was grateful; a few more minutes' postponement would be won by driving them home.

He asked, "How was the concert?"

"Groovy," one boy said from the back seat.

"It bit," the other said.

"It was O.K.," Dickie said, moderate by nature, so reasonable that in his childhood the unreason of the world had given him headaches, stomach aches, nausea. When the second friend had been dropped off at his dark house, the boy blurted, "Dad, my eyes are killing me with hay fever! I'm out there cutting that mothering grass all day!"

"Do we still have those drops?"

"They didn't do any good last summer."

"They might this." Richard swung a U-turn on the empty street. The drive home took a few minutes. The mountain was here, in his throat. "Richard," he said, and felt the boy, slumped and rubbing his eyes, go tense at his tone, "I didn't come to meet you just to make your life easier. I came because your mother and I have some news for you, and you're a hard man to get ahold of these days. It's sad news."

"That's O.K." The reassurance came out soft, but quick, as if released from the tip of a spring.

Richard had feared that his tears would return and choke him, but the boy's manliness set an example, and his voice issued forth steady and dry. "It's sad news, but it needn't be tragic news, at least for you. It should have no practical effect on your life, though it's bound to have an emotional effect. You'll work at your job, and go back to school in September. Your mother and I are really proud of what you're making of your life; we don't want that to change at all."

"Yeah," the boy said lightly, on the intake of his breath, holding himself up. They turned the corner; the church they went to loomed like a gutted fort. The home of the woman Richard hoped to marry stood across the green. Her bedroom light burned.

"Your mother and I," he said, "have decided to separate. For the summer. Nothing legal, no divorce yet. We want to see how it feels. For some years now, we haven't been doing enough for each other, making each other as happy as we should be. Have you sensed that?"

"No," the boy said. It was an honest, unemotional answer: true or false in a quiz.

Glad for the factual basis, Richard pursued, even garrulously, the details. His apartment across town, his utter accessibility, the split vacation arrangements, the advantages to the children, the added mobility and variety of the summer. Dickie listened, absorbing. "Do the others know?"

"Yes."

"How did they take it?"

"The girls pretty calmly. John flipped out; he shouted and ate a cigarette and made a salad out of his napkin and told us how much he hated school."

His brother chuckled. "He did?"

"Yeah. The school issue was more upsetting for him than Mom and me. He seemed to feel better for having exploded."

"He did?" The repetition was the first sign that he was stunned.

"Yes. Dickie, I want to tell you something. This last hour, waiting for your train to get in, has been about the worst of my life. I hate this. *Hate* it. My father would have died before doing it to me." He felt immensely lighter, saying this. He had dumped the mountain on the boy. They were home. Moving swiftly as a shadow, Dickie was out of the car, through the bright kitchen. Richard called after him, "Want a glass of milk or anything?"

"No thanks."

"Want us to call the course tomorrow and say you're too sick to work?"

"No, that's all right." The answer was faint, delivered at the door to his room; Richard listened for the slam that went with a tantrum. The door closed normally, gently. The sound was sickening.

Joan had sunk into that first deep trough of sleep and was slow to awake. Richard had to repeat, "I told him."

"What did he say?"

"Nothing much. Could you go say goodnight to him? Please."

She left their room, without putting on a bathrobe. He sluggishly changed back into his pajamas and walked down the hall. Dickie was already in bed, Joan was sitting beside him, and the boy's bedside clock radio was murmuring music. When she stood, an inexplicable light—the moon?—outlined her body through the nightie. Richard sat on the warm place she had indented on the child's narrow mattress. He asked him, "Do you want the radio on like that?"

"It always is."

"Doesn't it keep you awake? It would me."

"No."

"Are you sleepy?"

"Yeah."

"Good. Sure you want to get up and go to work? You've had a big night."

"I want to."

Away at school this winter he had learned for the first time that you can go short of sleep and live. As an infant he had slept with an immobile, sweating intensity that had alarmed his babysitters. In adolescence he had often been the first of the four children to go to bed. Even now, he would go slack in the middle of a television show, his sprawled legs hairy and brown. "O.K. Good boy. Dickie, listen. I love you so much, I never knew how much until now. No matter how this works out, I'll always be with you. Really."

Richard bent to kiss an averted face but his son, sinewy, turned and with wet cheeks embraced him and gave him a kiss, on the lips, passionate as a woman's. In his father's ear he moaned one word, the crucial, intelligent word: *"Why?"*

Why. It was a whistle of wind in a crack, a knife thrust, a window thrown open on emptiness. The white face was gone, the darkness was featureless. Richard had forgotten why.

ALICE MUNRO

The Children Stay

Thirty years ago, a family was spending a holiday together on the east coast of Vancouver Island. A young father and mother, their two small daughters, and an older couple, the husband's parents.

What perfect weather. Every morning, every morning it's like this, the first pure sunlight falling through the high branches, burning away the mist over the still water of Georgia Strait. The tide out, a great empty stretch of sand still damp but easy to walk on, like cement in its very last stage of drying. The tide is actually less far out; every morning, the pavilion of sand is shrinking, but it still seems ample enough. The changes in the tide are a matter of great interest to the grandfather, not so much to anyone else.

Pauline, the young mother, doesn't really like the beach as well as she likes the road that runs behind the cottages for a mile or so north till it stops at the bank of the little river that runs into the sea.

If it wasn't for the tide, it would be hard to remember that this is the sea. You look across the water to the mountains on the mainland, the ranges that are the western wall of the continent of North America. These humps and peaks coming clear now through the mist and glimpsed here and there through the trees, by Pauline as she pushes her daughter's stroller along the road, are also of interest to the grandfather. And to his son Brian, who is Pauline's husband. The two men are continually trying to decide which is what. Which of these shapes are actual continental mountains and which are improbable heights of the islands that ride in front of the shore? It's hard to sort things out when the array is so complicated and parts of it shift their distance in the day's changing light.

But there is a map, set up under glass, between the cottages and the beach. You can stand there looking at the map, then looking at what's in front of you, looking back at the map again, until you get things sorted out. The grandfather and Brian do this every day, usually getting into an argument—though you'd think there would not be much room for disagreement with the map right there. Brian chooses to see the map as inexact. But his father will not hear a word of criticism about any aspect of this place, which was his choice for the holiday. The map, like the accommodation and the weather, is perfect.

Brian's mother won't look at the map. She says it boggles her mind. The men laugh at her, they accept that her mind is boggled. Her husband believes that this is because she is a female. Brian believes that it's because she's his mother. Her concern is always about whether anybody is hungry yet, or thirsty, whether the children have their sun hats on and have been rubbed with protective lotion. And what is the strange bite on Caitlin's arm that doesn't look like the bite of a mosquito? She makes her husband wear a floppy cotton hat and thinks that Brian should wear one too—she reminds him of how sick he got from the sun, that summer they went to the Okanagan, when he was a child. Sometimes Brian says to her, "Oh, dry up, Mother." His tone is mostly affectionate, but his father may ask him if that's the way he thinks he can talk to his mother nowadays.

"She doesn't mind," says Brian.

"How do you know?" says his father.

"Oh for Pete's sake," says his mother.

———————

Pauline slides out of bed as soon as she's awake every morning, slides out of reach of Brian's long, sleepily searching arms and legs. What wakes her are the first squeaks and mutters of the baby, Mara, in the children's room, then the creak of the crib as Mara—sixteen months old now, getting to the end of babyhood—pulls herself up to stand hanging on to the railing. She continues her soft amiable talk as Pauline lifts her out—Caitlin, nearly five, shifting about but not waking, in her nearby bed—and as she is carried into the kitchen to be changed, on the floor. Then she is settled into her stroller, with a biscuit and a bottle of apple juice, while Pauline gets into her sundress and sandals, goes to the bathroom, combs out her hair—all as quickly and quietly as possible. They leave the cottage; they head past some other cottages for the bumpy unpaved road that is still mostly in deep morning shadow, the floor of a tunnel under fir and cedar trees.

The grandfather, also an early riser, sees them from the porch of his cottage, and Pauline sees him. But all that is necessary is a wave. He and Pauline never have much to say to each other (though sometimes there's an affinity they feel, in the midst of some long-drawn-out antics of Brian's or some apologetic but insistent fuss made by the grandmother; there's an awareness of not looking at each other, lest their look should reveal a bleakness that would discredit others).

On this holiday Pauline steals time to be by herself—being with Mara is still almost the same thing as being by herself. Early morning walks, the late-morning hour when she washes and hangs out the diapers. She could have had another hour or so in the afternoons, while Mara is napping. But Brian has fixed up a shelter on the beach, and he carries the playpen down every day, so that Mara can nap there and Pauline won't have to absent herself. He says his parents may be offended if she's always sneaking off. He agrees though that she does need some time to go over her lines for the play she's going to be in, back in Victoria, this September.

Pauline is not an actress. This is an amateur production, but she is not even an amateur actress. She didn't try out for the role, though it happened that she had already read the play. *Eurydice* by Jean Anouilh. But then, Pauline has read all sorts of things.

She was asked if she would like to be in this play by a man she met at a barbecue, in June. The people at the barbecue were mostly teachers and their wives or husbands—it was held at the house of the principal of the high school where Brian teaches. The woman who taught French was a widow—she had brought her grown son who was staying for the summer with her and working as a night clerk in a downtown hotel. She told everybody that he had got a job teaching at a college in western Washington State and would be going there in the fall.

Jeffrey Toom was his name. "Without the *B*," he said, as if the staleness of the joke wounded him. It was a different name from his mother's because she had been widowed twice, and he was the son of her first husband. About the job he said, "No guarantee it'll last, it's a one-year appointment."

What was he going to teach?

"Dram-ah," he said, drawing the word out in a mocking way.

He spoke of his present job disparagingly, as well.

"It's a pretty sordid place," he said. "Maybe you heard—a hooker was killed there last winter. And then we get the usual losers checking in to OD or bump themselves off."

People did not quite know what to make of this way of talking and drifted away from him. Except for Pauline.

"I'm thinking about putting on a play," he said. "Would you like to be in it?" He asked her if she had ever heard of a play called *Eurydice*.

Pauline said, "You mean Anouilh's?" and he was unflatteringly surprised. He immediately said he didn't know if it would ever work out. "I just thought it might be interesting to see if you could do something different here in the land of Noël Coward."

Pauline did not remember when there had been a play by Noël

Coward put on in Victoria, though she supposed there had been several. She said, "We saw *The Duchess of Malfi* last winter at the college. And the little theater did *A Resounding Tinkle*, but we didn't see it."

"Yeah. Well," he said, flushing. She had thought he was older than she was, at least as old as Brian (who was thirty, though people were apt to say he didn't act it), but as soon as he started talking to her, in this offhand, dismissive way, never quite meeting her eyes, she suspected that he was younger than he'd like to appear. Now with that flush she was sure of it.

As it turned out, he was a year younger than she was. Twenty-five.

She said that she couldn't be Eurydice; she couldn't act. But Brian came over to see what the conversation was about and said at once that she must try it.

"She just needs a kick in the behind," Brian said to Jeffrey. "She's like a little mule, it's hard to get her started. No, seriously, she's too self-effacing, I tell her that all the time. She's very smart. She's actually a lot smarter than I am."

At that Jeffrey did look directly into Pauline's eyes—impertinently and searchingly—and she was the one who was flushing.

He had chosen her immediately as his Eurydice because of the way she looked. But it was not because she was beautiful. "I'd never put a beautiful girl in that part," he said. "I don't know if I'd ever put a beautiful girl on stage in anything. It's too much. It's distracting."

So what did he mean about the way she looked? He said it was her hair, which was long and dark and rather bushy (not in style at that time), and her pale skin ("Stay out of the sun this summer") and most of all her eyebrows.

"I never liked them," said Pauline, not quite sincerely. Her eyebrows were level, dark, luxuriant. They dominated her face. Like her hair, they were not in style. But if she had really disliked them, wouldn't she have plucked them?

Jeffrey seemed not to have heard her. "They give you a sulky look and that's disturbing," he said. "Also your jaw's a little heavy and that's sort of Greek. It would be better in a movie where I could get you close up. The routine thing for Eurydice would be a girl who looked ethereal. I don't want ethereal."

As she walked Mara along the road, Pauline did work at the lines. There was a speech at the end that was giving her trouble. She bumped the stroller along and repeated to herself, "'You are terrible, you know, you are terrible like the angels. You think everybody's going forward, as brave and bright as you are—oh, don't look at me, please, darling, don't look at me—perhaps I'm not what you wish I was, but I'm here, and I'm warm, I'm kind, and I love you. I'll give you all the happiness I can. Don't look at me. Don't look. Let me live.'"

She had left something out. "'Perhaps I'm not what you wish I was, but you feel me here, don't you? I'm warm and I'm kind—'"

She had told Jeffrey that she thought the play was beautiful.

He said, "Really?" What she'd said didn't please or surprise him—he seemed to feel it was predictable, superfluous. He would never describe a play in that way. He spoke of it more as a hurdle to be got over. Also a challenge to be flung at various enemies. At the academic snots—as he called them—who had done *The Duchess of Malfi*. And at the social twits—as he called them—in the little theater. He saw himself as an outsider heaving his weight against these people, putting on his play—he called it his—in the teeth of their contempt and opposition. In the beginning Pauline thought that this must be all in his imagination and that it was more likely these people knew nothing about him. Then something would happen that could be, but might not be, a coincidence. Repairs had to be done on the church hall where the play was to be performed, making it unobtainable. There was an unexpected increase in the cost of printing advertising posters. She found herself seeing it his way. If you were going to be around him much, you almost had to see it his way—arguing was dangerous and exhausting.

"Sons of bitches," said Jeffrey between his teeth, but with some satisfaction. "I'm not surprised."

The rehearsals were held upstairs in an old building on Fisgard Street. Sunday afternoon was the only time that everybody could get there, though there were fragmentary rehearsals during the week. The retired harbor pilot who played Monsieur Henri was able to attend every rehearsal, and got to have an irritating familiarity with everybody else's lines. But the hairdresser—who had experience only with Gilbert and Sullivan but now found herself playing Eurydice's mother—could not leave her shop for long at any other time. The bus driver who played her lover had his daily employment as well, and so had the waiter who played Orphée (he was the only one of them who hoped to be a real actor). Pauline had to depend on sometimes undependable high-school baby-sitters—for the first six weeks of the summer Brian was busy teaching summer school—and Jeffrey himself had to be at his hotel job by eight o'clock in the evenings. But on Sunday afternoons they were all there. While other people swam at Thetis Lake, or thronged Beacon Hill Park to walk under the trees and feed the ducks, or drove far out of town to the Pacific beaches, Jeffrey and his crew labored in the dusty high-ceilinged room on Fisgard Street. The windows were rounded at the top as in some plain and dignified church, and propped open in the heat with whatever objects could be found—ledger books from the 1920s belonging to the hat shop that had once operated downstairs, or pieces of wood left over from the picture frames made by the artist whose canvases were now stacked against one wall and apparently abandoned. The glass was grimy, but outside the sunlight bounced off the sidewalks, the empty gravelled parking lots, the low stuccoed buildings, with what seemed a special Sunday brightness. Hardly anybody moved through these downtown streets. Nothing was open except the occasional hole-in-the-wall coffee shop or fly-specked convenience store.

Pauline was the one who went out at the break to get soft drinks and coffee. She was the one who had the least to say about the play and the way it was going—even though she was the only one who had read it before—because she alone had never done any acting.

So it seemed proper for her to volunteer. She enjoyed her short walk in the empty streets—she felt as if she had become an urban person, someone detached and solitary, who lived in the glare of an important dream. Sometimes she thought of Brian at home, working in the garden and keeping an eye on the children. Or perhaps he had taken them to Dallas Road—she recalled a promise—to sail boats on the pond. That life seemed ragged and tedious compared to what went on in the rehearsal room—the hours of effort, the concentration, the sharp exchanges, the sweating and tension. Even the taste of the coffee, its scalding bitterness, and the fact that it was chosen by nearly everybody in preference to a fresher-tasting and maybe more healthful drink out of the cooler seemed satisfying to her. And she liked the look of the shop windows. This was not one of the dolled-up streets near the harbor—it was a street of shoe- and bicycle-repair shops, discount linen and fabric stores, of clothes and furniture that had been so long in the windows that they looked secondhand even if they weren't. On some windows sheets of golden plastic as frail and crinkled as old cellophane were stretched inside the glass to protect the merchandise from the sun. All these enterprises had been left behind just for this one day, but they had a look of being fixed in time as much as cave paintings or relics under sand.

When she said that she had to go away for the two-week holiday Jeffrey looked thunderstruck, as if he had never imagined that things like holidays could come into her life. Then he turned grim and slightly satirical, as if this was just another blow that he might have expected. Pauline explained that she would miss only the one Sunday—the one in the middle of the two weeks—because she and Brian were driving up the island on a Monday and coming back on a Sunday morning. She promised to get back in time for rehearsal. Privately she wondered how she would do this—it always took so much longer than you expected to pack up and get away. She wondered if she could possibly come back by herself, on the morning bus. That would probably be too much to ask for. She didn't mention it.

She couldn't ask him if it was only the play he was thinking about, only her absence from a rehearsal that caused the thundercloud. At the moment, it very likely was. When he spoke to her at rehearsals there was never any suggestion that he ever spoke to her in any other way. The only difference in his treatment of her was that perhaps he expected less of her, of her acting, than he did of the others. And that would be understandable to anybody. She was the only one chosen out of the blue, for the way she looked—the others had all shown up at the audition he had advertised on the signs put up in cafés and bookstores around town. From her he appeared to want an immobility or awkwardness that he didn't want from the rest of them. Perhaps it was because, in the latter part of the play, she was supposed to be a person who had already died.

Yet she thought they all knew, the rest of the cast all knew, what was going on, in spite of Jeffrey's offhand and abrupt and none too civil ways. They knew that after every one of them had straggled off home, he would walk across the room and bolt the staircase door. (At first Pauline had pretended to leave with the rest and had even got into her car and circled the block, but later such a trick had come to seem insulting, not just to herself and Jeffrey, but to the others whom she was sure would never betray her, bound as they all were under the temporary but potent spell of the play.)

Jeffrey crossed the room and bolted the door. Every time, this was like a new decision, which he had to make. Until it was done, she wouldn't look at him. The sound of the bolt being pushed into place, the ominous or fatalistic sound of the metal hitting metal, gave her a localized shock of capitulation. But she didn't make a move, she waited for him to come back to her with the whole story of the afternoon's labor draining out of his face, the expression of matter-of-fact and customary disappointment cleared away, replaced by the live energy she always found surprising.

"So. Tell us what this play of yours is about," Brian's father said. "Is it one of those ones where they take their clothes off on the stage?"

"Now don't tease her," said Brian's mother.

Brian and Pauline had put the children to bed and walked over to his parents' cottage for an evening drink. The sunset was behind them, behind the forests of Vancouver Island, but the mountains in front of them, all clear now and hard-cut against the sky, shone in its pink light. Some high inland mountains were capped with pink summer snow.

"Nobody takes their clothes off, Dad," said Brian in his booming schoolroom voice. "You know why? Because they haven't got any clothes on in the first place. It's the latest style. They're going to put on a bare-naked *Hamlet* next. Bare-naked *Romeo and Juliet*. Boy, that balcony scene where Romeo is climbing up the trellis and he gets stuck in the rosebushes—"

"Oh, Brian," said his mother.

"The story of Orpheus and Eurydice is that Eurydice died," Pauline said. "And Orpheus goes down to the underworld to try to get her back. And his wish is granted, but only if he promises not to look at her. Not to look back at her. She's walking behind him—"

"Twelve paces," said Brian. "As is only right."

"It's a Greek story, but it's set in modern times," said Pauline. "At least this version is. More or less modern. Orpheus is a musician travelling around with his father—they're both musicians—and Eurydice is an actress. This is in France."

"Translated?" Brian's father said.

"No," said Brian. "But don't worry, it's not in French. It was written in Transylvanian."

"It's so hard to make sense of anything," Brian's mother said with a worried laugh. "It's so hard, with Brian around."

"It's in English," Pauline said.

"And you're what's-her-name?"

She said, "I'm Eurydice."

"He get you back okay?"

"No," she said. "He looks back at me, and then I have to stay dead."

"Oh, an unhappy ending," Brian's mother said.

"You're so gorgeous?" said Brian's father skeptically. "He can't stop himself from looking back?"

"It's not that," said Pauline. But at this point she felt that something had been achieved by her father-in-law, he had done what he meant to do, which was the same thing that he nearly always meant to do, in any conversation she had with him. And that was to break through the structure of some explanation he had asked her for, and she had unwillingly but patiently given, and, with a seemingly negligent kick, knock it into rubble. He had been dangerous to her for a long time in this way, but he wasn't particularly so tonight.

But Brian did not know that. Brian was still figuring out how to come to her rescue.

"Pauline is gorgeous," Brian said.

"Yes indeed," said his mother.

"Maybe if she'd go to the hairdresser," his father said. But Pauline's long hair was such an old objection of his that it had become a family joke. Even Pauline laughed. She said, "I can't afford to till we get the veranda roof fixed." And Brian laughed boisterously, full of relief that she was able to take all this as a joke. It was what he had always told her to do.

"Just kid him back," he said. "It's the only way to handle him."

"Yeah, well, if you'd got yourselves a decent house," said his father. But this like Pauline's hair was such a familiar sore point that it couldn't rouse anybody. Brian and Pauline had bought a handsome house in bad repair on a street in Victoria where old mansions were being turned into ill-used apartment buildings. The house, the street, the messy old Garry oaks, the fact that no basement had been blasted out under the house, were all a horror to Brian's father. Brian usually agreed with him and tried to go him one further. If his father pointed at the house next door all crisscrossed with black fire escapes, and asked what kind of neighbors they had, Brian said, "Really poor people, Dad. Drug addicts." And when his father wanted to know how it was heated, he'd said, "Coal furnace. Hardly any of them left these days, you can get coal really cheap. Of course it's dirty and it kind of stinks."

So what his father said now about a decent house might be some kind of peace signal. Or could be taken so.

Brian was an only son. He was a math teacher. His father was a civil engineer and part owner of a contracting company. If he had hoped that he would have a son who was an engineer and might come into the company, there was never any mention of it. Pauline had asked Brian whether he thought the carping about their house and her hair and the books she read might be a cover for this larger disappointment, but Brian had said, "Nope. In our family we complain about just whatever we want to complain about. We ain't subtle, ma'am."

Pauline still wondered, when she heard his mother talking about how teachers ought to be the most honored people in the world and they did not get half the credit they deserved and that she didn't know how Brian managed it, day after day. Then his father might say, "That's right," or, "I sure wouldn't want to do it, I can tell you that. They couldn't pay me to do it."

"Don't worry Dad," Brian would say. "They wouldn't pay you much."

Brian in his everyday life was a much more dramatic person than Jeffrey. He dominated his classes by keeping up a parade of jokes and antics, extending the role that he had always played, Pauline believed, with his mother and father. He acted dumb, he bounced back from pretended humiliations, he traded insults. He was a bully in a good cause—a chivvying cheerful indestructible bully.

"Your boy has certainly made his mark with us," the principal said to Pauline. "He has not just survived, which is something in itself. He has made his mark."

Your boy.

Brian called his students boneheads. His tone was affectionate, fatalistic. He said that his father was the King of the Philistines, a pure and natural barbarian. And that his mother was a dishrag, good-natured and worn out. But however he dismissed such people, he could not be long without them. He took his students on camping trips. And he could not imagine a summer without this shared holiday. He was mortally afraid, every year, that Pauline would refuse to go along. Or that, having agreed to go, she was going to be miserable, take offense at something his father said, complain about how much time she had to spend with his mother, sulk because there was no way they could do anything by themselves. She might decide to spend all day in their own cottage, reading and pretending to have a sunburn.

All those things had happened, on previous holidays. But this year she was easing up. He told her he could see that, and he was grateful to her.

"I know it's an effort," he said. "It's different for me. They're my parents and I'm used to not taking them seriously."

Pauline came from a family that took things so seriously that her parents had got a divorce. Her mother was now dead. She had a distant, though cordial, relationship with her father and her two much older sisters. She said that they had nothing in common. She knew Brian could not understand how that could be a reason. She saw what comfort it gave him, this year, to see things going so well. She had thought it was laziness or cowardice that kept him from breaking the arrangement, but now she saw that it was something far more positive. He needed to have his wife and his parents and his children bound together like this, he needed to involve Pauline in his life with his parents and to bring his parents to some recognition of her—though the recognition, from his father, would always be muffled and contrary, and from his mother too profuse, too easily come by, to mean much. Also he wanted Pauline to be connected, he wanted the children to be connected, to his own childhood—he wanted these holidays to be linked to holidays of his childhood with their lucky or unlucky weather, car troubles or driving records, boating scares, bee stings, marathon Monopoly games, to all the things that he told his mother he was bored to death hearing about. He wanted pictures from this summer to be taken, and fitted into his mother's album, a continuation of all the other pictures that he groaned at the mention of.

The only time they could talk to each other was in bed, late at night. But they did talk then, more than was usual with them at home, where Brian was so tired that often he fell immediately asleep. And in ordinary daylight it was often hard to talk to him because of his jokes. She could see the joke brightening his eyes (his coloring was very like hers—dark hair and pale skin and gray eyes, but her eyes were cloudy and his were light, like clear water over stones). She could see it pulling at the corners of his mouth, as he foraged among your words to catch a pun or the start of a rhyme— anything that could take the conversation away, into absurdity. His whole body, tall and loosely joined together and still almost as skinny as a teenager's, twitched with comic propensity. Before she married him, Pauline had a friend named Gracie, a rather grumpy-looking girl, subversive about men. Brian had thought her a girl whose spirits needed a boost, and so he made even more than the usual effort. And Gracie said to Pauline, "How can you stand the nonstop show?"

"That's not the real Brian," Pauline had said. "He's different when we're alone." But looking back, she wondered how true that had ever been. Had she said it simply to defend her choice, as you did when you had made up your mind to get married?

So talking in the dark had something to do with the fact that she could not see his face. And that he knew she couldn't see his face.

But even with the window open on the unfamiliar darkness and stillness of the night, he teased a little. He had to speak of Jeffrey as Monsieur le Directeur, which made the play or the fact that it was a French play slightly ridiculous. Or perhaps it was Jeffrey himself, Jeffrey's seriousness about the play, that had to be called in question.

Pauline didn't care. It was such a pleasure and a relief to her to mention Jeffrey's name.

Most of the time she didn't mention him; she circled around that pleasure. She described all the others, instead. The hairdresser and the harbor pilot and the waiter and the old man who claimed to have once acted on the radio. He played Orphée's father and gave Jeffrey the most trouble, because he had the stubbornest notions of his own, about acting.

The middle-aged impresario Monsieur Dulac was played by a twenty-four-year-old travel agent. And Mathias, who was Eurydice's former boyfriend, presumably around her own age, was played by the manager of a shoe store, who was married and a father of children.

Brian wanted to know why Monsieur le Directeur hadn't cast these two the other way round.

"That's the way he does things," Pauline said. "What he sees in us is something only he can see."

For instance, she said, the waiter was a clumsy Orphée.

"He's only nineteen, he's so shy Jeffrey has to keep at him. He tells him not to act like he's making love to his grandmother. He has to tell him what to do. *Keep your arms around her a little longer, stroke her here a little.* I don't know how it's going to work—I just have to trust Jeffrey, that he knows what he's doing."

"'Stroke her here a little'?" said Brian. "Maybe I should come around and keep an eye on these rehearsals."

When she had started to quote Jeffrey, Pauline had felt a giving-way in her womb or the bottom of her stomach, a shock that had travelled oddly upwards and hit her vocal cords. She had to cover up this quaking by growling in a way that was supposed to be an imitation (though Jeffrey never growled or ranted or carried on in any theatrical way at all).

"But there's a point about him being so innocent," she said hurriedly. "Being not so physical. Being awkward." And she began to talk about Orphée in the play, not the waiter. Orphée has a problem with love or reality. Orphée will not put up with anything less than perfection. He wants a love that is outside of ordinary life. He wants a perfect Eurydice.

"Eurydice is more realistic. She's carried on with Mathias and with Monsieur Dulac. She's been around her mother and her mother's lover. She knows what people are like. But she loves Orphée. She loves him better in a way than he loves her. She loves him better because she's not such a fool. She loves him like a human person."

"But she's slept with those other guys," Brian said.

"Well with Mr. Dulac she had to, she couldn't get out of it. She didn't want to, but probably after a while she enjoyed it, because after a certain point she couldn't help enjoying it."

So Orphée is at fault, Pauline said decidedly. He looks at Eurydice on purpose, to kill her and get rid of her because she is not perfect. Because of him she has to die a second time.

Brian, on his back and with his eyes wide open (she knew that because of the tone of his voice) said, "But doesn't he die too?"

"Yes. He chooses to."

"So then they're together?"

"Yes. Like Romeo and Juliet. *Orphée is with Eurydice at last.* That's what Monsieur Henri says. That's the last line of the play. That's the end." Pauline rolled over onto her side and touched her cheek to Brian's shoulder—not to start anything but to emphasize what she said next. "It's a beautiful play in one way, but in another it's so silly. And it isn't really like *Romeo and Juliet* because it isn't bad luck or circumstances. It's on purpose. So they don't have to go on with life and get married and have kids and buy an old house and fix it up and—"

"And have affairs," said Brian. "After all, they're French."

Then he said, "Be like my parents."

Pauline laughed. "Do they have affairs? I can imagine."

"Oh sure," said Brian. "I meant their life.

"Logically I can see killing yourself so you won't turn into your parents," Brian said. "I just don't believe anybody would do it."

"Everybody has choices," Pauline said dreamily. "Her mother and his father are both despicable in a way, but Orphée and Eurydice don't have to be like them. They're not corrupt. Just because she's slept with those men doesn't mean she's corrupt. She wasn't in love then. She hadn't met Orphée. There's one speech where he tells her that everything she's done is sticking to her, and it's disgusting. Lies she's told him. The other men. It's all sticking to her forever. And then of course Monsieur Henri plays up to that. He tells Orphée that he'll be just as bad and that one day he'll walk down the street with Eurydice and he'll look like a man with a dog he's trying to lose."

To her surprise, Brian laughed.

"No," she said. "That's what's stupid. It's not inevitable. It's not inevitable at all."

They went on speculating, and comfortably arguing, in a way that was not usual, but not altogether unfamiliar to them. They had done this before, at long intervals in their married life—talked half the night about God or fear of death or how children should be educated or whether money was important. At last they admitted to being too tired to make sense any longer, and arranged themselves in a comradely position and went to sleep.

Finally a rainy day. Brian and his parents were driving into Campbell River to get groceries, and gin, and to take Brian's father's car to a garage, to see about a problem that had developed on the drive up from Nanaimo. This was a very slight problem, but there was the matter of the new-car warranty's being in effect at present, so Brian's father wanted to get it seen to as soon as possible. Brian had to go along, with his car, just in case his father's car had to be left in the garage. Pauline said that she had to stay home because of Mara's nap.

She persuaded Caitlin to lie down, too—allowing her to take her music box to bed with her if she played it very softly. Then Pauline spread the script on the kitchen table and drank coffee and went over the scene in which Orphée says that it's intolerable, at last, to stay in two skins, two envelopes with their own blood and oxygen sealed up in their solitude, and Eurydice tells him to be quiet.

"Don't talk. Don't think. Just let your hand wander, let it be happy on its own."

Your hand is my happiness, says Eurydice. Accept that. Accept your happiness.

Of course he says he cannot.

Caitlin called out frequently to ask what time it was. She turned up the sound of the music box. Pauline hurried to the bedroom door and hissed at her to turn it down, not to wake Mara.

"If you play it like that again I'll take it away from you. Okay?"

But Mara was already rustling around in her crib, and in the next few minutes there were sounds of soft, encouraging conversation from Caitlin, designed to get her sister wide awake. Also of the music being quickly turned up and then down. Then of Mara rattling the crib railing, pulling herself up, throwing her bottle out onto the floor, and starting the bird cries that would grow more and more desolate until they brought her mother.

"I didn't wake her," Caitlin said. "She was awake all by herself. It's not raining anymore. Can we go down to the beach?"

She was right. It wasn't raining. Pauline changed Mara, told Caitlin to get her bathing suit on and find her sand pail. She got into her own bathing suit and put her shorts over it, in case the rest of the family arrived home while she was down there. ("Dad doesn't like the way some women just go right out of their cottages in their bathing suits," Brian's mother had said to her. "I guess he and I just grew up in other times.") She picked up the script to take it along, then laid it down. She was afraid that she would get too absorbed in it and take her eyes off the children for a moment too long.

The thoughts that came to her, of Jeffrey, were not really thoughts at all—they were more like alterations in her body. This could happen when she was sitting on the beach (trying to stay in the half shade of a bush and so preserve her pallor, as Jeffrey had ordered) or when she was wringing out diapers or when she and Brian were visiting his parents. In the middle of Monopoly games, Scrabble games, card games. She went right on talking, listening, working, keeping track of the children, while some memory of her secret life disturbed her like a radiant explosion. Then a warm weight settled, reassurance filling up all her hollows. But it didn't last, this comfort leaked away, and she was like a miser whose windfall has vanished and who is convinced such luck can never strike again. Longing buckled her up and drove her to the discipline of counting days. Sometimes she even cut the days into fractions to figure out more exactly how much time had gone.

She thought of going into Campbell River, making some excuse, so that she could get to a phone booth and call him. The cottages had no phones—the only public phone was in the hall of the lodge. But she did not have the number of the hotel where Jeffrey worked. And besides that, she could never get away to Campbell River in the evening. She was afraid that if she called him at home in the daytime his mother the French teacher might answer. He said his mother hardly ever left the house in the summer. Just once, she had taken the ferry to Vancouver for the day. Jeffrey had phoned Pauline to ask her to come over. Brian was teaching, and Caitlin was at her play group.

Pauline said, "I can't. I have Mara."

Jeffrey said, "Who? Oh. Sorry." Then "Couldn't you bring her along?"

She said no.

"Why not? Couldn't you bring some things for her to play with?"

No, said Pauline. "I couldn't," she said. "I just couldn't." It seemed too dangerous to her, to trundle her baby along on such a guilty expedition. To a house where cleaning fluids would not be bestowed on high shelves, and all pills and cough syrups and cigarettes and buttons put safely out of reach. And even if she escaped poisoning or choking, Mara might be storing up time bombs—memories of a strange house where she was strangely disregarded, of a closed door, noises on the other side of it.

"I just wanted you," Jeffrey said. "I just wanted you in my bed."

She said again, weakly, "No."

Those words of his kept coming back to her. *I wanted you in my bed.* A half-joking urgency in his voice but also a determination, a practicality, as if "in my bed" meant something more, the bed he spoke of taking on larger, less marital dimensions.

Had she made a great mistake with that refusal? With that reminder of how fenced in she was, in what anybody would call her real life?

The beach was nearly empty—people had got used to its being a rainy day. The sand was too heavy for Caitlin to make a castle or dig an irrigation system—projects she would only undertake with her father, anyway, because she sensed that his interest in them was wholehearted, and Pauline's was not. She wandered a bit forlornly at the edge of the water. She probably missed the presence of other children, the nameless instant friends and occasional stone-throwing water-kicking enemies, the shrieking and splashing and falling about. A boy a little bigger than she was and apparently all by himself stood knee-deep in the water farther down the beach. If these two could get together it might be all right; the whole beach experience might be retrieved. Pauline couldn't tell whether Caitlin was now making little splashy runs into the water for his benefit or whether he was watching her with interest or scorn.

Mara didn't need company, at least for now. She stumbled towards the water, felt it touch her feet and changed her mind, stopped, looked around, and spotted Pauline. "Paw. Paw," she said, in happy recognition. "Paw" was what she said for "Pauline," instead of "Mother" or "Mommy." Looking around overbalanced her—she sat down half on the sand and half in the water, made a squawk of surprise that turned to an announcement, then by some determined ungraceful maneuvers that involved putting her weight on her hands, she rose to her feet, wavering and triumphant. She had been walking for half a year, but getting around on the sand was still a challenge. Now she came back towards Pauline, making some reasonable, casual remarks in her own language.

"Sand," said Pauline, holding up a clot of it. "Look. Mara. Sand."

Mara corrected her, calling it something else—it sounded like "whap." Her thick diaper under her plastic pants and her terry cloth playsuit gave her a fat bottom, and that, along with her plump cheeks and shoulders and her sidelong important expression, made her look like a roguish matron.

Pauline became aware of someone calling her name. It had been called two or three times, but because the voice was unfamiliar she had not recognized it. She stood up and waved. It was the woman who worked in the store at the lodge. She was leaning over the balcony and calling, "Mrs. Keating. Mrs. Keating? Telephone, Mrs. Keating."

Pauline hoisted Mara onto her hip and summoned Caitlin. She and the little boy were aware of each other now—they were both picking up stones from the bottom and flinging them out into the water. At first she didn't hear Pauline, or pretended not to.

"Store," called Pauline. "Caitlin. Store." When she was sure Caitlin would follow—it was the word "store" that had done it, the reminder of the tiny store in the lodge where you could buy ice

cream and candy and cigarettes and mixer—she began the trek
across the sand and up the flight of wooden steps above the sand
and the salal bushes. Halfway up she stopped, said, "Mara, you
weigh a ton," and shifted the baby to her other hip. Caitlin banged
a stick against the railing.

"Can I have a Fudgsicle? Mother? Can I?"

"We'll see."

"Can I please have a Fudgsicle?"

"Wait."

The public phone was beside a bulletin board on the other side
of the main hall and across from the door to the dining room. A
bingo game had been set up in there, because of the rain.

"Hope he's still hanging on," the woman who worked in the
store called out. She was unseen now behind her counter.

Pauline, still holding Mara, picked up the dangling receiver and
said breathlessly, "Hello?" She was expecting to hear Brian telling
her about some delay in Campbell River or asking her what it was
she had wanted him to get at the drugstore. It was just the one
thing—calamine lotion—so he had not written it down.

"Pauline," said Jeffrey. "It's me."

Mara was bumping and scrambling against Pauline's side, anxious to get down. Caitlin came along the hall and went into the
store, leaving wet sandy footprints. Pauline said, "Just a minute, just
a minute." She let Mara slide down and hurried to close the door
that led to the steps. She did not remember telling Jeffrey the name
of this place, though she had told him roughly where it was. She
heard the woman in the store speaking to Caitlin in a sharper voice
than she would use to children whose parents were beside them.

"Did you forget to put your feet under the tap?"

"I'm here," said Jeffrey. "I didn't get along well without you. I
didn't get along at all."

Mara made for the dining room, as if the male voice calling out
"Under the *N*—" was a direct invitation to her.

"Here. Where?" said Pauline.

She read the signs that were tacked up on the bulletin board beside the phone.

No Person under Fourteen Years of Age Not Accompanied by Adult Allowed in Boats or Canoes.

Fishing Derby.

Bake and Craft Sale, St. Bartholomew's Church.

Your Life Is in Your Hands. Palms and Cards Read. Reasonable and Accurate. Call Claire.

"In a motel. In Campbell River."

Pauline knew where she was before she opened her eyes. Nothing surprised her. She had slept but not deeply enough to let go of anything.

She had waited for Brian in the parking area of the lodge, with the children, and had asked him for the keys. She had told him in front of his parents that there was something else she needed, from Campbell River. He asked, What was it? And did she have any money?

"Just something," she said, so he would think that it was tampons or birth control supplies, that she didn't want to mention. "Sure."

"Okay but you'll have to put some gas in," he said.

Later she had to speak to him on the phone. Jeffrey said she had to do it.

"Because he won't take it from me. He'll think I kidnapped you or something. He won't believe it."

But the strangest thing of all the things that day was that Brian did seem, immediately, to believe it. Standing where she had stood not so long before, in the public hallway of the lodge—the bingo game over now but people going past, she could hear them, people on their way out of the dining room after dinner—he said, "Oh. Oh. Oh. Okay" in a voice that would have to be quickly controlled, but that seemed to draw on a supply of fatalism or foreknowledge that went far beyond that necessity.

As if he had known all along, all along, what could happen with her.

"Okay," he said. "What about the car?"

He said something else, something impossible, and hung up, and she came out of the phone booth beside some gas pumps in Campbell River.

"That was quick," Jeffrey said. "Easier than you expected."

Pauline said, "I don't know."

"He may have known it subconsciously. People do know."

She shook her head, to tell him not to say anymore, and he said, "Sorry." They walked along the street not touching or talking.

They'd had to go out to find a phone booth because there was no phone in the motel room. Now in the early morning looking around at leisure—the first real leisure or freedom she'd had since she came into that room—Pauline saw that there wasn't much of anything in it. Just a junk dresser, the bed without a headboard, an armless up-holstered chair, on the window a venetian blind with a broken slat and curtain of orange plastic that was supposed to look like net and that didn't have to be hemmed, just sliced off at the bottom. There was a noisy air conditioner—Jeffrey had turned it off in the night and left the door open on the chain, since the window was sealed. The door was shut now. He must have got up in the night and shut it.

This was all she had. Her connection with the cottage where Brian lay asleep or not asleep was broken, also her connection with the house that had been an expression of her life with Brian, of the way they wanted to live. She had no furniture anymore. She had cut herself off from all the large solid acquisitions like the washer and dryer and the oak table and the refinished wardrobe and the chandelier that was a copy of the one in a painting by Vermeer. And just as much from those things that were particularly hers—the pressed-glass tumblers that she had been collecting and the prayer rug which was of course not authentic, but beautiful. Especially from those things. Even her books, she might have lost. Even her clothes. The skirt and blouse and sandals she had put on for the trip to Campbell River might well be all she had now to her name. She would never go back to lay claim to anything. If Brian got in touch with her to ask what was to be done with things, she would tell him to do what he liked—throw everything into garbage bags and take it to the dump, if that was what he liked. (In fact she knew that he would probably pack up a trunk, which he did, sending on, scrupulously, not only her winter coat and boots but things like the waist cincher she had worn at her wedding and never since, with the prayer rug draped over the top of everything like a final statement of his generosity, either natural or calculated.)

She believed that she would never again care about what sort of rooms she lived in or what sort of clothes she put on. She would not be looking for that sort of help to give anybody an idea of who she was, what she was like. Not even to give herself an idea. What she had done would be enough, it would be the whole thing.

What she was doing would be what she had heard about and read about. It was what Anna Karenina had done and what Madame Bovary had wanted to do. It was what a teacher at Brian's school had done, with the school secretary. He had run off with her. That was what it was called. Running off with. Taking off with. It was spoken of disparagingly, humorously, enviously. It was adultery taken one step further. The people who did it had almost certainly been having an affair already, committing adultery for quite some time before they became desperate or courageous enough to take this step. Once in a long while a couple might claim their love was unconsummated and technically pure, but these people would be thought of—if anybody believed them—as being not only very serious and high-minded but almost devastatingly foolhardy, almost in a class with those who took a chance and gave up everything to go and work in some poor and dangerous country.

The others, the adulterers, were seen as irresponsible, immature, selfish, or even cruel. Also lucky. They were lucky because the sex they had been having in parked cars or the long grass or in each other's sullied marriage beds or most likely in motels like this one must surely have been splendid. Otherwise they would never have got such a yearning for each other's company at all costs or such a faith that their shared future would be altogether better and different in kind from what they had in the past.

Different in kind. That was what Pauline must believe now—that there was this major difference in lives or in marriages or unions between people. That some of them had a necessity, a fatefulness, about them that others did not have. Of course she would have said the same thing a year ago. People did say that, they seemed to believe that, and to believe that their own cases were all of the first, the special kind, even when anybody could see that they were not and that these people did not know what they were talking about. Pauline would not have known what she was talking about.

It was too warm in the room. Jeffrey's body was too warm. Conviction and contentiousness seemed to radiate from it, even in sleep. His torso was thicker than Brian's; he was pudgier around the waist. More flesh on the bones, yet not so slack to the touch. Not so good-looking in general—she was sure most people would say that. And not so fastidious. Brian in bed smelled of nothing. Jeffrey's skin, every time she'd been with him, had had a baked-in, slightly oily or nutty smell. He didn't wash last night—but then, neither did she. There wasn't time. Did he even have a toothbrush with him? She didn't. But she had not known she was staying.

When she met Jeffrey here it was still in the back of her mind that she had to concoct some colossal lie to serve her when she got home. And she—they—had to hurry. When Jeffrey said to her that he had decided that they must stay together, that she would come with him to Washington State, that they would have to drop the play because things would be too difficult for them in Victoria, she had looked at him just in the blank way you'd look at somebody the moment that an earthquake started. She was ready to tell him all the reasons why this was not possible, she still thought she was going to tell him that, but her life was coming adrift in that moment. To go back would be like tying a sack over her head.

All she said was "Are you sure?"

He said, "Sure." He said sincerely, "I'll never leave you."

That did not seem the sort of thing that he would say. Then she realized he was quoting—maybe ironically—from the play. It was what Orphée says to Eurydice within a few moments of their first meeting in the station buffet.

So her life was falling forwards; she was becoming one of those people who ran away. A woman who shockingly and incomprehensibly gave everything up. For love, observers would say wryly. Meaning, for sex. None of this would happen if it wasn't for sex.

And yet what's the great difference there? It's not such a variable procedure, in spite of what you're told. Skins, motions, contact, results. Pauline isn't a woman from whom it's difficult to get results. Brain got them. Probably anybody would, who wasn't wildly inept or morally disgusting.

But nothing's the same, really. With Brian—especially with Brian, to whom she has dedicated a selfish sort of goodwill, with whom she's lived in married complicity—there can never be this stripping away, the inevitable flight, the feelings she doesn't have to strive for but only to give in to like breathing or dying. That she believes can only come when the skin is on Jeffrey, the motions made by Jeffrey, and the weight that bears down on her has Jeffrey's heart in it, also his habits, thoughts, peculiarities, his ambition and loneliness (that for all she knows may have mostly to do with his youth).

For all she knows. There's a lot she doesn't know. She hardly knows anything about what he likes to eat or what music he likes to listen to or what role his mother plays in his life (no doubt a mysterious but important one, like the role of Brian's parents). One thing she's pretty sure of—whatever preferences or prohibitions he has will be definite.

She slides out from under Jeffrey's hand and from under the top sheet which has a harsh smell of bleach, she slips down to the floor where the bedspread is lying and wraps herself quickly in that rag of greenish-yellow chenille. She doesn't want him to open his eyes and see her from behind and note the droop of her buttocks. He's seen her naked before, but generally in a more forgiving moment.

She rinses her mouth and washes herself, using the bar of soap that is about the size of two thin squares of chocolate and firm as stone. She's hard-used between the legs, swollen and stinking. Urinating takes an effort, and it seems she's constipated. Last night when they went out and got hamburgers she found she could not eat. Presumably she'll learn to do all these things again, they'll resume their natural importance in her life. At the moment it's as if she can't quite spare the attention.

She has some money in her purse. She has to go out and buy a toothbrush, toothpaste, deodorant, shampoo. Also vaginal jelly. Last night they used condoms the first two times but nothing the third time.

She didn't bring her watch and Jeffrey doesn't wear one. There's no clock in the room, of course. She thinks it's early—there's still an early look to the light in spite of the heat. The stores probably won't be open, but there'll be someplace where she can get coffee.

Jeffrey has turned onto his other side. She must have wakened him, just for a moment.

They'll have a bedroom. A kitchen, an address. He'll go to work. She'll go to the Laundromat. Maybe she'll go to work too. Selling things, waiting on tables, tutoring students. She knows French and Latin—do they teach French and Latin in American high schools? Can you get a job if you're not an American? Jeffrey isn't.

She leaves him the key. She'll have to wake him to get back in. There's nothing to write a note with, or on.

It is early. The motel is on the highway at the north end of town, beside the bridge. There's no traffic yet. She scuffs along under the cottonwood trees for quite a while before a vehicle of any kind rumbles over the bridge—though the traffic on it shook their bed regularly late into the night.

Something is coming now. A truck. But not just a truck—there's a large bleak fact coming at her. And it has not arrived out of nowhere—it's been waiting, cruelly nudging at her ever since she woke up, or even all night.

Caitlin and Mara.

Last night on the phone, after speaking in such a flat and controlled and almost agreeable voice—as if he prided himself on not being shocked, not objecting or pleading—Brian cracked open. He said with contempt and fury and no concern for whoever might hear him, "Well then—what about the kids?"

The receiver began to shake against Pauline's ear.

She said, "We'll talk—" but he did not seem to hear her.

"The children," he said, in this same shivering and vindictive voice. Changing the word "kids" to "children" was like slamming a board down on her—a heavy, formal, righteous threat.

"The children stay," Brian said. "Pauline. Did you hear me?"

"No," said Pauline. "Yes. I heard you but—"

"All right. You heard me. Remember. The children stay."

It was all he could do. To make her see what she was doing, what she was ending, and to punish her if she did so. Nobody would blame him. There might be finagling, there might be bargaining, there would certainly be humbling of herself, but there it was like a round cold stone in her gullet, like a cannonball. And it would remain there unless she changed her mind entirely. The children stay.

Their car—hers and Brian's—was still sitting in the motel parking lot. Brian would have to ask his father or his mother to drive him up here today to get it. She had the keys in her purse. There were spare keys—he would surely bring them. She unlocked the car door and threw her keys on the seat and locked the door on the inside and shut it.

Now she couldn't go back. She couldn't get into the car and drive back and say that she'd been insane. If she did that he would forgive her, but he'd never get over it and neither would she. They'd go on, though, as people did.

She walked out of the parking lot, she walked along the sidewalk, into town.

The weight of Mara on her hip, yesterday. The sight of Caitlin's footprints on the floor.

Paw. Paw.

She doesn't need the keys to get back to them, she doesn't need the car. She could beg a ride on the highway. Give in, give in, get back to them any way at all, how can she not do that?

A sack over her head.

A fluid choice, the choice of fantasy, is poured out on the ground and instantly hardens; it has taken its undeniable shape.

This is acute pain. It will become chronic. Chronic means that it will be permanent but perhaps not constant. It may also mean that you won't die of it. You won't get free of it, but you won't die of it. You won't feel it every minute, but you won't spend many days without it. And you'll learn some tricks to dull it or banish it, trying not to end up destroying what you incurred this pain to get. It isn't his fault. He's still an innocent or a savage, who doesn't know there's a pain so durable in the world. Say to yourself, You lose them anyway. They grow up. For a mother there's always waiting this private slightly ridiculous desolation. They'll forget this time, in one way or another they'll disown you. Or hang around till you don't know what to do about them, the way Brian has.

And still, what pain. To carry along and get used to until it's only the past she's grieving for and not any possible present.

———

Her children have grown up. They don't hate her. For going away or staying away. They don't forgive her, either. Perhaps they wouldn't have forgiven her anyway, but it would have been for something different.

Caitlin remembers a little about the summer at the lodge, Mara nothing. One day Caitlin mentions it to Pauline, calling it "that place Grandma and Grandpa stayed at."

"The place we were at when you went away," she says. "Only we didn't know till later you went away with Orphée."

Pauline says, "It wasn't Orphée."

"It wasn't Orphée? Dad used to say it was. He'd say, 'And then your mother ran away with Orphée.'"

"Then he was joking," says Pauline.

"I always thought it was Orphée. It was somebody else then."

"It was somebody else connected with the play. That I lived with for a while."

"Not Orphée."

"No. Never him."

ANDRE DUBUS

The Winter Father

for Pat

The Jackman's marriage had been adulterous and violent, but in its last days, they became a couple again, as they might have if one of them were slowly dying. They wept together, looked into each other's eyes without guile, distrust, or hatred, and they planned Peter's time with the children. On his last night at home, he and Norma, tenderly, without a word, made love. Next evening, when he got home from Boston, they called David and Kathi in from the snow and brought them to the kitchen.

David was eight, slender, with light brown hair nearly to his shoulders, a face that was still pretty; he seemed always hungry, and Peter liked watching him eat. Kathi was six, had long red hair and a face that Peter had fallen in love with, a face that had once been pierced by glass the shape of a long dagger blade. In early spring a year ago: he still had not taken the storm windows off the screen doors; he was bringing his lunch to the patio, he did not know Kathi was following him, and holding his plate and mug he had pushed the door open with his shoulder, stepped outside, heard the crash and her scream, and turned to see her gripping then pulling the long shard from her cheek. She got it out before he reached her. He picked her up and pressed his handkerchief to the wound, mid-way between her eye and throat, and held her as he phoned his doc-

105

tor who said he would meet them at the hospital and do the stitching himself because it was cosmetic and that beautiful face should not be touched by residents. Norma was not at home. Kathi lay on the car seat beside him and he held his handkerchief on her cheek, and in the hospital he held her hands while she lay on the table. The doctor said it would only take about four stitches and it would be better without anesthetic, because sometimes that puffed the skin, and he wanted to fit the cut together perfectly, for the scar; he told this very gently to Kathi, and he said as she grew, the scar would move down her face and finally would be under her jaw. Then she and Peter squeezed each other's hands as the doctor stitched and she gritted her teeth and stared at pain.

She was like that when he and Norma told them. It was David who suddenly cried, begged them not to get a divorce, and then fled to his room and would not come out, would not help Peter load his car, and only emerged from the house as Peter was driving away: a small running shape in the dark, charging the car, picking up something and throwing it, missing, crying *You bum You bum You bum . . .*

Drunk that night in his apartment whose rent he had paid and keys received yesterday morning before last night's grave lovemaking with Norma, he gained through the blur of bourbon an intense focus on his children's faces as he and Norma spoke: We fight too much, we've tried to live together but can't; you'll see, you'll be better off too, you'll be with Daddy for dinner on Wednesday nights, and on Saturdays and Sundays you'll do things with him. In his kitchen he watched their faces.

Next day he went to the radio station. After the news at noon he was on; often, as the records played, he imagined his children last night, while he and Norma were talking, and after he was gone. Perhaps she took them out to dinner, let them stay up late, flanking her on the couch in front of the television. When he talked he listened to his voice: it sounded as it did every weekday afternoon. At four he was finished. In the parking lot he felt as though, with stooped shoulders, he were limping. He started the forty-minute drive northward, for the first time in twelve years going home to empty rooms. When he reached the town where he lived he stopped at a small store and bought two lamb chops and a package of frozen peas. *I will take one thing at a time,* he told himself. Crossing the sidewalk to his car, in that short space, he felt the limp again, the stooped shoulders. He wondered if he looked like a man who had survived an accident which had killed others.

That was on a Thursday. When he woke Saturday morning, his first thought was a wish: that Norma would phone and tell him they were sick, and he should wait to see them Wednesday. He amended his wish, lay waiting for his own body to let him know it was sick, out for the weekend. In late morning he drove to their coastal town; he had moved fifteen miles inland. Already the snow-ploughed streets and country roads leading to their house felt like parts of his body: intestines, lung, heart-fiber lying from his door to theirs. When they were born he had smoked in the waiting room with the others. Now he was giving birth: stirruped, on his back, waves of pain. There would be no release, no cutting of the cord. Nor did he want it. He wanted to grow a cord.

Walking up their shovelled walk and ringing the doorbell, he felt at the same time like an inept salesman and a con man. He heard their voices, watched the door as though watching the sounds he heard, looking at the point where their faces would appear, but when the door opened he was looking at Norma's waist; then up to her face, lipsticked, her short brown hair soft from that morning's washing. For years she had not looked this way on a Saturday morning. Her eyes held him: the nest of pain was there, the shyness, the coiled anger; but there was another shimmer: she was taking a new marriage vow: This is the way we shall love our children now; watch how well I can do it. She smiled and said: "Come in out of the cold and have a cup of coffee."

In the living room he crouched to embrace the hesitant children. Only their faces were hesitant. In his arms they squeezed, pressed, kissed. David's hard arms absolved them both of Wednesday night. Through their hair Peter said pleasantly to Norma that he'd skip the coffee this time. Grabbing caps and unfurling coats, they left the house, holding hands to the car.

He showed them his apartment: they had never showered behind glass; they slid the doors back and forth. Sand washing down the drain, their flesh sunburned, a watermelon waiting in the refrigerator . . .

"This summer—"

They turned from the glass, looked up at him.

"When we go to the beach. We can come back here and shower."

Their faces reflected his bright promise, and they followed him to the kitchen; on the counter were two cans of kidney beans, Jalapeño peppers, seasonings. Norma kept her seasonings in small jars, and two years ago when David was six and came home bullied and afraid of next day at school, Peter asked him if the boy was bigger than he was, and when David said "A lot," and showed him the boy's height with one hand, his breadth with two, Peter took the glass stopper from the cinnamon jar, tied it in a handkerchief corner, and struck his palm with it, so David would know how hard it was, would believe in it. Next morning David took it with him. On the schoolground, when the bully shoved him, he swung it up from his back pocket and down on the boy's forehead. The boy cried and went away. After school David found him on the sidewalk and hit his jaw with the weapon he had sat on all day, chased him two blocks swinging at his head, and came home with delighted eyes, no damp traces of yesterday's shame and fright, and Peter's own pain and rage turned to pride, then caution, and he spoke gently, told David to carry it for a week or so more, but not to use it unless the bully attacked; told him we must control our pleasure in giving pain.

Now reaching into the refrigerator he felt the children behind him; then he knew it was not them he felt, for in the bathroom when he spoke to their faces he had also felt a presence to his rear, watching, listening. It was the walls, it was fatherhood, it was himself. He was not an early drinker but he wanted an ale now; looked at the brown bottles long enough to fear and dislike his reason for wanting one, then he poured two glasses of apple cider and, for himself, cider and club soda. He sat at the table and watched David slice a Jalapeño over the beans, and said: "Don't ever touch one of those and take a leak without washing your hands first."

"Why?"

"I did it once. Think about it."

"Wow."

They talked of flavors as Kathi, with her eyes just above rim-level of the pot, her wrists in the steam, poured honey, and shook paprika, basil, parsley, Worcestershire, wine vinegar. In a bowl they mixed ground meat with a raw egg: jammed their hands into it, fingers touching; scooped and squeezed meat and onion and celery between their fingers; the kitchen smelled of bay leaf in the simmering beans, and then of broiling meat. They talked about the food as they ate, pressing thick hamburgers to fit their mouths, and only then Peter heard the white silence coming at them like afternoon snow. They cleaned the counter and table and what they had used; and they spoke briefly, quietly, they smoothly passed things; and when Peter turned off the faucet, all sound stopped, the kitchen was multiplied by silence, the apartment's walls grew longer, the floors wider, the ceilings higher. Peter walked the distance to his bedroom, looked at his watch, then quickly turned to the morning paper's television listing, and called: "Hey! *The Magnificent Seven*'s coming on."

"All *right*," David said, and they hurried down the short hall, light footsteps whose sounds he could name: Kathi's, David's, Kathi's. He lay between them, bellies down, on the bed.

"Is this our third time or fourth?" Kathi said.

"I think our fourth. We saw it in a theater once."

"I could see it every week," David said.

"Except when Charles Bronson dies," Kathi said. "But I like when the little kids put flowers on his grave. And when he spanks them."

The winter sunlight beamed through the bedroom window, the afternoon moving past him and his children. Driving them home he imitated Yul Brynner, Eli Wallach, Charles Bronson; the children praised his voices, laughed, and in front of their house they kissed him and asked what they were going to do tomorrow. He said he didn't know yet; he would call in the morning, and he watched them go up the walk between snow as high as Kathi's waist. At the door they turned and waved; he tapped the horn twice, and drove away.

That night he could not sleep. He read *Macbeth*, woke propped against the pillows, the bedside lamp on, the small book at his side. He put it on the table, turned out the light, moved the pillows down, and slept. Next afternoon he took David and Kathi to a movie.

He did not bring them to his apartment again, unless they were on the way to another place, and their time in the apartment was purposeful and short: Saturday morning cartoons, then lunch before going to a movie or museum. Early in the week he began reading the movie section of the paper, looking for matinees. Every weekend they went to a movie, and sometimes two, in their towns and other small towns and in Boston. On the third Saturday he took them to a PG movie which was bloody and erotic enough to make him feel ashamed and irresponsible as he sat between his children in the theater. Driving home, he asked them about the movie until he believed it had not frightened them, or made them curious about bodies and urges they did not yet have. After that, he saw all PG movies before taking them, and he was angry at mothers who left their children at the theater and picked them up when the movie was over; and left him to listen to their children exclaiming at death, laughing at love; and often they roamed the aisles going to the concession stand, and distracted him from this weekly entertainment, which he suspected he waited for and enjoyed more than David and Kathi. He had not been an indiscriminate moviegoer since he was a child. Now what had started as a duty was pleasurable, relaxing. He knew that beneath this lay a base of cowardice. But he told himself it would pass. A time would come when he and Kathi and David could sit in his living room, talking like three friends who had known each other for eight and six years.

Most of his listeners on weekday afternoons were women. Between love songs he began talking to them about movie ratings. He said not to trust them. He asked what they felt about violence and sex in movies, whether or not they were bad for children. He told them he didn't know; that many of the fairy tales and all the comic books of his boyhood were violent; and so were the westerns and serials on Saturday afternoons. But there was no blood. And he chided the women about letting their children go to the movies alone.

He got letters and read them in his apartment at night. Some thanked him for his advice about ratings. Many told him it was all right for him to talk, he wasn't with the kids every afternoon after school and all weekends and holidays and summer; the management of the theater was responsible for quiet and order during the movies; they were showing the movies to attract children and they were glad to take the money. The children came home happy and did not complain about other children being noisy. Maybe he should stop going to matinees, should leave his kids there and pick them up when it was over. *It's almost what I'm doing,* he thought; and he stopped talking about movies to the afternoon women.

He found a sledding hill: steep and long, and at its base a large frozen pond. David and Kathi went with him to buy his sled, and with a thermos of hot chocolate they drove to the hill near his apartment. Parked cars lined the road, and children and some parents were on the hill's broad top. Red-faced children climbed back, pulling their sleds with ropes. Peter sledded first; he knew the ice on the pond was safe, but he was beginning to handle fatherhood as he did guns: always as if they were loaded, when he knew they were not. There was a satisfaction in preventing even dangers which did not exist.

The snow was hard and slick, rushed beneath him; he went over a bump, rose from the sled, nearly lost it, slammed down on it, legs outstretched, gloved hands steering around the next bump but not the next one suddenly rising toward his face, and he pressed against the sled, hugged the wood-shock to his chest, yelled with delight at children moving slowly upward, hit the edge of the pond and sledded straight out, looking at the evergreens on its far bank. The sled stopped near the middle of the pond; he stood and waved to the top of the hill, squinting at sun and bright snow, then two silhouettes waved back and he saw Kathi's long red hair. Holding the sled's rope he walked on ice, moving to his left as David started down and Kathi stood waiting, leaning on her sled. He told himself he was a fool: had lived winters with his children, yet this was the first sled he had bought for himself; sometimes he had gone with them because they asked him to, and he had used their sleds. But he had never found a sledding hill. He had driven past them, seen the small figures on their crests and slopes, but no more. Watching David swerve around a bump and Kathi, at the top, pushing her sled, then dropping onto it, he forgave himself; there was still time; already it had begun.

But on that first afternoon of sledding he made a mistake: within an hour his feet were painfully cold, his trousers wet and his legs cold; David and Kathi wore snow pants. Beneath his parka he was sweating. Then he knew they felt the same, yet they would sled as long as he did, because of the point and edges of divorce that pierced and cut all their time together.

"I'm freezing," he said. "I can't move my toes."

"Me too," David said.

"Let's go down one more time," Kathi said.

Then he took them home. It was only three o'clock.

After that he took them sledding on weekend mornings. They brought clothes with them, and after sledding they went to his apartment and showered. They loved the glass doors. On the first day they argued about who would shower first, until Peter flipped a coin and David won and Peter said Kathi would have the first shower next time and they would take turns that way. They showered long and when Peter's turn came the water was barely warm and he was quickly in and out. Then in dry clothes they ate lunch and went to a movie.

Or to another place, and one night drinking bourbon in his living room, lights off so he could watch the snow falling, the yellowed, gentle swirl at the corner streetlight, the quick flakes at his window, banking on the sill, and across the street the grey-white motion lowering the sky and making the evergreens look distant, he thought of owning a huge building to save divorced fathers. Free admission. A place of swimming pool, badminton and tennis courts, movie theaters, restaurants, soda fountains, batting cages, a zoo, an art gallery, a circus, aquarium, science museum, hundreds of restrooms, two always in sight, everything in the tender charge of women trained in first aid and Montessori, no uniforms, their only style warmth and cheer. A father could spend entire days there, weekend after weekend, so in winter there would not be all this planning and driving. He had made his cowardice urbane, mobile, and sophisticated; but perhaps at its essence cowardice knows it is apparent: he believed David and Kathi knew that their afternoons at the aquarium, the Museum of Fine Arts, the Science Museum, were houses Peter had built, where they could be together as they were before, with one difference: there was always entertainment.

Frenetic as they were, he preferred weekends to the Wednesday nights when they ate together. At first he thought it was shyness. Yet they talked easily, often about their work, theirs at school, his as a disc jockey. When he was not with the children he spent much time thinking about what they said to each other. And he saw that, in his eight years as a father, he had been attentive, respectful, amusing; he had taught and disciplined. But no: not now: when they were too loud in the car or they fought, he held onto his anger, his heart buffetted with it, and spoke calmly, as though to another man's children, for he was afraid that if he scolded as he had before, the day would be spoiled, they would not have the evening at home, the sleeping in the same house, to heal them; and they might not want to go with him next day or two nights from now or two days. During their eight and six years with him, he had shown them love, and made them laugh. But now he knew that he had remained a secret from them. What did they know about him? What did he know about them?

He would tell them about his loneliness, and what he had learned about himself. When he wasn't with them, he was lonely all the time, except while he was running or working, and sometimes at the station he felt it waiting for him in the parking lot, on the highway, in his apartment. He thought much about it, like an athletic man considering a sprained ligament, changing his exercises to include it. He separated his days into parts, thought about each one, and learned that all of them were not bad. When the alarm woke him in the winter dark, the new day and waiting night were the grey of the room, and they pressed down on him, fetid repetitions bent on smothering his spirit before he rose from the bed. But he got up quickly, made the bed while the sheets still held his warmth, and once in the kitchen with coffee and newspaper he moved into the first part of the day: bacon smell and solemn disc jockeys with classical music, an hour or more at the kitchen table, as near-peaceful as he dared hope for; and was grateful for too, as it went with him to the living room, to the chair at the southeast window where, pausing to watch traffic and look at the snow and winter branches of elms and maples in the park across the street, he sat in sun-warmth and entered the cadence of Shakespeare. In midmorning, he Vaselined his face and genitals and, wearing layers of nylon, he ran two and a half miles down the road which, at his corner, was a town road of close houses but soon was climbing and dropping past farms and meadows; at the crest of a hill, where he could see the curves of trees on the banks of the Merrimack, he turned and ran back.

The second part began with ignition and seat belt, driving forty minutes on the highway, no buildings or billboards, low icicled cliffs and long white hills, and fields and woods in the angled winter sun, and in the silent car he received his afternoon self: heard the music he had chosen, popular music he would not listen to at home but had come to accept and barely listen to at work, heard his voice in mime and jest and remark, often merry, sometimes showing off and knowing it, but not much, no more than he had earned. That part of his day behind glass and microphone, with its comfort drawn from combining the familiar with the spontaneous, took him to four o'clock.

The next four hours, he learned, were not only the time he had to prepare for, but also the lair of his loneliness, the source of every quick chill of loss, each sudden whisper of dread and futility: for if he could spend them with a woman he loved, drink and cook and eat with her while day changed to night (though now, in winter, night came as he drove home), he and this woman huddled in the light and warmth of living room and kitchen, gin and meat, then his days until four and nights after eight would demand less from him of will, give more to him of hopeful direction. After dinner he listened to jazz and read fiction or watched an old movie on television until, without lust or even the need of a sleeping woman beside him, he went to bed: a blessing, but a disturbing one. He had assumed, as a husband and then an adulterous one, that his need for a woman was as carnal as it was spiritual. But now celibacy was easy; when he imagined a woman, she was drinking with him, eating dinner. So his most intense and perhaps his only need for a woman was then; and all the reasons for the end of his marriage became distant, blurred, and he wondered if the only reason he was alone now was a misogyny he had never recognized: that he did not even want a woman except at the day's end, and had borne all the other hours of woman-presence only to have her comfort as the clock's hands moved through their worst angles of the day.

Planning to tell all this to David and Kathi, knowing he would need gin to do it, he was frightened, already shy as if they sat with him now in the living room. A good sign: if he were afraid, then it took courage; if it took courage, then it must be right. He drank more bourbon than he thought he did, and went to bed excited by intimacy and love.

He slept off everything. In the morning he woke so amused at himself that, if he had not been alone, he would have laughed aloud. He imagined telling his children, over egg rolls and martinis and Shirley Temples, about his loneliness and his rituals to combat it. And *that* would be his new fatherhood, smelling of duck sauce and hot mustard and gin. Swallowing aspirins and orange juice, he saw clearly why he and the children were uncomfortable together, especially at Wednesday night dinners: when he lived with them, their talk had usually dealt with the immediate (I don't like playing with Cindy anymore; she's too bossy. I wish it would snow; it's no use being cold if it doesn't snow); they spoke at dinner and breakfast and, during holidays and summer, at lunch; in the car and stores while running errands; on the summer lawn while he prepared charcoal; and in their beds when he went to tell them goodnight; most of the time their talk was deep only because it was affectionate and tribal, sounds made between creatures sharing the same blood. Now their talk was the same, but it did not feel the same. They talked in his car and in places he took them, and the car and each place would not let them forget they were there because of divorce.

So their talk had felt evasive, fragile, contrived, and his drunken answer last night had been more talk: courageous, painful, honest. *My God,* he thought, as in a light snow that morning he ran out of his hangover, into lucidity. *I was going to have a Goddamn therapy session with my own children.* Breathing the smell of new snow and winter air he thought of this fool Peter Jackman, swallowing his bite of pork fried rice, and saying: And what do you feel at school? About the divorce, I mean. Are you ashamed around the other kids? He thought of the useless reopening and sometimes celebrating of wounds he and Norma had done with the marriage counselor, a pleasant and smart woman, but what could she do when all she had to work with was wounds? After each session he and Norma had driven home, usually mute, always in despair. Then, running faster, he imagined a house where he lived and the children came on Friday nights and stayed all weekend, played with their friends during the day, came and left the house as they needed, for food, drink, bathroom, diversion, and at night they relaxed together as a family; saw himself reading as they painted and drew at the kitchen table . . .

That night they ate dinner at a seafood restaurant thirty minutes from their town. When he drove them home he stayed outside their house for a while, the three of them sitting in front for warmth; they talked about summer and no school and no heavy clothes and no getting up early when it was still dark outside. He told them it was his favorite season too because of baseball and the sea. Next morning when he got into his car, the inside of his windshield was iced. He used the small plastic scraper from his glove compartment. As he scraped the middle and right side, he realized the grey ice curling and falling from the glass was the frozen breath of his children.

At a bar in the town where his children lived, he met a woman. This was on a Saturday night, after he had taken them home from the Museum of Fine Arts. They had liked Monet and Cézanne, had shown him light and color they thought were pretty. He told them Cézanne's *The Turn in the Road* was his favorite, that every time he came here he stood looking at it and he wanted to be walking up that road, toward the houses. But all afternoon he had known they were restless. They had not sledded that morning. Peter had gone out drinking the night before, with his only married friend who could leave his wife at home without paying even a subtle price, and he had slept through the time for sledding, had apologized when they phoned and woke him, and on the drive to the museum had told them he and Sibley (whom they knew as a friend of their mother too) had been having fun and had lost track of time until the bar closed. So perhaps they wanted to be outdoors. Or perhaps it was the old resonance of place again, the walls and ceiling of the museum, even the paintings telling them: You are here because your father left home.

He went to the bar for a sandwich, and stayed. Years ago he had come here often, on the way home from work, or at night with Norma. It was a neighborhood bar then, where professional fishermen and lobstermen and other men who worked with their hands drank, and sometimes brought their wives. Then someone from Boston bought it, put photographs and drawings of fishing and pleasure boats on the walls, built a kitchen which turned out quiche and crêpes, hired young women to tend the bar, and musicians to play folk and bluegrass. The old customers left. The new ones were couples and people trying to be a couple for at least the night, and that is why Peter stayed after eating his sandwich.

Within an hour she came in and sat at the bar, one empty chair away from him: a woman in her late twenties, dark eyes and light brown hair. Soon they were talking. He liked her because she smiled a lot. He also liked her drink: Jack Daniel's on the rocks. Her name was Mary Ann; her last name kept eluding him. She was a market researcher, and like many people Peter knew, she seemed to dismiss her work, though she was apparently good at it; her vocation was recreation: she skied down and across; backpacked; skated; camped; ran and swam. He began to imagine doing things with her, and he felt more insidious than if he were imagining passion: he saw her leading him and Kathi and David up a mountain trail. He told her he spent much of his life prone or sitting, except for a daily five-mile run, a habit from the Marine Corps (she gave him the sneer and he said: Come on, that was a long time ago, it was peacetime, it was fun), and he ran now for the same reasons everyone else did, or at least everyone he knew who ran: the catharsis, which kept his body feeling good, and his mind more or less sane. He said he had not slept in a tent since the Marines; probably because of the Marines. He said he wished he did as many things as she did, and he told her why. Some time in his bed during the night, she said: "They probably did like the paintings. At least you're not taking them to all those movies now."

"We still go about once a week."

"Did you know Lennie's has free matinees for children? On Sunday afternoons?"

"No."

"I have a divorced friend; she takes her kids almost every Sunday."

"Why don't we go tomorrow?"

"With your kids?"

"If you don't mind."

"Sure. I like kids. I'd like to have one of my own, without a husband."

As he kissed her belly he imagined her helping him pitch the large tent he would buy, the four of them on a weekend of cold brook and trees on a mountainside, a fire, bacon in the skillet . . .

In the morning he scrambled their eggs, then phoned Norma. He had a general dislike of telephones: talking to his own hand gripping plastic, pacing, looking about the room; the timing of hanging up was tricky. Nearly all these conversations left him feeling as disconnected as the phone itself. But talking with Norma was different: he marvelled at how easy it was. The distance and disembodiment he felt on the phone with others were good here. He and Norma had hurt each other deeply, and their bodies had absorbed the pain: it was the stomach that tightened, the hands that shook, the breast that swelled then shrivelled. Now fleshless they could talk by phone, even with warmth, perhaps alive from the time when their bodies were at ease together. He thought of having a huge house where he could live with his family, seeing Norma only at meals, shared for the children, he and Norma talking to David and Kathi; their own talk would be on extension phones in their separate wings: they would discuss the children, and details of running the house. This was of course the way they had finally lived, without the separate wings, the phones. And one of their justifications as they talked of divorce was that the children would be harmed, growing up in a house with parents who did not love each other, who rarely touched, and then by accident. There had been moments near the end when, brushing against each other in the kitchen, one of them would say: Sorry. Now as Mary Ann Brighi (he had waked knowing her last name) spread jam on toast, he phoned.

"I met this woman last night."

Mary Ann smiled; Norma's voice did.

"It's about time. I was worried about your arm going."

"What about you?"

"I'm doing all right."

"Do you bring them home?"

"It's not them, and I get a sitter."

"But he comes to the house? To take you out?"

"Peter?"

"What."

"What are we talking about?"

"I was wondering what the kids would think if Mary Ann came along this afternoon."

"What they'll think is Mary Ann's coming along this afternoon."

"You're sure that's all?"

"Unless you fuck in front of them."

He turned his face from Mary Ann, but she had already seen his blush; he looked at her smiling with toast crumbs on her teeth. He wished he were married and lovemaking was simple. But after cleaning the kitchen he felt passion again, though not much; in his mind he was introducing the children to Mary Ann. He would make sure he talked to them, did not leave them out while he talked to her. He was making love while he thought this; he hoped they would like her; again he saw them hiking up a trail through pines, stopping for Kathi and David to rest; a sudden bounding deer; the camp beside the stream; he thanked his member for doing its work down there while the rest of him was in the mountains in New Hampshire.

As he walked with David and Kathi he held their hands; they were looking at her face watching them from the car window.

"She's a new friend of mine," he said. "Just a friend. She wants to show us this night club where children can go on Sunday afternoons."

From the back seat they shook hands, peered at her, glanced at Peter, their eyes making him feel that like adults they could sense when people were lovers; he adjusted the rearview mirror, watched their faces, decided he was seeing jumbled and vulnerable curiosity: Who was she? Would she marry their father? Would they like her? Would their mother be sad? And the night club confused them.

"Isn't that where people go drink?" Kathi said.

"It's afternoon too," David said.

Not for Peter; the sky was grey, the time was grey, dark was coming, and all at once he felt utterly without will; all the strength he had drawn on to be with his children left him like one long spurt of arterial blood: all his time with his children was grey, with night coming; it would always be; nothing would change: like three people cursed in an old myth they would forever be thirty-three and eight and six, in this car on slick or salted roads, going from one place to another. He disapproved of but understood those divorced fathers who fled to live in a different pain far away. Beneath his despair, he saw himself and his children sledding under a lovely blue sky, heard them laughing in movies, watching in awe like love a circling blue shark in the aquarium's tank; but these seemed beyond recapture.

He entered the highway going south, and that quick transition of hands and head and eyes as he moved into fast traffic snapped him out of himself, into the sound of Mary Ann's voice: with none of the rising and falling rhythm of nursery talk, she was telling them, as if speaking to a young man and woman she had just met, about Lennie's. How Lennie believed children should hear good music, not just the stuff on the radio. She talked about jazz. She hummed some phrases of "Somewhere Over the Rainbow," then improvised. They would hear Gerry Mulligan today, she said, and as she talked about the different saxophones, Peter looked in the mirror at their listening faces.

"And Lennie has a cook from Tijuana in Mexico," Mary Ann said. "She makes the best chili around."

Walking into Lennie's with a pretty woman and his two healthy and pretty children, he did not feel like a divorced father looking for something to do; always in other places he was certain he looked that way, and often he felt guilty when talking with waitresses. He paid the cover charge for himself and Mary Ann and she said: All right, but I buy the first two rounds, and he led her and the children to a table near the bandstand. He placed the children between him and Mary Ann. Bourbon, Cokes, bowls of chili. The room was filling and Peter saw that at most tables there were children with parents, usually one parent, usually a father. He watched his children listening to Mulligan. His fingers tapped the table with the drummer. He looked warmly at Mary Ann's profile until she turned and smiled at him.

Often Mulligan talked to the children, explained how his saxophone worked; his voice was cheerful, joking, never serious, as he talked about the guitar and bass and piano and drums. He clowned laughter from the children in the dark. Kathi and David turned to each other and Peter to share their laughter. During the music they listened intently. Their hands tapped the table. They grinned at Peter and Mary Ann. At intermission Mulligan said he wanted to meet the children. While his group went to the dressing room he sat on the edge of the bandstand and waved the children forward. Kathi and David talked about going. Each would go if the other would. They took napkins for autographs and, holding hands, walked between tables and joined the children standing around Mulligan. When it was their turn he talked to them, signed their napkins, kissed their foreheads. They hurried back to Peter.

"He's *neat*," Kathi said.

"What did you talk about?"

"He asked our names," David said.

"And if we liked winter out here."

"And if we played an instrument."

"What kind of music we liked."

"What did you tell him?"

"Jazz like his."

The second set ended at nearly seven; bourbon-high, Peter drove carefully, listening to Mary Ann and the children talking about Mulligan and his music and warmth. Then David and Kathi were gone, running up the sidewalk to tell Norma, and show their autographed napkins, and Peter followed Mary Ann's directions to her apartment.

"I've been in the same clothes since last night," she said.

In her apartment, as unkempt as his, they showered together, hurried damp-haired and chilled to her bed.

"This is the happiest day I've had since the marriage ended," he said.

But when he went home and was alone in his bed, he saw his cowardice again. All the warmth of his day left him, and he lay in the dark, knowing that he should have been wily enough to understand that the afternoon's sweetness and ease meant he had escaped: had put together a family for the day. That afternoon Kathi had spilled a Coke; before Peter noticed, Mary Ann was cleaning the table with cocktail napkins, smiling at Kathi, talking to her under the music, lifting a hand to the waitress.

Next night he took Mary Ann to dinner and driving to her apartment, it seemed to him that since the end of his marriage, dinner had become disproportionate: alone at home it was a task he forced himself to do, with his children it was a fragile rite, and with old friends who alternately fed him and Norma he felt vaguely criminal. Now he must once again face his failures over a plate of food. He and Mary Ann had slept little the past two nights, and at the restaurant she told him she had worked hard all day, yet she looked fresh and strong, while he was too tired to imagine making love after dinner. With his second martini, he said: "I used you yesterday. With my kids."

"There's a better word."

"All right: needed."

"I knew that."

"You did?"

"We had fun."

"I can't do it anymore."

"Don't be so hard on yourself. You probably spend more time with them now than when you lived together."

"I do. So does Norma. But that's not it. It's how much I wanted your help, and started hoping for it. Next Sunday. And in summer: the sort of stuff you do, camping and hiking; when we talked about it Saturday night—"

"I knew that too. I thought it was sweet."

He leaned back in his chair, sipped his drink. Tonight he would break his martini rule, have a third before dinner. He loved women who knew and forgave his motives before he knew and confessed them.

But he would not take her with the children again. He was with her often; she wanted a lover, she said, not love, not what it still did to men and women. He did not tell her he thought they were using each other in a way that might have been cynical, if it were not so frightening. He simply followed her, became one of those who make love with their friends. But she was his only woman friend, and he did not know how many men shared her. When she told him she would not be home this night or that weekend, he held his questions. He held onto his heart too, and forced himself to make her a part of the times when he was alone. He had married young, and life to him was surrounded by the sounds and touches of a family. Now in this foreign land he felt so vulnerably strange that at times it seemed near madness as he gave Mary Ann a function in his time, ranking somewhere among his running and his work.

When the children asked about her, he said they were still friends. Once Kathi asked why she never came to Lennie's anymore, and he said her work kept her pretty busy and she had other friends she did things with, and he liked being alone with them anyway. But then he was afraid the children thought she had not liked them; so, twice a month, he brought Mary Ann to Lennie's.

He and the children went every Sunday. And that was how the cold months passed, beginning with the New Year, because Peter and Norma had waited until after Christmas to end the marriage: the movies and sledding, museums and aquarium, the restaurants; always they were on the road, and whenever he looked at his car he thought of the children. How many conversations while looking through the windshield? How many times had the doors slammed shut and they re-entered or left his life? Winter ended slowly. April was cold and in May Peter and the children still wore sweaters or windbreakers, and on two weekends there was rain, and everything they did together was indoors. But when the month ended, Peter thought it was not the weather but the patterns of winter that had kept them driving from place to place.

Then it was June and they were out of school and Peter took his vacation. Norma worked, and by nine in the morning he and Kathi and David were driving to the sea. They took a large blanket and tucked its corners into the sand so it wouldn't flap in the wind, and they lay oiled in the sun. On the first day they talked of winter, how they could feel the sun warming their ribs, as they had watched it warming the earth during the long thaw. It was a beach with gentle currents and a gradual slope out to sea but Peter told them, as he had every summer, about undertow: that if ever they were caught in one, they must not swim against it; they must let it take them out and then they must swim parallel to the beach until the current shifted and they could swim back in with it. He could not imagine his children being calm enough to do that, for he was afraid of water and only enjoyed body-surfing near the beach, but he told them anyway. Then he said it would not happen because he would always test the current first.

In those first two weeks the three of them ran into the water and body-surfed only a few minutes, for it was too cold still, and they had to leave it until their flesh was warm again. They would not be able to stay in long until July. Peter showed them the different colors of summer, told them why on humid days the sky and ocean were paler blue, and on dry days they were darker, more beautiful, and the trees they passed on the roads to the beach were brighter green. He bought a whiffle ball and bat and kept them in the trunk of his car and they played at the beach. The children dug holes, made castles, Peter watched, slept, and in late morning he ran. From a large thermos they drank lemonade or juice; and they ate lunch all day, the children grazing on fruit and the sandwiches he had made before his breakfast. Then he took them to his apartment for showers, and they helped carry in the ice chest and thermos and blanket and their knapsack of clothes. Kathi and David still took turns showering first, and they stayed in longer, but now in summer the water was still hot when his turn came. Then he drove them home to Norma, his skin red and pleasantly burning; then tan.

When his vacation ended they spent all sunny weekends at the sea, and even grey days that were warm. The children became braver about the cold, and forced him to go in with them and body-surf. But they could stay longer than he could, and he left to lie on the blanket and watch them, to make sure they stayed in shallow water. He made them promise to wait on the beach while he ran. He went in the water to cool his body from the sun, but mostly he lay on the blanket, reading, and watching the children wading out to the breakers and riding them in. Kathi and David did not always stay together. One left to walk the beach alone. Another played with strangers, or children who were there most days too. One built a castle. Another body-surfed. And, often, one would come to the blanket and drink and take a sandwich from the ice chest, would sit eating and drinking beside Peter, offer him a bite, a swallow. And on all those beach days Peter's shyness and apprehension were gone. It's the sea, he said to Mary Ann one night.

And it was: for on that day, a long Saturday at the beach, when he had all day felt peace and father-love and sun and salt water, he had understood why now in summer he and his children were as he had yearned for them to be in winter: they were no longer confined to car or buildings to remind them why they were there. The long beach and the sea were their lawn; the blanket their home; the ice chest and thermos their kitchen. They lived as a family again. While he ran and David dug in the sand until he reached water and Kathi looked for pretty shells for her room, the blanket waited for them. It was the place they wandered back to: for food, for drink, for rest, their talk as casual as between children and father arriving, through separate doors, at the kitchen sink for water, the refrigerator for an orange. Then one left for the surf; another slept in the sun, lips stained with grape juice. He had wanted to tell the children about it, but it was too much to tell, and the beach was no place for such talk anyway, and he also guessed they knew. So that afternoon when they were all lying on the blanket, on their backs, the children flanking him, he simply said: "Divorced kids go to the beach more than married ones."

"Why?" Kathi said.

"Because married people do chores and errands on weekends. No kid-days."

"I love the beach," David said.

"So do I," Peter said.

He looked at Kathi.

"You don't like it, huh?"

She took her arm from her eyes and looked at him. His urge was to turn away. She looked at him for a long time; her eyes were too tender, too wise, and he wished she could have learned both later, and differently; in her eyes he saw the car in winter, heard its doors closing and closing, their talk and the sounds of heater and engine and tires on the road, and the places the car took them. Then she held his hand, and closed her eyes.

"I wish it was summer all year round," she said.

He watched her face, rosy tan now, lightly freckled; her small scar was already lower. Holding her hand, he reached over for David's, and closed his eyes against the sun. His legs touched theirs. After a while he heard them sleeping. Then he slept.

Lee K. Abbott

Once Upon a Time

I would not want to be one of those memoirists who begin a recollection by saying, "Attention, people, there is a dead dog in these pages," but, alas, I am and there is. In fact, now that I puzzle it through from the higher ground of time and distance, I see not one but two dead dogs. My wife, Vicki, who is suing me for divorce and without whom I once thought it inconceivable to live, says we dare not treat our pets—the cats and dogs, even the reptiles only the odd truly love—with more irony, or indifference, than we treat ourselves. It is a truism (no more original or startling than the vast blue sky our heaven is here in southern New Mexico) that you can tell much about a person by the way he treats his animals: brutes for brutes, she once explained, lapdogs for the lovely inside. They are our analogues, these hounds. Us without the fret-filled, overlarge brain. Us would we only bound and bark and fetch when the urge strikes us.

The dog that concerns me first is the one, waterlogged and huge, I dragged from a pond in Capitan, New Mexico, over a month ago. We were staying in Lincoln, population fifty-two, a wide swerve in the road, where my father-in-law, a bronze sculptor and tyrannical zoning commission chairman, has his dream house. It was in the guest quarters out back where Vicki, level-headed as the Republican state senator she is, said we could go to repair the rot-weakened timbers that were our marriage. "We will do nothing here but sleep and eat and talk," she said, and for five days, watched over by the part-time artists and cowboys and rich folks who are my in-laws' buddies, that's exactly what we did. We hiked the one street of that town—a crumbling United States highway—from the stuccoed adobe courthouse Billy the Kid once blasted his way out of at one end, to the narrow bridgeworks the Army Corps of Engineers was putting riprap around that summer. Late enough at night to watch the deer trot down out of the mountain behind us to feast on pears and apples in the orchards (or on my mother-in-law's garden of lettuce and yellow corn), Vicki and I recognized the strangers we'd become to each other since our courting days as sophomores at the University of New Mexico. Yes, we were proud of our kids, Debbie and Bobby Phelps, Jr., and still carefree enough to try the watusi or the frug at the Mimbres Valley Country Club over in Deming, where we live (and where I sell more Chevrolets than any other car dealer in our deserts). As Christians, we were satisfied, not smug, and a bit humbled by the charitable, lofty view we took of humankind; we had all the virtues—thrift, honesty, a respect for the creature parts of us—but by the fifth day it was clear, but unspoken, that we did not have love, the one thing that was to make our lives wonderful, no matter how narrow or deprived they might otherwise be.

On the fifth day we drove the eighteen miles of switchbacks and dangerous hills to Capitan, which is a no-account crossroads of necessary businesses—a laundry, a Piggly Wiggly market, a post office—known to the big world as the town nearest the birthplace of Smokey the Bear (whose face, by the way, is seen on signs and paper bags and calendars often enough to bring out the hating half of you). "Let's play tennis," Vicki had suggested, and so there we were, roasted by a sun you can get damn tired of, bouncing to and fro in a chain-link–enclosed rectangle of green concrete not ten paces from a highway intersection a drunk could doze in fearlessly.

I played this game in a frenzy, I tell you. The sportsman in me, that nagging wild-haired infant inside who knows only perfection and how far short of it we are, was in high form that day. He raged at her for being too slow. And too clumsy. He picked on her swing, which was too fussy and full of elbow to be choice. He begged her to pay attention, for crying out loud, and to stop kidding around. "Oh," she scolded once, "just shut up, you!" She threw him the finger once, and told him—that ugly loud-mouth sore loser inside me—to blow it out his ear. We were fighting, our medium an optic orange Wilson tennis ball and two Prince racquets her daddy had made us the loan of. I tried, I confess, to drive a serve down her throat, or catch her in the fanny (she was laughing at my shorts, I remember, and speaking satirically about the skinny, lazy man's legs I have). "Ah-hah," she said, hands on her hips, her cum laude chin in the air the way it gets when an Albuquerque Democrat makes an ass out of himself in public. "You're useless," she said. "I could just beat the pants off you, Bobby Joe."

By the second set we had forsaken talking in favor of blasting that ball back and forth. Grim, unhappy people, we were. This was work, not play. Our sweat and grunts had become the wet and sounds of average folks trying to prove the impossible by hurling themselves, time and time again, against a wall too high, too wide and too thick to get over or around or through. Funny thing is, while she glared and scowled, I loved her. I swatted and she flailed, and all I could wonder about—in the deeper tissues of my brain where, I believe, juice and joy are one—was how much I loved that outraged woman over there. I loved how the Dunlap's department store shorts creeped up her butt, and how she bit her lip in frustration, and the child's yip-yip noise she made charging the net. Love, the force and want of it, ripped through the center of me, leaving me to be king and clown both. There it is, I kept telling myself. And I can't have it. It has legs and good breasts and makes a loud song in bed, and I don't have it anymore. I thought to hop the net, but was hobbled by the pride in me. Longingly and wholeheartedly, I imagined myself as the sort of man, wearing a red carnation in his lapel, who appears at a woman's door with a fancy-wrapped box of Valentine candy, plus a typed sonnet of his own composition, full of faith in the fairy tale Hallmark tells us about male-female relations. I tried to apologize once, but what tumbled out, made gibberish by the stubborn grown-up I am, was only "Guh, guh, guh," which Vicki looked mindful over but finally shook away with a shrug. "Hit the ball, Bobby Joe Phelps," she ordered. She stood hundreds and hundreds and hundreds of yards away now, I believed. I let go a deep breath, one from my flat and sore feet. "Yes, ma'am," I said. Silently, I went to the service line. I had shut down inside, gone still as a ghost town; there was nothing in the flesh of me but wind and dry, cracked organs. "Ready?" I almost snarled; but when I turned around, she was spun away from me and pointing.

"Look," she was saying. Adjacent to our court was an acre of grasses and weeds and gnarled plant life that is supposed to be government's idea of the ground cover and landscape we have here in the Southwest—pigweed and nutgrass and cacti and mesquite bushes, growth that needs no water to be hearty and is a pain to yank free of your lilies or roses or other foreign flowers—each patch of it identified by a sign saying what to avoid eating and how the world might have looked hundreds of years before white men settled here. A part of this space, nearest us and big as a public putting green, was a pond, green and silly and wrong for our arid earth. "What is it?" I said, and then, as if thrown into gear again, the picture in front of me lurched and got loud. "It's *drownding*," a woman was hollering. "It's *drownding*." For a second I wondered what English she'd learned, and then Vicki was saying to me, "It's a dog, Bobby Joe. Over there."

A ball squeezed in one hand, too-expensive racquet in the other, I watched a dog—an important one, it turned out—thrash up and down three or four times in that pond, its struggle mostly over and futile. In the park, citizens were going whichaway in confusion, and somebody, in a too-vowely Odessa-like voice, was yelling, "I can't swim," and Vicki was telling me to run over there and pull that dog out, goddammit. I looked at my sneakers, which were Adidas and not bought for wading in muck, and waited for my thoughts to turn generous. Yonder, Vicki had her woman's fist up, tiny but capable, and was shaking it my way. "Bobby Joe," she said. Her voice was warning only. "Okay," I said, attending to the husband half of me; I had been told what to do and now, reluctantly and stupidly, I was doing it.

I hated that dog I wrestled out of that scummy water—hated it for the dumb, hairy thing it was to have panicked and to have gone down and down and down; hated it for its awkward weight and sloppy jaws and useless limp legs; hated it because I was soaked and it was already dead and because my wife, usually sensible as a banker, was the first among the half-dozen on the slippery bank where I dropped the animal to insist I push on its chest, under the ribs, respirate it or resuscitate it or just do some damn thing. "Jesus, Vicki," I said. "It's too late, all right?" It lay beside me, a collarless mongrel that might have been half wild in the first place, red and black, the product of years and years of just hunching and eating and sleeping full at night. "Just try," she said, "it's better than nothing." I studied her and it, my wife and the thing she was currently rooting for. I thought about the constellations sometimes seen hereabouts—Andromeda, Cepheus, Cassiopeia; I thought, seriously and too long, about our hometown pals—Walt Scoggins, J.B. and Bonnie Streeter, old Bucky Waters—and the life-affirming Labor Day bar-b-que we throw. A man stood next to Vicki, and I remember thinking how nifty his Stetson-like cowboy hat was and how, were I a less domestic man, I'd like to buy it and soon enough swagger into a saloon for a shot of Wild West red-eye. "Five minutes," I told her. "I'll do it for five minutes."

Hardly a minute later she shoved me aside, forced all forty-one of her years into my shoulder and told me to move the hell out of the way. "You coward," she snapped. In her voice was the farm girl and rodeo queen and double-A basketball forward she'd once been. "He was doing it all wrong," she said; and I saw the woman for whom the dog was *drowning* nod and make a face I could not take the measure of. Vicki was amazing, she was. Straddling that dog, she pushed the heels of her hands under its ribcage. She called that dog a low-down bastard and used other language I'd once heard her throw a Sinclair Oil lobbyist out of her office with; deep in me, it was comforting to think that the dog, from its black hereafter, might be reached with such talk and thus come howling back into the here-and-now. "Come on, dog," she said. "Don't you dare quit on me." I felt like a stranger now, no more related to this drama than I am to those catastrophes we hear about from China. I was here, all mostly good six feet of me; and she was there, on her knees, in the mud. I was in a car going hither or in a plane bound for the make-believe outlands of Timbuktu; and she, a woman with a familiar name and a laugh I used to know in darkness, was in a different place and time, me merely a dumbbell to read about one day.

And then it was over. A cloud had gone by, changed shapes a dozen times, and was now a milky streak at the horizon. "What?" I said. She was standing near me, her expression empty space that could not be read into or be made warmly human. I was going to learn something, I knew. Working on that dog, trying to put its magic back, she had come to a decision about us. The dog, the stink and bulk of him, was a 3-D thing she'd spent time and feeling on, and now she had come to me again, another beast that was maybe already gone to her. I could smell me, I remember. Part English Leather my daughter, Debbie, had given me for Christmas, part athletics, part pond water. Watching Vicki, I recalled some things I knew: my first fistfight, the warped dreams I often shake from, how money feels in my wallet. My arm had an itch I would not scratch;

my brain a need I could not act on. Everything hereabouts—these average citizens, that scraggly cottonwood, this infernal air we breathe—was both itself and not, and it was simple to believe that what held me here on earth was cheap, weak and loose.

"You want me to go," I said. Her head went *yes* a little and I could feel the separate, common strings of me pop free. "Where?" I asked. Immediately, I saw how things would be henceforth: the Triangle Drive-In, where I eat chicken-fried steak and bullshit with Del Cruz, the five-bedroom home I only drive by now, the remote-control TV I watch too much of in the duplex I rent on Olive Street. "Go away, Bobby Joe," Vickie said. "I don't care where."

So I did.

The other dog that died was named Gigi Babette Regis III, a black registered toy poodle, its mother Babette Coco Village, its father Regis Antoine Pierre II; and that fine dog—which was called Sheri—had papers that went back to the days when Indians fought palefaces and travel by steamship was a big damn deal. An ordinary house pet, it was—in the innocent years long before Vicki and I flew apart one month ago—her dog and, sad to say, I actually killed it.

Coming home from work one night, after drinking Jack Daniel's that was no good for me and after making calls to women I had no right to know or to bother, I pulled into my driveway and felt a bump that, I hoped then, could not have been live or meaningful. It was dark on that side of the house and I remember saying to myself, "Bobby, you ought to put the car in the garage." On the radio was the music I buy, what is sung about in Houston and Nashville, unashamed and from the heart of things. This was 1975, when our news concerned Jim "Catfish" Hunter and hoodlums named Mitchell and Haldeman and John D. Erlichman, and I owned a half-million dollars of shiny inventory the better businessmen at Honda and Datsun aimed to make me swallow whole. I sat in my driveway for a time, muttering, "Shit, shit, shit," and then, careful as any drunk, I eased my Impala into the garage. Things will get better, I told myself.

At first, I tried to ignore the black lump her dead dog was. I watched Marvin Stapleton's house across the way and noted the banging coming from his garage. In the east, the moon was partly up, shining down on the sixty barren flat miles between me and another town of workaday folks. I remembered the bit of dirty Spanish I knew and the faraway countries of Persia and France I intended to visit. That dog was Vicki's practically all its life. She had raised it, taught it the customary tricks—to sit and to heel, to roll over and to beg—and now there would be nothing to sleep in the curl of her in our big bed. Hell, I liked it too, that silly poodle. It came when called, did its business outdoors as it ought. It liked to ride on my lap and chase whatever I tossed. In its way, it was as steadfast a pal as any human I'd known as long. Truth to tell, though from a breed often vain as the royalty I've read about, that dog probably thought of itself as a mutt, not as twenty-five pounds of muscle worth over five hundred dollars to folks with breeding kennels.

Vicki took it well, I thought. She switched off the shoot-'em-up Karl Malden was starring in and looked at me squarely, nothing in her eyes about the cross-hearted, angry thing this should have been. "Tell me that again, Bobby," she said. I'd seen her look before, but for a moment I couldn't place it. "Say it again, Bobby." I heard the children in the living room, Bobby Jr. trying to learn what nine times x was and Debbie being helpful with advice about integers. I took in the character of my rec room, the two golf trophies I'd won and the nine-point buck I'd bow-shot one winter in the Gila Forest. It was this way, I told her. It was dark, I was indecisive and maybe not concentrating as one should, and well, it was a mistake. "An accident," she said. Her hand went through her hair twice, and instantly I recognized her expression. I'd seen it the summer before when, near the shallow end of the club pool, I'd confessed to sleeping with my accountant, Mildred Tanner. Against the sun, she'd shaded her eyes and said, quietly, "Bobby, you're a stupid man." Now, she lighted a menthol cigarette, and the present came rushing back.

"Tell me again, Bobby. Slowly, this time." A cloud of smoke came my way, and I realized I was frightened. This is fury, I told myself. This is rage without the volume and lashing out. "What do you want to know?" I asked. She used silence the way actors do, knowing it had weight and color and shape. Then: "What were you thinking of, tell me that." I heard myself again: how I'd been at the Thunderbird Lounge with Jimmy Stokes and the Clute brothers; how, between jokes and drinks, we'd fixed the world and pitched ourselves high up on the heap we saw. I'd listened to Uncle Roy and the Red Creek Wranglers, I told her, and was especially impressed by the wild notes they reached. I re-created my wandering ride home, up Fir Street and down Iron, onto I-10 for twenty miles of trucks roaring past. "I want to know what was on your mind," she said. "I want to know what sort of person you are." I was thinking about shoes then, I said, how new ones are a pleasure and yet polishing a chore. I had thought about running, which I was once fair at, and how much I hated the paperwork that buying and selling are. And then, while my house made mechanical noises and something jetlike could be heard flying overhead, it was her turn.

"This is what you'll do," she said. This was it, she was really saying. I was not to disappoint, or hurt, her again. I was to shave every morning, including weekends. I was to get my hair cut twice a month. I was to stop cussing. I was to cast aside my affection for bombing America's enemies. "Go to the linen closet," she said, "and get out one of the monogrammed bath towels. Put the dog in the towel, and in the backyard, by the upright willow, dig a hole." Were I to fail her again, she was saying, in a month or a year or even ten years, I was finished. There was no such thing as accident. There was only us and the busy world itself. There was only her and me, and events that were the true expression of us. No bad luck. No misfortune. No happenstance. Just the sad character I was and the grief I left behind me. "Tell me," she actually said, "when you're done."

What do I see, now that this story has moved sufficiently backward? I see a man whose favorite food was spaghetti and whose happiest color was the yellow you find on certain doctors and dentists at the golf course. I see him—this man I am related to only by time and specific memories—at work in his backyard around midnight, his ordinary world asleep and tending toward dreamland. But what can be done to express his state of mind? It's like watching home movies. You know the names of these folks—Uncle Boots, your granny, that toddler who is the fat, grinning image of you—but you do not know, though you think you do, the secret insides of them. They are only light and shadow, sound and movement; then they are vanished.

My jacket folded over one willow limb, I dug a proper hole in the hour I was outside alone. I kept my thoughts to the work I did in the place I was: the dirt, the shovel, the ache in my spine, the blisters that would appear in the morning. Then I knocked on the window to tell Vicki to come out. She was beautiful, I remember, all leg and arm and heroine's shiny hair; and I did well to resist the desire to grab her and hold on. "I'm sorry," I said. She looked at me as if I were a guy she'd bumped fenders with at the supermarket. "It's kind of cold, isn't it, Bobby?" This was only polite talk; it wasn't nighttime in March she was thinking of. "You want to say something?" she asked. "It is a burial, after all." She stood next to the hole, staring down at the towel and the lump underneath, and I could think of no words to explain that and me both. "Go over there a minute, Bobby," she said. I saw her slippers and the blue robe that was a birthday gift, and as if I had a real weight to drag, I went some paces away. Once upon a time, she was an expert dancer, able to throw herself heedlessly into the steps we knew. She could play bridge too. And knit well enough to give her handiwork as presents. I'd seen her ride her daddy's meanest horse, a gelding named Scooter, and slug it when it misbehaved. I remembered her favorite books and the French history she liked to study, and then, in what was the climax of this night, she came toward me and said all right, I could cover the hole now. "Be sure to clean up before you go inside," she said. "Mrs. Tipton waxed the floors today."

She was asleep when I came in. I put on my pajamas, and when I lay down, I was surprised that the world didn't tilt more. Our house was silent, Vicki was mostly still, and I was wondering about the jobs I'd accomplish by noon. This, I see now, was the true end of us; there would be only years and one more dead dog to make it plain for me. But this night, my clock radio showing how late it was, I was counting the employees I had, thirty-one, and visualizing the new showroom I was building, and telling myself that everything—Vicki, our children, me—was all right. I was happy, I told myself. Lord, I was very, very happy.

The Children

Hobbits and Hobgoblins

The world whispers to those who listen. Secrets collide in the air with visions of truth and particles of fancy. *Listen.* Hear the murmurs of owls speaking of buried treasures, the sparrows conversing over great battles of yore, the squirrels telling tales in hushed voices of the time an angel lighted on the shoulders of a young girl and allowed her to see the ghosts of her future. The voices canter about unceasing, sibilant and silken and silvery in the ether, containing all the wisdom of the great world; all the knowledge ever needed floats about in the air simply to be heeded, contained in faint hummings slightly louder than the chiming of the spheres. Any boy can hear. If he only listens.

Malcolm sits in his grandmother's chair, a great chair it is. In truth, a throne once owned by an Egyptian empress. Malcolm knows. She sat here, as he does, nibbling peacock's brain and honey-covered hippopotamus eyes, fanned from behind by a Nubian, naked but for a blindingly white turban and gold bracelets. He fans Malcolm now, an idle coloring book in Malcolm's lap while the gossamer plumes create an imperial breeze. Malcolm sighs.

"Brandon, I'm really tired of discussing it."

"Don't call me Brandon again, Denise. It's Fetasha. Fetasha Yakob."

"Jesus, Brandon—"

"Denise!"

Malcolm's father cannot see it, but a cobra slithers about his feet. Malcolm can see it. He does not worry. Malcolm knows it will not harm his father. The snake has a bright red hood and is striped like a barber's pole in orange and black. It has no venom; but it can breathe fire when it is angry.

"You have no respect for me or my beliefs."

"Brandon, *you* have no respect for you or your beliefs. You've changed your damn mind so much you don't even know what you believe."

"Don't use language like that in front of the kid."

"Jesus, Brandon. He's six."

"Exactly. Set an example."

"Mother, can you believe this?"

"Hm."

Malcolm grins when he sees that his grandmother, who sits ignoring his quarreling parents, trying to read a magazine, has a hobbit on her lap. The hobbit's name is Fidor. He winks at Malcolm. Fidor's orange hair is pulled back in a long ponytail and he wiggles his big toes in contentment, enjoying the grown-ups' argument.

"*You* are the one who hasn't held a job in ten fucking years."

"Denise. The boy."

"Don't come into my house and lecture me on how I should raise my son, Brandon. My god, you haven't seen him in three months and suddenly you've decided you can't live without him."

"He's my son, Denise."

"You noticed. Finally. Took you six years."

"Don't be mean, Denise. There's no reason."

Malcolm is pleased to see that the blue cockatoo—a very rare creature, with the ability to fly through walls—is perched atop his mother's head. The blue cockatoo sings in a Tibetan dialect taught to it by the great pirate Yeheman, a friend of Malcolm's who invited him onto his flying pirate ship, the galleon *Celestial,* once. Yeheman wanted to take Malcolm on an expedition to the other side of the sun. But Malcolm had to go to school. Yeheman left the blue cockatoo with Malcolm as a bond of friendship. The cockatoo is named Qwnpft.

"The answer is no, Brandon. No."

"The name is Fetasha, Denise. It means 'search' in Amharic, the Ethiopian tongue."

"I don't care. No. You can't take him."

"Only for a month, Denise."

"Not for a day."

"I have rights, you know."

"Sue me."

"Denise. I am his father."

"Brandon, I was there. For both events. The conception and the delivery. I know who the father is."

"You're trying to be funny, Denise. This is not productive."

"You're being flaky, Brandon. This is not sane."

The curtains are covered with speckled lizards, they chirp like birds and create melodies in eight-part harmony; gifts from the Maharajah of Zamzeer. He keeps sending gifts to Malcolm to gain his hand in marriage for his royal daughter, the ugly Princess Zamaha. Malcolm plans to hold out.

"Mother, do you hear what your *former* son-in-law proposes to do?"

"Hm."

Fidor giggles and slaps his knees; Qwnpft trills in Tibetan. Yamor, the black winged horse, another gift from the Maharajah, wanders into the room, up to Malcolm, and nuzzles him softly behind the ear. Yamor is lonely and wants to go for a fly. But Malcolm can't right now. His parents are arguing.

"Denise, I know how to take care of him. He'll be well looked after."

"Brandon—"

"*Fetasha!*"

"*What*ever. You can't even look after yourself. How on earth do you expect me to allow you to take my son to Jamaica for a month? Has this Rastafarian bullshit really messed your mind up that much?"

"Denise. Your language."

"I cussed like a sailor when you met me, remember? That's what you liked about me, or so you said."

A green orangutan hangs from the ceiling lamp; giant fire-red Amazonian toads play leapfrog in the thick carpet; a yerple sea turtle swims the length of the room, turning somersaults as he completes laps over everyone's head. Underneath the coffee table perch three demons, Ksiel, Lahatiel, and Shaftiel, whom Malcolm caught a week ago trying to punish a knight. He has made them his slaves. They smoke long pipes of blue tobacco, which puffs up in pungent clouds of pink.

Today is Malcolm's sixth birthday. Jerome, Sheniqua, Perry, William, Davenport, Clarise, Sheryl, Tameka, Yuko, Bharati, John, Björn, Ali, Federica, Francesca, and Kwame came to his party. School will be over in three weeks, his grandmother says, and he will be taken from his Kingdom in the Land of New Jersey to his summer residence in the Land of the Carolinas, to rule with his Imperial cousins at the Imperial Palace at Tims-on-the-Creek. But now his father, who used to be a sorcerer named Mahammet al-Saddin and has now become this Prince Fetasha Yakob, plans to steal him away to the island principality of Jamaica, where rules, Malcolm has heard tell, the sinister Lord Jam-Ka. His father must need him to do serious battle. But Prince Fetasha must convince the Empress, his mother. Malcolm is worried.

"Just stop asking, Brandon. You are not going to let my son smoke ganja and commune with Ja and fiddle with some crystal around his neck. And what on earth are you wearing anyhow, Brandon? You look like . . . Jesus, what does he look like, Mama?"

"Hm."

"What's that around your neck?"

"Cowrie shells. And the name is Bran—I mean Fetasha."

"Your name is Brandon Church Harrington, okay? And that's what I'm going to call you."

"You continue to disrespect me, just as you always did. That's what ruined our marriage."

"O Lord, here we go. How dare you—"

Prince Fetasha came to Malcolm's party as a surprise. He tiptoed around back, in through the wood, and made a grand entrance in the backyard, coming through the hedges. He scared Malcolm's friends. Malcolm was surprised and happy. Malcolm's mother was angry. They fail to "communicate," his mother once told him. They're just from different worlds, child, his grandmother said. His grandmother likes Prince Fetasha. He likes Prince Fetasha too.

"How can a man, a black man, with your background, with a degree from Morehouse with Honors, no less, with a J.D. from fucking Yale, *fucking Yale,* go around with his head twigged up like a reggae singer, wearing—what the hell is it you have on, Brandon? I liked last year's getup much better—Do you know how much you'd be pulling down now if . . . ? I have to take a Valium every time I think about it—"

"It's always money with you."

"*You* were the one born with a trust fund, okay? Don't talk to me about money. I worked my way through med school, fool. *You* don't even pay alimony, which I could still contest."

"I don't *caaarre* about money, Denise. Can't you get that through—"

"You don't *caaarre* about anything. Except your hair."

Malcolm's mother, the Empress of the Kingdom of Orange, in the Land of New Jersey, is a baby doctor, a pediatrician. Her office has walls of tangerine and licorice and lime and lemon and blueberry. Grandmother, the Queen Mother, takes him there sometimes. All their subjects, waiting for an audience, sit in the candy-flavored room playing with blocks and trucks and rainbow-assorted animals—toys Malcolm now finds boring. The Empress doesn't have any video games there.

"Okay, for the last time—now I'm going to say this slowly, Mr. Rasta, so you can possibly, perhaps, maybe, understand me: Under. No. Circumstance. Will. I. Allow. You. To. Take. My. Son—the one who's sitting over there in that chair. With. You. Any. Where. Not Jamaica. Not Ethiopia. Not Newark. Not New York. Not to the convenience store down the road. After your last escapade, Mr. 'I'll-have-him-back-Sunday-night,' Malcolm is OFF LIMITS. If you want to see him, you do it *here*. There he is. Now look."

"Denise. You're being unreasonable again."

"Unreasonable? Again? Need I remind you that you kid-napped—"

"Kidnapped is unfa—"

"You were gone for a week—"

"Should we really be arguing in fron—"

"—instead of a weekend."

"—of him?"

Malcolm likes to go to the Savage Land with Prince Fetasha. He likes the caverns and the canyons, the mountains of steel and glass. They speak in loud booming voices. Sometimes they scream. The roads are wide and black with strange hieroglyphics painted about them, and the inhabitants rush about, surely chased by some monster like Godzilla or Smaug or Bigfoot. Prince Fetasha, when he was Mahammet al-Saddin, carried Malcolm on his shoulders when they were in the Savage Land. He could smell the scent on his father called M-cents. Malcolm liked the smell. Prince Fetasha's hair is in long black snakes like Medusa's. He says they are called dead-locks. Malcolm likes to play with his father's deadlocks. They feel spongy and soft, and they smell of M-cents. Once Fetasha, who was then Mahammet al-Saddin, gave Malcolm a necklace of shells like the one he's wearing now. The shells told Malcolm where a magic amulet, long lost, lay in Africa. But when he got home his mother, the Empress, tore the shells from his neck and said he might get a funjus from them and threw them into the trash compactor. The amulet will never be found.

"Denise."

"No."

Yamor, the black winged horse, is getting antsy, and the floating yerple turtle seems to be slowing down. A mask on the wall winks at Malcolm, and the hobbit is climbing down off his grandmother's lap. Malcolm stands up, and his wing'd sandals take him across the room to his mother and father.

"Mom, can I get some deadlocks like Daddy's?"

His mother, the Empress, raises her hands in the air and rolls her eyes—the look she has when his grandmother says his mother is "disgusted with the world again." His father, Prince Fetasha, pats him on the head. But before either of them say anything, his grandmother pops her magazine shut.

"Okay, Boo"—his grandmother always calls him Boo—"time for your bath and bed, birthday boy. It's been a big day."

Malcolm's grandmother, the Queen Mother of the Empress, sells castles and palaces when she's not being Queen Mother. They call her a Real Tor and she wears a man's jacket with a house decal on the breast just like his F-16 decal. Each day she meets people looking for a new castle. Sometimes she takes him with her. People make very strange noises when they look about and ask the Queen Mother weird questions. Malcolm likes to explore the castles, looking for ghosts and lost elves, always on the lookout for hobgoblins, his sworn enemies.

Sometimes his grandmother, the Queen Mother, takes him to the movies and gives him candy and makes him swear he won't tell his mother, the Empress, since she'd be "disgusted with the world." Malcolm isn't allowed to have candy. But he sneaks plenty.

In the bathroom his grandmother helps him undress. He lifts his arms to get his shirt off. The water sloshes into the tub with a river's rush. The Queen Mother sprinkles the secret magic special potion into the water and it begins to bubble like a witch's cauldron.

"Okay, soldier. In you go."

"Gramma?"

"Hmmm?"

"Am I going to go to Jamaica with Daddy?"

"I doubt it very seriously."

"Will I get to go to New York with him?"

"I don't think so baby. Not for a while."

"Can I get deadlocks like his?"

"Hell no."

"Why?"

"Into the water."

The silly octopus with the glasses caresses Malcolm's ankle as he steps into the water; the bubbles tickle his hind parts as he eases down. When each one pops it says a magic word. The water is warm and heavy and fun.

"Now don't forget to wash behind your ears."

The Queen Mother leaves, and Malcolm closes his eyes and says the magic words and—Qwiza!—he is a merman with a fishtail wide as the dining-room table, its scales diamond-shaped and sparkling and the color of oil on water, and it flops gracefully in the air like a sail in the wind. When Malcolm is in the water he is transformed into the Lord of the Sea (a part-time job), and he must save his Dominion from the evil sea-wizard Nptananan who takes on many forms, his favorite being that of a merwolf with fangs like a viper.

Malcolm knows when it is about time for his grandmother to come to fetch him out of the water, "so your skin won't wrinkle," she says, so in a flash he turns back into a boy. He lathers himself with the secret magic special potion soap that will make him invincible to arrows and bullets and swords and hexes. He remembers to wash behind his ears.

Grandmother, the Queen Mother, dries him off in the huge

towel that could eat him whole—yet another gift from the Maharajah. In times of trouble, with the right magic words, it becomes a flying towel.

After saying good night to the Empress and the former Prince-Consort Fetasha, who once was the Crown Prince Mahammet al-Saddin, Malcolm is tucked into bed, the Nubian still fanning him. The yerple turtle sleeps bobbing in the air current; the lizards are aligned on the curtain in the pattern of the family coat-of-arms; the flying horse, Yamor, is ZZZZZZing on the floor, his wings fluttering ever so gently with each breath; Fidor, the hobbit, is curled underneath the covers with Malcolm; Qwnpft, the blue cockatoo, nestles in Malcolm's hair; and the barber-pole–striped cobra coils into a perfect O at Malcolm's feet. The demons, Ksiel, Lahatiel, and Shaftiel, are secure in the closet and Malcolm can smell the pink smoke as it wafts up from underneath the door.

"Sweet dreams, Boo. Happy birthday."

"'Night."

The Archangel Rafael, right on schedule, appears in the corner when the lights go out, his blazing sword at the ready.

Voices drift up through the ventilation shaft.

"Denise, you know it would really be a good experience for him at his age."

"I've already paid for his trip down South with Mama."

"Money, money, money."

"I know, I know. I was the Marxist once, remember? I still . . . well, you know . . ."

"Oh, yeah, the occasional freebie at the clinic, the volunteer work at the soup kitchen, the checks to Amnesty and the NAACP and Klanwatch and Greenpeace. You mean the payoffs for the guilt ghosts?"

"Now who's being mean? I'm not going to be a hypocrite, Bran—Fe—I can't. Mr. Dreadlocks. I've worked hard for this life. If you don't like it, fuck you and the horse you rode in on. It's my life, okay? I'm the one going to Capitalist Hell."

"But do you have to take Malcolm with you? I just don't want my son to grow up to be a vain, pampered, spoiled, over-educated, suburbanite airhead with no sense of history and no sense of self."

"Like you, you mean?"

"Hey, I'm trying, okay? At least I'm—"

"Well, so am I."

". . ."

". . ."

"Look, I don't want to take the bus to the PATH to the subway to home."

"Brandon? I don't know why you won't just buy a car."

"Can I . . . ? Well . . . you know . . ."

"Oh, you're such a baby, Brandon; a cute baby, but a thirty-six-year-old baby just the same."

"Please, Dr. Harrington, ma'am, *please*. I'll wash your turbo-engined-diesel-guzzling-air-polluting-whatever-the-hell-it-is in the morning. Please . . ."

"Stop that. You know . . . I'm . . . ooooh . . . Now quit that. Brandon. *Brandon*. You . . ."

". . ."

". . ."

"Remember the time we got ourselves holed up for a whole weekend and listened to nothing but Carmen McRae and ate nothing but fruit and did it till we were sore?"

"Hmmmmmm . . . Where do you plan to sleep?"

"Right here."

"But Mama'll . . ."

"She *is* a grown woman, you know."

". . ."

". . ."

"I do like the way those feel."

Through the open window Malcolm can see four red eyes aflame. He knows they belong to the hobgoblins, Gog and Magog, on the lookout for him, lurking in the whispering New Jersey night. But the Archangel will protect him and there is no cause for worry. The castle is secure. The drawbridge is drawn. The Imperial Family is one. And he is six years old.

Once in a great while, now and again, deep within dreams of dreams of dreams, we may chance to hear our true selves speak, and in those words are kept the keys to ourselves; but we must listen softly, listen soundly, listen silently, or we may never hear our voices telling tales of who we are.

WENDI KAUFMAN

Helen on Eighty-Sixth Street

I hate Helen. That's all I can say. I hate her. Helen McGuire is playing Helen, so Mr. Dodd says, because, out of the entire sixth grade, she most embodies Helen of Troy. Great. Helen McGuire had no idea who Helen of Troy even was! When she found out, well, you should have seen her—flirting with all the boys, really acting the part. And me? Well, I know who Helen was. I am pissed.

My mother doesn't understand. Not that I expected she would. When I told her the news, all she said was "Ah, the face that launched a thousand ships." She didn't even look up from her book. Later, at dinner, she apologized for quoting Marlowe. Marlowe is our cat.

At bedtime I told my mother, "You should have seen the way Helen acted at school. It was disgusting, flirting with the boys."

Mom tucked the sheets up close around my chin, so that only my head was showing, my body covered mummy style. "Vita," she said, "it sounds like she's perfect for the part."

So, I can't play Helen. But, to make it worse, Mr. Dodd said I have to be in the horse. I can't believe it. The horse! I wanted to be one of the Trojan women—Andromache, Cassandra, or even Hecuba. I know all their names. I told Mr. Dodd this, and then I showed him I could act. I got really sad and cried out about the thought of the body of my husband, Hector, being dragged around the walls of my city. I wailed and beat my fist against my chest. "A regular Sarah Heartburn" was all he said.

"Well, at least you get to be on the winning team," my mother said when I told her about the horse. This didn't make me feel any better. "It's better than being Helen. It's better than being blamed for the war," she told me.

Mom was helping me make a shield for my costume. She said every soldier had a shield that was big enough to carry his body off the field. I told her I wasn't going to be a body on the field, that I was going to survive, return home.

"Bring the shield, just in case," she said. "It never hurts to have a little help."

Mom and I live on West Eighty-sixth Street. We have lived in the same building, in the same apartment, my entire life. My father has been gone for almost three years. The truth is that he got struck with the wanderlust—emphasis on "lust," my mother says—and we haven't heard from him since.

"Your father's on his own odyssey," my mother said. And now it's just me and Mom and Marlowe and the Keatses, John and John, our parakeets, or "pair of Keats," as Mom says. When I was younger, when Dad first left and I still believed he was coming back, it made me happy that we still lived in the same building. I was happy because he would always know where to find us. Now that I am older, I know the city is not that big. It is easy to be found and easy to stay lost.

And I also know not to ask about him. Sometimes Mom hears things through old friends—that he has travelled across the ocean, that he is living on an island in a commune with some people she called "the lotus eaters," that he misses us.

Once I heard Mr. Farfel, the man who's hanging around Mom now, ask why she stayed in this apartment after my father left. "The rent's stabilized," she told him, "even if the relationship wasn't."

At school, Helen McGuire was acting weird because I'm going to be in the horse with Tommy Aldridge. She wanted to know what it's like: "Is it really cramped in there? Do you have to sit real close together?"

I told her it's dark, and we must hold each other around the waist and walk to make the horse move forward. Her eyes grew wide at this description. "Lucky you," she said.

Lucky me? She gets to stand in the center of the stage alone, her white sheet barely reaching the middle of her thighs, and say lines like "This destruction is all my fault" and "Paris, I do love you." She gets to cry. Why would she think I'm lucky? The other day at rehearsal, she was standing onstage waiting for her cue, and I heard Mrs. Reardon, the stage manager, whisper, "That Helen is as beautiful as a statue."

At home Old Farfel is visiting again. He has a chair in Mom's department. The way she describes it, a chair is a very good thing. Mom translates old books written in Greek and Latin. She is working on the longest graduate degree in the history of Columbia University. "I'll be dead before I finish," she always says.

Old Farfel has been coming around a lot lately, taking Mom and me to dinner at Italian places downtown. I don't like to be around when he's over.

"I'm going to Agamemnon's apartment to rehearse," I told Mom.

Old Farfel made a small laugh, one that gets caught in the back of the throat and never really makes it out whole. I want to tell him to relax, to let it out. He smells like those dark cough drops, the kind that make your eyes tear and your head feel like it's expanding. I don't know how she can stand him.

"Well, the play's the *thing*," Old Farfel said. "We're all just players strutting and fretting our hour on the stage." Mom smiled at this, and it made me wish Old Farfel would strut his hours at his apartment and not at our place. I hate the way he's beginning to come around all the time.

When I get back from rehearsal, Mom is spinning Argus. It's what she does when she gets into one of her moods. Argus, our dog, died last summer when I was away at camp. My mother can't stand to part with anything, so she keeps Argus, at least his ashes, in a blue-and-white vase that sits on our mantel.

Once I looked into the vase. I'd expected to see gray stuff, like the ash at the end of a cigarette. Instead, there was black sand and big chunks of pink like shells, just like at the beach.

My mother had the vase down from the mantel and was twirling it in her hands. I watched the white figures on it turn, following each other, running in a race that never ends.

"Life is a cycle," my mother said. The spinning made me dizzy. I didn't want to talk about life. I wanted to talk about Helen.

"Helen, again with Helen. Always Helen," my mother said. "You want to know about Helen?"

I nod my head.

"Well, her father was a swan and her mother was too young to have children. You don't want to be Helen. Be lucky you're a warrior. You're too smart to be ruled by your heart."

"And what about beauty? Wasn't she the most beautiful woman in the world?" I asked.

Mom looked at the Greek vase. "Beauty is truth, truth beauty—that is all ye need to know."

She is not always helpful.

"Manhattan is a rocky island," Mom said at dinner. "There is no proper beach, no shore." My mother grew up in the South, near the ocean, and there are times when she still misses the beach. Jones,

Brighton, or even Coney Island beaches don't come close for her. I know when she starts talking about the water that she's getting restless. I hope this means that Old Farfel won't be hanging around too long.

Every night I write a letter to my father. I don't send them—I don't know where to send them—but, still, I write them. I keep the letters at the back of my closet in old shoeboxes. I am on my third box. It's getting so full that I have to keep the lid tied down with rubber bands.

I want to write, "Mom is talking about the water again. I think this means she is thinking of you. We are both thinking of you, though we don't mention your name. Are you thinking of us? Do you ever sit on the shore at night and wonder what we're doing, what we're thinking? Do you miss us as much as we miss you?"

But instead I write, "I am in a play about the Trojan War. I get to wear a short white tunic, and I ambush people from inside a big fake horse. Even though we win the war, it will be many, many years before I return home. Until I see my family again. In this way, we are the same. I will have many adventures. I will meet giants and witches and see strange lands. Is that what you are doing? I wish you could come to the play."

Old Farfel is going to a convention in Atlanta. He wants Mom to go with him. From my bed, I can hear them talking about it in the living room. It would be good for her, he says. I know that Mom doesn't like to travel. She can't even go to school and back without worrying about the apartment—if she turned the gas off, if she fed the cat, if she left me enough money. She tells him that she'll think about it.

"You have to move on, Victoria," he tells her. "Let yourself go to new places."

"I'm still exploring the old places," she says.

He lets the conversation drop.

Mom said once that she travelled inside herself when Dad left. I didn't really understand, but it was one of the few times I saw her upset. She was sitting in her chair, at her desk, looking tired. "Mom, are you in there?" I waved my hand by her face.

"I'm not," she said. "I'm on new ground. It's a very different place."

"Are you thinking about Dad?"

"I was thinking how we all travel differently, Vita. Some of us don't even have to leave the house."

"Dad left the house."

"Sometimes it's easier to look outside than in," she said.

That night I dreamed about a swan. A swan that flies in circles over the ocean. This is not the dark water that snakes along the West Side Highway and slaps against the banks of New Jersey but the real ocean. Open water. Salty, like tears.

At play practice, I watch the other girls dress up as goddesses and Trojan women. They wear gold scarves wound tight around their necks and foreheads. They all wear flowers in their hair and flat pink ballet slippers. I wear a white sheet taken from my bed. It is tied around the middle with plain white rope. I also wear white sneakers. I don't get to wear a gold scarf or flowers. Mr. Dodd wrote this play himself and is very picky about details. Tommy Aldridge, my partner in the horse, was sent home because his sheet had Ninja Turtles on it. "They did not have Ninja Turtles in ancient Greece," Mr. Dodd said.

Mr. Dodd helps Helen McGuire with her role. "You must understand," he tells her, "Helen is the star of the show. Men have travelled great distances just to fight for her. At the end, when you come onstage and look at all the damage you've caused, we must believe you're really upset by the thought that this is all your fault."

Helen nods and looks at him blankly.

"Well, at least try to think of something really sad."

———

Old Farfel is taking Mom out to dinner again. It's the third time this week. Mom says it is a very important dinner, and I am not invited. Not that I would want to go, but I wasn't even asked. Mom brought in takeout, some soup and a cheese sandwich, from the coffee shop on the corner.

I eat my soup, alone in the kitchen, from a blue-and-white paper cup. I remember once at a coffee shop Mom held the same type of cup out in front of me.

"See this building, Vita?" she said. She pointed to some columns that were drawn on the front of her cup. It wasn't really a building—more like a cartoon drawing. "It's the Parthenon," she said. "It's where the Greeks made sacrifices to Athena."

"How did they make sacrifices?" I asked.

"They burned offerings on an altar. They believed this would bring them what they wanted. Good things. Luck."

I finish my soup and look at the tiny building on the cup. In between the columns are the words "Our Pleasure to Serve You." I run my fingers across the flat lines of the Parthenon and trace the roof. I can almost imagine a tiny altar and the ceremonies that were performed there.

It is then that I get an idea. I find a pair of scissors on Mom's desk and cut through the thick white lip of the cup toward the lines of the little temple. I cut around the words "Our Pleasure to Serve You." Then I take the temple and the words and glue them to the back of my notebook. The blue-and-white lines show clearly against the cardboard backing. I get Argus's big metal water bowl from the kitchen and find some matches from a restaurant Old Farfel took us to for dinner.

In my room I put on my white sheet costume and get all my letters to Dad out from the back of the closet. I know that I must say something, to make this more like a ceremony. I think of any Greek words I know: *spanakopita, moussaka, gyro.* They're only food words, but it doesn't matter. I decide to say them anyway. I say them over and over out loud until they blur into a litany, my own incantation: "*Spanakopitamoussakaandgyro, Spanakopitamoussakaandgyro, Spanakopitamoussakaandgyro.*"

As I say this, I burn handfuls of letters in the bowl. I think about what I want: to be Helen, to have my father come back. Everything I have ever heard says that wishes are granted in threes, so I throw in the hope of Old Farfel's leaving.

I watch as the words burn. Three years of letters go up in smoke and flame. I see blue-lined paper turn to black ashes; I see pages and pages, months and years, burn, crumble, and then disappear. The front of my white sheet has turned black from soot, and my eyes water and burn.

When I am done, I take the full bowl of ashes and hide it in the vase on the mantel, joining it with Argus. My black hands smudge the white figures on the vase, until their tunics become as sooty as my own. I change my clothes and open all the windows, but still Mom asks, when she comes home, about the burning smell. I told her I was cooking.

She looked surprised. Neither of us cooks much. "No more burnt offerings when I'm not home," she said. She looked upset and distracted, and Old Farfel didn't give that stifled laugh of his.

It's all my fault. Helen McGuire got chicken pox. Bad. She has been out of school for almost two weeks. I know my burning ceremony did this. "The show must go on," Mr. Dodd said when Achilles threw up the Tater Tots or when Priam's beard got caught in Athena's hair, but this is different. This is Helen. And it's my fault.

I know all her lines. Know them backward and forward. I have stood in our living room, towel tied around my body, and acted out the entire play, saying every line for my mother. When Mr. Dodd made the announcement about Helen at dress rehearsal, I stood up, white bedsheet slipping from my shoulders, and said in a loud, clear voice, "The gods must have envied me my beauty, for now my name is a curse. I have become hated Helen, the scourge of Troy."

Mr. Dodd shook his head and looked very sad. "We'll see, Vita. She might still get better," he said.

Helen McGuire recovered, but she didn't want to do the part because of all the pockmarks that were left. Besides, she wanted to be inside the horse with Tommy Aldridge. Mr. Dodd insisted that she still be Helen until her parents wrote that they didn't want her to be pressured, they didn't want to *do any further damage,* whatever that means. After that, the part was mine.

Tonight is the opening, and I am so excited. Mom is coming without Old Farfel. "He wasn't what I wanted," she said. I don't think she'll be seeing him anymore.

"What is beautiful?" I ask Mom before the play begins.

"Why are you so worried all the time about beauty? Don't you know how beautiful you are to me?"

"Would Daddy think I was beautiful?"

"Oh, Vita, he *always* thought you were beautiful."

"Would he think I was like Helen?"

She looked me up and down, from the gold lanyard snaked through my thick hair to my too tight pink ballet slippers.

"He would think you're more beautiful than Helen. I'm almost sorry he won't be here to see it."

"*Almost* sorry?"

"Almost. At moments like this—you look so good those ancient gods are going to come alive again with envy."

"What do you mean, come alive again? What are you saying about the gods?"

"Vita, Greek polytheism is an extinct belief," she said, and laughed. And then she stopped and looked at me strangely. "When people stopped believing in the gods, they no longer had power. They don't exist anymore. You must have known that."

Didn't I get the part of Helen? Didn't Old Farfel leave? I made all these things happen with my offering. I know I did. I don't believe these gods disappeared. At least not Athena.

"I don't believe you."

She looked at me, confused.

"You can't know for sure about the gods. And who knows? Maybe Daddy will even be here to see it."

"Sure," she said. "And maybe this time the Trojans will win the war."

I stand offstage with Mr. Dodd and wait for my final cue. The dry-ice machine has been turned on full blast and an incredible amount of fake smoke is making its way toward the painted backdrop of Troy. Hector's papier-mâché head has accidentally slipped from Achilles' hand and is now making a hollow sound as it rolls across the stage.

I peek around the thick red curtain, trying to see into the audience. The auditorium is packed, filled with parents and camcorders. I spot my mom sitting in the front row, alone. I try to scan the back wall, looking for a sign of him, a familiar shadow. Nothing.

Soon I will walk out on the ramparts, put my hand to my forehead, and give my last speech. "Are you sure you're ready?" Mr. Dodd asks. I think he's more nervous than I am. "Remember," he tells me, "this is Helen's big moment. Think loss." I nod, thinking nothing.

"Break a leg," he says, giving me a little push toward the stage. "And try not to trip over the head."

The lights are much brighter than I had expected, making me squint. I walk through the smoky fog toward center stage.

"It is I, the hated Helen, scourge of Troy."

With the light on me, the audience is in shadow, like a big pit, dark and endless. I bow before the altar, feeling my tunic rise. "Hear my supplication," I say, pulling down a bit on the back of my tunic.

"Do not envy me such beauty—it has wrought only pain and despair."

I can hear Mr. Dodd, offstage, loudly whispering each line along with me.

"For this destruction, I know I will be blamed."

I begin to recite Helen's wrongs—beauty, pride, the abdication of Sparta—careful to enunciate clearly. "Troy, I have come to ask you to forgive me."

I'm supposed to hit my fist against my chest, draw a hand across my forehead, and cry loudly. Mr. Dodd has shown me this gesture, practiced it with me in rehearsal a dozen times—the last line, my big finish. The audience is very quiet. In the stillness there is a hole, an empty pocket, an absence. Instead of kneeling, I stand up, straighten my tunic, look toward the audience, and speak the line softly: "And to say goodbye."

There is a prickly feeling up the back of my neck. And then applause. The noise surrounds me, filling me. I look into the darkened house and, for a second, I can hear the beating of a swan's wings, and, then, nothing at all.

MICHAEL CHABON

The Halloween Party

Whenever Nathan Shapiro regarded Eleanor Parnell, it was like looking at a transparent overlay in the *World Book Encyclopedia*. In his mind he would flip back and forth from today's deep-voiced, black-haired, chain-smoking, heavy-breasted woman in a red sheath dress or tight dungarees, gracefully working the cork from another bottle of pink California wine, to the vague, large, friendly woman in plaids who had fed him year after year on Cokes and deviled-ham sandwiches, whose leaves he had raked for seven autumns now, and who still lay somewhere underneath the new Eleanor, like the skeleton of a frog beneath the bright chaos of its circulatory system.

It was only since Nathan had turned fourteen and found himself privy to the reckless conversation of divorcées—of those half-dozen funny, sad women with whom his mother had surrounded herself—that he had discovered Eleanor Parnell to be a woman of bad habits and of enterprises that ended in disaster. They said that she baked and consumed marijuana desserts, and that she liked to spend Christmas Eve playing blackjack in Las Vegas, alone. She drove her scarlet Alfa Romeo with the abandon of someone who, as Mrs. Shapiro pointed out, had always been very unlucky.

When she was hardly older than Nathan was now, Eleanor had

spent two triumphant years on the L.P.G.A. tour; then she'd fallen from a horse and broken her left elbow. Nathan had seen her trophies once, in a glass cabinet up in Eleanor and Major Ray's bedroom. Her real-estate company went down under a hailstorm of lawsuits and threats of criminal prosecution, which Nathan and his mother had read about in the Huxley *New Idea* and even, eventually, in *The Washington Post*. Cayenne, her New Orleans-style restaurant in Huxley Mall, closed after only a few months. And there had been a pale little baby, a redhead named Sullivan, who lived so briefly that Ricky, Nathan's little brother, did not even remember him.

All these tales of misfortune, all the melancholy under Eleanor's eyes and around her mouth, had the surprising—to Nathan—effect of causing him to fall helplessly in love. It began one August when, after a hiatus of several years, he resumed his ancient habit of visiting the Parnells' house every day, for soft drinks and conversation with Eleanor. He was driven to her, at first, simply by loneliness and by the sadness of boredom. Ricky was gone—he had gone to live in Boston with their father the previous spring—and during the tedious, spectacular afternoons of August the house was distressingly empty. All month, Mrs. Shapiro, who was a nurse, had to work late on the ward, so Nathan ate dinner with his friend Edward St. John and Edward's bohemian family more often than usual, and he was glad to spend the last afternoons of the summer down the street at the Parnells'. Major Ray—Major Raymond Parnell, of Galveston, Texas—did not get home from the base until seven o'clock, and Nathan would sit in the kitchen until Major Ray's boisterous arrival, watching Eleanor smoke cigarettes and squeeze lemons into her diet Coke, of which she drank sixty ounces a day—enough, as Major Ray often declared, to reanimate a dead body. She would ask Nathan for his opinions on hair styles, decorating, ecology, religion, and music, and he would offer them only after a good deal of consideration, in an airy, humorous, pedantic tone of voice, which he borrowed, without knowing it, from his father. Eleanor had treated him without condescension when he was a little boy, and she now listened to him with an intentness that was both respectful and amused, as though she half expected him to tell her something new.

Nathan's love for Eleanor followed hard on the heels of his long-awaited and disastrous growth spurt, and it wrenched him every bit as much, until his chest ached from the sudden and irregular expansion of his feelings. In the mirror the sight of his heavy-rimmed eyeglasses and unfortunate complexion; of the new, irregular largeness of his body, of his suddenly big—his fat—stomach, would send him off on giddy binges of anxiety. He ate sweet snacks and slept badly and jumped at loud sounds. The sight of Eleanor's red Alfa Romeo—the sight of any red car—disturbed him. He was filled with deep compassion for animals and children, in particular for Nickel Boy, the Parnells' dog, a sensitive, courtly old beagle. In fact, Nathan spoke at length to Nickel Boy about his feelings for Eleanor, even though he knew that talking to a dog was not really talking but, as he had read in *Psychology Today,* simply making a lot of comforting sounds in order to secrete some enzyme that would lower his own blood pressure and slow his pulse.

Every night before he switched off the lamp, and every morning when he awoke, he took out the collection of photographs of Eleanor Parnell he had pilfered from his mother's album and looked deeply into each of them, trying to speak to Eleanor with the telepathy of love. In his freshman-English class they arrived at the writing of poetry, and Nathan, startled into action, composed haiku, limericks, odes, and cinquains to Eleanor, as well as an acrostic sonnet, the first letters of whose lines daringly spelled out E-L-E-A-N-O-R P-A-R-N-E-L-L; whenever, in these poems, he referred to her directly, he called her Jennifer—like "Eleanor" a dactyl.

On the Saturday before the start of his freshman year of high school, as Nathan wandered home through the woods from Edward's house, trying to walk erect, he saw Eleanor under the tulip poplars, in a battered pith helmet, wildly shooting down wasps' nests with the pistol nozzle of a garden hose. Great golden, malevolent wasps had been something of a problem all summer, but after all the rain in July they proliferated and flew into the houses at suppertime.

"Is it working?" called Nathan, trotting toward her. One of the things he loved about Eleanor was her inventiveness, however doomed.

"Oh, no," Eleanor said. As soon as she glimpsed Nathan she began to laugh, and the stream of water shivered and fell to the ground. Her laugh, which was the first thing Nathan remembered noticing about Eleanor, had always been odd—raucuous and dark, like a cartoon magpie's or spider's—but lately it had come for Nathan to be invested with the darkness of sex and the raucousness of having survived misfortune. She had been in the sun too long, and her face was bright red. "No one was supposed to see me doing this. Do you think this is a bad idea? They look pretty pissed off. Major Ray thought this wasn't a good idea." Major Ray did not appreciate Eleanor.

"I disagree," said Nathan, gazing up at the treetops, where the wasps had hung their cities of paper. A dense golden cloud of wasps wavered around them. "There's a lot less of them now."

"Do you think so?" said Eleanor. She took off her hat and stared upward. Her bangs clung to her damp, sunburned forehead.

"Yes," said Nathan. "I guess you drowned them. Or maybe the impact kills them. Of the water." The cloud of wasps widened and descended. "Uh, Eleanor. Could I— Maybe I should try it."

"All right," said Eleanor. She handed him the squirting, hissing nozzle and then, solemnly, the pith helmet, all the while keeping an eye on the insects and biting her lip. Almost immediately Nathan got the feeling that a blanket, or a net, was about to fall on him. Eleanor jumped backward with a cry, and Nathan was left to fight off the wasps with his lunatic weapon, which he did for fifteen valiant seconds. Then he ran, with Eleanor behind him. He tore around the front of the Parnells' house, crossed the front lawn, and ran out onto Les Adieux Circle. At the center of the cul-de-sac lay a round patch of grass, planted with a single, frail oak tree. No one on the street knew who was supposed to mow this island and so it generally went unmown, and, according to the local children's legend, it harbored a family of field rats. He and Eleanor fell into the weeds, and Nathan's eyeglasses, which were photosensitive and had darkened in the afternoon sunshine, flew from his face. Dazzled, frightened, he rolled laughing in her rosy arms, and they embraced like a couple of fortunate castaways. Then, his heart pounding, he scrambled to his knees and sought the comforting weight, the protection of his glasses.

Of the four stings that Nathan received, three were on his thigh and one was on his shoulder. Eleanor took him into the house, up the stairs, and into the bedroom, where blue laundry lay folded on the big bed and where Eleanor's gold trophies, like so many miniature Mormon temples, sat shining dimly in their cabinet. Then she led him into the bathroom, lowered the lid onto the toilet, and sat him down.

"Roll up your cutoffs, Nathan," she said. She found a box of baking soda and mixed a little with some tap water in the plastic bathroom cup. Nathan pulled upward on the frazzled leg of his shorts and tried to keep from crying. She knelt beside him to daub his pale, fat, blistered thigh. Nathan flinched, but the paste was cool, and he was overcome with gratitude. He didn't know what to do, and so he stared at the parting of her hair, at Eleanor's miraculous scalp, white and fine as polished wood.

"I guess Major Ray was right," said Eleanor. "It wasn't such a hot idea." She cackled nervously, and it was a relief to Nathan to see that she also felt that something weird was happening—such a relief that he began to cry, although he hated crying more than anything else in the world.

"Oh, Jesus, does it hurt, honey?" Eleanor said. "I'm sorry, I'm sorry. Does it hurt?"

This expression of concern made Nathan inordinately happy,

and he tried to tell her it didn't hurt a bit, but he was too miserable to speak. He was frightened by the zeal of his crying, but it felt too good to stop. So he covered his face and hee-hawed like a child.

Eleanor stopped ministering to his wasp stings and sat back on her heels, regarding Nathan. A different kind of concern entered her face, and all at once she looked very sad. "What's the matter, Nathan?" she said.

But Nathan told no one, not even Edward, to whom he generally confided all his ludicrous amours. The two boys had supported and amused one another through a long series of fanciful loves, but until now the objects of their affections had always been unattainable, unlikely, and laughable: a prom queen, a postwoman, the earth-sciences teacher Miss Patocki, or the disturbing Sabina McFay, Edward's nineteen-year-old neighbor, who was half Vietnamese and rode a motorcycle. Not so Eleanor Parnell; she was unattainable and farfetched, but she was not at all laughable, and Nathan said nothing to Edward about her.

When he learned, from his mother, that he had been invited to the Parnells' Halloween party, he was flattered and struck with fear, and during the abject, optimistic weeks that followed he resolved to declare his feelings to Eleanor Parnell once and for all at this party. For ten days his head was filled with whispered, intricate repartee.

At dusk on Halloween, just as the youngest and most carefully chaperoned of the demons and nurses and mice were beginning to make their rounds, Nathan and Edward were standing in the living room of the Shapiros' house, drawing pictures with colored pencils onto Mrs. Shapiro's arms, back, and shoulders. Nathan's mother sat on a horsehide ottoman, in blue fishnet tights, blue high-heeled shoes, and a strapless Popsickle-blue bathing suit, laughing and complaining that the boys were pressing too hard as they drew anchors, hearts, thunderbolts, and snakes across her skin. The boys dipped the tips of the pencils into a jar of water, which made the colors run rich. As the drawings began to predominate over un-marked patches of skin, Nathan put his crimson pencil down and stepped back, as if to admire their handiwork.

"I think that's enough tattoos, Mom," he said.

"Is that so?" said his mother.

"Personally," said Edward, inspecting her. "I think a big, you know, triumphant eagle, with a javelin in its claw, right here under your neck, would look really cool, Mrs. Shapiro. Rose."

"That sounds fine, Edward," said Mrs. Shapiro.

Nathan looked at his friend, who began to paint a gray, scream-ing eagle. Nothing about his voice or studious little face indicated that he felt anything but the enthusiasm of art. As a matter of fact, his drawings were much better than Nathan's—bold, well drafted, easily recognizable; the snakes Nathan had drawn looked kind of like sewing needles, or flattened teaspoons.

"If you think about it," said Edward, in the careful but dazed way he had of propounding his many insights, "the symbol of our coun-try is a really warlike symbol."

"Hmm," said Mrs. Shapiro. "Isn't that interesting?"

When her costume was finally complete, and Nathan regarded her in all her fiery, gay motley, his heart sank, and he was seized with doubts about the costume he'd decided on. After much inde-cision and agonized debate with Edward, whose father was an avant-garde artist, Nathan had decided upon a *conceptual* Hal-loween costume. He had made a coat hanger into a wire ring that sat like a diadem on his brow, bent the end of it so that it would stand up over the back of his head, then made a small loop into which he could screw a light bulb. When he wore this contraption the light bulb seemed to hang suspended a few inches above him, and the wire was, in a dim room, practically invisible. He was going to the Parnells' Halloween party, in Edward's excited formulation, as a guy in the process of having a good idea for a costume.

The whole notion now struck Nathan as childish, and anemic, and it bothered him that the light bulb would never actually be lit up, and would just bob there, gray and dull, atop his head, as though he were really going to Eleanor's party as a guy in the process of having a *bad* idea for a costume. The truth was that Nathan felt so keenly how plain, how squat and clumsy he had become—his belly had begun to strain against the ribbed elastic of his new gym shorts, and his mother had received his last school pictures with a fond, motherly, devastating sigh—that he regretted having passed up the opportunity of concealing himself, if only for one night, in the raiment of a robot or a king.

"Cool," said Edward, standing up straight and blowing gently on the eagle tattoo.

Mrs. Shapiro rose from the ottoman, went to the chrome mirror that had been one of his parents' last joint purchases, and seemed greatly pleased by the apparition that she saw there. She hadn't wanted them to illustrate her face, and now it rose pale and almost shockingly bare from her shoulders. "You did a great job," she said. "I like the hula girl, Edward," she added, looking down at her right biceps.

"Make a muscle," he said. He went to the mirror and took hold of her right arm and wrist. Nathan followed.

"Flex your arm," said Edward.

Mrs. Shapiro flexed her arm. Nathan leaned over his friend's shoulder to watch the hula girl do a rudimentary bump and grind. He looked around for something to stand on, to get a better view, and his glance fell upon the matching chrome wastebasket, which stood beside the mirror, but when he balanced himself on its edge and peered down at the dancing tattoo the wastebasket immediately gave way. Nathan's eyeglasses, which for weeks he'd been meaning to tighten, slipped from his face, and when he fell he landed on them with a gruesome crunch.

"Oh, no," said Mrs. Shapiro. "Not again."

"I'm sorry, Mom," said Nathan.

"Are you all right? Did you hurt yourself?"

Edward, laughing, held out his hand to Nathan to pull him to his feet.

"You're insane, Dr. Lester," he said.

"You're deranged, Madame LaFarge," said Nathan, automatically. He looked at his friend and his tattooed mother gazing down upon him with a kind of mild, perfunctory concern. They turned to one another and laughed. A barrage of miniature-demon knocks rang out against the front door of the house. Nathan passed a hand before his eyes, blinked, and shook his head.

"I can see," he said flatly.

After Edward went home, he and his mother sat down at the kitchen table that smelled of 409 and called Ricky in Boston, to find out how his trick-or-treating had gone and to tell him that Nathan could see without his glasses. This was a development that ophthalmologists had been calling for since Nathan was five and had donned his first little owlish pair of horn-rims. Though its coming to pass was certainly something of a shock, it did not surprise him, especially now, when the behavior of his body was so continually shocking, and when so many of the ancient fixtures of his life—his slight form, his smooth face, his father and brother— were vanishing one by one.

Anne, his stepmother, answered the phone but went immediately to find Ricky, as she always did, and it occurred to Nathan for the first time that he was never particularly kind to her. He looked at the receiver, wishing he could run after her, and waited for Ricky to pick up his extension. His brother had just come in from trick-or-treating and was almost delirious with sated greed.

"Almond Roca, Nate!" he exulted. "Popcorn balls that are orange!"

"You can't eat the ones that aren't wrapped. Throw away the popcorn balls."

"Why?"

"Razor blades," said Nathan. He missed his brother so badly that it made him nervous to speak to Ricky on the phone. They talked to each other three times a week, but they could never generate any real silliness, and Nathan, in spite of himself, was always irritable and mocking, or stern.

"Yeah," Ricky said excitedly. "Halloween razor blades. Oh, my God, Nate, someone gave me raisin bread! *Raisin bread,* Nate!"

"I don't believe it," said Nathan. "Ricky, guess what?"

"I bet it was Mrs. Gilette. Hey, what are you going to be? Galactus?"

Ricky had spent his entire life waiting for Nathan to dress as Galactus, the World Eater, for Halloween, which was something Nathan a long time ago had said he was going to do, not dreaming that Ricky would never forget it, and would even come to regard it as the greatest and most magical of all the magical promises that his older brother had ever broken. In this instance Nathan felt more guilty than usual about having to tell Ricky the sorry truth, and he swiveled around in his chair so that his mother wouldn't be able to see his face.

"I'm going as a guy in the process of having a good idea for a costume," he mumbled.

"Huh?"

"You wouldn't understand it."

"I don't understand it because it's dumb," said Ricky. "I can tell it must be dumb."

"Go to hell," said Nathan.

"Nathan," said Mrs. Shapiro.

"Go to hell *you,*" said Ricky.

"Guess what? I can see without my glasses." Nathan spun around to face his mother, and she looked at him with mild amazement.

"You mean you never have to wear them ever again?" said Ricky. Absently he added, "Now you won't be so ugly."

This thought had not occurred to Nathan. He heard the sound of a plastic bag full of candy bars being rummaged around in and felt that he had exhausted Ricky's attention span, just when he most needed to speak to him. This incompleteness was why Nathan had first come to hate talking on the telephone to his father, in the days of his parents' trial separation. Ricky tore open a wrapper and began to chew. Bit-O-Honey, from the sound of it. Nathan pictured his brother surrounded by candy, lying in his fancy bedroom in Boston on his bed shaped like a racing car. It was a big bedroom, with a large, empty alcove at the back, which Ricky claimed to be afraid of entering. Nathan imagined the Boston Halloween night through the windows in the dark alcove as Ricky would see it from his speeding bed. "The big brother is always uglier," Ricky said.

"I know you're only teasing me," said Nathan. As he had several times before, he felt very far away from his brother just then, as he felt far from Anne and his father and mother and everyone he knew, isolated in his love and anxiety, but for the first time the void around him seemed to offer a new perspective, as though he were standing safely on top of a house in the midst of a great flood. He had no desire to return Ricky's insults. He looked at Mrs. Shapiro, who, although she didn't know what Ricky had said, nodded her head. "I know I'm not ugly," said Nathan.

"No," said the sleepy little boy in Boston, flowing off away from Nathan on his bed of sweets. "You have nice shoulders."

It was as Nathan walked with his mother through the woods to the Parnells' house that he began to feel distinctly altered. These trees were going to be cut down soon, to make way for three new houses, and as he strode, barefaced, across the little wood, there seemed a particular clarity to the starlit Halloween air, a sharpness that hitherto he had only smelled, and the sight of the world struck him with the austere flavor of smoke and dead leaves. Up the street the beam of a child's flashlight tumbled to the ground, igniting the red oak leaves that littered the Parnells' lawn, and then flew upward, illuminating the bare tops of previously invisible trees.

"I can't believe it," said Nathan. "I must be cured."

"You look very nice without your glasses," said his mother. "You look like your father."

"Dad wears glasses."

"He didn't always," she said. She shivered in her coat, which was made from rabbits and had been the gift of Humberto, the Brazilian professional soccer player she had dated last winter.

"Do you think my concept is stupid, Mom?"

"I just don't really understand it, Nathan," said his mother. "I never really understand your jokes. I'm sure lots of people will think it's hilarious."

They came to the short incline of yellow lawn which rose to the cedar planks of the Parnells' front porch, and which was transected by a crooked line of stepping-stones that led to the shallow goldfish pond beside the front door. Major Ray had been stationed for five years in Yokohama during the sixties, and the Parnells had returned with a houseful of Japanese things. The carved pumpkin shared the porch with a stone lamp shaped like a pointed Japanese house, and as Nathan and his mother stepped up to the front door—you could already hear them inside, dozens of laughing adults—it struck him that a jack-o'-lantern was truly a lantern. His last thought before Eleanor threw open the door was an idea for a science-fiction novel in which the denizens of a distant world furnished their lives with various giant vegetables, carving out their beds, dressing in long, curly peels, illuminating their homes with the light of pumpkins. Then the door flew open. In all his anxiety over his own wardrobe, in all the editing and revision of the tortured sentence he intended that night jauntily to pronounce to Eleanor, he had forgotten to wonder about what she might wear, and he found himself taken completely by surprise.

Nathan had been prey, of course, to night fantasies of Eleanor Parnell. He concocted these happy narratives of seduction with the same thoroughness he brought to all his imaginary projects, such as Davor, the Golden Planet, and the vast turnpike, each of its rest stops and motor courts carefully named, that he had once mapped across two hundred pages of his loose-leaf notebook. He had envisioned Mrs. Parnell in all manner of empty rooms, and on desert beaches, and under a remote lean-to in the Far West, but during these trysts she remained demurely clothed. (At those crucial moments when Eleanor began to remove her garments, Nathan's vision tended to falter.) But he had never imagined her in a black leather bikini, black cape, black boots, and black visor with a great pointed pair of black leather ears.

"I'm Batman," Eleanor said, giving Nathan a dry kiss on the cheek. "You look wonderful," she said to Mrs. Shapiro. She stepped back to examine Nathan, and her eyes narrowed within their moon-shaped black windows. "Nathan, you're a— You're a lamp. You're a lamppost."

"Oh, no," said Mrs. Shapiro.

"That's right," said Nathan the Lamppost. "Ha, ha." He could not say whether it was desire he felt for her or total, irredeemable embarrassment.

"Nathan," said his mother. "You are not a lamp. Tell her."

"Come in," said Eleanor. "We're in the Yellow Room. So what are you, Nathan?"

She drew them into the house, taking their hands in her own, as was her habit. The Yellow Room was filled, as Nathan had known it would be, with alcohol and disco music and adulthood in its most intimidating aspect. Two dozen men and women in costume— Nathan spotted a knight, a baseball player, and some sort of witch or hag—held their drinks and shouted mildly at each other over the agitated music, and five or six couples were dancing in the middle of the room. Ever since his mother had become a single woman she had increasingly involved herself, it seemed, with adults who liked to dance—a sight that for Nathan had not lost its novelty. He especially enjoyed watching the diligent men as they jogged in place.

"O.K., I give up," Eleanor said. She turned to face him and Nathan stopped dead. "No, I don't." A pinched look crossed her face as she scanned his body, and she seemed to take in for the first time the poverty of Nathan's lamentable concept. Nathan blushed and looked away, though this was partly because he feared he had already looked too many times at her breasts and at her radiant stomach.

"Are you supposed to be Thomas Edison? Is that it? Are you Thomas Alva Edison?"

Nathan forced himself to meet the humiliation of her sympathetic gaze. He opened his mouth to explain, to tell her that he was indeed the Wizard of Menlo Park, on the verge of stealing fire.

"He's a guy in the process of having a good idea for a costume," said Mrs. Shapiro, crossing her arms and shrugging her tattooed shoulders. "What do you think of that?"

"Nathan," said Eleanor, smiling at Nathan and taking his chin between the long fingers of her hand. "You're such a strange young man."

She laughed her magpie's laugh, and in her hooded eyes Nathan read both pain and amusement, as though she already knew that he loved her. Then she turned away from him, and the two women put their arms around one another—a habit his mother had picked up from Eleanor, who had learned it from Major Ray, who put his arm around everybody. They went to the long table, draped by a black paper tablecloth, that served as the bar. Major Ray, wearing his Bruce Wayne smoking jacket, came over to hug Mrs. Shapiro. He said something to her, she laughed, and then he led her off to one side, so that Eleanor was left momentarily alone. For a moment Nathan, suffused with the careless, wild-haired courage of an inventor, contemplated Eleanor in her racy suit. He took a step toward her, then another, tentatively, gathering all his strength, as though about to throw a heavy switch that would, if his calculations were correct, bring light to a hundred cities and ten thousand darkened rooms. He was going to ask her to dance—that was all. In the few seconds before he reached her bat-winged side he searched his memory for a suave line or smooth invitation from some movie, but all he could think of at that moment was *Young Mr. Lincoln.* "Eleanor," he said, "I would like to dance with you in the worst way."

Eleanor smiled, then leaned close to him and put her hand on his shoulder, her lips to his ear. For a long time she hesitated. "I know a couple of very bad ways," she said at last, "but you're too young for them, Nathan."

"I suppose so," he said, almost happily. He doffed his wire hat and set it down on the bar. There was now nothing on his face or his temples, and he felt light, almost headless, as he imagined he would feel on the brilliant evening he tried liquor for the first time. He took her hand, peacefully, and put it over his eyes, then covered her visor with his own damp palm. They stood a moment in this darkness. Then he said, "Guess who I am now."

RUSSELL BANKS

―――――

Queen for a Day

The elder of the two boys, Earl, turns from the dimly lit work-table, a door on sawhorses, where he is writing. He pauses a second and says to his brother, "Cut that out, willya? Getcha feet off the walls."

The other boy says, "Don't tell me what to do. You're not the boss of this family, you know." He is dark-haired with large brown eyes, a moody ten-year-old lying bored on his cot with sneakered feet slapped against the faded green floral print wallpaper.

Earl crosses his arms over his bony chest and stares down at his brother from a considerable height. The room is cluttered with model airplanes, schoolbooks, papers, clothing, hockey sticks and skates, a set of barbells. Earl says, "We're supposed to be doing homework, you know. If she hears you tramping your feet on the walls, she'll come in here screaming. So get your damned feet off the wall. I ain't kidding."

"She can't hear me. Besides, you ain't doing homework. And *I'm* reading," he says, waving a geography book at him.

The older boy sucks his breath through his front teeth and glares. "You really piss me off, George. Just put your goddamned feet down, will you? I can't concentrate with you doing that, rub-bing your feet all over the wallpaper like you're doing. It makes me

180

all distracted." He turns back to his writing, scribbling with a ball-point pen on lined paper in a schoolboy's three-ring binder. Earl has sandy blond hair and pale blue eyes that turn downward at the corners and a full red mouth. He's more scrawny than skinny, hard and flat-muscled, and suddenly tall for his age, making him a head taller than his brother, taller even than their mother now, too, and able to pat their sister's head as if he were a full-grown adult already.

He turned twelve eight months ago, in March, and in May their father left. Their father is a union carpenter who works on projects in distant corners of the state—schools, hospitals, post offices—and for a whole year the man came home only on weekends. Then, for a while, every other weekend. Finally, he was gone for a month, and when he came home the last time, it was to say goodbye to Earl, George, and their sister Louise, and to their mother, too, of course, she who had been saying (for what seemed to the children years) that she never wanted to see the man again anyhow, ever, un-der any circumstances, because he just causes trouble when he's home and more trouble when he doesn't come home, so he might as well stay away for good. They can all get along better without him, she insisted, which was true, Earl was sure, but that was before the man left for good and stopped sending them money, so that now, six months later, Earl is not so sure anymore that they can get along better without their father than with him.

It happened on a Sunday morning, a day washed with new sun-shine and dry air, with the whole family standing somberly in the kitchen, summoned there from their rooms by their mother's taut, high-pitched voice, a voice that had an awful point to prove. "Come out here! Your father has something important to say to you!"

They obeyed, one by one, and gathered in a line before their fa-ther, who, dressed in pressed khakis and shined work shoes and cap, sat at the kitchen table, a pair of suitcases beside him, and in front of him a cup of coffee, which he stirred slowly with a spoon. His eyes were red and filled with dense water, the way they almost al-ways were on Sunday mornings, from his drinking the night before, the children knew, and he had trouble looking them in the face, because of the sorts of things he and their mother were heard saying to one another when they were at home together late Saturday nights. On this Sunday morning it was only a little worse than usual—his hands shook some, and he could barely hold his cigarette; he let it smolder in the ashtray and kept on stirring his coffee while he talked. "Your mother and me," he said in his low, roughened voice, "we've decided on some things you kids should know about." He cleared his throat. "Your mother, she thinks you oughta hear it from me, though I don't quite know so much about that as she does, since it isn't completely my idea alone." He studied his coffee cup for a few seconds.

"They should hear it from you because it's what you *want!*" their mother finally said. She stood by the sink, her hands wringing each other dry, and stared over at the man. Her face was swollen and red from crying, which, for the children, was not an unusual thing to see on a Sunday morning when their father was home. They still did not know what was coming.

"Adele, it's *not* what I want," he said. "It's what's got to be, that's all. Kids," he said, "I got to leave you folks for a while. A long while. And I won't be comin' back, I guess." He grabbed his cigarette with thumb and forefinger and inhaled the smoke fiercely, then placed the butt back into the ashtray and went on talking, as if to the table: "I don't want to do this, I hate it, but I got to. It's too hard to explain, and I'm hoping that someday you'll understand it all, but I just . . . I just got to live somewheres else now."

Louise, the little girl, barely six years old, was the only one of the three children who could speak. She said, "Where are you going, Daddy?"

"Upstate," he said. "Back up to Holderness, where I been all along. I got me an apartment up there, small place."

"That's not all he's got up there!" their mother said.

"Adele, I can walk outa here right this second," he said smoothly.

"I don't hafta explain a damned thing, if you keep that kinda stuff up. We had an agreement."

"Yup, yup. Sorry," she said, pursing her lips, locking them with an invisible key, throwing the key away.

Finally, Earl could speak. "Will . . . will you come and see us, or can we come visit you, on weekends and like that?" he asked his father.

"Sure, son, you can visit me, anytime you want. It'll take a while for me to get the place set up right, but soon's I get it all set up for kids, I'll call you, and we'll work out some nice visits. I shouldn't come here, though, not for a while. You understand."

Earl shook his head somberly up and down, as if his one anxiety concerning this event had been put satisfactorily to rest.

George had turned his back on his father, however, and now he was taking tiny, mincing half-steps across the linoleum-covered kitchen floor toward the outside door. Then he stopped a second, opened the door and stood on the landing at the top of the stairs, and no one tried to stop him, because he was doing what they wanted to do themselves, and then they heard him running pell-mell, as if falling, down the darkened stairs, two flights, to the front door of the building, heard it slam behind him, and knew he was gone, up Perley Street, between parked cars, down alleys, to a hiding place where they knew he'd stop, sit, and bawl, knew it because it was what they wanted to do themselves, especially Earl, who was too old, too scared, too confused and too angry. Instead of running away and bawling, Earl said, "I hope everyone can be more happy now."

His father smiled and looked at him for the first time and clapped him on the shoulder. "Hey, son," he said, "you, you're the man of the house now. I know you can do it. You're a good kid, and listen, I'm proud of you. Your mother, your brother and sister, they're all going to need you a hell of a lot more than they have before, but I know you're up to it, son. I'm countin' on ya," he said, and he stood up and rubbed out his cigarette. Then he reached beyond Earl with both hands and hugged Earl's little sister, lifted her off her feet and squeezed her tight, and when the man set her down, he wiped tears away from his eyes. "Tell Georgie . . . well, maybe I'll see him downstairs or something. He's upset, I guess. . . ." He shook Earl's hand, drew him close, quickly hugged him and let go and stepped away. Grabbing up his suitcases, in silence, without looking over once at his wife or back at his children, he left the apartment.

For good. "And good riddance, too," as their mother immediately started saying to anyone who would listen. Louise said she missed her daddy, but she seemed to be quickly forgetting that, since for most of her life he had worked away from home, and George, who stayed mad, went deep inside himself and said nothing about it at all, and Earl—who did not know how he felt about their father's abandoning them, for he knew that in many ways it was the best their father could do for them and in many other ways it was the worst—spoke of the man as if he had died in an accident, as if their mother were a widow and they half orphaned. This freed him, though he did not know it then, to concentrate on survival, survival for them all, which he now understood to be his personal responsibility, for his mother seemed utterly incapable of guaranteeing it and his brother and sister, of course, were still practically babies. Often, late at night, lying in his squeaky, narrow cot next to his brother's, Earl would say to himself, "I'm the man of the house now," and somehow just saying it, over and over, "I'm the man of the house now," like a prayer, made his terror ease back away from his face, and he could finally slip into sleep.

Now, with his father gone six months and their mother still fragile, still denouncing the man to everyone who listens, and even to those who don't listen but merely show her their faces for a moment or two, it's as if the man were still coming home weekends drunk and raging against her and the world, were still betraying her, were telling all her secrets to another woman in a motel room in the northern part of the state. It's as if he were daily abandoning her and their three children over and over again, agreeing to send money and then sending nothing, promising to call and write letters and then going silent on them, planning visits and trips together on weekends and holidays and then leaving them with not even a forwarding address, forbidding them, almost, from adjusting to a new life, a life in which their father and her husband does not betray them anymore.

Earl decides to solve their problems himself. He hatches and implements, as best he can, plans, schemes, designs, all intended to find a substitute for the lost father. He introduces his mother to his hockey coach, who turns out to be married and a new father; and he invites in for breakfast and to meet his ma the cigar-smoking vet with the metal plate in his skull who drops off the newspapers at dawn for Earl to deliver before school, but the man turns out to dislike women actively enough to tell Earl so, right to his face: "No offense, kid, I'm sure your ma's a nice lady, but I got no use for 'em is why I'm single, not 'cause I ain't met the right one yet or something"; and to the guy who comes to read the electric meter one afternoon when Earl's home from school with the flu and his mother's at work down at the tannery, where they've taken her on as an assistant bookkeeper, Earl says that he can't let the man into the basement because it's locked and he'll have to come back later when his mom's home, so she can let him in herself, and the man says, "Hey, no problem, I can use last month's reading and make the correction next month," and waves cheerfully goodbye, leaving Earl suddenly, utterly, shockingly aware of his foolishness, his pathetic, helpless longing for a man of the house.

For a moment, he blames his mother for his longing and hates her for his fantasies. But then quickly he forgives her and blames himself and commences to concoct what he thinks of as more realistic, more dignified plans, schemes, designs: sweepstakes tickets, lotteries, raffles—Earl buys tickets on the sly with his paper route money. And he enters contests, essay contests for junior high school students that provide the winner with a week-long trip for him and a parent to Washington, D.C., and the National Spelling Bee, which takes Earl only to the county level before he fails to spell "alligator" correctly. A prize, any kind of award from the world outside their tiny, besieged family, Earl believes, will make their mother happy at last. He believes that a prize will validate their new life somehow and will thus separate it, once and for all, from their father. It will be as if their father never existed.

"So what are you writing now?" George demands from the bed. He walks his feet up the wall as high as he can reach, then retreats. "I know it ain't homework, you don't write that fast when you're doing homework. What is it, a *love* letter?" He leers.

"No, asshole. Just take your damned feet off the wall, will you? Ma's gonna be in here in a minute screaming at both of us." Earl closes the notebook and pushes it away from him carefully, as if it is the Bible and he has just finished reading aloud from it.

"I wanna see what you wrote," George says, flipping around and setting his feet, at last, onto the floor. He reaches toward the notebook. "Lemme see it."

"C'mon, willya? Cut the shit."

"Naw, lemme see it." He stands up and swipes the notebook from the table as Earl moves to protect it.

"You little sonofabitch!" Earl says, and he clamps onto the notebook with both hands and yanks, pulling George off his feet and forward onto Earl's lap, and they both tumble to the floor, where they begin to fight, swing fists and knees, roll and grab, bumping against furniture in the tiny, crowded room, until a lamp falls over, books tumble to the floor, model airplanes crash. In seconds, George is getting the worst of it and scrambles across the floor to the door, with Earl crawling along behind, yanking his brother's shirt with one hand and pounding at his head and back with the other, when suddenly the bedroom door swings open, and their mother stands over them. Grabbing both boys by their collars, she shrieks, "What's the matter with you! What're you doing! What're you doing!" They stop and collapse into a bundle of legs and arms, but she goes on shrieking at them. "I can't *stand* it when you fight! Don't you know that? I can't *stand* it!"

George cries, "I didn't do anything! I just wanted to see his homework!"

"Yeah, sure," Earl says. "Sure. Innocent as a baby."

"Shut up! Both of you!" their mother screams. She is wild-eyed, glaring down at them, and, as he has done so many times, Earl looks at her face as if he's outside his body, and he sees that she's not angry at them at all, she's frightened and in pain, as if her sons are little animals, rats or ferrets, with tiny, razor-sharp teeth biting at her ankles and feet.

Quickly, Earl gets to his feet and says, "I'm sorry, Ma. I guess I'm just a little tired or something lately." He pats his mother on her shoulder and offers a small smile. George crawls on hands and knees back to his bed and lies on it, while Earl gently turns their mother around and steers her back out the door to the living room, where the television set drones on, Les Paul and Mary Ford, playing their guitars and singing bland harmonies. "We'll be out in a few minutes for *Dobie Gillis,* Ma. Don't worry," Earl says.

"Jeez," George says. "How can she stand that Les Paul and Mary Ford stuff? Yuck. Even Louise goes to bed when it comes on, and it's only what, six-thirty?"

"Yeah. Shut up."

"Up yours."

Earl leans down and scoops up the fallen dictionary, pens, airplanes and lamp and places them back on the worktable. The black binder he opens squarely in front of him, and he says to his brother, "Here, you wanta see what I was writing? Go ahead and read it. I don't care."

"I don't care, either. Unless it's a *love* letter!"

"No, it's not a *love* letter."

"What is it, then?"

"Nothing," Earl says, closing the notebook. "Homework."

"Oh," George says, and he starts marching his feet up the wall and back again.

Nov. 7, 1953

Dear Jack Bailey,

I think my mother should be queen for a day because she has suffered a lot more than most mothers in this life and she has come out of it very cheerful and loving. The most important fact is that my father left her alone with three children, myself (age 12 1/2), my brother George (age 10), and my sister Louise (age 6). He left her for another woman though that's not the important thing, because my mother has risen above all that. But he refuses to send her any child support money. He's been gone over six months and we still haven't seen one cent. My mother went to a lawyer but the lawyer wants $50 in advance to help her take my father to court. She has a job as assistant bookkeeper down at Belvedere's Tannery downtown and the pay is bad, barely enough for our rent and food costs in fact, so where is she going to get $50 for a lawyer?

Also my father was a very cruel man who drinks too much and many times when he was living with us when he came home from work he was drunk and he would beat her. This has caused her and us kids a lot of nervous suffering and now she sometimes has spells which the doctor says are serious, though he doesn't know exactly what they are.

We used to have a car and my father left it with us when he left (a big favor) because he had a pickup truck. But he owed over $450 on the car to the bank so the bank came and repossessed the car. Now my mother has to walk everywhere she goes which is hard and causes her varicose veins and takes a lot of valuable time from her day.

My sister Louise needs glasses the school nurse said but "Who can pay for them?" my mother says. My paper route gets a little money but it's barely enough for school lunches for the three of us kids which is what we use it for.

My mother's two sisters and her brother haven't been too help-ful because they are Catholic, as she is and the rest of us, and they don't believe in divorce and think that she should not have let my father leave her anyhow. She needs to get a divorce but no one ex-cept me and my brother George think it is a good idea. Therefore my mother cries a lot at night because she feels so abandoned in this time of her greatest need.

The rest of the time though she is cheerful and loving in spite of her troubles and nervousness. That is why I believe that this courageous long-suffering woman, my mother, should be Queen for a Day.

Sincerely yours,
Earl Painter

Several weeks slide by, November gets cold and gray, and a New Hampshire winter starts to feel inevitable again, and Earl does not receive the letter he expects. He has told no one, especially his mother, that he has written to Jack Bailey, the smiling, mustachioed host of the *Queen for a Day* television show, which Earl happened to see that time he was home for several days with the flu, bored and watching television all afternoon. Afterwards, delivering pa-pers in the predawn gloom, in school all day, at the hockey rink, do-ing homework at night, he could not forget about the television show, the sad stories told by the contestants about their illness, poverty, neglect, victimization and, always, their bad luck, luck so bad that you feel it's somehow deserved. The studio audience seemed genuinely saddened, moved to tears, even, by Jack Bailey's recitation of these narratives, and then elated afterwards, when the winning victims, all of them middle-aged women, were rewarded with refrigerators, living room suites, vacation trips, washing ma-chines, china, fur coats and, if they needed them, wheelchairs, prosthetic limbs, twenty-four-hour nursing care. As these women wept for joy, the audience applauded, and Earl almost applauded too, alone there in the dim living room of the small, cold, and threadbare apartment in a mill town in central New Hampshire.

Earl knows that those women's lives surely aren't much different from his mother's life, and in fact, if he has told it right, if somehow he has got into the letter what he has intuited is basically wrong with his mother's life, it will be obvious to everyone in the audience that his mother's life is actually much worse than that of many or perhaps even most of the women who win the prizes. Earl knows that though his mother enjoys good health (except for "spells") and holds down a job and is able to feed, house, and clothe her children, there is still a deep, essential sadness in her life that, in his eyes, none of the contestants on *Queen for a Day* has. He believes that if he can just get his description of her life right, other people—Jack Bailey, the studio audience, millions of people all over America watching it on television—*everyone* will share in her sadness, so that when she is rewarded with appliances, furniture and clothing, maybe even a trip to Las Vegas, then everyone will share in her elation, too. Even he will share in it.

Earl knows that it is not easy to become a contestant on *Queen for a Day*. Somehow your letter describing the candidate has first to move Jack Bailey, and then your candidate has to be able to communicate her sufferings over television in a clear and dramatic way. Earl noticed that some of the contestants, to their own apparent disadvantage, downplayed the effect on them of certain tragedies— a child with a birth defect, say, or an embarrassing kind of operation or a humiliating dismissal by an employer—while playing up other, seemingly less disastrous events, such as being cheated out of a small inheritance by a phony siding contractor or having to drop out of hairdressing school because of a parent's illness, and when the studio audience was asked to show the extent and depth of its compassion by having its applause measured on a meter, it was always the woman who managed to present the most convincing mixture of courage and complaint who won.

Earl supposes that what happens is that Jack Bailey writes or maybe telephones the writer of the letter nominating a particular woman for *Queen for a Day* and offers him and his nominee the opportunity to come to New York City's Radio City Music Hall to tell her story in person, and then, based on how she does in the audition, Jack Bailey chooses her and two other nominees for a particular show, maybe next week, when they all come back to New York City to tell their stories live on television. Thus, daily, when Earl arrives home, he asks Louise and George, who normally get home from school an hour or so earlier than he, if there's any mail for him, any letter. You're sure? Nothing? No phone calls, either?

"Who're you expectin' to hear from, lover boy, your *girl*friend?" George grins, teeth spotted with peanut butter and gobs of white bread.

"Up yours," Earl says, and heads into his bedroom, where he dumps his coat, books, hockey gear. It's becoming clear to him that if there's such a thing as success, he's evidently a failure. If there's such a thing as a winner, he's a loser. I oughta go on that goddamned show myself, he thinks. Flopping onto his bed face-first, he wishes he could keep on falling, as if down a bottomless well or mine shaft, into darkness and warmth, lost and finally blameless, gone, gone, gone. And soon he is asleep, dreaming of a hockey game, and he's carrying the puck, dragging it all the way up along the right, digging in close to the boards, skate blades flashing as he cuts around behind the net, ice chips spraying in white fantails, and when he comes out on the other side, he looks down in front of him and can't find the puck, it's gone, dropped off behind him, lost in his sweeping turn, the spray, the slash of the skates and the long sweeping arc of the stick in front of him. He brakes, turns, and heads back, searching for the small black disk.

At the sound of the front door closing, a quiet click, as if someone is deliberately trying to enter the apartment silently, Earl wakes from his dream, and he hears voices from the kitchen, George and Louise and his mother:

"Hi, Mom. We're just makin' a snack, peanut butter sand-wiches."

"Mommy, George won't give me—"

"Don't eat it directly off the knife like that!"

"Sorry, I was jus'—"

"You heard me, mister, don't answer back!"

"Jeez, I was jus'—"

"I don't *care* what you were doing!" Her voice is trembling and quickly rising in pitch and timbre, and Earl moves off his bed and comes into the kitchen, smiling, drawing everyone's attention to him, the largest person in the room, the only one with a smile on his face, a relaxed, easy, sociable face and manner, normalcy itself, as he gives his brother's shoulder a fraternal squeeze, tousles his sister's brown hair, nods hello to his mother and says, "Hey, you're home early, Ma. What happened, they give you guys the rest of the day off?"

Then he sees her face, white, tight, drawn back in a cadaverous grimace, her pale blue eyes wild, unfocused, rolling back, and he says, "Jeez, Ma, what's the matter, you okay?"

Her face breaks into pieces, goes from dry to wet, white to red, and she is weeping loudly, blubbering, wringing her hands in front of her like a maddened knitter. "Aw-w-w-w!" she wails, and Louise and George, too, start to cry. They run to her and wrap her in their arms, crying and begging her not to cry, as Earl, aghast, sits back in his chair and watches the three of them wind around each other like snakes moving in and out of one another's coils.

"Stop!" he screams at last. "Stop it! All of you!" He pounds his fists on the table. "Stop crying, all of you!"

And they obey him, George first, then their mother, then Louise, who goes on staring into her mother's face. George looks at his feet, ashamed, and their mother looks pleadingly into Earl's face, expectant, hopeful, as if knowing that he will organize everything.

In a calm voice, Earl says, "Ma, tell me what happened. Just say it slowly, you know, and it'll come out okay, and then we can all talk about it, okay?"

She nods, and slowly George unravels his arms from around her neck and steps away from her, moving to the far wall of the room, where he stands and looks out the window and down to the bare yard below. Louise snuggles her face in close to her mother and sniffles quietly.

"I . . . I lost my job. I got fired today," their mother says. "And it wasn't my fault," she says, starting to weep again, and Louise joins her, bawling now, and George at the window starts to sob, his small shoulders heaving.

Earl shouts, "Wait! Wait a minute, Ma, just *tell* me about it. Don't cry!" he commands her, and she shudders, draws herself together again and continues.

"I . . . I had some problems this morning, a bunch of files I was supposed to put away last week sometime got lost. And everybody was running around like crazy looking for them, 'cause they had all these figures from last year's sales in 'em or something, I don't know. Anyhow, they were important, and I was the one who was accused of losing them. Which I didn't! But no one could find them, until finally they turned up on Robbie's desk, down in shipping, which I couldna done since I never go to shipping anyhow. But just the same, Rose blamed me, because she's the head bookkeeper and she was the last person to use the files, and she was getting it because they needed them upstairs, and . . . well, you know, I was just getting yelled at and yelled at, and it went on after lunch . . . and, I don't know, I just started feeling dizzy and all, you know, like I was going to black out again? And I guess I got scared and started talking real fast, so Rose took me down to the nurse, and I did black out then. Only for a few seconds, though, and when

I felt a little better, Rose said maybe I should go home for the rest of the day, which is what I wanted to do anyhow. But when I went back upstairs to get my pocketbook and coat and my lunch, because I hadn't been able to eat my sandwich, even, I was so nervous and all, and then Mr. Shandy called me into his office. . . ." She makes a twisted little smile, helpless and confused, and quickly continues. "Mr. Shandy said I should maybe take a lot of time off. Two weeks sick leave with pay, he said, even though I was only working there six months. He said that would give me time to look for another job, one that wouldn't cause me so much worry, he said. So I said, 'Are you firing me?' and he said, 'Yes, I am,' just like that. 'But it would be better for you all around,' he said, 'if you left for medical reasons or something.'"

Earl slowly exhales. He's been holding his breath throughout, though from her very first sentence he has known what the outcome would be. Reaching forward, he takes his mother's hands in his, stroking them as if they were an injured bird. He doesn't know what will happen now, but somehow he is not afraid. Not really. Yet he knows that he should be terrified, and when he says this to himself, *I should be terrified,* he answers by observing simply that this is not the worst thing. The worst thing that can happen to them is that one or all of them will die. And because he is still a child, or at least enough of a child not to believe in death, he knows that no one in his family is going to die. He cannot share this secret comfort with anyone in the family, however. His brother and sister, children completely, cannot yet know that death is the worst thing that can happen to them; they think this is, that their mother has been fired from her job, which is why they are crying. And his mother, no longer a child at all, cannot believe with Earl that the worst thing will not happen, for this is too much like death and may somehow lead directly to it, which is why she is crying. Only Earl can refuse to cry. Which he does.

———

Later, in the room she shares with her daughter, their mother lies fully clothed on the double bed and sleeps, and it grows dark, and while George and Louise watch television in the gloom of the living room, Earl writes:

Nov. 21, 1953

Dear Jack Bailey,

Maybe my first letter to you about why my mother should be queen for a day did not reach you or else I just didn't write it good enough for you to want her on your show. But I thought I would write again anyhow, if that's okay, and mention to you a few things that I left out of that first letter and also mention again some of the things in that letter, in case you did not get it at all for some reason (you know the Post Office). I also want to mention a few new developments that have made things even worse for my poor mother than they already were.

First, even though it's only a few days until Thanksgiving my father who left us last May, as you know, has not contacted us about the holidays or offered to help in any way. This makes us mad though we don't talk about it much since the little kids tend to cry about it a lot when they think about it, and me and my mother think it's best not to think about it. We don't even know how to write a letter to my father, though we know the name of the company that he works for up in Holderness (a town in New Hampshire pretty far from here) and his sisters could tell us his address if we asked, but we won't. A person has to have some pride, as my mother says. Which she has a lot of.

We will get through Thanksgiving all right because of St. Joseph's Church, which is where we go sometimes and where I was confirmed and my brother George (age 10) took his first communion last year and where my sister Louise (age 6) goes to catechism class. St. Joe's (as we call it) has turkeys and other kinds of food for people who can't afford to buy one so we'll do okay if my mother goes down there and says she can't afford to buy a turkey for her family on Thanksgiving. This brings me to the new developments.

My mother just got fired from her job as assistant bookkeeper at the tannery. It wasn't her fault or anything she did. They just fired her because she has these nervous spells sometimes when there's a lot of pressure on her, which is something that happens a lot these days because of my father and all and us kids and the rest of it. She got two weeks of pay but that's the only money we have until she gets another job. Tomorrow she plans to go downtown to all the stores and try to get a job as a saleslady now that Christmas is coming and the stores hire a lot of extras. But right now we don't have any money for anything like Thanksgiving turkey or pies, and we can't go down to Massachusetts to my mother's family, Aunt Dot's and Aunt Leona's and Uncle Jerry's house, like we used to because (as you know) the bank repossessed the car. And my father's sisters and all who used to have Thanksgiving with us, sometimes, have taken our father's side in this because of his lies about us and now they won't talk to us anymore.

I know that lots and lots of people are poor as us and many of them are sick too, or crippled from polio and other bad diseases. But I still think my mother should be Queen for a Day because of other things.

Because even though she's poor and got fired and has dizzy spells and sometimes blacks out, she's a proud woman. And even though my father walked off and left all his responsibilities behind, she stayed here with us.

And in spite of all her troubles and worries, she really does take good care of his children. One look in her eyes and you know it.

Thank you very much for listening to me and considering my mother for the Queen for a Day television show.

Sincerely,
Earl Painter

The day before Thanksgiving their mother is hired to start work the day after Thanksgiving, in gift wrapping at Grover Cronin's on Moody Street, and consequently she does not feel ashamed for accepting a turkey and a bag of groceries from St. Joe's. "Since I'm working, I don't think of it as charity. I think of it as a kind of loan," she explains to Earl as they walk the four blocks to the church.

It's dark, though still late afternoon, and cold, almost cold enough to snow, Earl thinks, which makes him think of Christmas, which in turn makes him cringe and tremble inside and turn quickly back to now, to this very moment, to walking with his tiny, brittle-bodied mother down the quiet street, past houses like their own—triple-decker wood-frame tenements, each with a wide front porch like a bosom facing the narrow street below, lights on in kitchens in back, where mothers make boiled supper for kids cross-legged on the living room floor watching *Kukla, Fran and Ollie,* while dads trudge up from the mills by the river or drive in from one of the plants on the Heights or maybe walk home from one of the stores downtown, the A&P, J.C. Penney's, Sears—the homes of ordinary families, people exactly like them. But with one crucial difference, for a piece is missing from the Painter family, a keystone, making all other families, in Earl's eyes, wholly different from his, and for an anxious moment he envies them. He wants to turn up a walkway to a strange house, step up to the door, open it and walk down the long, dark, sweet-smelling hallway to the kitchen in back, say hi and toss his coat over a chair and sit down for supper, have his father growl at him to hang his coat up and wash his hands first, have his mother ask about school today, how did hockey practice go, have his sister interrupt to show her broken dolly to their father, beg him to fix it, which he does at the table next to his son, waiting for supper to be put on the table, all of them relaxed, happy, relieved that tomorrow is a holiday, a day at home with the family, no work, no school, no hockey practice. Tomorrow, he and his father and his brother will go to the high school football game at noon and will be home by two to help set the table.

Earl's mother says, "That job down at Grover Cronin's? It's only, it's a temporary job, you know." She says it as if uttering a slightly shameful secret. "After Christmas I get let go."

Earl jams his hands deeper into his jacket pockets and draws his chin down inside his collar. "Yeah, I figured."

"And the money, well, the money's not much. It's almost nothing. I added it up, for a week and for a month, and it comes out to quite a lot less than what you and me figured out in that budget, for the rent and food and all. What we need. It's less than what we need. Never mind Christmas, even. Just regular."

They stop a second at a curb, wait for a car to pass, then cross the street and turn right. Elm trees loom in black columns overhead; leafless branches spread out in high arcs and cast intricate shadows on the sidewalk below. Earl can hear footsteps click against the pavement, his own off-beat, long stride and her short, quick one combining in a stuttered rhythm. He says, "You gotta take the job, though, doncha? I mean, there isn't anything else, is there? Not now, anyhow. Maybe soon, though, Ma, in a few days, maybe, if something at the store opens up in one of the other departments, dresses or something. Bookkeeping, maybe. You never know, Ma."

"No, you're right. Things surprise you. Still . . ." She sighs, pushing a cloud of breath out in front of her. "But I am glad for the turkey and the groceries. We'll have a nice Thanksgiving, anyhow," she chirps.

"Yeah."

They are silent for a few seconds, still walking, and then she says, "I been talking to Father LaCoy, Earl. You know, about . . . about our problems. I been asking his advice. He's a nice man, not just a priest, you know, but a kind man too. He knows your father, he knew him years and years ago, when they were in high school together. He said he was a terrible drinker even then. And he said . . . other things, he said some things the other morning that I been thinking about."

"What morning?"

"Day before yesterday. Early. When you were doing your papers. I felt I just had to talk to someone, I was all nervous and worried, and I needed to talk to someone here at St. Joe's anyhow, 'cause I wanted to know about how to get the turkey and all, so I came over, and he was saying the early mass, so I stayed and talked with him a while afterwards. He's a nice priest, I like him. I always liked Father LaCoy."

"Yeah. What'd he say?" Earl knows already what the priest said, and he pulls himself further down inside his jacket, where his insides seem to have hardened like an ingot, cold and dense, at the exact center of his body.

Up ahead, at the end of the block, is St. Joseph's, a large, squat parish church with a short, broad steeple, built late in the last century of pale yellow stone cut from a quarry up on the Heights and hauled across the river in winter on sledges. "Father LaCoy says that your father and me, we should try to get back together. That we should start over, so to speak."

"And you think he's right," Earl adds.

"Well, not exactly. Not just like that. I mean, he knows what happened. He knows all about your father and all, I told him, but he knew anyhow. I told him how it was, but he told me that it's not right for us to be going on like this, without a father and all. So he said, he told me, he'd like to arrange to have a meeting in his office at the church, a meeting between me and your father, so we could maybe talk some of our problems out. And make some compromises, he said."

Earl is nearly a full head taller than his mother, but suddenly, for the first time since before his father left, he feels small, a child again, helpless, dependent, pulled this mysterious way or that by the obscure needs and desires of adults. "Yeah, but how come . . .

how come Father LaCoy thinks Daddy'll even listen? He doesn't *want* us!"

"I know, I know," his mother murmurs. "But what can I do? What else can I do?"

Earl has stopped walking and shouts at his mother, like a dog barking at the end of a leash: "He can't even get in touch with Daddy! He doesn't even know where Daddy is!"

She stops and speaks in a steady voice. "Yes, he can find him all right. I told him where Daddy was working and gave him the name of McGrath and Company and also Aunt Ellie's number too. So he can get in touch with him, if he wants to. He's a priest."

"A priest can get in touch with him but his own wife and kids can't!"

His mother has pulled up now and looks at her son with a hardness in her face that he can't remember having seen before. She tells him, "You don't understand. I know how hard it's been for you, Earl, all this year, from way back, even, with all the fighting, and then when your father went away. But you got to understand a little bit how it's been for me, too. I can't . . . I can't do this all alone like this."

"Do you love Daddy?" he demands. "*Do* you? After . . . after everything he's done? After hitting you like he did all those times, and the yelling and all, and the drinking, and then, then the worst, after leaving us like he did! Leaving us and running off with that *girl*friend or whatever of his! And not sending any money! Making you hafta go to work, with us kids coming home after school and nobody at home. Ma, he *left* us! Don't you know that? He *left* us!" Earl is weeping now. His skinny arms wrapped around his own chest, tears streaming over his cheeks, the boy stands straight-legged and stiff on the sidewalk in the golden glow of the streetlight, his wet face crossed with spidery shadows from the elm trees, and he shouts, "I *hate* him! I hate him, and I never want him to come back again! If you let him come back, I swear it, I'm gonna run away! I'll leave!"

His mother says, "Oh, no, Earl, you don't mean that," and she reaches forward to hold him, but he backs fiercely away.

"No! I do mean it! If you let him back into our house, I'm leaving."

"Earl. Where will you go? You're just a boy."

"Ma, so help me, don't treat me like this. I can go lotsa places, don't worry. I can go to Boston, I can go to Florida, I can go to lotsa places. All I got to do is hitchhike. I'm not a little kid anymore," he says, and he draws himself up and looks down at her.

"You *don't* hate your father."

"Yes, Ma. Yes, I do. And you should hate him too. After all he did to you."

They are silent for a moment, facing each other, looking into each other's pale blue eyes. He is her son, his face is her face, not his father's. Earl and his mother have the same sad, downward-turning eyes, like teardrops, the same full red mouth, the same clear voice, and now, at this moment, they share the same agony, a life-bleeding pain that can be stanched only with a lie, a denial.

She says, "All right, then. I'll tell Father LaCoy. I'll tell him that I don't want to talk to your father, it's gone too far now. I'll tell him that I'm going to get a divorce." She opens her arms, and her son steps into them. Above her head, his eyes jammed shut, he holds on to his tiny mother and sobs, as if he's learned that his father has died.

His mother says, "I don't know when I'll get the divorce, Earl, but I'll do it. Things'll work out. They have to. Right?" she asks, as if asking a baby who can't understand her words.

He nods. "Yeah . . . yeah, things'll work out," he says.

They let go of one another and walk slowly on toward the church.

Dec. 12, 1953

Dear Jack Bailey,
    Yes, it's me again and this is my third letter asking you to make my mother Adele Painter into queen for a day. Things are much

worse now than last time I wrote to you. I had to quit the hockey team so I could take an extra paper route in the afternoons because my mother's job at Grover Cronin's is minimum wage and can't pay our bills. But that's okay, it's only junior high so it doesn't matter like if I was in high school as I will be next year. So I don't really mind.

My mother hasn't had any of her spells lately, but she's still really nervous and cries a lot and yells a lot at the kids over little things because she's so worried about money and everything. We had to get winter coats and boots this year used from the church, St. Joe's, and my mom cried a lot about that. Now that Christmas is so close everything reminds her of how poor we are now, even her job which is wrapping gifts. She has to stand on her feet six days and three nights a week so her varicose veins are a lot worse than before, so when she comes home she usually has to go right to bed.

My brother George comes home now after school and takes care of Louise until I get through delivering papers and can come home and make supper for us, because my mother's usually at work then. We don't feel too sad because we've got each other and we all love each other but it is hard to feel happy a lot of the time, especially at Christmas.

My mother paid out over half of one week's pay as a down payment to get a lawyer to help her get a divorce from my father and get the court to make him pay her some child support, but the lawyer said it might take two months for any money to come and the divorce can't be done until next June. The lawyer also wrote a letter to my father to try and scare him into paying us some money but so far it hasn't worked. So it seems like she spent that money on the lawyer for nothing. Everything just seems to be getting worse. If my father came back the money problems would be over.

Well, I should close now. This being the third time I wrote in to nominate my mother for Queen for a Day and so far not getting any answer, I guess it's safe to say you don't think her story is sad enough to let her go on your show. That's okay because there are

*hundreds of women in America whose stories are much sadder
than my mom's and they deserve the chance to win some prizes on
your show and be named queen for a day. But my mom deserves
that chance too, just as much as that lady with the amputated legs
I saw and the lady whose daughter had that rare blood disease and
her husband died last year. My mom needs recognition just as
much as those other ladies need what they need. That's why I keep
writing to you like this. I think this will be my last letter though.
I get the picture, as they say.*

Sincerely,
Earl Painter

The Friday before Christmas, Earl, George, Louise, and their
mother are sitting in the darkened living room, George sprawled
on the floor, the others on the sofa, all of them eating popcorn from
a bowl held in Louise's lap and watching *The Jackie Gleason Show,*
when the phone rings.

"You get it, George," Earl says.

Reggie Van Gleason III swirls his cape and cane across the tiny
screen in front of them, and the phone goes on ringing. "Get it
yourself," says George. "I always get it and it's never for me."

"Answer the phone, Louise," their mother says, and she suddenly laughs at one of Gleason's moves, a characteristic high-
pitched peal that cuts off abruptly, half a cackle that causes her
sons, as usual, to look at each other and roll their eyes in shared embarrassment. She's wearing her flannel bathrobe and slippers,
smoking a cigarette, and drinking from a glass of beer poured from
a quart bottle on the floor beside her.

Crossing in front of them, Louise cuts to the corner table by the
window and picks up the phone. Her face, serious most of the time
anyhow, suddenly goes dark, then brightens, wide-eyed. Earl
watches her, and he knows who she is listening to. She nods, as if
the person on the other end can see her, and then she says, "Yes,
yes," but no one, except Earl, pays any attention to her.

After a moment, the child puts the receiver down gently and returns to the sofa. "It's Daddy," she announces. "He says he wants to talk to the boys."

"I don't want to talk to him," George blurts, and stares straight ahead at the television.

Their mother blinks, opens and closes her mouth, looks from George to Louise to Earl and back to Louise again. "It's Daddy?" she says. "On the telephone?"

"Uh-huh. He says he wants to talk to the boys."

Earl crosses his arms over his chest and shoves his body back into the sofa. Jackie Gleason dances delicately across the stage, a graceful fat man with a grin.

"Earl?" his mother asks, eyebrows raised.

"Nope."

The woman stands up slowly and walks to the phone. Their mother speaks to their father; all three children watch carefully. She says, "Nelson?" and nods, listening, now and then opening her mouth to say something, closing it when she's interrupted. "Yes, yes," she says, and, "yes, they're both here." She listens again, then says, "Yes, I know, but I should tell you, Nelson, the children . . . the boys, they feel funny about talking to you. Maybe . . . maybe you could write a letter first or something. It's sort of . . . hard for them. They feel very upset, you see, especially now, with the holidays and all. We're all very upset and worried. And with me losing my job and having to work down at Grover Cronin's and all. . . ." She nods, listens, her face expressionless. "Well, Lord knows, that would be very nice. It would have been very nice a long time ago, but no matter. We surely need it, Nelson." She listens again, longer this time, her face gaining energy and focus as she listens. "Yes, yes, I know. Well, I'll see, I'll ask them again. Wait a minute," she says, and puts her hand over the receiver and says, "Earl, your father wants to talk to you. He really does." She smiles wanly.

Earl squirms in his seat, crosses and uncrosses his legs, looks away from his mother to the wall opposite. "I got nothin' to say to him."

"Yes, but . . . I think he wants to say some things to you, though. Can't hurt to let him say them."

Silently, the boy gets up from the couch and crosses the room to the phone. As she hands him the receiver, his mother smiles with a satisfaction that bewilders and instantly angers him.

"H'lo," he says.

"H'lo, son. How're ya doin', boy?"

"Okay."

"Attaboy. Been a while, eh?"

"Yeah. A while."

"Well, I sure am sorry for that, you know, that it's been such a while and all, but I been going through some hard times myself. Got laid off, didn't work for most of the summer because of that damned strike. You read about that in the papers?"

"No."

"How's the paper route?"

"Okay."

"Hey, son, look, I know it's been tough for a while, believe me, I know. It's been tough for us all, for everyone. So I know whatcha been going through. No kidding. But it's gonna get better, things're gonna be better now. And I want to try and make it up to you guys a little, what you hadda go through this last six months or so. I want to make it up to you guys a little, you and Georgie and Louise. Your ma too. If you'll let me. Whaddaya say?"

"What?"

"Whaddaya say you let me try to make it up a little to you?"

"Sure. Why not? Try."

"Hey, listen, Earl, that's quite a attitude you got there. We got to do something about that, eh? Some kind of attitude, son. I guess things've done a little changing around there since the old man left, eh? Eh?"

"Sure they have. What'd you expect? Everything'd stay the same?" Earl hears his voice rising and breaking into a yodel, and his eyes fill with tears.

"No, of course not. I understand, son. I understand. I know I've made some big mistakes this year, lately. Especially with you kids, in dealing with you kids. I didn't do it right, the leaving and all. It's hard, Earl, to do things like that right. I've learned a lot. But hey, listen, everybody deserves a second chance. Right? Right? Even your old man?"

"I guess so. Yeah."

"Sure. Damn right," he says, and then he adds that he'd like to come by tomorrow afternoon and see them, all of them, and leave off some Christmas presents. "You guys got your tree yet?"

Earl can manage only a tiny, cracked voice: "No, not yet."

"Well, that's good, real good. 'Cause I already got one in the back of the truck, a eight-footer I cut this afternoon myself. There's lotsa trees out in the woods here in Holderness. Not many people and lotsa trees. Anyhow, I got me a eight-footer, Scotch pine. Them are the best. Whaddaya think?"

"Yeah. Sounds good."

His father rattles on, while Earl feels his chest tighten into a knot, and tears spill over his cheeks. The man repeats several times that he's really sorry about the way he's handled things these last few months, but it's been hard for him, too, and it's hard for him even to say this, he's never been much of a talker, but he knows he's not been much of a father lately, either. That's all over now, though, over and done with, he assures Earl; it's all a part of the past. He's going to be a different man now, a new man. He's turned over a new leaf, he says. And Christmas seems like the perfect time for a new beginning, which is why he called them tonight and why he wants to come by tomorrow afternoon with presents and a tree and help set up and decorate the tree with them, just like in the old days. "Would you go for that? How'd that be, son?"

"Daddy?"

"Yeah, sure, son. What?"

"Daddy, are you gonna try to get back together with Mom?" Earl looks straight at his mother as he says this, and though she pretends to be watching Jackie Gleason, she is listening to his every word, he knows. As is George, and probably even Louise.

"Am I gonna try to get back together with your mom, eh?"

"Yeah."

"Well . . . that's a hard one, boy. You asked me a hard one." He is silent for a few seconds, and Earl can hear him sipping from a glass and then taking a deep draw from his cigarette. "I'll tell ya, boy. The truth is, she don't want me back. You oughta know that by now. I left because *she* wanted me to leave, son. I did some wrong things, sure, lots of 'em, but I did not want to leave you guys. No, right from the beginning, this thing's been your mom's show, not mine."

"Daddy, that's a lie."

"No, son. No. We fought a lot, your mom and me, like married people always do. But I didn't want to leave her and you kids. She told me to. And now, look at this—*she's* the one bringing these divorce charges and all, not me. You oughta see the things she's charging me with."

"What about . . . what about her having to protect herself? You know what I mean. I don't want to go into any details, but you know what I mean. And what about your *girl*friend?" he sneers.

His father is silent for a moment. Then he says, "You sure have got yourself an attitude since I been gone. Listen, kid, there's lots you don't know anything about, that nobody knows anything about, and there's lots more that you *shouldn't* know anything about. You might not believe this, Earl, but you're still a kid. You're a long ways from being a man. So don't go butting into where you're not wanted and getting into things between your mom and me that you can't understand anyhow. Just butt out. You hear me?"

"Yeah. I hear you."

"Lemme speak to your brother."

"He doesn't want to talk to you," Earl says, and he looks away from George's face and down at his own feet.

"Put your mother on, Earl."

"None of us wants to talk to you."

"Earl!" his mother cries. "Let me have the phone," she says, and she rises from the couch, her hand reaching toward him.

Earl places the receiver in its cradle. Then he stands there, looking into his mother's blue eyes, and she looks into his.

She says, "He won't call back."

Earl says, "I know."

SHERMAN ALEXIE

*Because My Father Always Said He Was
the Only Indian Who Saw Jimi Hendrix Play
"The Star-Spangled Banner" at Woodstock*

During the sixties, my father was the perfect hippie, since all the hippies were trying to be Indians. Because of that, how could anyone recognize that my father was trying to make a social statement?

But there is evidence, a photograph of my father demonstrating in Spokane, Washington, during the Vietnam war. The photograph made it onto the wire service and was reprinted in newspapers throughout the country. In fact, it was on the cover of *Time*.

In the photograph, my father is dressed in bell-bottoms and flowered shirt, his hair in braids, with red peace symbols splashed across his face like war paint. In his hands my father holds a rifle above his head, captured in that moment just before he proceeded to beat the shit out of the National Guard private lying prone on the ground. A fellow demonstrator holds a sign that is just barely visible over my father's left shoulder. It read MAKE LOVE NOT WAR.

The photographer won a Pulitzer Prize, and editors across the country had a lot of fun creating captions and headlines. I've read many of them collected in my father's scrapbook, and my favorite was run in the *Seattle Times*. The caption under the photograph read DEMONSTRATOR GOES TO WAR FOR PEACE. The editors capitalized on my father's Native American identity with other headlines like ONE WARRIOR AGAINST WAR and PEACEFUL GATHERING TURNS INTO NATIVE UPRISING.

Anyway, my father was arrested, charged with attempted murder, which was reduced to assault with a deadly weapon. It was a high-profile case so my father was used as an example. Convicted and sentenced quickly, he spent two years in Walla Walla State Penitentiary. Although his prison sentence effectively kept him out of the war, my father went through a different kind of war behind bars.

"There was Indian gangs and white gangs and black gangs and Mexican gangs," he told me once. "And there was somebody new killed every day. We'd hear about somebody getting it in the shower or wherever and the word would go down the line. Just one word. Just the color of his skin. Red, white, black, or brown. Then we'd chalk it up on the mental scoreboard and wait for the next broadcast."

My father made it through all that, never got into any serious trouble, somehow avoided rape, and got out of prison just in time to hitchhike to Woodstock to watch Jimi Hendrix play "The Star-Spangled Banner."

"After all the shit I'd been through," my father said, "I figured Jimi must have known I was there in the crowd to play something like that. It was exactly how I felt."

Twenty years later, my father played his Jimi Hendrix tape until it wore down. Over and over, the house filled with the rockets' red glare and the bombs bursting in air. He'd sit by the stereo with a cooler of beer beside him and cry, laugh, call me over and hold me tight in his arms, his bad breath and body odor covering me like a blanket.

Jimi Hendrix and my father became drinking buddies. Jimi Hendrix waited for my father to come home after a long night of drinking. Here's how the ceremony worked:

1. I would lie awake all night and listen for the sounds of my father's pickup.

2. When I heard my father's pickup, I would run upstairs and throw Jimi's tape into the stereo.

3. Jimi would bend his guitar into the first note of "The Star-Spangled Banner" just as my father walked inside.

4. My father would weep, attempt to hum along with Jimi, and then pass out with his head on the kitchen table.

5. I would fall asleep under the table with my head near my father's feet.

6. We'd dream together until the sun came up.

The days after, my father would feel so guilty that he would tell me stories as a means of apology.

"I met your mother at a party in Spokane," my father told me once. "We were the only two Indians at the party. Maybe the only two Indians in the whole town. I thought she was so beautiful. I figured she was the kind of woman who could make buffalo walk on up to her and give up their lives. She wouldn't have needed to hunt. Every time we went walking, birds would follow us around. Hell, tumbleweeds would follow us around."

Somehow my father's memories of my mother grew more beautiful as their relationship became more hostile. By the time the divorce was final, my mother was quite possibly the most beautiful woman who ever lived.

"Your father was always half crazy," my mother told me more than once. "And the other half was on medication."

But she loved him, too, with a ferocity that eventually forced her to leave him. They fought each other with the kind of graceful anger that only love can create. Still, their love was passionate, unpredictable, and selfish. My mother and father would get drunk and leave parties abruptly to go home and make love.

"Don't tell your father I told you this," my mother said. "But there must have been a hundred times he passed out on top of me. We'd be right in the middle of it, he'd say *I love you,* his eyes would roll backwards, and then out went his lights. It sounds strange, I know, but those were good times."

I was conceived during one of those drunken nights, half of me formed by my father's whiskey sperm, the other half formed by my mother's vodka egg. I was born a goofy reservation mixed drink, and my father needed me just as much as he needed every other kind of drink.

One night my father and I were driving home in a near-blizzard after a basketball game, listening to the radio. We didn't talk much. One, because my father didn't talk much when he was sober, and two, because Indians don't need to talk to communicate.

"Hello out there, folks, this is Big Bill Baggins, with the late-night classics show on KROC, 97.2 on your FM dial. We have a request from Betty in Tekoa. She wants to hear Jimi Hendrix's version of 'The Star-Spangled Banner' recorded live at Woodstock."

My father smiled, turned the volume up, and we rode down the highway while Jimi led the way like a snowplow. Until that night, I'd always been neutral about Jimi Hendrix. But, in that near-blizzard with my father at the wheel, with the nervous silence caused by the dangerous roads and Jimi's guitar, there seemed to be more to all that music. The reverberation came to mean something, took form and function.

That song made me want to learn to play guitar, not because I wanted to be Jimi Hendrix and not because I thought I'd ever play for anyone. I just wanted to touch the strings, to hold the guitar tight against my body, invent a chord, and come closer to what Jimi knew, to what my father knew.

"You know," I said to my father after the song was over, "my generation of Indian boys ain't ever had no real war to fight. The first Indians had Custer to fight. My great-grandfather had World War I, my grandfather had World War II, you had Vietnam. All I have is video games."

My father laughed for a long time, nearly drove off the road into the snowy fields.

"Shit," he said. "I don't know why you're feeling sorry for your-self because you ain't had to fight a war. You're lucky. Shit, all you had was that damn Desert Storm. Should have called it Dessert Storm because it just made the fat cats get fatter. It was all sugar and whipped cream with a cherry on top. And besides that, you didn't even have to fight it. All you lost during that war was sleep because you stayed up all night watching CNN."

We kept driving through the snow, talked about war and peace.

"That's all there is," my father said. "War and peace with noth-ing in between. It's always one or the other."

"You sound like a book," I said.

"Yeah, well, that's how it is. Just because it's in a book doesn't make it not true. And besides, why the hell would you want to fight a war for this country? It's been trying to kill Indians since the very beginning. Indians are pretty much born soldiers anyway. Don't need a uniform to prove it."

Those were the kinds of conversations that Jimi Hendrix forced us to have. I guess every song has a special meaning for someone somewhere. Elvis Presley is still showing up in 7-11 stores across the country, even though he's been dead for years, so I figure music just might be the most important thing there is. Music turned my father into a reservation philosopher. Music had powerful medicine.

"I remember the first time your mother and I danced," my father told me once. "We were in this cowboy bar. We were the only real cowboys there despite the fact that we're Indians. We danced to a Hank Williams song. Danced to that real sad one, you know. 'I'm So Lonesome I Could Cry.' Except your mother and I weren't lonesome or crying. We just shuffled along and fell right goddamn down into love."

"Hank Williams and Jimi Hendrix don't have much in com-mon," I said.

"Hell, yes, they do. They knew all about broken hearts," my fa-ther said.

"You sound like a bad movie."

"Yeah, well, that's how it is. You kids today don't know shit about romance. Don't know shit about music either. Especially you Indian kids. You all have been spoiled by those drums. Been hearing them beat so long, you think that's all you need. Hell, son, even an Indian needs a piano or guitar or saxophone now and again."

My father played in a band in high school. He was the drummer. I guess he'd burned out on those. Now, he was like the universal defender of the guitar.

"I remember when your father would haul that old guitar out and play me songs," my mother said. "He couldn't play all that well but he tried. You could see him thinking about what chord he was going to play next. His eyes got all squeezed up and his face turned all red. He kind of looked that way when he kissed me, too. But don't tell him I said that."

Some nights I lay awake and listened to my parents' lovemaking. I know white people keep it quiet, pretend they don't ever make love. My white friends tell me they can't even imagine their own parents getting it on. I know exactly what it sounds like when my parents are touching each other. It makes up for knowing exactly what they sound like when they're fighting. Plus and minus. Add and subtract. It comes out just about even.

Some nights I would fall asleep to the sounds of my parents' lovemaking. I would dream Jimi Hendrix. I could see my father standing in the front row in the dark at Woodstock as Jimi Hendrix played "The Star-Spangled Banner." My mother was at home with me, both of us waiting for my father to find his way back home to the reservation. It's amazing to realize I was alive, breathing and wetting my bed, when Jimi was alive and breaking guitars.

I dreamed my father dancing with all these skinny hippie women, smoking a few joints, dropping acid, laughing when the rain fell. And it did rain there. I've seen actual news footage. I've seen the documentaries. It rained. People had to share food. People got sick. People got married. People cried all kinds of tears.

But as much as I dream about it, I don't have any clue about what it meant for my father to be the only Indian who saw Jimi Hendrix play at Woodstock. And maybe he wasn't the only Indian there. Most likely there were hundreds but my father thought he was the only one. He told me that a million times when he was drunk and a couple hundred times when he was sober.

"I was there," he said. "You got to remember this was near the end and there weren't as many people as before. Not nearly as many. But I waited it out. I waited for Jimi."

A few years back, my father packed up the family and the three of us drove to Seattle to visit Jimi Hendrix's grave. We had our photograph taken lying down next to the grave. There isn't a gravestone there. Just one of those flat markers.

Jimi was twenty-eight when he died. That's younger than Jesus Christ when he died. Younger than my father as we stood over the grave.

"Only the good die young," my father said.

"No," my mother said. "Only the crazy people choke to death on their own vomit."

"Why you talking about my hero that way?" my father asked.

"Shit," my mother said. "Old Jesse WildShoe choked to death on his own vomit and he ain't anybody's hero."

I stood back and watched my parents argue. I was used to these battles. When an Indian marriage starts to fall apart, it's even more destructive and painful than usual. A hundred years ago, an Indian marriage was broken easily. The woman or man just packed up all their possessions and left the tipi. There were no arguments, no discussions. Now, Indians fight their way to the end, holding onto the last good thing, because our whole lives have to do with survival.

After a while, after too much fighting and too many angry words had been exchanged, my father went out and bought a motorcycle. A big bike. He left the house often to ride that thing for hours, sometimes for days. He even strapped an old cassette player to the gas tank so he could listen to music. With that bike, he learned something new about running away. He stopped talking as much, stopped drinking as much. He didn't do much of anything except ride that bike and listen to music.

Then one night my father wrecked his bike on Devil's Gap Road and ended up in the hospital for two months. He broke both his legs, cracked his ribs, and punctured a lung. He also lacerated his kidney. The doctors said he could have died easily. In fact, they were surprised he made it through surgery, let alone survived those first few hours when he lay on the road, bleeding. But I wasn't surprised. That's how my father was.

And even though my mother didn't want to be married to him anymore and his wreck didn't change her mind about that, she still came to see him every day. She sang Indian tunes under her breath, in time with the hum of the machines hooked into my father. Although my father could barely move, he tapped his finger in rhythm.

When he had the strength to finally sit up and talk, hold conversations, and tell stories, he called for me.

"Victor," he said. "Stick with four wheels."

After he began to recover, my mother stopped visiting as often. She helped him through the worst, though. When he didn't need her anymore, she went back to the life she had created. She traveled to powwows, started to dance again. She was a champion traditional dancer when she was younger.

"I remember your mother when she was the best traditional dancer in the world," my father said. "Everyone wanted to call her sweetheart. But she only danced for me. That's how it was. She told me that every other step was just for me."

"But that's only half of the dance," I said.

"Yeah," my father said. "She was keeping the rest for herself. Nobody can give everything away. It ain't healthy."

"You know," I said, "sometimes you sound like you ain't even real."

"What's real? I ain't interested in what's real. I'm interested in how things should be."

My father's mind always worked that way. If you don't like the things you remember, then all you have to do is change the memories. Instead of remembering the bad things, remember what happened immediately before. That's what I learned from my father. For me, I remember how good the first drink of that Diet Pepsi tasted instead of how my mouth felt when I swallowed a wasp with the second drink.

Because of all that, my father always remembered the second before my mother left him for good and took me with her. No. I remembered the second before my father left my mother and me. No. My mother remembered the second before my father left her to finish raising me all by herself.

But however memory actually worked, it was my father who climbed on his motorcycle, waved to me as I stood in the window, and rode away. He lived in Seattle, San Francisco, Los Angeles, before he finally ended up in Phoenix. For a while, I got postcards nearly every week. Then it was once a month. Then it was on Christmas and my birthday.

On a reservation, Indian men who abandon their children are treated worse than white fathers who do the same thing. It's because white men have been doing that forever and Indian men have just learned how. That's how assimilation can work.

My mother did her best to explain it all to me, although I understood most of what happened.

"Was it because of Jimi Hendrix?" I asked her.

"Part of it, yeah," she said. "This might be the only marriage broken up by a dead guitar player."

"There's a first time for everything, enit?"

"I guess. Your father just likes being alone more than he likes being with other people. Even me and you."

Sometimes I caught my mother digging through old photo albums or staring at the wall or out the window. She'd get that look on her face that I knew meant she missed my father. Not enough to want him back. She missed him just enough for it to hurt.

On those nights I missed him most I listened to music. Not always Jimi Hendrix. Usually I listened to the blues. Robert Johnson mostly. The first time I heard Robert Johnson sing I knew he understood what it meant to be Indian on the edge of the twenty-first century, even if he was black at the beginning of the twentieth. That must have been how my father felt when he heard Jimi Hendrix. When he stood there in the rain at Woodstock.

Then on the night I missed my father most, when I lay in bed and cried, with that photograph of him beating that National Guard private in my hands, I imagined his motorcycle pulling up outside. I knew I was dreaming it all but I let it be real for a moment.

"Victor," my father yelled. "Let's go for a ride."

"I'll be right down. I need to get my coat on."

I rushed around the house, pulled my shoes and socks on, struggled into my coat, and ran outside to find an empty driveway. It was so quiet, a reservation kind of quiet, where you can hear somebody drinking whiskey on the rocks three miles away. I stood on the porch and waited until my mother came outside.

"Come on back inside," she said. "It's cold."

"No," I said. "I know he's coming back tonight."

My mother didn't say anything. She just wrapped me in her favorite quilt and went back to sleep. I stood on the porch all night long and imagined I heard motorcycles and guitars, until the sun rose so bright that I knew it was time to go back inside to my mother. She made breakfast for both of us and we ate until we were full.

EDMUND WHITE

Cinnamon Skin

W hen I was a kid, I was a Buddhist and an atheist, but I kept
making bargains with God: if he'd fulfill a particular wish,
I'd agree to believe in him. He always came through, but I still
withheld my faith, which shows, perhaps, how unreasonable ra-
tionality can be.

One of God's miracles occurred when I was thirteen. I was
spending most of that year with my father in Cincinnati; my
mother, a psychologist, thought I needed the proximity of a man,
even though my father then ignored me and was uninterested in
teaching me baseball or tennis, sports in which he excelled. My father and stepmother were going to Mexico for a winter holiday that
would not, alas, fall during my Christmas school break, although it
was unlikely that he would have invited me even if I had been free,
since the divorce agreement specified nothing about winter vaca-
tions. One long weekend, I returned to Chicago to see my mother
and sister, and fell on my knees beside my bed in the dark and
prayed that I'd be invited to come along anyway. The next morning
my mother received a telegram from my father asking me to join
him in Cincinnati the following day for a three-week car trip to
Acapulco. He'd already obtained advance assignments from my
teachers; he would supervise my homework.

My mother had a phobia about speaking to my father, and spent thirty-five years without ever hearing his voice. If vocal communication was forbidden, the exchange of cordial but brief tactical notes or telegrams was acceptable, provided it didn't occur regularly. My mother's generation believed in something called *character,* and it was established through self-discipline. Anyway, my mother suggested that I phone my father, since court etiquette prevented her from doing so.

The next day I took the train to Cincinnati; it was the James Whitcomb Riley, named after the Hoosier Poet ("When the frost is on the punkin," one of his odes begins). At the end of each car, there were not scenes of rural Indiana, as one might have expected, but, instead, large reproductions of French Impressionist paintings—hayricks, water lilies, Notre-Dame, mothers and children *en fleurs* . . . This train, which I took twice a month to visit my dad when I was living with my mom, or to visit Mom when I was living with Dad, was the great forcing shed of my imagination: no one knew me; I was free to become anyone. I told one startled neighbor that I was English and in America for the first time, affecting an accent so obviously fabricated and snobbish that it eventually provoked a smile. I told another I had leukemia but was in remission. Another time I said that both my parents had just died in a car crash, and I was going to live with a bachelor uncle. Once I chatted up a handsome young farmer, his face stiff under its burn, his T-shirt incapable of containing the black hair sprouting up from under it; he inspired a tragic opera that I started writing the next week; it was called "Orville."

On this trip, my imagination was busy with a thick guidebook on Mexico I'd checked out of the public library. I read everything I could about Toltecs, Aztecs, and Mayans; but the astrology bored me, as did the bloody attacks and counterattacks, and one century blended into another without a single individual's emerging out of the plumed hordes—until the tragic Montezuma (a new opera subject, even more heartrending than Orville, whose principal attribute had been a smell of Vitalis hair tonic and, more subtly, of starch and ironing, a quality difficult to render musically).

The year was 1953; my father and stepmother rode in the front of his new, massive Cadillac—shiny pale-blue metal and chrome and, inside, an oiled, dark-blue leather with shag carpet—and I had so much space in the back seat that I could stretch out full length, slightly nauseated from the cigars that my father chain-smoked and his interminable monologues about the difference between stocks and bonds. While in the States, he listened to broadcasts of the news, the stock reports, and sporting events, three forms of impersonal entertainment that I considered to be as tedious as the Toltecs' battles.

I lay in the back seat, knocking my legs together in an agony of unreleased desire. My head filled with vague daydreams, as randomly rotating as the clouds I could see up above through the back window. In those days, the speed limit was higher than now and the roads were just two-lane meanders; there was no radar and no computers, and if a cop stopped us for speeding my father tucked a five-dollar bill under his license and instantly we were urged on our way with a cheerful wave and a "Y'all come back, yuh heah?" My father then resumed his murderous speed, lunging and turning and braking and swearing, and I hid so I wouldn't witness, white-knuckled, the near-disasters. As night fell, the same popular song, the theme song from the film *Moulin Rouge,* was played over and over again on station after station, like a flame being passed feebly from torch to torch in a casual marathon.

We stopped in Austin, Texas, to see my grandfather, who was retired and living alone in a small wooden house he rented. He was famous locally for his "nigger" jokes, which he collected in self-published books with titles such as *Let's Laugh, Senegambian Sizzles, Folks Are Funny,* and *Chocolate Drops from the South,* and he made fun of me for saying "Cue" Klux Klan instead of "Koo"—an organization he'd once belonged to, and accepted as a harmless if stern fraternity. He was dull, like my father, though my father was different: whereas my grandfather was gregarious but disgustingly self-absorbed, my father was all facts, all business, misanthropic, his racism genial and condescending, though his anti-Semitism was virulent and reeked of hate. He wanted as little contact as possible with other people. And while he liked women, he regarded them as silly and flighty and easy to seduce; they excited men but weren't themselves sexual, although easily tricked into bed. Men he despised, even boys.

My stepmother, Kay, was "cockeyed and harelipped," according to my mother, although the truth was she simply had a lazy eye that wandered in and out of focus and an everted upper lip that rose on one side like Judy Garland's whenever she hit a high note. Kay read constantly, anything at all; she'd put down *Forever Amber* to pick up *War and Peace*, trade in *Désirée* for *Madame Bovary*, but the next day she couldn't remember a thing about what she'd been reading. My father, who never finished a book, always said, when the subject of literature came up, "You'll have to ask Kay about that. She's the reader in this family." He thought novels were useless, even corrupting; if he caught me reading he'd find me a chore to do, such as raking the lawn.

My father liked long-legged redheads in high heels and short nighties, if his addiction to *Esquire* and its illustrations was any indication, but my stepmother was short and dumpy, like my mother, though less intelligent. She'd been brought up on a farm in northern Ohio by a scrawny father in bib overalls and a pretty, calm, round-faced mother from Pennsylvania Dutch country, who said "mind" for "remember." ("Do you mind that time we went to the caves in Kentucky?") Kay had done well in elocution class, and even now she could recite mindless doggerel with ringing authority—and with the sort of steely diction and hearty projection that are impossible to tune out. She could paint—watercolors of little Japanese maidens all in a row, or kittens or pretty flowers—and her love of art led her to be a volunteer at the art museum, where she worked three hours a week in the gift shop run by the Ladies' Auxiliary. Oh, she had lots of activities and belonged to plenty of clubs—the Ladies' Luncheon Club and the Queen City Club and the Keyboard Club.

Kay had spent her twenties and thirties being a shrewd, feisty office "gal" who let herself be picked up by big bored businessmen out for a few laughs and a roll in the hay with a good sport. She always had a joke or a wisecrack to dish up, she'd learned how to defend herself against a grabby drunk, and she always knew the score. I'm not sure how I acquired this information about her early life. Probably from my mother, who branded Kay a Jezebel, an unattractive woman with secret sexual power, someone like Wallis Simpson. After Kay married my father, however, and moved up a whole lot of social rungs, she pretended to be shocked by the very jokes she used to deliver. She adopted the endearingly dopey manner of the society matron immortalized in Helen E. Hokinson's *New Yorker* cartoons. Dad gave her an expensive watch that dangled upside down from a brooch (so that only Kay could read it), which she pinned to her lapel: a bow of white and yellow gold studded with beautiful lapis lazuli. Her skirts became longer, her voice softer, her hair grayer, and she replaced her native sassiness with an acquired innocence. She'd always been cunning rather than intelligent, but now she appeared to become naïve as well, which in our milieu was a sign of wealth: only rich women were sheltered; only the overprotected were unworldly. As my real mother learned to fend for herself, my stepmother learned to feign incompetence.

Such astute naïveté, of course, was only for public performance. At home, Kay was as crafty as ever. She speculated out loud about other people's motives and pieced together highly unflattering scenarios based on the slimmest evidence. Every act of kindness was considered secretly manipulative, any sign of generosity profoundly selfish. She quizzed me for hours about my mother's finances (turbulent) and love life (usually nonexistent, sometimes disastrous). She was, of course, hoping that Mother would remarry so Dad wouldn't have to pay out the monthly alimony. My sister was disgusted that I'd betray our mother's secrets, but Kay bewitched me. We had few entertainments and spent long, tedious hours together in the stifling Cincinnati summer heat, and I'd been so carefully sworn to silence by my mother that, finally, when one thing came out, I told all. I was thrilled to have a promise to break.

Kay and my father fought all the time. She'd pester him to do something or challenge him over a trivial question of fact until he exploded: "God damn it, Kay, shut your goddam mouth, you don't know what the hell you're talking about, and I don't want to hear one more goddam word out of your mouth! I'm warning you to shut it and shut it now. Got it?"

"Oh, E.*V*," she wailed (his nickname; his middle name was Valentine), "you don't have to talk to me that way, you're making me sick, physically sick, my heart is pounding, and, look, I'm sweating freely, I'm soaked right through, my underarms are drenched, and you know—my high *blood* pressure." Here she'd break off and begin blubbering. She had only to invoke her blood pressure ("Two hundred and fifty over a hundred and ten," she'd mysteriously confide) in order to win the argument and subdue my red-faced father. I pictured the two of them as thermometers in which the mounting mercury was about to explode through the upper tip. Kay constantly referred to her imminent death, often adding, "Well, I won't be around much longer to irritate you with my remarks, which you find so *stupid* and *ignorant*."

My father filled his big house with Mahler, and played it throughout the night; he went to sleep at dawn. And the more socially successful Kay became the less she conformed to his hours. They scarcely saw each other. During the hot Cincinnati days, while

Daddy slept in his air-conditioned room, Kay and I spent the idle hours talking to each other. I bit my nails; she paid me a dollar a nail to let them grow. When they came in, I decided I wanted them longer and longer and shaped like a woman's; Kay promised to cut them as I desired, but each time she tricked me and trimmed them short while I whined my feeble protests: "*C'mon.* I want them long and *pointy.* . . . Kay! You *promised!*" I danced for her in my underpants; once I did an elaborate (and very girly) striptease. As I became more and more feminine, she became increasingly masculine. She put one leg up and planted her foot on the chair seat, hugging her knee to her chest as a guy might. I felt I was dancing for a man.

Perhaps she watched me because she was bored and had nothing else to do. Or perhaps she knew these games attached me to her with thrilling, erotic bonds; in the rivalry with my mother for my affections, she was winning.

Or perhaps she got off on me. I remember that she gave me long massages with baby oil as I lay on the Formica kitchen table in my underpants, and I sprang a boner. Her black maid watched us and smiled benignly. Her name was Naomi and she'd worked for Kay one day a week ironing before Kay married; afterward she moved in as a full-time, live-in employee in my father's big house. She knew Kay's earlier incarnation as a roaring girl and no doubt wondered how far she'd go now.

In fact, she went very far. Once when I told her I was constipated she had me mount the Formica table on all fours and administered a hot-water enema out of a blue rubber pear she filled and emptied three times before permitting me to go to the toilet and squirt it out.

My whole family was awash with incestuous desires. When my real mother was drunk (as she was most nights), she'd call out from her bed and beg me to rub her back, then moan with pleasure as I kneaded the cool, sweating dough. My sister was repulsed by our mother's body, but I once walked in on her and my father in his study in Cincinnati. She must have been fourteen or fifteen. She was sitting in a chair and he stood behind her, brushing her long blond hair and quietly crying. (It was the only time I ever saw him cry.) Later she claimed she and Daddy had made love. She said she and I'd done it in an upper berth on the night train from Chicago to Cincinnati once, but I can't quite be sure I remember it.

When I was twelve, Kay was out of town once and Daddy took me to dinner at the Gourmet Room, a glass-walled dome on top of the Terrace Hilton. The restaurant had a mural by Miró and French food. Daddy drank a lot of wine and told me I had my mother's big brown eyes. He said boys my age were rather like girls. He said there wasn't much difference between boys and girls my age. I was thrilled. I tried to be warm and intuitive and seductive.

Now, as we approached the Mexican border, Kay started teasing me: "I hope you have on very clean underpants, Eddie, because the Mexican police strip-search every tourist and if they find skid marks in your Jockey shorts they may not let you in."

My father thought this was a terrific joke and with his thin-lipped smile nodded slowly and muttered, "She's serious, and she's a hundred per cent right."

Although I worried about my panties, I half hoped that a brown-skinned, mustachioed guard in a sweat-soaked uniform would look into them, and at my frail, naked body: even though I was convinced that I'd never been uglier. I had a brush cut Kay had forced on me ("You'll be hot if you don't get all that old hair out of your face"), and my white scalp showed through it. I wore glasses with enormous black frames and looked like an unappealing quiz kid, without the budding intellectual's redeeming brashness. I was ashamed of my recently acquired height, cracking voice, and first pubic hairs, and I posed in front of the foggy bathroom mirror with a towel turban around my head and my penis pushed back and concealed between my legs. In public, I'd fold into myself like a Swiss Army knife, hoping to occupy as little space as possible.

But at the border the guards merely waved us through after querying my father about the ten cartons of Cuban cigars in the trunk (Dad had to grease a few palms to convince them the cigars were for his own use, not for resale). We drove down the two-lane Pan-American Highway from the Rio Grande through an endless flat cactus desert into the mountains. Kay encouraged me to wave at the tiny, barefoot Indians walking along the highway in their bright costumes, their raven-black hair hanging straight down to their shoulders. Sometimes they'd shake their fists at our retreating fins, but I seemed to be the only one who noticed.

From the highway, we seldom saw villages or even houses, although from time to time we noticed a red flag that had been tossed into the top of a mesquite tree. Daddy said the flag signified that a cow had just been slaughtered. "Since they don't have refrigeration," he informed us through a cloud of cigar smoke, his tiny yellow teeth revealed in a rare smile, "they must sell all the edible parts of the animal and cook them within a few hours." I don't know how he knew that, although he had grown up in Texas, worked summers as a cowboy, and must have known many Mexicans. I was struck by his equanimity in contemplating such shameful poverty, which would have disgusted him had we still been in the States; in Mexico, he smiled benignly at it, as though it were an integral part of a harmonious whole.

My father had a passion for travelling long hours and making record time. He also had ironclad kidneys. Kay had to stop to pee every hour. Perhaps her blood-pressure medicine was a diuretic. "Anyway," she whined, "I don't understand why we have to rush like this. What's the hurry? For Pete's sake, E.V., we're in a foreign country and we should take a gander at it. *No es problema?*"

Before her marriage, when she was still just my father's secretary and "mistress" (my mother's lurid, old-fashioned word), Kay would have said, "For Christ's sake." If she now replaced "Christ" with "Pete," she did so as part of her social beatification. She might actually have said "take a gander" when she was a farm girl in northern Ohio, but now it was placed between gently inverted commas to suggest that she was citing, with mild merriment but without contempt, an endearingly rural but outdated Americanism. Like many English-speaking North Americans, she thought foreign languages were funny, as though no one would ordinarily speak one except as a joke. *"No es problema?"* was her comic contribution to the mishap of being in Mexico, the verbal equivalent of a jumping bean.

Halfway to Mexico City we stopped at a beautiful old colonial-style hotel that had what it advertised as the world's largest porch, wrapped around it on all four sides. Meek Indian women were eternally on all fours scrubbing tiles the garnet color of fresh scabs still seeping blood. That night, Kay and Dad and I walked past banana trees spotlit orange and yellow and a glowing swimming pool that smelled of sulfur. *"Pee-you,"* Kay said, holding her little nose with her swollen, red-nailed fingers.

"It's a sulfur spa, Kay," Dad explained. "The Mexicans think it has curative powers."

We entered a roomy, high-ceilinged cave in which a band was playing sophisticated rumbas. The headwaiter, broad and tall as a wardrobe, wore a double-breasted jacket.

"*Uno* whiskey," Dad said once we were seated, showing off for our benefit. "Y two Coca-Cola *por favorita.*"

"*Sí, señor!*" the headwaiter shouted before he reclaimed his dignity by palming the order off with lofty disdain on a passing Indian busboy in a collarless blue jacket.

All the other guests at the hotel appeared to be rich Mexicans. No one around us was speaking English. The most attractive couple I'd ever seen were dancing an intricate samba, chatting and smiling to each other casually while their slender hips swivelled into and out of provocative postures, and their small, expensively shod feet shuffled back and forth in a well-rehearsed, syncopated trot.

Daddy was decked out in a pleated jacket with side tabs that opened up to accommodate extra girth; I think it was called a Havana shirt. Suddenly both he and Kay looked impossibly sexless in their pale, perspiring bodies. In my blood the marimbas had lit a crackling fire, a fiery longing for the Mexican couple before me, their bodies expert and sensual, their manner light and sophisticated—a vision of a civilized sexuality I'd never glimpsed before. Outside, however, the heavy sulfur smell somehow suggested an animal in rut, just as the miles of unlit rural night around the cave made me jumpy. There was nowhere to go, and the air was pungent with smoke from hearths and filled with the cry of cocks; in the distance were only the shadowy forms of the mountains.

In Mexico City, we stayed in a nineteen-thirties hotel on the Reforma. There were then only two million people in "México," as the citizens called their beautiful city, with a proud use of synecdoche. People swarmed over our car at each stoplight, proffering lottery tickets, but we kept our windows closed and sailed down the spacious boulevards. We saw the Ciudad Universitaria under construction outside town, with its bold mural by Diego Rivera—a lien on a bright future, a harbinger of progress. We visited the Museum of Modern Art and ate in a French restaurant, Normandie, a few blocks away. We ascended the hill to the fortress castle of Chapultepec, where the Austrian rulers, the lean Maximilian, the pale Carlota, had lived. We were poled in barques through floating gardens and climbed the Aztecs' step pyramids.

We were accompanied everywhere by one of Daddy's business associates and his wife. After I corrected this man ("Not the eighteenth century," I snapped, "that was in the *sixteenth*"), Daddy drew me aside and said, "Never contradict another person like that, especially someone older. Just say 'I may be wrong but I thought I read somewhere . . .' or 'What do I know, but it seems . . .' Got it? Best to let it just go by, but if you must correct him do it that way. And by the way, don't say you *love* things. Women say that. Rather, say you *like* things."

I had always been proud of noticing the fatuous remarks made by adults. Now I was appalled to learn that my father had been vexed by things I said. I was half flattered by his attention (he was looking at me, after all) but also half irritated at how he wanted me to conform to his idea of a man.

We went to Cuernavaca and saw the flower-heavy walls of its mansions, then to Taxco, where Kay bought a very thin silver bracelet worked into interlocking flowers. The heat made her heavy perfume, Shalimar, smell all the stronger; its muskiness competed with my father's cigar smoke. Only I had no smell at all. Daddy warned us to look for tarantulas in our shoes before we put them on.

We arrived in Acapulco, still a chic beach resort, not the paved-over fast-food hellhole it would become, and stayed at the Club de Pesca. I had a room to myself on a floor above my father and Kay's. The manager had delivered baskets of soft and slightly over-ripe fruit to our rooms; after a day, the pineapple smelled pungent.

One night we went to a restaurant in a hotel on top of a cliff and watched teen-age boys in swimsuits shed their silk capes and kneel before a spotlit statue of the Virgin, then plunge a hundred and fifty feet down into the waves flowing into and out of a chasm. Their timing had to be exact or they'd be dashed on the rocks. They had superb, muscled bodies, tan skin, glinting religious medals, and long black hair slicked back behind their ears. Afterward, the divers walked among the crowd, passing a hat for coins, their feet huge, their faces pale behind their tans, their haughty smiles at odds with the look of shock in their eyes.

The popular song that year in Mexico was "Piel Canela" ("Cinnamon Skin"), an ode to a beautiful mulatto girl. In the States, reference to color was considered impolite, although everyone told racist jokes in private; here, apparently, a warm brown color was an attribute of beauty. In the afternoons on the beach, young water-ski instructors stretched their long brown arms and legs, adjusting themselves inside their swimsuits, offering to give lessons to pale tourists, both male and female. We gringos had a lot to learn from them.

A singer and movie star from Argentina, Libertad Lamarque, was staying in our hotel. When we rode up in the elevator with her, she was wearing a tailored white linen suit and had a clipped, snowy-white Chihuahua on a leash. It turned out that her room was next to mine. I became friendly with her daughter—I don't remember how we met. Although Libertad was in exile from Perón's Argentina, her daughter still lived most of the time in Buenos Aires, where she sang American ballads in a night club. One night she volunteered to sing "You Go to My Head" at the Club de Pesca—yes, that must be how I met her. I went up to congratulate her and was surprised to discover she scarcely spoke English, though she sang it without an accent.

Libertad's daughter must have found me amusing, or perhaps docile, or a convenient alibi for her midday mid-ocean pastimes. She invited me to go out on her speedboat late the next morning; after dropping anchor, she and the handsome Indian driver kissed and embraced for an hour. I didn't know what to do with my eyes, so I watched. The sun was hot but the breeze constant. That night I was so burned Kay had to wrap me in sheets drenched in cold water.

I moaned and turned for two days and nights in wet sheets. A local doctor came and went. My fever soared. In my confused, feverish thoughts I imagined that I'd been burned by the vision of that man and woman clawing at each other on the varnished doors that folded down over the speedboat's powerful motor.

The man who had accompanied Libertad's daughter on the piano was a jowly Indian in his late thirties. Perhaps he smiled at me knowingly or held my hand a second too long when we were introduced, but I honestly can't remember his giving me the slightest sign of being interested in me. And yet I became determined to seduce him. My skin was peeling in strips, like long white gauze, revealing patches of a cooked-shrimp pink underneath. My mirror told me the effect wasn't displeasing; in fact the burn brought out my freckles and gave me a certain raffishness. Perhaps soon I, too, would have cinnamon skin. Until now, I'd resembled a newly shorn sheep.

One night at ten, my well-sauced father, atypically genial, sent me off to bed with a pat on the shoulder. But, instead of undressing and going to sleep, I prepared myself for a midnight sortie. I showered in the tepid water that smelled of chlorine and pressed my wet brush-cut hair flat against my skull. From my chest I coaxed off another strip of dead skin; I felt I was unwinding a mummy. I soaked myself in a cheap aftershave made by Mennen and redolent of the barbershop (witch hazel and limes). I sprinkled the toilet water onto the sheets. I put on a fresh pair of white Jockey underpants and posed in front of the mirror. I rolled the waistband down until it revealed just a tuft of newly sprouting pubic hair. I danced my version of the samba toward the mirror and back again. I wriggled out of my undershorts, turned, and examined my buttocks. I kissed my shoulder, then stood on tiptoe and looked at my chest, belly button, penis.

At last, my watch told me it was midnight. I dressed in shorts and a pale-green shirt and new sandals and headed down toward the bar. My legs looked as long and silky as those of Dad's pinups. I stood beside the piano and stared holes through the musician; I hoped he could smell my aftershave. He didn't glance up at me once, but I felt he was aware of my presence.

He took his break between sets and asked me if I wanted to walk to the end of the dock. When we got there we sat on a high-backed bench, which hid us from view. We looked out across the harbor at the few lights on the farther shore, one of them moving. A one-eyed car or a motor scooter climbed the road and vanished over the crest of a hill. A soft warm breeze blew in over the Pacific.

Some people lived their whole lives beside the restless, changeable motions of the ocean, rocked by warm breezes night and day, their only clothing the merest concession to decency, their bodies constantly licked by water and wind. I who had known the cold Chicago winters, whose nose turned red and hands blue in the arctic temperatures, whose scrotum shrank and feet went numb, who could scarcely guess the gender, much less discern the degree of beauty, under those moving gray haystacks of bonnets, mittens, overcoats, and scarves—here, in Mexico, I felt my body, browned and peeled into purity, expand and relax.

The pianist and I held hands. He said, "I could come up to your room after I get off at four in the morning."

"I'm in Room 612," I said.

I looked over my shoulder and saw my very drunk father weaving his way toward me. When he was halfway out the dock, I stood up and hailed him.

"Hi, Daddy," I said. "I just couldn't sleep. I decided to come down and relax. Do you know Pablo, the pianist from the bar?" I made up the name out of thin air.

"Hello, Pablo." They shook hands. "Now you better get to bed, young man."

"O.K. Good night, Daddy. Good night, Pablo."

Back in my room, I looked at the luminescent dial on my watch as it crept toward two, then three. I had no idea what sex would be like; in truth, I had never thought about it. I just imagined our first embrace would be as though we were in a small wooden boat floating down a river by moonlight. Pablo and I would live here by the sea; I'd learn to make tortillas.

I woke to the sound of shouts in the hall. Oh, no! I'd given Pablo not my room number, 610, but that of Libertad Lamarque, 612. I could hear her angry denunciations in Spanish and Pablo's timid murmurs. At last, she slammed her door shut and I opened mine. I hissed for him to come in. He pushed past me, I shut the door, and he whispered curses in Spanish against me. He sat on the edge of the bed, a mountain that had become a volcano. I knelt on the floor before him and looked up with meek eyes, pleading for forgiveness.

I was appalled by the mistake in room numbers. In my fantasies love was easy, a costume drama, a blessed state that required neither skill nor aptitude but was conferred—well, on *me*, simply because I wanted it so much and because, even if I wasn't exactly worthy of it, I would become so once love elected me. Now my hideous error showed me that I wasn't above mishaps and that a condition of cinematic bliss wasn't automatic.

Pablo undressed. He didn't kiss me. He pulled my underpants down, spit on his wide, stubby cock, and pushed it up my ass. He didn't hold me in his arms. My ass hurt like hell. I wondered if I'd get blood or shit on the sheets. He was lying on top of me, pushing my face and chest into the mattress. He plunged in and out. It felt like I was going to shit and I hoped I would be able to hold it in. I was afraid I'd smell and repulse him. He smelled of old sweat. His fat belly felt cold as it pressed against my back. He breathed a bit harder, then abruptly stopped his movements. He pulled out and stood up. He must have ejaculated. It was in me now. He headed for the bathroom, switched on the harsh light, washed his penis in the bowl, and dried it off with one of the two small white towels that the maid brought every day. He had to stand on tiptoe to wash his cock properly in the bowl.

I sat on the edge of the bed and put my underpants back on. The Indian dressed and put one finger to his lips as he pulled open the door and stuck his head out to see if all was clear. Then he was gone.

A couple of years later, when my dad found out I was gay, he said, "It's all your mother's fault, I bet. When did it first happen?" He was obsessed with such technicalities.

"I was with *you*, Daddy," I said, triumphant. "It was in Acapulco that time, with the Indian who played the piano in the Club de Pesca."

A year later, after he'd made another trip with Kay to Acapulco, he told me he'd asked a few questions and learned that the pianist had been caught molesting two young boys in the hotel and had been shot dead by the kids' father, a rich Mexican from Mexico

City. I never knew whether the story was true or just a cautionary tale dreamed up by Daddy. Not that he ever had much imagination.

Recently I was in Mexico City to interview Maria Felix, an old Mexican movie star. She kept me waiting a full twenty-four hours while she washed her hair (as she explained). I wandered around the city, still in ruins from a recent earthquake. The beautiful town of two million had grown into a filthy urban sprawl of slums where twenty-four million people now lived and milled around and starved.

I returned to my hotel. My room was on the fifteenth floor of a shoddy tower. I had an overwhelming desire—no, not a desire, a compulsion—to jump from the balcony. It was the closest I ever came to suicide. I sealed the glass doors and drew the curtains, but still I could feel the pull. I left the room, convinced that I'd jump if I stayed there another moment.

I walked and walked, and I cried as I went, my body streaked by passing headlights. I felt that we'd been idiots back then, Dad and Kay and I, but we'd been full of hope and we'd come to a beautiful Art Deco hotel, the Palacio Nacional, and we'd admired the castle in Chapultepec Park and the fashionable people strolling up and down the Reforma. We'd been driving in Daddy's big Cadillac, Kay was outfitted in her wonderfully tailored Hattie Carnegie suit, with the lapel watch Daddy had given her dangling from the braided white and yellow gold brooch studded with lapis lazuli.

Now they were both dead, and the city was dirty and crumbling, and the man I was travelling with was sero-positive, and so was I. Mexico's hopes seemed as dashed as mine, and all the goofy innocence of that first thrilling trip abroad had died, my boyhood hopes for love and romance faded, just as the blue in Kay's lapis had lost its intensity year after year, until it ended up as white and small as a blind eye.

ALICE ELLIOTT DARK

Close

Tasha sounded like a name out of a romance novel. Just this side of cloying. But great on her.

She was in his thoughts when Ian woke up. Immediately he buried his face in the pillow and moaned, but there was no relief in it. She'd been so close in this particular dream that he caught the exact scent of the skin between her nose and upper lip and, as if in slow motion, saw the muscles in her cheeks tighten as she looked up at him and smiled. He'd reached out to touch her and automatically snapped awake; that was how thoroughly he'd incorporated the precariousness of his situation. He couldn't even dream of her without feeling guilty, couldn't think of her without his stomach sloshing. The intensity of what he felt for her still surprised him; he didn't know where it came from or what to do about it. What he did know was that he had to do something, and soon. Tasha'd delivered an ultimatum. Choose, she pleaded, I can't take it anymore.

All right, he'd agreed. The truth was, he couldn't take it either. Ian was a married man, about to become a father, a responsible, reliable, thirty-one-year-old guy. Not a kid anymore. And not the type to have an affair—at least not until Tasha. He wasn't cut out for it, hated the deceptions and the juggling; he believed in marriage, for God's sake. Although he had no idea how he'd do it, he had to decide, and it had to be soon.

This weekend, he told himself. By Sunday night he'd have an answer for Tasha. He would choose—but how? He loved them both. He knew how crappy that sounded, but it was true. Tasha had nothing to do with his feelings for his wife, Margot. He wished she did; then at least he'd have an excuse, albeit a shopworn one. As it was, he had no explanation for his behavior except that he was a jerk, a heel, a selfish bastard—epithets that had ruined his sleep for weeks. He was definitely ready to lead a clean life again. But with whom?

At least this weekend he'd have time to think without being swayed by seeing either of them. He was on a business trip, in a businessman's motel, in a room with two beds, a refrigerator, a microwave, a television enhanced by several premium channels, a hair dryer, a phone (two, actually; there was also one in the bathroom)—*and* he'd brought along his laptop. "It's like an apartment in Tokyo," he'd joked to Margot when they'd spoken the night before. He could have gone home already—he'd finished his meetings—but he'd stayed on to have a look at the house where he'd lived as a child. He hadn't seen it since he was twelve, when it was sold during his parents' divorce. Tasha'd asked him to take her there, which was impossible, of course—at least for the moment. Margot also wanted to see it, had been suggesting it for years, but he'd always steered her toward less loaded destinations. Then this business trip came up. When he looked at the map, he saw he'd be only a few miles from the house.

"Oh, let's go," Margot had said. "Let's have one last fling before the baby comes. We'll take pictures, so we can show him later where you grew up."

He'd winced at the word "fling" and swiftly agreed to her suggestion. They'd made the plans, but in the end she'd decided it was getting too late in the pregnancy to travel that far from her doctor.

"Promise you'll take us again?" she said, meaning her and the

baby, his coming-right-up son. Us was already *them.* It was tempt-
ing to resent that, to feel left out; in other words, to use it to justify
Tasha. He fought the urge, though—he wasn't a complete sleaze.

"Of course," he agreed. "In fact, let's wait until we can all go together." He felt himself trying to buy time. He'd avoided that house
and would be happy to go on doing so.

"No, no. You go. You can't miss this opportunity!" Margot shook
her head, as if the very idea was madness. "I want a full report."

He sighed and sat up. A shard of sun was inching across the
mauve rug, while a prism somewhere had tossed rainbows on the
dark wood of the bedside table. Idly he dipped his hand into the pool
of color and was transported immediately back to a fall day in his
childhood dining room. He'd just come home from school and happened to walk in at the moment when the pine table was strewn with
a display of spectral flags toward which he automatically reached.
To his surprise, the flags had no substance. When he tried to grasp
them, he ended up with an empty fist striped with colored light and
a fretful wish that no one had seen him make such a fool of himself.

No such luck. His mother watched the whole episode from the
kitchen door and the incident became a family story. Supposedly it
demonstrated cuteness on his part, but he didn't feel cute. Even now,
he found the anecdote humiliating and wondered that no one else
recognized the pathos in the image of a boy who thought he could
hold rainbows. For Ian the moment had become emblematic of his
whole youth, which he thought of as a series of internal longings the
pursuit of which either left him empty-handed or got him in trouble.
Eventually he decided that the longings themselves must be off-base
and had trained himself to live by a code of principles rather than according to his private emotions. Tasha was an exception that under-
scored the rule. He should break it off with her . . . but on the other
hand, he thought, maybe it was time he tried again to listen to his inner voices. Maybe he was old enough to make his impulses work.

He glanced at the clock. It was only six, too early to disturb anyone. He couldn't call Tasha anyway, not until he had an answer for

her, and he didn't want to wake Margot. He realized the person he really wanted to talk to was Bill, his father. Bill would listen without judgment, but he'd have a clear idea of what Ian should do. He wouldn't even mind being woken up to talk; what were dads for? He lived alone in a breezy house in Key West, which he'd bought dirt cheap in the seventies after Ian's mother dumped him for being a loser—signified by his refusal to stop being a painter even when his work didn't sell. His art did better in Florida, but he drank a lot and had never exactly landed on his feet, at least not in any northern sense. Nevertheless, Ian thought him the wisest person he knew and felt lucky to have him as a father. If anyone had the answer to this problem, it would be Bill.

Ian dialed the number. No answer. He felt better for trying, though, less alone. He tossed the covers back.

The fields were almost gone; it saddened him to see it. He'd run himself sick in those fields, run until his lungs felt scalded and his legs were so tight he feared the tendons would snap. Now it was one development after the next, expensive faux French houses sprouting incongruously from the old Indian land. As a kid he'd found lots of arrowheads buried in the dirt. He wondered if the construction workers bothered to collect the artifacts that they plowed up or if the children who lived in these sterile houses ever went exploring. Did anyone even think about what had been there once?

It wasn't all bad news, however. Though much of the land had been ruined, the lay of it was the same, the streets still making for a bumpy ride that reminded him of pioneers being jostled on their buckboard wagons. With the windows down, the sharp clean scents of forsythia and thawing ground lent his flimsy rental car the purity of his old Raleigh three-speed, and he found himself instinctively shifting his weight as he maneuvered along the twisting roads that were known for disorienting even the locals. This is good, he thought—good to remember who he was before women.

The radio featured an album side of early Springsteen, and that seemed right, too.

He took the "back way" to Mill Rock Road and felt a pang as he turned the final corner and entered the street. The shade trees had grown, but the curbs were still buried under the detritus of leaves and mock oranges and black walnuts, a natural arsenal perfect for chucking at cars. He noticed the Millers had a red door now and an addition had been built onto the side of Drew Adams's, except they weren't the Millers' or the Adamses' houses anymore; all the mail-boxes declared new names. At the front of every property, large leaf bags sat lined up for collection by the township in compliance with the spate of laws against leaf burning that had overtaken the suburbs since he was a kid. That was too bad, he thought. He'd loved look-ing out his window at night and seeing a circle of embers shining in the back yard, then lying down on sheets that smelled of cooked leaves. In the afternoons, he'd send the buoyant ashes flying with a stamp of his foot and write his name surreptitiously on the blind side of the garage with the tip of a charred stick. What did kids do now, he wondered. What was childhood without campfires? Some-how or other, he thought, he'd give his own son that experience.

He swallowed repeatedly as he approached the end of the cul-de-sac, site of his family's house. The night before he'd fantasized about ringing the doorbell and asking to have a look around. He'd even lingered over an image of himself pointing out to the current children the spot in the attic where he'd carved his name in the rafters. What he hadn't imagined was what he saw now—a care-fully lettered green-and-white For Sale sign planted in the middle of the front yard. It threw him for a moment; was it really possible that someone other than his heartless mother was capable of aban-doning this house? He realized he still held to the notion that she was singularly insensitive. Now *that* was an insight for Margot, he thought; she was always encouraging him to do some therapy. Maybe she was right, he told himself quickly, not wanting to feel snippy toward her. His chest ached, though, from missing Tasha.

A face appeared at one of the upstairs windows. He gave a reassuring wave and pointed to the realtor's sign, meaning to suggest he'd return under official auspices, that he wasn't some creep casing the joint. As he drove off it occurred to him that it was actually a stroke of luck that the house was for sale. He could take a look without making a big deal of it. Tasha would want him to go for it, to make the most of the opportunity; Margot would be thrilled if he brought her the realtor's write-up so she'd have a picture, details, stats. Of course, depending on what he decided about the future, he might not have the chance to tell one or the other of them much about this part of his trip. But that was a concern for later, when he'd made a decision. At the moment, he knew that they each would like him to take a tour. It seemed the least he could do.

"May I use the phone?" he asked. "I have a calling card."

The receptionist smiled and wheeled her chair to the far end of her desk to give him privacy. It was a moot point, however; his father still didn't answer. Ian shrugged and handed the receiver back.

"Anything important?" the receptionist asked sympathetically.

"It can wait," Ian said. In this context, importance surely denoted a business problem. Yet the woman behind the desk seemed to hint at a willingness to be a sounding board. Ian felt a wad of emotion rise behind his ribs as he contemplated what a relief it would be to spill his guts. Why not confide in her? It would be like talking to a stranger in a bar, harmless and comforting. He tapped his fingers on the desk and opened his mouth to speak. "Uh," he began, then felt a knot the size of a squash ball settle at the base of his throat. He drummed his fingers more rapidly, shrugged again, and walked back to the sofa where he'd originally been told to wait. There was a listings book on a coffee table and he was beginning to thumb through it when Tommy Wood came rushing through the door. His good leather shoes grated on the tile, a sound that Ian associated with work, focus, success. Good for Tommy, he thought—

or Tom now, surely. The receptionist spoke to him, leaning eagerly forward, and pointed over at Ian. Tom turned toward him wearing his professional mask, then broke into a grin.

"Ian Flynn. What do you know." Tom's handshake was dry and warm.

"More than I did the last time you saw me, I hope," Ian laughed. They'd been classmates.

Tom didn't take this as a joke. "That's good," he said solemnly. He hadn't let go yet, and now brought his other hand up, pressing Ian's hand into a sandwich. "Not everyone can claim that."

Ian blushed, feeling he'd misrepresented himself. "Well, I don't know if I can, either," he backpedaled.

Tom gazed at him with a ministerial benevolence. It was a look Ian recognized but rarely encountered in New York, Dale Carnegie redux. He had to stifle an impulse to laugh, and the laughter caught in his chest like a pill swallowed dry. Tom led Ian to his office and showed him to a chair that afforded a view of what appeared to be the only raw field left along the commercial strip. A pretty woman in a burgundy pantsuit came in and handed them each a fragrant cup of coffee. She called Tom "Mr. Wood," but said it in an exaggerated, almost facetious way that made the hair rise on Ian's arms. He tried to appear preoccupied as they exchanged glances, but he registered every nuance. As she left, Ian automatically craned toward the picture of Tom's wife and kids on the desk.

"I married Kay Nelson," Tom said, following Ian's gaze. "Do you remember her?"

"Sure. She looks great." Ian inspected the photograph more thoroughly, but he couldn't separate her out from the river of girls who'd been at the junior high, all of whom had astonished him. In the picture, Kay Nelson Wood—he doubted women kept their names around here—looked like Pam Dawber from *Mork & Mindy,* a pretty brunette. He wondered if she suspected anything.

"We have twin girls, Ruthie and Miranda. Do you have a family?" Tom asked.

Ian still thought of his parents and sibs as his family. He wondered if that would change when his kid was born. "My wife is pregnant."

To Ian's surprise, Tom made a revolted frown that did away with the Dale Carnegie demeanor. "That's a drag. I mean, it's great about the baby, but jeez. Let's just say that was not my favorite moment, and it lasted thirty-eight weeks. Maybe you're into it, though. Some guys really are."

Ian had a sudden memory of Tommy clutching his stomach and rolling on the ground in a pastiche of pain after someone had appeared in the locker room brandishing a used tampon in a plastic bag. Ian had envied his show of squeamishness; his sisters had bullied that out of him and enjoined him to be respectful and mature about everything to do with girls' bodies. Now he felt a bubble of mirth in his gut at the prospect of admitting his own discombobulation, for the truth was he couldn't get used to the way Margot looked pregnant. She'd always had pretty limbs which, if anything, had been improved by the layer of extra fat plumping her skin. She was as ripe and glowing as a polished apple; he could feel himself blush Harrison Fordishly when he looked at her. Most remarkably, her former moodiness was miraculously gone, osmosed into the hormone bath that had swept her off to a tranquil, dreamy place from which she gazed out at him as if he were far, far away. He couldn't get used to it. He leaned forward.

"You know what happened once?" Ian said. "I was walking on Fifth Avenue and I saw a woman waving at me from across the street. I cringed for her, waving like that to a stranger. Then I realized she was my wife!"

Tommy nodded. "Yeah, it's weird. And those sonograms! Kay kept looking at the tape, oohing and aahing. I finally asked her how she knew those were our kids. Who's to say they don't show the same tape to everybody?"

"Good point," Ian said. "I never thought of that."

"Kay told me that wasn't funny."

"I'm sure. Margot has no sense of humor about it, either. And every time she has a doctor appointment, she goes into one of the baby shops on Madison Avenue and buys a new outfit. We're going broke dressing someone who doesn't even exist yet!"

Tom leaned back in his chair and fiddled with a pen. "And guess what? It only gets worse. Your marriage is basically over, pal. From now on, you're a meal ticket. You'll walk into the house at night and you'll feel like a stranger. Remember that Talking Heads song where he says, 'This is not my beautiful house, this is not my beautiful wife'? Pretty soon that will *start* making sense!"

Ian got the reference and acknowledged it with the sort of grimace one makes at a pun. Part of him cringed at being drawn into a conversation that was clearly heading in the direction of disloyalty, but another part clamored with relief at the prospect of confession. He hadn't told anybody about his situation. Bill was going to be the first, whenever Ian was finally able to reach him. Yet perhaps it would be better to get advice from someone his own age? He didn't know Tommy, but then again he did; he knew him in the way that one knows childhood friends, a visceral knowing that included habits and proclivities that had since been quashed. He and Tommy knew each other's families, how their houses had smelled, what they ate, and how they treated each other. That had validity, Ian thought. There were truths there that outweighed much of what had happened since. And chances were, he wouldn't see Tommy again anyway; there was no crossover between their lives. He decided to take the risk.

"So what would you do if you met somebody else?"

Tommy laughed. "I've met a lot of other people."

"Someone special, I mean."

There was a pause. Tommy tapped his pen against his palm and glanced at the door through which the woman in the burgundy pantsuit had disappeared. Ian breathed lightly, from the top of his chest. His pulse roared.

"I'd be careful," Tom said without looking up.

"Yeah." Ian felt queasy. He wasn't sure if Tommy was making a confession or offering a warning.

"You have to consider the kids." Now Tommy raised his eyes. "Right?"

Ian nodded. His parents had gotten the first divorce among their crowd, although many others weren't far behind, Tommy's parents included. "Right," he muttered. He wondered briefly if he could convince Tasha to go on as they were, but the thought fluttered from his mind like a leaf, dead and spiraling. It was useless.

Tommy smiled, a salesman again. "So you heard your parents' old house was for sale. Are you really interested, or do you just want to take a look?"

"B," Ian said.

"Hey, why not? You know who lives there, don't you? Wallace Muldoon. Speaking of divorce!"

"You're kidding. Wallace lives there now?"

Ian reached for the phone. "Not for much longer, I guess. I know he'd get a kick out of seeing you. Why don't you have some more coffee while I try to reach him? I'm pretty busy today, but you could go over without me, couldn't you? And if you decide you want to make a bid, you'll call me back."

Before Ian could protest—he usually limited himself to a cup a day—the woman in the burgundy pantsuit appeared and poured refills for them both.

Had snow been in the forecast? Ian hadn't paid attention. All he knew was that while he was in Tom's office the sky whitened, and as he reached his car the windshield was budding fat, wet flakes.

He'd loved Christmas in the Mill Rock Road house. His parents knew how to celebrate, that was for sure. His mother wound strands of ribbon and pine around the bannister and sprayed powdered snow stencils onto the windows. Bill made a big deal out of getting the tree. They sold them at the firehouse, where the volunteer firemen created a festive atmosphere by dressing up in bits and pieces of Santa costumes and roasting chestnuts and marshmallows over old oil barrels filled with fragrant logs.

Everyone knew everyone else, and the kids hurled snowballs and played hide and seek among the merchandise while the parents exchanged last-minute invitations and details of holiday plans. Eventually choices were made and the great, shivering trees were tied to the tops of station wagons for the ride home. See you at church, people called out of frosty windows. See you later at the Flynns'! Trails of warm breath rose like breakaway balloons through the crisp air as dozens of hands—mittens, gloves—waved merry goodbyes. All around the neighborhood lights were draped over bushes and wound around fence posts; at night, the separate plots converged into a single entity and it was impossible to tell where one property ended and the next began. It was all for one and one for all, a charming, glittery place in the universe where the meaning of life was clear, children were safe, and families stayed together.

Ian sighed. He wished he could make himself believe that he'd actually be doing his son a favor by leaving now rather than possibly later, but he knew that was just wishful b.s. He sifted through Tommy's statements again and decided that, taking all factors into consideration, his advice had been to stay with Margot. All right, all right, Ian thought, nodding—who could argue with that? But the comeback was swift and obvious; Tom didn't know Tasha. Ian wasn't sure he could stand to never spend a Christmas with her.

Wallace answered the door and grabbed Ian into a bear hug. Although Ian couldn't have predicted what he'd grow up to look like, he saw Wallace as basically the same, small-eyed and chinless. Now he was heavy and balding but his childhood face shone through. He still looked like trouble for the teacher.

"This is perfect," Wallace bellowed. "Everyone's out. You want a beer?"

Ian pointed to the window. "It's getting slippery out there. I'd better not."

Wallace opened the fridge. "I'm not going anywhere. At least not today." He popped the tab on the can and ran to the sink, cupping the escaping froth. "Not that it matters what I do anymore. Here's to marriage," he toasted sarcastically. "Are you married?"

Ian nodded. "And expecting."

"Then I'll try to spare you my current vitriol." He swigged hard. "Although I can't claim I didn't bring this on myself."

"How?" Ian asked.

"You don't want to know."

"Yeah, I do." Wallowing with Wallace. Why not?

Wallace caught the hint in his tone and squinted more ferociously. "Okay, but let me give you the tour first. All the rooms are pretty much the same . . ."

They were. It was weird. As Ian walked through the house, he was easily able to remember everything, and none of it hurt as much as he'd expected. His initials were still on the rafter and that gave him a buzz, but otherwise, to his chagrin, it was just a house. Once, during college, he'd been in a car that drove nearby, and he'd purposely slept until they were clear of the area. He couldn't stand the idea of seeing it occupied by other people. It was his, his touchstone, the haven of stability and comfort that had formed a needed counterbalance to his parents' troubles. Or so he'd thought. Now he felt an idiot for having made so much of it over the years. Luckily Wallace kept up a constant patter as they moved about so Ian didn't have to say much. He confined his comments to murmurs of appreciation when Wallace indicated pride in a particular corner or room. Ian's old room, for instance, now contained a loft bed with a desk underneath it that Wallace had built himself for his son.

"It has to stay here," Wallace said regretfully. "I can't take it apart. I didn't think I'd have to."

Ian gave his arm a steadying squeeze. "So what happened?" He'd seen enough and was ready to talk.

Wallace shrugged. "I met someone."

Ian knew that, it had been clear from their exchange in the kitchen, but it was still exciting to hear it stated, and so casually. "Oh."

"Oh is right. Come on, let's go into the den. In case they come back."

They clambered downstairs and into what used to be, in Ian's day, a combination play/ironing/guest room, the decor muddled and in flux. It occurred to him now that it was the room that reflected the true state of his family, as opposed to the show of propriety put forth by the dining room or the pretension of the living room. He closed his eyes for a moment and remembered it; how clear it had been for anyone willing to look at the clues that his mother had been on her way out the door for a long time before she finally left. There'd been travel brochures and fashion magazines in piles along the wainscoting, all wizened from handling. He wondered what nook of the apartment showed his state of mind but he couldn't place anything in particular. He thought he was too close to see himself clearly; he was in it too deep.

"I'm going to miss this room," Wallace said.

Ian cast a glance around. The space was a pastiche of masculinity, complete with a Foosball table and a mounted collection of beer coasters. It depressed him, but he welcomed that sensation. It fit with the snow and his worries. Wallace pointed him to a beat-up old leather armchair; he couldn't remember when he'd felt as physically comfortable. To complete the picture, Wallace lit up a cigar.

"You mind if I take a nap?" Ian joked.

"It's good, eh? I call it my home away from home at home. I'll be sorry to leave this, too."

"So—are you going to be with your friend?" Ian was amazed his voice didn't crack like a kid's.

"Funny you should ask that. That's the million-dollar question in my mind. What happened was, my wife found out and raised hell and made appointments with shrinks and all this crap, so I broke it off with Susan. I bought into the whole thing of owing the marriage a second chance; that sounded reasonable. I mean, we've got three kids. Then my wife says she just can't get over it and never will and wants a divorce. So I call Susan but she says it's too late—how could she ever trust me again?"

"Wow."

"I know. I mean it would be funny if it weren't so fucking frustrating."

Ian shuddered. It wasn't funny. He could picture the scenario all too well. "So what are you going to do?"

"Well, we have to sell this place. She's going to get a smaller house and I'm moving to an apartment in Philadelphia. I want to get a loft, you know? I'd have room for when the kids come over, and for some partying, too."

"Isn't it hard to live here now?"

Wallace gave a gruesome laugh. "It's sick is what it is. It doesn't help with Susan, either. But all our money—of which there isn't any, anyway—it's all frozen. I can't move out. I can't do anything. They say marriage is a trap, but it's nothing compared to this!"

Ian nodded. What could he say?

"The worst part is, I have no one to blame but myself. I wanted to be with Susan, but I was too fucking chicken to do it when I had the chance. Now it's looking like I never will."

Suddenly Ian felt like laughing. The conversation was absurdly apropos. Who am I, he thought, Ebenezer Scrooge, being haunted? The reference brought him back to images of Christmas, and again he felt the tears rise. Wallace switched the subject to Ian, but Ian focused on work and anecdotes rather than telling his story. He didn't know how it ended yet.

That night he woke up with a swollen heart. It was only one o'clock but he dressed and went out to the lobby to stave off the stabbing thoughts that were liable to come in the dark. No one else was up, and the building was swathed in the quiet that fell after snow. Ian walked to the shelf of books in the front parlor. A handwritten index card—an attempt at calligraphy—instructed guests to take or leave the volumes as they wished. His eyes lit on a collection of Fitzgerald; perfect. He reached for it greedily, looking forward to having his own mood of regret and longing put into words. "Winter Dreams," he thought, or maybe even "Babylon Revisited," which always made his throat constrict. This was good—a familiar route to help him toward an unknown destination. He didn't kid himself that there weren't other people who knew how he was feeling, but F. Scott could put it into words.

After settling himself, however, on a rather scratchy sofa, he began to probe the image on the dust jacket; he realized it was the same edition his father had kept on his bedside table when Ian was a small boy. The lamp nearby cast a comfortable light on the text, but the words of even his favorite stories blurred under the pressure of his driving thoughts. It was not the first time that he'd felt so alone, but always before he'd assumed the extremity of the feeling was temporary. Now he felt utterly desolate, hopeless. His former methods of staying tough and impenetrable seemed to have forsaken him; as if wanting to get away from himself, he sprang off the sofa and began to pace.

Absentmindedly he wove a path in and out of the furniture until he ended up by the pay phone in the foyer. Of course; he'd been headed toward a telephone all along. As he lifted the receiver, it occurred to him that in spite of her instructions not to call until he'd made a choice, on some level Tasha was waiting for him to call, and that she would see it as a strength rather than a weakness when he finally did. He thought of her face as it looked in an attitude of pleasure and how thoroughly it moved him to be a source of happiness for her. She made him feel ten feet tall. Even in his current anguish the memory of her voice stood out from his own internal chatter, and he heard again her remonstrations.

"You'll be alive and I'll be alive but we won't be married to each other?"

She was right; it was nuts. He knew the shape of her telephone number by heart and pressed it without looking at the buttons, thereby feeling a sense of dominion over the mechanics of the situation that translated, for a heady moment, into a belief that he was doing the right thing. But when the telephone began to ring . . . he couldn't call Tasha. Hadn't his sisters taught him years earlier to assume that no meant no? As he replaced the receiver in its cradle he thought he heard her voice, and her hopeful tone filled him with a remorse that literally doubled him over. When he could breathe again, he walked outside.

The moon lit the frosted cars in the parking lot as efficiently as a series of lamps. He crossed the street and followed the path by the riverbank. The snow had mostly melted, although there was still some in strips along the branches and held in clumps of downed leaves. Out of a childhood habit, he skidded down the bank to examine a beaver dam and was gratified to see it studded with the same brands of candy wrappers he remembered from twenty years earlier. The bits of foil and aluminum bottle caps that littered the silt bottom shone a precious light up toward the sky. He and Tasha had often spoken about how deeply they appreciated the natural world, and he'd said she was all of nature to him. It was true; no matter how hard he fought it, she was present in these lacy branches, this spongy earth. She was a part of his life, a presence. If that made him a terrible person, he'd have to live with it.

He went back to the lobby and pressed Bill's number.

"Dad?"

"Ian! I just walked in. What are you doing up? I thought you kept bankers' hours."

"I have to ask your advice."

"Shoot, son."

"I will. But first—guess where I went today. Mill Rock Road."

"Do I need a beer to hear about this? I think so. Hold on a minute." There was a pause, then all the noises of a flip top being ripped away. "Okay. Here I am. So how was the place?"

"Chilly."

"Those old houses are always chilly at this time of year. The damp seeps right through the walls."

"I saw my initials still carved in the attic."

"How about the trees? How big is the lilac now?"

"I didn't notice."

"I planted that for your mother on the anniversary of our first full year in the house. In those days, it was all she asked for, if you can believe it!"

Ian felt a rush of embarrassment, as if he were responsible for his mother's descent into materialism. "I'm sorry, Dad."

"How is she, anyway?"

"Fine. As always."

"Looking forward to her next grandchild?"

"I think so. She says she is."

Bill sighed. "She loves babies. Count yourself lucky. I'm sure she'll come over whenever you want, to baby-sit so you and Margot can get some time alone to remember why you liked each other. We didn't have that. Our families lived too far away."

"Is that what happened? You forgot how you felt in the beginning?" Ian felt himself grasping and angling toward his confession, his plea for help.

"Oh, I don't know. It was a long time ago, son."

"But you must still think about it."

"Not if I can help it."

"Really?"

"Really. As a matter of fact, let's change the subject right now. Tell me about the house," he said.

"Wait, Dad—" Ian was trying to figure out a way to launch into his Tasha story when he had a sudden image of Margot wearing his sweatshirt. When he'd spoken to her earlier, she said it was hard for her to sleep without him; maybe she was awake now? Maybe he should get in the car and go home early to surprise her. Before Tasha, he would have done that.

"Ian? Are you there?"

"I'm here, Dad."

"It must have been hard, eh? I mean, I couldn't go back there. Not if you paid me."

"Yes, you could," Ian said automatically. Then he winced and wished he could take it back. Who was he to say what Bill could or could not handle? Bill had bought that house. It had been his life, his marriage that went wrong there. Ian cleared his throat. "And someone *is* paying me," he said, hoping he sounded light. "I'm on a beeswax trip. The trip to the house was a tax deduction."

They laughed. "Okay," Bill went along with the joke. "Maybe if I got paid enough." There was a pause. "So what did you want to ask me?"

"Never mind. I think I figured it out."

"Are you sure?"

"No!" Ian laughed. "But I will be. I think it's something I have to deal with on my own."

"Fine. So back to the house . . ."

Ian wound the phone cord around his finger. "Dad? I'm kind of tired. Can I call you tomorrow?"

"I'm not going anywhere."

"I'll call you."

Back in his room, Ian got into bed and pulled the covers up. It was so dark he saw nothing even with his eyes wide open.

"I need a sign," he said aloud, but it didn't work any magic. The room was still and silent, absent of even the whisper of a passing car.

PETER HO DAVIES

Small World

Is it cheating? Wilson asks himself, watching her sprinkle salt on the bridge of skin between her thumb and index finger. Is it cheating to sleep with an ex-girlfriend? The question forms slowly, hangs there. He's been drinking all night. *They've* been drinking all night. First the grown-up drinks: martinis before dinner, a nice merlot with, a cognac after. And now, at the bar, shots. Against the cold, she says, nodding at the snow falling past the neon lattice of a Guinness sign in the window. For old times' sake.

He takes the salt shaker from her and makes a small pile of crystals on his own hand. Stray grains bounce and scatter on the bar. She lowers her head, glances up at him from under her brows, and he dips his own face, reaches out his tongue, draws it through the salt.

He is aware of her head tipping back beside him as he throws his own shot down.

Well, is it? he asks himself, eyes watering. With an ex?

He supposes so. Technically. But surely, the casuist inside him, the Jesuit schoolboy, wonders, surely there's some dispensation. After all, it's not someone new. It's someone old. Someone who pre-dates your wife. Someone you've cheated on already (so you owe her) or who's cheated on you (so you're owed). Not cheated on in the conventional sense, maybe, while you were still together, a couple, an *item*, but cheated on in a primordial sense. That moment of guilt, of memory, of *comparison* between the last fuck and the latest.

He bites down on the lime.

That moment.

He blinks the tears from his eyes, and sees she is laughing at him.

"You used to be a better drinker," she says. There's a rime of salt on her lower lip, and in reflex he licks his own.

"Out of practice," he tells her, but not why. Apart from rare nights sitting up alone in front of the tube with a glass of Bushmills, he's sworn off, to make it easier for his wife to go without during her pregnancy.

"A regular churchgoer," she teases, but he shakes his head. "You infidel."

In the Back Bay everything has changed. The Big Dig seems to have buried everything Wilson remembers. On Atlantic he doesn't recognize any of the stores. Near Fenway a bar he thought he recalled going to with his father is a sub shop. He's in actuarial research, an underwriter of new risks—next-generation chips, satellites, freak weather patterns—attending a conference on risk assessment at BU. When he tries to take two Berkeley mathematicians to dinner, nothing is where it's supposed to be. "I thought you grew up here," one of them says, laughing, and he tells them sharply, "Somerville. Not Boston." Finally, freezing, they go to the Pru, to the Top of the Hub, like any fucking tourists. And so he sits there, surrounded by the conference crowd, looking down on the city he grew up in. He can see the John Hancock building, the light on top red for snow. He can see the Citgo sign. He can see the river. He looks down on his childhood from behind double glazing.

Later, at the hotel, he calls his wife. He wants the reassurance of talking to someone who knows him. But she's not home yet. It's eight o'clock in California. She's in patent law, and he remembers she planned to work late while he was away. He calls her office, but she's not there either. In transit, then.

Bored, he glances at the price list for the minibar, flicks through the phone book. On a whim he looks for his own name. There it is, a string of them, like a list of descendants, but none of the initials are his, or his father's. The last memory he has of Somerville is the family kitchen, in '76. He'd known it was coming, and he was ready for them with his anger. His mother told him the divorce wouldn't change the way they felt about him: "We both still love you just the same." His father nodded, but Wilson said he didn't believe it. "You used to say you loved each other," he sneered. She tried to explain that it was different, what they felt for him and what they felt for each other, but he told her, "It's love, isn't it? It's all love." And something about the way he said it, how he looked at her, the bitterness, the anger, as if it were her fault that she was being cheated on, reduced her to tears for the first time in the whole sorry business. She jerked back from the table and went up to her bedroom—hers alone now—not wanting his father to see her tears. And they'd been left alone, he and his old man, who hadn't been home for a week, who was only there now for this last family meeting.

"Now look what you've done," his father said, and Wilson laughed bitterly. Slowly, ruefully, his dad smiled too, recognizing that he'd lost the power to make his son feel guilty. Because Wilson didn't feel guilty—not then, at least, although later guilt would be almost all he felt—just frustrated. It wasn't that he thought his mother was lying. He didn't distrust her, or even his father, when they said they loved him. He simply didn't trust their capacity for love, which was even worse.

"What can I say?" his father asked, but Wilson just looked away. His father got up, poured himself a shot, said, "Listen," and told Wilson about his birth. How Wilson had been a preemie, how the doctors had put him in the ICN, in an incubator, and his parents had watched him through a plate glass window, his mother from a wheelchair. "You were a marvel," his father said. "So small. So pink. Curled up, with your tiny fists to your chest."

"Spare me," Wilson said, but his father pushed on.

"We loved you that much. We both felt it—we expected it, of course, but it still surprised us, hey, how intense it was."

He stopped for a moment and glanced at Wilson, who said flatly, "So what?"

"So," his father replied a little roughly, "so afterwards, after we brought you home and we got to thinking about how much we loved you, we realized that what we'd felt before, what we thought was love, for each other, it wasn't the same thing."

He paused, and Wilson looked over and saw that he was staring at him.

"Does that explain it any better?"

And Wilson nodded, unable to speak, because it did; he did understand. He understood that his parents loved him and he understood that he'd driven them apart.

He tries his wife again, punching in the calling-card numbers deliberately, but hangs up before the machine cuts in. In the phone book, he looks for old friends. Dick Keane. Ryan Lynch. No listings. Dan Murphy could be any one of a dozen D. Murphys. The thought of calling them all makes Wilson feel tired. Dan, he thinks. Got Angela Quinn, the redhead, pregnant at sixteen, married her, dropped out. He looks for a listing of D. and A. Murphy. Nothing. Even the high school dropouts are gone. And because he has given up hope, he looks idly, flicking through the pages, just trying to remember names and faces. That's how he finds Joyce's name. J. Limerick. It has to be her. Joyce, he thinks. Still going by her own name. Limerick. He writes the number down, the hotel pen on the hotel pad. He'll never use it, after all. After all these years. He remembers getting her old number, the first time. The piece of paper he kept it on, soft and fuzzy from being folded and unfolded, tucked in a wallet for years, long after he'd moved away, long after he could have still called her.

And in the middle of it all the phone rings, as if he's willed it, and he jumps because he doesn't believe in such things.

"Hello?" he says.

"Hello yourself," his wife says.

She asks him what he's doing and he tells her, "Nothing. Debating whether to break into my minibar."

"Too sad," she says. "You don't want to be drinking alone."

"Vodka, Scotch, tiny tequilas. That's pretty good company. A whole miniature world of booze."

"Not to mention those ten-dollar macadamias," she says. "Whoever invented those things must have made a killing."

"Unless the legend is true and they were once free," he tells her. "Now all that's left is the vestigial free mint on the pillow."

She laughs with relief. They've fought. She didn't want him to take this trip. So now she says she loves him. "We miss you." And it takes him a moment to understand she means herself and the baby. She asks him to hold on a second, and the line goes quiet. He wonders where she's gone, and then she's back. "Could you hear her?" And he realizes she's been holding the phone to her belly. "Say something," she tells him, and the line goes quiet again. "Like what?" he asks. "Hello?" And then he falls silent, listening. He imagines her lying back on the sofa, dress unbuttoned, pressing the receiver to her stomach, round as a globe. It reminds him of the nurse running the ultrasound wand over her gooseflesh, the sonar pulse of the baby's heart and the grainy pixelled image he keeps in his wallet of the tucked, clenched form, a smudged question mark curled inside her. All he can hear now, very faintly, is the sea, waves, like in a shell. He thinks it's the rubbing of the plastic on his wife's belly, the tiny slap and suck of her skin.

Afterward he sits in bed, chewing his chocolate mint, reading *What to Expect When You're Expecting*. The compressor of the minibar cuts out with a shiver of glass.

His wife is in her third trimester, and they haven't had sex in a long time. At first he was too protective of her, then she was too sick in the mornings, now she's just too big. It's uncomfortable, impossible. When he's in the mood, she fears for the baby. When he's not, she says he doesn't find her attractive anymore. He tells her she's paranoid; she tells him he missed his chance.

Instead, he's taken to masturbating, for the first time in years, in the shower or when she goes out for groceries. The A&P has never sounded so sexy to him. It makes him feel furtive, caught halfway between infidelity and adolescence, by turns ashamed and angry. Tonight, still on West Coast time, he can't sleep, touches himself, stops. He realizes with dismay that he misses the risk of being caught, wants her to catch him. At least, he tells himself, he doesn't do it to images of her. But when he finally sleeps he dreams of sex with her on top, her hard, heavy belly held over him, pinning him down, forcing the air from his chest, and when he wakes it is on the verge of a wet dream. He stumbles into the arctic whiteness of the bathroom, squinting against the fluorescent glare of his own reflection. In the morning, before he leaves, he puts the piece of hotel notepaper with the phone number in his pocket.

He carries it around all day at the conference. At lunch he tells the mathematicians from the night before, trying to sound casual but trying to prove he's *from* here, and regrets it at once. They give him shit, and it's like being back in high school. For dinner they want to go to the Bull and Finch and he blows them off, thinking, *Geeks!* Instead, he drives his rental car along the river: Storrow to the Longfellow Bridge with its salt-and-pepper pots, Mem. Drive, Mass. Ave to Central, Harvard Square, and finally to Johnny D's in Davis Square. After he parks he just walks for a while, slipping in the snow, until it feels like the roads are the same, the sidewalks, the gradients. He sees the streets of chainlink fences. He sees the statues of the Virgin in every third yard. Mary on the half-shell, he remembers, grinning. Slummerville. It's coming back. He returns to the bar. Orders a beer. Asks for the phone.

She must think he's one of those telesales people, but then he says his name and there's a pause and her voice changes. "What a coincidence," she says; she just moved back to town six months ago. Afterward, waiting for her, he mouths the words to himself: What a coincidence. Small world. What's that line? he asks himself. In a big enough universe, anything can happen. And in a small enough world, he thinks. Something about the odds of it, he decides, the odds of his being here, of her still being in town, of its really being her, makes it feel implacably innocent—not like a choice, more like an accident of fate.

She teaches at the high school now, Joyce. "Substitute," she says, "but they say it'll be permanent in the spring." Her husband's a consultant for an educational software firm. He visits schools and colleges all over the country to give presentations. "This week St. Louis, I think." Wilson says he's in insurance but doesn't want her to think he's a claims adjuster.

"I was never very good with numbers," she reminds him, but he tries to tell her that what he does isn't traditional insurance: writing policies for cars, houses, even lives is just accounting, but with new ventures there aren't any statistics. "Risk assessment isn't even about numbers, really," he says. "It doesn't matter if the chance of a car wreck is a million times higher than the probability of a radiation leak. People want to take their own risks, not have others impose them. Plus it's not the size of the risk that counts, it's the size of the consequences. The chance of getting caught might be vanishing, but if the penalty is bad enough, it changes the equation."

She tells him, "It all sounds very Catholic," and he lets it drop.

They make light, competitive small talk over dinner. Who remembers what. SAT scores. Colleges. Catching up with each other. Her honeymoon was on St. Barts. His handicap is fifteen. Her husband's is twelve. "One to me," she laughs, licking her finger and drawing a line in the air. She has three kids—three!—she says; six, five, and two; boy, girl, boy. "Wow," he responds.

"You wouldn't be so wowed if you had any yourself, I'm thinking?" she says, and he smiles and looks in his drink and slowly shakes his head.

"Okay, okay," he says. "You win. Game over."

She tells him she'll drink to that, and after a moment she asks after his parents and he after hers, and it doesn't seem odd to him that these are their common points of reference.

He dated her while his parents' marriage fell apart. Back then, in their Irish Catholic enclave (not quite a neighborhood, but a kind of satellite, a moon of Southie, the main Irish community), he was the first kid he knew whose parents were divorcing. It made him feel watched, the worst thing for a fifteen-year-old. He felt as if he were on a cliff, on the edge of something, feeling that pressure at the back of his knees to jump before he fell. So he broke a few windows, got in some fights, drank. Tried to cut a tragic figure by wearing black and listening to the Clash. And people—kids, their parents—shook their heads but let him get away with it, made allowances. Joyce was the only one who wouldn't tolerate him. She was in all honors classes, he in math only. When he made fun of her last name—"There once was a girl from Nantucket"—she came right back: "Who told some chickenshit to shut it." He called her *cunt* and she told him, "Using your parents as an excuse *is* chickenshit." Everyone else's gentle sympathy made him want to smash things; her frankness just made him want to talk. So he told her about his parents. And she was by turns curious, sad, outraged in ways that magnified his feelings. He told her he loved her, and it was such a relief to have someone to say it to. He even nursed a fantasy that his love for her could somehow inspire his parents. He touched her constantly in front of them, even though it made her squirm with embarrassment. Always an arm around her, holding hands, thigh to thigh. But his parents ignored them or, worse, seemed goaded to fight in front of her, until she insisted he spend more time at her place.

Joyce's parents, Mike and Moira, must have known about his home life, but they never talked about it, not a word, just welcomed him, treated him as if his being there every evening and all weekend were entirely normal. He became a fixture, ate with them, watched TV, took his turn washing up when Moira handed him a dishtowel, even went to church with them. Mike had been wary of Wilson at first, his reputation as a bad kid. Early on he'd taken him down to the basement, shown him his shotgun, his rifle, as if to say, *You're not so tough.* But Wilson's eyes had just lit up at the sight of the guns, their oily sheen. Besides, he knew Mike liked him. Joyce was the eldest of three girls, and Wilson figured her father enjoyed having a boy around (if only because he preferred to think of Wilson as a brother rather than a boyfriend to Joyce). It made him feel the value of being a son again, even as he felt guilty for cheating on his own parents.

One weekend when Joyce was down with the flu, Wilson looked so lost that Mike even invited him hunting. "Really?" "Sure," Mike said, although he had Moira call Wilson's mother for permission. "Hunting in New Hampster?" Joyce croaked, when Wilson was allowed to see her. "I know you don't want to turn into your dad. Just don't go turning into mine."

It was Wilson's first time, but he didn't admit it until Mike had parked the station wagon and they'd waded out into the snowy woods, for fear the trip would be canceled. Mike stopped in his tracks. "Your dad never took you?" he said, and then fell silent, embarrassed to have mentioned the unmentionable and for seeming to criticize. Wilson told him it was okay, but Mike was subdued all morning. At lunch he tried clumsily to apologize: "I could kick myself." Wilson, in trying to make him feel better, found himself talking about his parents. And once he began, unable to stop. Something about the woods, the cold, the guns beside them, the crouched anticipation of a deer, made him voluble. He even told Mike a dream he'd had of flicking through an old family photo album from back to front, seeing himself and his parents as they were now and then, as the pages turned, getting younger and younger. His father's hairline, his mother's hemline. Wilson himself playing with lost, broken toys, miraculously found and restored. Dropping to all fours, crawling, finally lifted up into their arms. "And in each photo they look happier and happier until in the very last, at the front of the book, they look as happy as I've ever seen them. And I'm gone."

He looked up and saw Mike staring at his hands, rotating the wedding ring on his finger. Wilson thought he was boring him, but then he saw him blinking, wiping his eyes. "The cold," Mike said when he saw Wilson staring, and Wilson looked away. He heard Mike pop a beer and in a moment felt the can being tapped against his arm.

"It's a mess, all right," Mike said, watching him drink. "But your folks, I'm sure they love you." And because it sounded like sympathy, because it sounded like a line of his parents', because he didn't want Mike to feel bad for him, Wilson said, "Fuck 'em." He meant it to be light, joky, a daring thing to say in front of an adult. But it didn't come out right. The coldness of the beer made him sound choked. There was a long pause, and then, as if in return, Mike told him how he'd met Moira, both of them in high school. "Married at seventeen, parents at eighteen." He shook his head. "We had no idea," he said. And Wilson nodded, overcome by this confidence and something more. Because wasn't that like him and Joyce? he thought. Wasn't that them? In high school. In love. "You understand, don't you?" her father was saying. And Wilson thought he did.

The week after, drunk on stolen whiskey, in bed with Joyce for the first time—Mike, Moira, and the girls out at the mall—they held each other, almost but not quite slept together. It was wonderful, clinging together on the brink of sex, and yet they never came as close again. A week later she told him it was over. And though he called and called, her phone just rang until Mike picked it up and stiffly told him not to call again. "Sorry, son," he said, while Wilson pleaded and cursed. "Sorry." A month later, Wilson and his mother were gone, first to his grandparents and then west.

So he and Joyce, over dinner and drinks, talk about their parents and not themselves.

Wilson's mother is remarried, he tells her, living in Lauderdale. His father is on Long Island with the latest in a string of girlfriends: the secretary he left Wilson's mother for; a waitress; now a nurse. "There are three things in every man's life he can be sure of," Wilson tells her in his father's voice. "Death, taxes, and a nurse." He shakes his head. "The nurse was his date at our wedding," he says. The funny thing, he tells her now, is that when he saw the wedding cake with its plastic bride and groom, he could think only of his parents, of their old wedding photo on the sideboard. He is silent a moment. After a second he asks about her folks, and she suggests the shots.

Her parents, she tells him at the bar, the drinks lined up before them, are splitting up, and it takes him a moment to realize she's serious. He feels himself groping for some fact, and she gives it to him. "Thirty-four years," she says, "they've been together. He's fifty-two and she's fifty-one." Wilson shakes his head as if to clear it. He feels something at the back of his throat, filling his chest. It's sorrow for her. He can feel his eyes prickling, and he blinks hard. He knows it's the drink, he knows it's nostalgia, some mutated self-pity, but still. She consoled him all those years ago, and now he leans in close, asks her how she's doing, and she gives a short laugh. She's been better. It's been bad. "I couldn't make sense of it for a long time. I wanted to punish them. I even threatened to stop them visiting their grandkids." She snaps a shot back and purses her lips. "I kept asking why, you know, why *bother*, and my mother got so angry. She's met someone else. She told me the way I looked at her it was as if her life was over, as if she couldn't change it." She pauses while the bartender fills their glasses. "And then I realized I was just angry at them. They're being so selfish. I kept thinking, what about me?"

"Well, what about you?" he says, and he takes her hand, and she lets him, but she says, "No. It's not like it was for you. You were a kid. I'm a grownup. I'm a mother, for crying out loud. It's not a tragedy. It's not the end of the world, really. How're you supposed to feel? I always thought you got through your teens and your parents were still together and you were safe somehow." She takes another shot and he matches her.

"Cheers," he says.

"Actually, you know how I feel?" she asks, her voice thick. "You really want to know?"

He tells her yes.

"I feel ridiculous." She is crying, and he puts his arm around her as she wipes the tears away and says again, "Ridiculous." She lays her head on his shoulder, and he worries for a moment that someone might catch them. But then he realizes there's no one left in his home town who knows him. No one except her. He smells her hair, and crazily, it's the same as sixteen years ago. He thinks of that time in bed. Touching her. It was the only time they were naked together. He remembers thinking how wonderful that was, to be naked with her, and how they had so much time, how they could wait for sex. He doesn't think either of them came that afternoon. They fell asleep, exhausted by desire, and woke in a panic to the sound of a door slamming downstairs. They dragged their clothes on like characters in a French farce, and he remembers almost laughing, not because it was funny but because he knew it would be, knew that they'd look back on it and it would be part of their history and they'd find it hysterical. *Do you remember when?* He was relieved that it was only her mother when they sauntered downstairs. He felt cocky, could hardly hide his grin, but she seemed preoccupied, too confused to notice. Mike had forgotten something at the store. If it had been him, Wilson thinks, he would have seen right through them.

Joyce excuses herself to go to the bathroom, and while she's away he thinks about reminding her of the story now, seeing if they can laugh about it, but he doesn't. He remembers something else. For two years afterward, until he lost his virginity freshman year of college, he had thought of that moment, masturbated to it, remained faithful to her.

When she comes back, she is weaving slightly.

"Boy," she says. "Get me out of here before someone sees me like this."

In the car outside the bar, he kisses her. It makes her laugh, and then she kisses him back. She tastes the same too, and the memory is sharp. "Shall we drive somewhere?" she asks. Her house is close—just a few blocks from her old home—but she doesn't want to go back like this. Mike still lives at the old place—she moved back, in fact, to be close to him—and he's sitting for her. Wilson's a little unsteady himself, wants to park, and without thinking about it does something they never did but he always wished they had. He drives them to the outskirts of town, to a small deserted lookout over Fresh Pond, the local lovers' lane. The dark water is frozen. They recline the seats. There's something about the childishness of it, the nostalgia of it, the ridiculousness—he catches one of his belt loops on the hand brake, she pushes the cigarette lighter in with her toe—that makes it seem less serious, not like faithlessness, not like betrayal, not like sex, at least not until it's over and the car windows are fogged and they pull their clothes on again. Or perhaps having started, neither of them has the heart to stop.

Afterward, they sit side by side, staring at the snow melting on the windshield. Her hair clip rests on the dash where she must have tossed it, the long curving teeth interlocked, like the fingers of folded hands. He holds the steering wheel and tries not to think. There is a hollow feeling in his stomach. He recognizes this. It's a tendency he has to make a bad thing worse, to tip accident into tragedy, jump before the fall. Every so often a breeze stirs the trees above them and a sudden shower of snow thumps hollowly onto the roof. Finally she says, "Well, that's one way to sober up." She needs to get back to her kids, and he starts the engine.

On the way, he says, "Unfinished business," and she says, "Yes," and what they both know is that it isn't unfinished anymore.

At her place she sits beside him for a few moments before going in. Wilson tells her he hopes it all works out. She nods. "The worst of it . . ." she says after a second. "The worst of it is that I always wondered about my parents. You know, when we were kids. I wondered about them, worried about them splitting up. They fought. A lot. When I was very young. Less when my sisters came along, but still sometimes with real hatred. It's one of the reasons I was drawn to you, I suppose. To see how bad it was. Only now," she says, "I wonder if they stayed together for us, my sisters and me. If we kept them together." She pulls her coat around her. "I guess it's not ridiculous I feel. It's guilty."

She looks across at him and he shakes his head.

"Parents," he says.

"And now I am one." She picks up her bag from between her feet, finds her keys. "If you don't want to turn into your parents, don't have kids, right?"

Cars shush past them on the pale street, snow piled on their roofs, six, eight, ten inches deep, like white luggage.

"Hey," he says quickly. "You know, I've always meant to ask." He actually blushes. "About us, what happened."

She plumps the bag on her lap, tells him she can hardly remember. "There was a fight. My mother and me. She thought you were dangerous, thought I'd get pregnant."

"What about your dad?"

"Stayed out of it, but then he always let her do the dirty work." She shrugs. "I told them I loved you"—and hearing her say it still gives him a strange thrill—"but even as I said it, I knew it wasn't true. In love with something, maybe. In love with love, but not each other."

Wilson lets it go. He isn't so sure, but he lets it go, and besides, they've had sex and it hasn't changed anything after all these years. He can still hear them when they lay together, him telling her he loved her, her telling him back. "We're so unoriginal," he'd said, and they had laughed.

She looks tired, exhausted.

"I've made things worse," he says, but she waves him off. "Just not better, huh?"

"You know," she says, looking at him sideways, "you don't have to compare everything. Your wife, me, our parents. Not everything's comparable."

"Right," he says.

"I'm happy," she says. "In my marriage. With my children. Really." He's quiet.

"Children don't fuck up marriages," she says. "Grownups do. You didn't fuck up your parents' marriage. Just don't fuck up your own."

"That's a little ironic," he says.

"And you're a shit to say so."

"She's pregnant," he tells her back, and she stares at him for a long beat.

"Motherfucker," she whispers.

There's a moment of stillness—the engine ticks off slow seconds—and then they both burst out laughing, fall against each other, shaking.

"You've never done this before," she says when she catches her breath. "Have you?"

He wipes his eyes, shrugs.

"Well, take it from me, it's not the end of the world. Sex isn't the only thing holding you together. Some people fight more when they have kids. You know why? Because they can."

She leans over and kisses him chastely on the cheek. So that's it, Wilson thinks. It occurs to him that he has been looking for some kind of out, but now he knows he's going to have to carry this night, swollen as he feels with it, forever.

"Hey," she says suddenly, one foot already on the snowy sidewalk. "Could you do me a favor? Would you take Dad home? He usually walks, but you know, on a night like this . . . And I'm not really up for driving him myself."

"Okay. Sure," Wilson says. "If you think it's a good idea."

"Just don't tell him we fooled around."

"I wasn't planning on it. So long as he doesn't bring it up."

"That's settled, then." She opens her door fully, and a snowy gust sweeps into the car. "I won't invite you in. You'd just get cold, and a new face'll excite the kids if they're still up. Wait here and I'll send him out in a sec."

Wilson watches her go, but she doesn't turn back. He shivers in the lingering draft and then sniffs the air, rolls the windows down one by one, then up again. He sees Mike come out and flashes his headlights.

"Evening," the older man says, climbing in. His hair is fine and silvery blond, almost like a child's, and his heavy, lined face is raw from the cold or drink, Wilson can't tell which.

"How've you been keeping?"

"Can't complain," Mike says, buckling up. "Course, seeing you doesn't make me feel any younger."

"You're looking great," Wilson tells him.

"Yeah? Joyce said you'd turned out a charmer."

There's an awkward silence, and Wilson pulls away from the curb too quickly. He feels a momentary panic as the car fishtails in the fresh snow. Mike grasps his door handle and Wilson says, "Sorry." It reminds him of a statistical anomaly, and in his nervousness he starts on a story about how in some countries the accident rates increase after seatbelts are made compulsory. The theory being that people feel safer and therefore drive more recklessly. "No kidding?" Mike says. "There's even a proposal," Wilson tells him, wondering what his point is but pressing on, "a thought experiment really, suggesting that accident rates would drop if we sprayed the roads with ice and stuck sharp metal spikes to every steering column."

"How about that," Mike says, and then, politely, "This handles nice, though," as if the car were Wilson's and not a rental.

"Here we are already," Wilson says, cheerful with relief.

Mike thanks him for the ride. He releases his belt and it slithers over his shoulder. "I'll get the rest of your news from Joycey, I expect."

"It was good to see you again," Wilson says. "And Joyce," he adds after a moment, feeling like he's walking out onto the frozen Charles. But Mike doesn't bat an eyelid.

"You too. She says you've done well for yourself. A kiddie on the way too?"

"Yeah," Wilson says, and then, because something more seems expected, he surprises himself. "You know what worries me? It's crazy. I worry I'm going to treat her like a pet. Love her the way you love a dog or a cat or something."

Mike is looking down, tugging at his knuckles. "If only it were that easy," he says, with a slow grin. He puts a hand on Wilson's forearm and squeezes. "God bless."

Wilson waits until he sees him go inside, worried he'll slip in the snow, and then waits some more. He used to stand on this corner nights, he remembers, after he left them, before he walked back to his own home. He liked to watch the lights go on and off—the hall, the stairs, bathrooms, bedrooms. When he told Joyce once, she said it must look like the end of *The Waltons*. "Goodnight, Pa, goodnight, Ma, goodnight, John Boy." She thought it was funny, but it hurt him. He used to stand there and think about their future.

But now he knows with certainty that it was all already over when he heard that door slam, as they leapt up, struggled into their clothes, covered their nakedness, that it was already over when he thought they'd be laughing about it for years to come, that the door had been slammed too hard, that it wasn't someone coming home but someone in fury leaving. They'd been caught.

He thinks about Mike's face in the woods when he told him how he felt about his own parents' breakup. Mike married at seventeen, a father at eighteen. And it occurs to Wilson that if anyone kept Joyce's parents together, it was him.

He starts the car, begins to trace his way back through the white, familiar streets to his hotel. McGrath to Monsignor O'Brien

Highway. But as he drives, another memory, something so oddly vivid he wonders if he dreamed it, comes back to him. Joyce was already asleep, but he had woken from a drowse, pulled the covers up and over his shoulder, and in doing so glanced at her body beneath them. It was a bright afternoon and the sunlight penetrated the comforter, so he could see her quite clearly. The sheets were rosy, a pastel shade he remembers distinctly because they were more girlish than she usually allowed herself to seem. He watched her for a moment in that warm, pink light, the soft folds surrounding her, watched her chest rising and falling with her breath, listened to her, fancying he could hear her heart—or was it his?—watched her curl into a loose ball, her knees tucked to her chest, her hands loosely cupped beneath her chin, and he was filled with a desire to protect her. And it was that desire, he thinks now, that filling, sweeping desire, that he first called love.

He finds himself driving faster, reckless in the snow, thinking about his wife and his about-to-be-child. She'll be home soon, he calculates. It's almost late enough to call.

The Afterlife

RAYMOND CARVER

Intimacy

I have some business out west anyway, so I stop off in this little town where my former wife lives. We haven't seen each other in four years. But from time to time, when something of mine appeared, or was written about me in the magazines or papers—a profile or an interview—I sent her these things. I don't know what I had in mind except I thought she might be interested. In any case, she never responded.

It is nine in the morning. I haven't called, and it's true I don't know what I am going to find.

But she lets me in. She doesn't seem surprised. We don't shake hands, much less kiss each other. She takes me into the living room. As soon as I sit down she brings me some coffee. Then she comes out with what's on her mind. She says I've caused her anguish, made her feel exposed and humiliated.

Make no mistake, I feel I'm home.

She says, But then you were into betrayal early. You always felt comfortable with betrayal. No, she says, that's not true. Not in the beginning, at any rate. You were different then. But I guess I was different too. Everything was different, she says. No, it was after you turned thirty-five, or thirty-six, whenever it was, around in there anyway, your mid-thirties somewhere, then you started in.

275

You really started in. You turned on me. You did it up pretty then. You must be proud of yourself.

She says, Sometimes I could scream.

She says she wishes I'd forget about the hard times, the bad times, when I talk about back then. Spend some time on the good times, she says. Weren't there some good times? She wishes I'd get off that other subject. She's bored with it. Sick of hearing about it. Your private hobby horse, she says. What's done is done and water under the bridge, she says. A tragedy, yes. God knows it was a tragedy and then some. But why keep it going? Don't you ever get tired of dredging up that old business?

She says, Let go of the past, for Christ's sake. Those old hurts. You must have some other arrows in your quiver, she says.

She says, You know something? I think you're sick. I think you're crazy as a bedbug. Hey, you don't believe the things they're saying about you, do you? Don't believe them for a minute, she says. Listen, I could tell them a thing or two. Let them talk to me about it, if they want to hear a story.

She says, Are you listening to me?

I'm listening, I say. I'm all ears, I say.

She says, I've really had a bellyful of it, buster! Who asked you here today anyway? I sure as hell didn't. You just show up and walk in. What the hell do you want from me? Blood? You want more blood? I thought you had your fill by now.

She says, Think of me as dead. I want to be left in peace now. That's all I want anymore is to be left in peace and forgotten about. Hey, I'm forty-five years old, she says. Forty-five going on fifty-five, or sixty-five. Lay off, will you.

She says, Why don't you wipe the blackboard clean and see what you have left after that? Why don't you start with a clean slate? See how far that gets you, she says.

She has to laugh at this. I laugh too, but it's nerves.

She says, You know something? I had my chance once, but I let it go. I just let it go. I don't guess I ever told you. But now look at me. Look! Take a good look while you're at it. You threw me away, you son of a bitch.

She says, I was younger then and a better person. Maybe you were too, she says. A better person, I mean. You had to be. You were better then or I wouldn't have had anything to do with you.

She says, I loved you so much once. I loved you to the point of distraction. I did. More than anything in the whole wide world. Imagine that. What a laugh that is now. Can you imagine it? We were so *intimate* once upon a time I can't believe it now. I think that's the strangest thing of all now. The memory of being that intimate with somebody. We were so intimate I could puke. I can't imagine ever being that intimate with somebody else. I haven't been.

She says, Frankly, and I mean this, I want to be kept out of it from here on out. Who do you think you are anyway? You think you're God or somebody? You're not fit to lick God's boots, or anybody else's for that matter. Mister, you've been hanging out with the wrong people. But what do I know? I don't even know what I know any longer. I know I don't like what you've been dishing out. I know that much. You know what I'm talking about, don't you? Am I right?

Right, I say. Right as rain.

She says, You'll agree to anything, won't you? You give in too easy. You always did. You don't have any principles, not one. Anything to avoid a fuss. But that's neither here nor there.

She says, You remember that time I pulled the knife on you?

She says this as if in passing, as if it's not important.

Vaguely, I say. I must have deserved it, but I don't remember much about it. Go ahead, why don't you, and tell me about it.

She says, I'm beginning to understand something now. I think I know why you're here. Yes. I know why you're here, even if you don't. But you're a slyboots. You know why you're here. You're on a fishing expedition. You're hunting for *material*. Am I getting warm? Am I right?

Tell me about the knife, I say.

She says, If you want to know, I'm real sorry I didn't use that knife. I am. I really and truly am. I've thought and thought about it, and I'm sorry I didn't use it. I had the chance. But I hesitated. I hesitated and was lost, as somebody or other said. But I should have used it, the hell with everything and everybody. I should have nicked your arm with it at least. At least that.

Well, you didn't, I say. I thought you were going to cut me with it, but you didn't. I took it away from you.

She says, You were always lucky. You took it away and then you slapped me. Still, I regret I didn't use that knife just a little bit. Even a little would have been something to remember me by.

I remember a lot, I say. I say that, then wish I hadn't.

She says, Amen, brother. That's the bone of contention here, if you hadn't noticed. That's the whole problem. But like I said, in my opinion you remember the wrong things. You remember the low, shameful things. That's why you got interested when I brought up the knife.

She says, I wonder if you ever have any regret. For whatever that's worth on the market these days. Not much, I guess. But you ought to be a specialist in it by now.

Regret, I say. It doesn't interest me much, to tell the truth. Regret is not a word I use very often. I guess I mainly don't have it. I admit I hold to the dark view of things. Sometimes, anyway. But regret? I don't think so.

She says, You're a real son of a bitch, did you know that? A ruthless, coldhearted son of a bitch. Did anybody ever tell you that?

You did, I say. Plenty of times.

She says, I always speak the truth. Even when it hurts. You'll never catch me in a lie.

She says, My eyes were opened a long time ago, but by then it was too late. I had my chance but I let it slide through my fingers. I even thought for a while you'd come back. Why'd I think that anyway? I must have been out of my mind. I could cry my eyes out now, but I wouldn't give you that satisfaction.

She says, You know what? I think if you were on fire right now, if you suddenly burst into flame this minute, I wouldn't throw a bucket of water on you.

She laughs at this. Then her face closes down again.

She says, Why in hell *are* you here? You want to hear some more? I could go on for days. I think I know why you turned up, but I want to hear it from you.

When I don't answer, when I just keep sitting there, she goes on.

She says, After that time, when you went away, nothing much mattered after that. Not the kids, not God, not anything. It was like I didn't know what hit me. It was like I had *stopped living*. My life had been going along, going along, and then it just stopped. It didn't just come to a stop, it screeched to a stop. I thought, If I'm not worth anything to him, well, I'm not worth anything to myself or anybody else either. That was the worst thing I felt. I thought my heart would break. What am I saying? It did break. Of course it broke. It broke, just like that. It's still broke, if you want to know. And so there you have it in a nutshell. My eggs in one basket, she says. A tisket, a tasket. All my rotten eggs in one basket.

She says, You found somebody else for yourself, didn't you? It didn't take long. And you're happy now. That's what they say about you anyway: "He's happy now." Hey, I read everything you send! You think I don't? Listen, I know your heart, mister. I always did. I knew it back then, and I know it now. I know your heart inside and out, and don't you ever forget it. Your heart is a jungle, a dark forest, it's a garbage pail, if you want to know. Let them talk to me if they want to ask somebody something. I know how you operate. Just let them come around here, and I'll give them an earful. I was there. I served, buddy boy. Then you held me up for display and ridicule in your so-called work. For any Tom or Harry to pity or pass judgment on. Ask me if I cared. Ask me if it embarrassed me. Go ahead, ask.

No, I say, I won't ask that. I don't want to get into that, I say.

Damn straight you don't! she says. And you know *why*, too!

She says, Honey, no offense, but sometimes I think I could shoot you and watch you kick.

She says, You can't look me in the eyes, can you?

She says, and this is exactly what she says, You can't even look me in the eyes when I'm talking to you.

So, okay, I look her in the eyes.

She says, Right. Okay, she says. Now we're getting someplace, maybe. That's better. You can tell a lot about the person you're talking to from his eyes. Everybody knows that. But you know something else? There's nobody in this whole world who would tell you this, but I can tell you. I have the right. I *earned* that right, sonny. You have yourself confused with somebody else. And that's the pure truth of it. But what do I know? they'll say in a hundred years. They'll say, Who was she anyway?

She says, In any case, you sure as hell have *me* confused with somebody else. Hey, I don't even have the same name anymore! Not the name I was born with, not the name I lived with you with, not even the name I had two years ago. What is this? What is this in hell all about anyway? Let me say something. I want to be left alone now. Please. That's not a crime.

She says, Don't you have someplace else you should be? Some plane to catch? Shouldn't you be somewhere far from here at this very minute?

No, I say. I say it again: No. No place, I say. I don't have anyplace I have to be.

And then I do something. I reach over and take the sleeve of her blouse between my thumb and forefinger. That's all. I just touch it that way, and then I just bring my hand back. She doesn't draw away. She doesn't move.

Then here's the thing I do next. I get down on my knees, a big guy like me, and I take the hem of her dress. What am I doing on the floor? I wish I could say. But I know it's where I ought to be, and I'm there on my knees holding on to the hem of her dress.

She is still for a minute. But in a minute she says, Hey, it's all right, stupid. You're so dumb, sometimes. Get up now. I'm telling you to get up. Listen, it's okay. I'm over it now. It took me a while to get over it. What do you think? Did you think it wouldn't? Then you walk in here and suddenly the whole cruddy business is back. I felt a need to ventilate. But you know, and I know, it's over and done with now.

She says, For the longest while, honey, I was inconsolable. *Inconsolable,* she says. Put that word in your little notebook. I can tell you from experience that's the saddest word in the English language. Anyway, I got over it finally. Time is a gentleman, a wise man said. Or else maybe a worn-out old woman, one or the other anyway.

She says, I have a life now. It's a different kind of life than yours, but I guess we don't need to compare. It's my life, and that's the important thing I have to realize as I get older. Don't feel *too* bad, anyway, she says. I mean, it's all right to feel a *little* bad, maybe. That won't hurt you, that's only to be expected after all. Even if you can't move yourself to regret.

She says, Now you have to get up and get out of here. My husband will be along pretty soon for his lunch. How would I explain this kind of thing?

It's crazy, but I'm still on my knees holding the hem of her dress. I won't let it go. I'm like a terrier, and it's like I'm stuck to the floor. It's like I can't move.

She says, Get up now. What is it? You still want something from me. What do you want? Want me to forgive you? Is that why you're doing this? That's it, isn't it? That's the reason you came all this way. The knife thing kind of perked you up, too. I think you'd forgotten about that. But you needed me to remind you. Okay, I'll say something if you'll just go.

She says, I forgive you.

She says, Are you satisfied now? Is that better? Are you happy? He's happy now, she says.

But I'm still there, knees to the floor.

She says, Did you hear what I said? You have to go now. Hey, stupid. Honey, I said I forgive you. And I even reminded you about the knife thing. I can't think what else I can do now. You got it made in the shade, baby. Come *on* now, you have to get out of here. Get up. That's right. You're still a big guy, aren't you. Here's your hat, don't forget your hat. You never used to wear a hat. I never in my life saw you in a hat before.

She says, Listen to me now. Look at me. Listen carefully to what I'm going to tell you.

She moves closer. She's about three inches from my face. We haven't been this close in a long time. I take these little breaths that she can't hear, and I wait. I think my heart slows way down, I think.

She says, You just tell it like you have to, I guess, and forget the rest. Like always. You been doing that for so long now anyway it shouldn't be hard for you.

She says, There, I've done it. You're free, aren't you? At least you think you are anyway. Free at last. That's a joke, but don't laugh. Anyway, you feel better, don't you?

She walks with me down the hall.

She says, I can't imagine how I'd explain this if my husband was to walk in this very minute. But who really cares anymore, right? In the final analysis, nobody gives a damn anymore. Besides which, I think everything that can happen that way has already happened. His name is Fred, by the way. He's a decent guy and works hard for his living. He cares for me.

So she walks me to the front door, which has been standing open all this while. The door that was letting in light and fresh air this morning, and sounds off the street, all of which we had ignored. I look outside and, Jesus, there's this white moon hanging in the morning sky. I can't think when I've ever seen anything so remarkable. But I'm afraid to comment on it. I am. I don't know what might happen. I might break into tears even. I might not understand a word I'd say.

She says, Maybe you'll be back sometime, and maybe you won't.

This'll wear off, you know. Pretty soon you'll start feeling bad again. Maybe it'll make a good story, she says. But I don't want to know about it if it does.

I say good-bye. She doesn't say anything more. She looks at her hands, and then she puts them into the pockets of her dress. She shakes her head. She goes back inside, and this time she closes the door.

I move off down the sidewalk. Some kids are tossing a football at the end of the street. But they aren't my kids, and they aren't her kids either. There are these leaves everywhere, even in the gutters. Piles of leaves wherever I look. They're falling off the limbs as I walk. I can't take a step without putting my shoe into leaves. Somebody ought to make an effort here. Somebody ought to get a rake and take care of this.

GRACE PALEY

Wants

I saw my ex-husband in the street. I was sitting on the steps of the new library.

Hello, my life, I said. We had once been married for twenty-seven years, so I felt justified.

He said, What? What life? No life of mine.

I said, O.K. I don't argue when there's real disagreement. I got up and went into the library to see how much I owed them.

The librarian said $32 even and you've owed it for eighteen years. I didn't deny anything. Because I don't understand how time passes. I have had those books. I have often thought of them. The library is only two blocks away.

My ex-husband followed me to the Books Returned desk. He interrupted the librarian, who had more to tell. In many ways, he said, as I look back, I attribute the dissolution of our marriage to the fact that you never invited the Bertrams to dinner.

That's possible, I said. But really, if you remember: first, my father was sick that Friday, then the children were born, then I had those Tuesday-night meetings, then the war began. Then we didn't seem to know them anymore. But you're right. I should have had them to dinner.

I gave the librarian a check for $32. Immediately she trusted me, put my past behind her, wiped the record clean, which is just what most other municipal and/or state bureaucracies will not do.

I checked out the two Edith Wharton books I had just returned because I'd read them so long ago and they are more apropos now than ever. They were *The House of Mirth* and *The Children*, which is about how life in the United States in New York changed in twenty-seven years fifty years ago.

A nice thing I do remember is breakfast, my ex-husband said. I was surprised. All we ever had was coffee. Then I remembered there was a hole in the back of the kitchen closet which opened into the apartment next door. There, they always ate sugar-cured smoked bacon. It gave us a very grand feeling about breakfast, but we never got stuffed and sluggish.

That was when we were poor, I said.

When were we ever rich? he asked.

Oh, as time went on, as our responsibilities increased, we didn't go in need. You took adequate financial care, I reminded him. The children went to camp four weeks a year and in decent ponchos with sleeping bags and boots, just like everyone else. They looked very nice. Our place was warm in winter, and we had nice red pillows and things.

I wanted a sailboat, he said. But you didn't want anything.

Don't be bitter, I said. It's never too late.

No, he said with a great deal of bitterness. I may get a sailboat. As a matter of fact I have money down on an eighteen-foot two-rigger. I'm doing well this year and can look forward to better. But as for you, it's too late. You'll always want nothing.

He had had a habit throughout the twenty-seven years of making a narrow remark which, like a plumber's snake, could work its way through the ear down the throat, halfway to my heart. He would then disappear, leaving me choking with equipment. What I mean is, I sat down on the library steps and he went away.

I looked through *The House of Mirth,* but lost interest. I felt extremely accused. Now, it's true, I'm short of requests and absolute requirements. But I do want *something.*

I want, for instance, to be a different person. I want to be the woman who brings these two books back in two weeks. I want to be the effective citizen who changes the school system and addresses the Board of Estimate on the troubles of this dear urban center.

I *had* promised my children to end the war before they grew up.

I wanted to have been married forever to one person, my ex-husband or my present one. Either has enough character for a whole life, which as it turns out is really not such a long time. You couldn't exhaust either man's qualities or get under the rock of his reasons in one short life.

Just this morning I looked out the window to watch the street for a while and saw that the little sycamores the city had dreamily planted a couple of years before the kids were born had come that day to the prime of their lives.

Well! I decided to bring those two books back to the library. Which proves that when a person or an event comes along to jolt or appraise me I *can* take some appropriate action, although I am better known for my hospitable remarks.

RICHARD FORD

Reunion

When I saw Mack Bolger, he was standing beside the bottom of the marble steps that bring travellers and passersby to and from the balcony of the main concourse in Grand Central. It was before Christmas last year, when the weather stayed so warm and watery the spirit seemed to go out of the season.

I was cutting through the terminal, as I often do on my way home from the publishing offices, on Fifty-first. I was, in fact, on my way to meet a new friend at Billy's. It was four o'clock on Friday, and the great station was athrong with citizens on their way somewhere, laden with baggage and precious packages, shouting goodbyes and greetings, flagging their arms, embracing, gripping each other with pleasure. Others, though, simply stood, as Mack Bolger was when I saw him, staring rather vacantly at the crowds, as if whomever he was there to meet for some reason hadn't come. Mack is a tall, handsome, well-put-together man who seems to see everything from a height. He was wearing a long gabardine over-coat of some deep-olive twill—an expensive coat, I thought, an Italian coat. His brown shoes were polished to a high gloss. His trouser cuffs hit them just right. And because he was without a hat he seemed even taller than what he was—perhaps six three. His hands were in his coat pockets, his smooth chin was slightly elevated, the way a middle-aged man's would be, and as if he thought he was extremely visible there. His hair was thinning a little in front, but it was carefully cut, and he was tanned, which caused his square face and prominent brow to appear heavy, almost artificially so, as though in a peculiar way the man I saw were not Mack Bolger but an effigy situated precisely there to attract my attention.

For a while, a year and a half before, I had been involved with Mack Bolger's wife, Beth Bolger. Oddly enough—only because all events that occur outside New York seem odd and fancifully unreal to New Yorkers—our affair had taken place in the city of St. Louis, that largely overlookable red brick abstraction that is neither West nor Middle West, neither South nor North; the city lost in the middle, as I think of it. I have always found it interesting that it was the home of T. S. Eliot and, only eighty-five years before that, the starting point of Western expansion. It is a place, I suppose, the world can't get away from fast enough.

What went on between Beth Bolger and me is hardly worth the words that would be required to explain it away. At any distance but the close range I saw it from, it was an ordinary adultery—spirited, thrilling, and then, after a brief while, when we had crossed the continent several times and caused as many people as possible unhappiness, embarrassment, and heartache, it became disappointing and ignoble and finally almost disastrous to those same people. Because it is the truth and serves to complicate Mack's unlikable dilemma and to cast him in a more sympathetic light, I will say that at one point he was forced to confront me (and Beth, as well) in a hotel room in St. Louis—a nice, graceful old barn called the Mayfair—with the result that I got banged around in a minor way and sent off into the downtown streets of St. Louis on a warmly humid autumn Sunday afternoon, without the slightest idea of what to do, ending up waiting for hours at the airport for a midnight flight back to New York. Apart from my dignity, I left behind and never saw again a brown silk Hermès scarf with tassels that my mother had given me for Christmas in 1971, a gift she felt was the nicest thing she'd ever seen and perfect for a man just starting life as an editor. I am glad she did not have to know about my losing it, or how it happened.

I also did not see Beth Bolger again, except for one sorrowful and bitter drink we had together in the theatre district last spring, a nervous, uncomfortable meeting we somehow felt obligated to have, and following which I walked away down Forty-seventh Street feeling that all of life was a sorry mess, while Beth went along to see *The Iceman Cometh*, which was playing then. We have not seen each other since that leavetaking, and, as I said, to tell more would not be quite worth the words.

But when I saw Mack Bolger standing in the great, crowded, holiday-bedecked concourse of Grand Central, looking rather vacant-headed but clearly himself, so far from the middle of the country, I was taken by a sudden, strange impulse—which was to walk straight across through the eddying currents of travellers and speak to him, just as you might speak to anyone you casually knew and had unexpectedly but not unhappily encountered. And not to impart anything, or to set in motion any particular action (to clarify history, for instance, or make amends), but just to speak and create an event where before there was none. And not an unpleasant event, or a provocative one. Just a dimensionless, unreverberant moment, a contact, unimportant in every other way. Life has few enough of these moments—the rest of it being involved so completely in the predictable and the obligated.

I knew a few things about Mack Bolger, about his life since we'd confronted each other semiviolently in the Mayfair Hotel. Beth had been happy to tell me during our woeful drink at the Espalier Bar in April. Our—Beth's and my—love affair was, of course, only one feature in the long devaluation and decline in her and Mack's marriage. This I'd understood. There were two children; Mack had been frantic to hold matters together for the sake of their futures. Beth was a portrait photographer who worked from home but craved engagement with the wide world outside University City—

craved it in the worst way, and was therefore basically unhappy with everything in her life. After my departure, she moved out of their house, took an apartment near the Gateway Arch, and for a time took a much younger lover. Mack, for his part in their upheaval, eventually quit his job as an executive for a large agribiz company, considered studying for the ministry, considered going on a missionary journey to Senegal or French Guiana; briefly took a young lover himself. One child had been arrested for shoplifting; the other had gotten admitted to Brown. There were months of all-night confrontations, some combative, some loving and revelatory, some derisory from both sides. Until everything that could be said or expressed or threatened was in its time said, expressed, threatened and a standstill was achieved by which they both stayed in their house but kept separate schedules, saw different new friends, had occasional dinners together, went to the Muny Opera, occasionally even slept together, but saw little hope (in Beth's case) of things turning out better than they were at the time of our joyless drink together and the O'Neill play. I'd assumed then that Beth was meeting someone else that evening, had someone in New York she was interested in, and I felt completely fine about it.

"It's really odd," Beth said, stirring her long, almost pure-white finger around the surface of her Kir Royale, staring not at me but at the glass rim where the pink liquid nearly exceeded its vitreous limits but did not, "we were so close." Her eyes rose to me, and she smiled affectionately. "You and I, I mean. Now I feel like I'm telling all this to an old friend. Or to my brother."

Beth is a tall, sallow-faced, big-boned, ash-blond woman who smokes too many cigarettes and whose hair always hangs down in her eyes like a forties Hollywood glamour girl's. This can be attractive, although it also causes her sometimes to seem to be spying on her own conversations.

"Well," I said, "it's all right to feel that way." I smiled back across the little round black-topped café table. It *was* all right. I had gone on. When I looked back on what we'd done, none of it except for what we'd done in bed made me feel good about life, or that the experience had been finally worth it. But I couldn't undo it. I don't believe the past can be repaired that way. It can only be exceeded. "Sometimes," I went on, "friendship's all we're after in the first place." This, I admit, I did not really believe.

"Mack's like a dog, you know," Beth said and flicked her hair away from her eyes. He was on her mind. "I kick him," she said, "and he tries to bring me things. It's pathetic. He's very interested in Tantric sex now, whatever that is. Do you know what that even is?"

"I don't like hearing this," I said stupidly, though it was true. "It sounds cruel."

"You're just afraid I'll say it about you, Johnny." She smiled and touched her damp fingertip to her lips, which were wonderful lips.

· "Afraid?" I said. "Afraid's really not the word, is it?"

"Well, then, whatever the word is." Beth turned her head quickly away and signalled the waiter for the check. She did not know how to be disagreed with. It always frightened her.

But that was all. I already said that our meeting was not a satisfying one.

Mack Bolger's pale-gray eyes caught me coming toward him well before I expected them to. We had seen each other only twice. Once at a fancy cocktail party given by an author I had come to St. Louis to wrest a book from. It was the time I had met his wife. And once more, at the Mayfair Hotel, when I'd taken an inept swing at him, and he'd slammed me against a wall and hit me in the face with the back of his hand. Perhaps you don't forget people you knock around. That becomes their place in your life. I, however, find it hard to recognize people when they're not where I believe they belong, and Mack Bolger belonged in St. Louis. But he was an exception.

Mack's eyes fixed on me, then left me, scanned the crowd uncomfortably, then found me again as I approached him. His large, tanned face took on an expression of stony unsurprise, as if he'd known I was somewhere in the terminal and a form of communication had already begun between us. Though, if anything, really, his face looked resigned—resigned to me, resigned to the situations the world foists on you unwilling, resigned to himself. It was what we had in common, though neither of us had a language which could express that. So, as I came into his presence, what I felt was an unexpected sympathy—for him, for having to see me now. And if I could've turned and walked straight away from him I would have.

"I just saw you," I said from the crowd, five feet before I expected to speak. My voice isn't loud, so that the theatrically nasal male voice announcing an arrival from Poughkeepsie on Track 34 seemed possibly to have blotted it out.

"Did you have something special in mind to tell me," Mack Bolger said. His eyes cast out again across the vaulted hall, where Christmas shoppers and overbundled passengers were moving in all directions. It occurred to me—shockingly—that he was waiting for Beth, and that in a moment's time I would be standing there facing her and Mack together, almost as I had in St. Louis. My heart actually struck two profound beats deep in my chest, then seemed for a moment to stop altogether. "How's your face?" Mack said without emotion, still scanning the crowd. "I didn't hurt you too bad, did I?"

"No," I said.

"You've grown a mustache." His eyes did not flicker toward me.

"Yes," I said. I'd forgotten about it, and for some reason felt ashamed, as if I looked absurd.

"Well," Mack said, "good." His voice was the one you would use to speak to someone in line beside you at the post office, someone you would never see again. Though there was also, just barely noticeable, a hint of what we used to call *juiciness* in his speech, some minor undispersable moisture in his cheek that one heard in each of his "s"s and "f"s. It was unfortunate, I thought. It robbed him of a small measure of gravity. I had not noticed it before, in the few overheated moments we'd had to exchange words.

He looked at me again, hands in his expensive Italian coat pockets, a coat that had heavy dark bone buttons and long, wide lapels. Too stylish for him, I thought, for the solid man he was. Mack and I were nearly the same height. But he was in every way larger and seemed to look down to me—something in the way he held his chin up. It was almost the opposite of the way Beth looked at me.

"I live here now," Mack said, without really addressing me. I noticed he had long, dark, almost feminine eyelashes and perfectly sized, perfectly shaped ears, which his new haircut put on nice display. He might've been forty—younger than I am—and looked more than anything like an army officer. A major. I thought of a letter Beth had shown me, written by Mack to her, containing the phrase "I want to kiss you all over. Yes I do. Macklin." Beth had rolled her eyes when she showed it to me. At another time she had talked to Mack on the telephone while we were in bed together naked. On that occasion she'd *kept* rolling her eyes at whatever he was saying—something, I gathered, about various difficulties he was having at work. Once we even engaged in a sexual act while she talked to him. I could hear his little, buzzing, fretful-sounding voice inside the receiver. But that was now erased. Everything Beth and I had done was over. All that remained of it was just this—a series of moments in the great train terminal, moments which, in their own way and in spite of everything, seemed correct, sturdy, almost classical in character, as if this later time were what really mattered, whereas the previous, passionate, linked, but now distant moments were merely preliminary.

"Did you buy a place?" I said to Mack Bolger, and unexpectedly felt a widely spreading vacancy open all around inside of me. It was such a preposterous thing to say.

Mack's eyes moved slowly to me, and his impassive expression, which had seemed to me to signify one thing—resignation—began to signify something different. I knew this because a small cleft appeared in his chin. "Yes," he said and let his eyes stay fixed on me. People were shouldering past us. I could smell some woman's heavy, hot-feeling perfume around my face. Music had commenced in the rotunda, making the moment feel clamorous, suffocating: "We three kings of Orient are . . ." "Yes," Mack Bolger said again, very emphatically, spitting the word from between his straight, white, nearly flawless teeth. He had grown up on a farm in Nebraska, had gone to a small college in Minnesota on a football scholarship, had then taken an M.B.A. at Harvard; had done well. All that life, all that experience was being brought into play now as self-control, dignity. It was strange that someone would call him a dog when he wasn't that at all. He was extremely admirable. "I bought an apartment on the Upper East Side," he said suddenly and blinked his eyes very rapidly. "I moved out in September. I have a new job. I'm living alone. Beth's not here. She's in Paris, where she's miserable— or I hope she is. We're getting a divorce. I'm waiting for my daughter to come down from boarding school. Is that all right? Does that seem all right to you? Does that satisfy your curiosity?"

"Yes," I said. "Of course." Mack was not angry. He was, instead, a thing that anger had no part of or at least had long been absent from, something akin to exhaustion, where the words you say are the only true words you *can* say. Myself, I did not think I'd ever felt that way. Always for me there had been a choice.

"Do you understand me?" Mack Bolger said. His thick athlete's brow slowly furrowed, as if he were studying a creature he didn't entirely understand, an anomaly of some kind, which perhaps I was.

"Yes," I said. "I'm sorry."

"Well, then," he said, and seemed suddenly embarrassed. He looked away, out over the crowd of swarming heads and faces, as if he'd just sensed someone coming. I looked toward where he was looking. No one was approaching us. Not Beth, not a daughter. Not anyone. Perhaps, I thought, it was all a lie. Or perhaps, I thought, for a moment I had lost consciousness, and this was not Mack Bolger at all, and I was dreaming everything. "Do you think there could be someplace else you could go now?" Mack said. His big, tanned, handsome face looked imploring and exhausted. Once Beth had said Mack and I looked alike. But we did not. That had been her fantasy. Without really looking at me again he said, "I would have a hard time introducing you to my daughter. I'm sure you can imagine that."

"Yes," I said. I looked around again, and this time I did see a pretty blond girl standing in the crowd, watching us from several steps away. She was holding a red nylon backpack by its straps. Something was causing her to stay away. Possibly her father had signalled her not to come near us. "Of course," I said. And by speaking I somehow made the girl's face break into a wide smile, a smile I recognized.

"Nothing's happened here," Mack said suddenly to me. He was staring at his daughter. From the pocket of his overcoat he had produced a tiny white box wrapped and tied with a red bow.

"I'm sorry?" I said. I was leaving. People were swirling noisily around us. The music seemed louder. I thought perhaps I'd misunderstood him. "I didn't hear you." I smiled in an entirely involuntary way.

"Nothing's happened today," Mack Bolger said. "Don't go away thinking anything happened here. Between you and me, I mean. *Nothing's* happened. I'm sorry I ever met you, that's all. Sorry I ever had to touch you. You make me feel ashamed." He still had the unfortunate dampness with his "s"s.

"Well," I said. "All right. I can understand."

He simply stepped away from me and began saying something toward the blond girl standing in the crowd smiling. What he said was "Boy, oh boy, do *you* look like a million bucks."

I walked on toward Billy's then, to the new arrangement I'd made that would take me on into the evening. I had been wrong, of

course, about the linkage of moments, and about what was preliminary and what was primary. It was a mistake, one I would not
make again. None of this was a good thing to have done. Though it
is such a large city here, so much larger than, say, St. Louis, I knew
I would not see him again.

MOLLY GILES

Pie Dance

I don't know what to do about my husband's new wife. She won't come in. She sits on the front porch and smokes. She won't knock or ring the bell, and the only way I know she's there at all is because the dog points in the living room. The minute I see Stray standing with one paw up and his tail straight out I say, "Shhh. It's Pauline." I stroke his coarse fur and lean on the broom and we wait. We hear the creak of a board, the click of a purse, a cigarette being lit, a sad, tiny cough. At last I give up and open the door. "Pauline?" The afternoon light hurts my eyes. "Would you like to come in?"

"No," says Pauline.

Sometimes she sits on the stoop, picking at the paint, and sometimes she sits on the edge of an empty planter box. Today she's perched on the railing. She frowns when she sees me and lifts her small chin. She wears the same black velvet jacket she always wears, the same formal silk blouse, the same huge dark glasses. "Just passing by," she explains.

I nod. Pauline lives thirty miles to the east, in the city, with Konrad. "Passing by" would take her one toll bridge, one freeway, and two backcountry roads from their flat. But lies are the least of our problems, Pauline's and mine, so I nod again, bunch my bathrobe a little tighter around my waist, try to cover one bare foot with the

297

other, and repeat my invitation. She shakes her head so vigorously the railing lurches. "Konrad," she says in her high young voice, "expects me. You know how he is."

I do, or I did—I'm not sure I know now—but I nod, and she flushes, staring so hard at something right behind me that I turn too and tell Stray, who is still posing in the doorway, to cancel the act and come say hello. Stray drops his front paw and pads forward, nose to the ground. Pauline blows cigarette smoke into the wisteria vine and draws her feet close to the railing. "What kind is it?" she asks, looking down.

I tell her we don't know, we think he's part Irish setter and part golden retriever; what happened was someone drove him out here to the country and abandoned him and he howled outside our house until one of the children let him come in. Pauline nods as if this were very interesting and says, "Oh really?" but I stop abruptly; I know I am boring. I am growing dull as Mrs. Dixon, Konrad's mother, who goes on and on about her poodle and who, for a time, actually sent us birthday cards and Christmas presents signed with a poodle paw print. I clasp the broom with both hands and gaze fondly at Stray. I am too young to love a dog; at the same time I am beginning to realize there isn't much to love in this world. So when Pauline says, "Can it do tricks?" I try to keep the rush of passion from my eyes; I try to keep my voice down.

"He can dance," I admit.

"How great," she says, swaying on the railing. "Truly great."

"Yes," I agree. I do not elaborate. I do not tell Pauline that at night, when the children are asleep, I often dance with him. Nor do I confess that the two of us, Stray and I, have outgrown the waltz and are deep into reggae. Stray is a gay and affable partner, willing to learn, delighted to lead. I could boast about him forever, but Pauline, I see, already looks tired. "And you?" I ask. "How have you been?"

For answer she coughs, flexing her small hand so the big gold wedding ring flashes a lot in the sun; she smiles for the first time and makes a great show of pounding her heart as she coughs. She doesn't look well. She's lost weight since the marriage and seems far too pale. "Water?" I ask. "Or how about tea? We have peppermint, jasmine, mocha, and lemon."

"Oh no!" she cries, choking.

"We've honey. We've cream."

"Oh no! But thank you! So much!"

After a bit she stops coughing and resumes smoking and I realize we both are staring at Stray again. "People," Pauline says with a sigh, "are so cruel. Don't you think?"

I do; I think yes. I tell her Stray was half-starved and mangy when we found him; he had been beaten and kicked, but we gave him raw eggs and corn oil for his coat and had his ear sewn up and took him to the vet's for all the right shots and look at him now. We continue to look at him now. Stray, glad to be noticed, and flattered, immediately trots to the driveway and pees on the wheel of Pauline's new Mustang. "Of course," I complain, "he's worse than a child."

Pauline bows her head and picks one of Stray's hairs off her black velvet jacket. "I guess," she says. She smiles. She really has a very nice smile. It was the first thing I noticed when Konrad introduced us; it's a wide smile, glamorous and trembly, like a movie star's. I once dreamt I had to kiss her and it wasn't bad, I didn't mind. In the dream Konrad held us by the hair with our faces shoved together. It was claustrophobic but not at all disgusting. I remember thinking, when I awoke: Poor Konrad, he doesn't even know how to punish people, and it's a shame, because he wants to so much. Later I noticed that Pauline's lips, when she's not smiling, are exactly like Konrad's, full and loose and purplish, sad. I wonder if when they kiss they feel they're making a mirror; I would. Whether the rest of Pauline mirrors Konrad is anyone's guess. I have never seen her eyes, of course, because of the dark glasses. Her hair is blonde and so fine that the tips of her ears poke through. She is scarcely taller than one of the children, and it is difficult to think of her as Konrad's "executive assistant"; she seems a child, dressed up. She favors what the magazines call the "layered look"—I suspect because she is ashamed of her bottom. She has thin shoulders but a heavy bottom. Well, I want to tell her, who is not ashamed of their bottom. If not their bottom their thighs or their breasts or their wobbly female bellies; who among us is perfect, Pauline.

Instead of saying a word of this, of course, I sigh and say, "Some days it seems all I do is sweep up after that dog." Stray, good boy, rolls in dry leaves and vomits some grass. As if more were needed, as if Stray and I together are conducting an illustrated lecture, I swish the broom several times on the painted porch floor. The straw scrapes my toes. What Pauline doesn't know—because I haven't told her and because she won't come inside—is that I keep the broom by the front door for show. I keep it to show the Moonies, Mormons, and Jehovah's Witnesses who stop by the house that I've no time to be saved, can't be converted. I use it to lean on when I'm listening, lean on when I'm not; I use it to convince prowlers of my prowess and neighbors of my virtue; I use it for everything, in fact, but cleaning house. I feel no need to clean house, and certainly not with a broom. The rooms at my back are stacked to the rafters with dead flowers and song sheets, stuffed bears and bird nests, junk mail and seashells, but to Pauline, perhaps, my house is vast, scoured, and full of light—to Pauline, perhaps, my house is in order. But who knows, with Pauline. She gives me her beautiful smile, then drops her eyes to my bathrobe hem and gives me her faint, formal frown. She pinches the dog hair between her fingers and tries to wipe it behind a leaf on the yellowing vine.

"I don't know how you manage" is what she says. She shakes her head. "Between the dog," she says, grinding her cigarette out on the railing, "and the children . . ." She sits huddled in the wan freckled sunlight with the dead cigarette curled in the palm of her hand, and after a minute, during which neither of us can think of one more thing to say, she lights up another. "It was the children," she says at last, "I really wanted to see."

"They'll be sorry they missed you," I tell her politely.

"Yes," Pauline says. "I'd hoped . . ."

"Had you but phoned," I add, just as politely, dropping my eyes and sweeping my toes. The children are not far away. They said they were going to the end of the lane to pick blackberries for pie, but what they are actually doing is showing their bare bottoms to passing cars and screaming "Hooey hooey." I know this because little Dixie Steadman, who used to baby-sit before she got her Master's Degree in Female Processes, saw them and called me. "Why are you letting your daughters celebrate their femininity in this burlesque?" Dixie asked. Her voice was calm and reasonable and I wanted to answer, but before I could there was a brisk papery rustle and she began to read rape statistics to me, and I had to hold the phone at arm's length and finally I put it to Stray's ear and even he yawned, showing all his large yellow teeth, and then I put the receiver down, very gently, and we tiptoed away. What I'm wondering now is what "hooey" means. I'd ask Pauline, who would be only too glad to look it up for me (her curiosity and industry made her, Konrad said, an invaluable assistant, right from the start), but I'm afraid she'd mention it to Konrad and then he would start threatening to take the children away; he does that; he can't help it; it's like a nervous tic. He loves to go to court. Of course he's a lawyer, he has to. Even so, I think he overdoes it. I never understood the rush to divorce me and marry Pauline; we were fine as we were, but he says my problem is that I have no morals and perhaps he's right, perhaps I don't. Both my divorce and Pauline's wedding were executed in court, and I think both by Judge Benson. The marriage couldn't have been statelier than the dissolution, and if I were Pauline, only twenty-four and getting married for the very first time, I would have been bitter. I would have insisted on white lace or beige anyway and candles and lots of fresh flowers, but Pauline is not one to complain. Perhaps she feels lucky to be married at all; perhaps she feels lucky to be married to Konrad. Her shoulders always droop a little when she's with him, I've noticed, and she listens to him with her chin tucked in and her wrists poised, as if she were waiting to take dictation. Maybe she adores him. But if she does she must learn not to take him too seriously or treat him as if he matters; he hates that; he can't deal with that at all. I should tell her this, but there are some things she'll have to find out for herself. All I tell her is that the girls are gone, up the lane, picking berries.

"How wonderful," she says, exhaling. "Berries."

"Blackberries," I tell her. "They grow wild here. They grow all over."

"In the city," she says, making an effort, "a dinky little carton costs eighty-nine cents." She smiles. "Say you needed three cartons to make one pie," she asks me, "how much would that cost?"

I blink, one hand on my bathrobe collar.

"Two-sixty-seven." Her smile deepens, dimples. "Two-sixty-seven plus tax when you can buy a whole frozen pie for one-fifty-six, giving you a savings of one-eleven at least. They don't call them convenience foods," Pauline says, "for nothing."

"Are you sure," I ask, after a minute, "you don't want some tea?"

"Oh no!"

"Some coffee?"

"Oh no!"

"A fast glass of wine?"

She chuckles, cheerful, but will not answer. I scan the sky. It's close, but cloudless. If there were to be a thunderstorm—and we often have thunderstorms this time of year—Pauline would have to come in. Or would she? I see her, erect and dripping, defiant.

"Mrs. Dixon," I offer, "had a wonderful recipe for blackber—"

"Mrs. Dixon?"

For a second I almost see Pauline's eyes. They are small and tired and very angry. Then she tips her head to the sun and the glasses cloud over again.

"Konrad's mother."

"Yes," she says. She lights another cigarette, shakes the match out slowly. "I know."

"A wonderful recipe for blackberry cake. She used to say that Konrad never liked pie."

"I know."

"Just cake."

"I know."

"What I found out, Pauline, is that he likes both."

"We never eat dessert," Pauline says, her lips small and sad again. "It isn't good for us and we just don't have it."

Stray begins to bark and wheel around the garden and a second later the children appear, Letty first, her blonde hair tangled and brambly like mine, then Alicia, brown-eyed like Konrad, and then Sophie, who looks like no one unless—yes—with her small proud head, a bit like Pauline. The children are giggling and they deliberately smash into each other as they zigzag down the driveway. "Oops," they cry, with elaborate formality, "do forgive me. My mistake." As they come closer we see that all three are scratched and bloody with berry juice. One holds a Mason jar half full and one has a leaky colander and one boasts a ruined pocket. Pauline closes her eyes tight behind her dark glasses and holds out her arms. The girls, giggling, jostle toward her. They're wild for Pauline. She tells them stories about kidnappers and lets them use her calculator. With each kiss the wooden railing rocks and lurches; if these visits keep up I will have to rebuild the porch, renew the insurance. I carry the berries into the kitchen, rinse them off, and set them to drain. When I come back outside Pauline stands alone on the porch. Stains bloom on her blouse and along her out-thrust chin.

"Come in," I urge, "and wash yourself off."

She shakes her head very fast and smiles at the floor. "No," she says. "You see, I have to go."

The children are turning handsprings on the lawn, calling "Watch me! me! me!" as Stray dashes between them, licking their faces. I walk down the driveway to see Pauline off. As I lift my hand to wave she turns and stares past me, toward the house; I turn too, see nothing, no one, only an old wooden homestead, covered with yellowing vines, a curtain aflutter in an upstairs window, a red door ajar on a dark brown room.

"Thank you," she cries. Then she throws her last cigarette onto the gravel and grinds it out and gets into her car and backs out the driveway and down to the street and away.

Once she turns the corner I drop my hand and bite the knuckles, hard. Then I look back at the house. Konrad steps out, a towel gripped to his waist. He is scowling; angry, I know, because he's spent the last half hour hiding in the shower with the cat litter box and the tortoise. He shouts for his shoes. I find them toed out in flight, one in the bedroom, one down the hall. As he hurries to tie them I tell him a strange thing has happened: it seems I've grown morals.

"What?" Konrad snaps. He combs his hair with his fingers when he can't find my brush.

"Us," I say. "You. Me. Pauline. It's a lot of hooey," I tell Konrad. "It is."

Konrad turns his face this way, that way, scrubs a space clear in the mirror. "Do you know what you're saying?" he says to the mirror.

I think. I think, Yes. I know what I'm saying. I'm saying goodbye. I'm saying, Go home.

And when he has gone and the girls are asleep and the house is night-still, I remember the pie. I roll out the rich dough, flute it, and fill it with berries and sugar, lemons and spice. We'll have it for breakfast, the children and I; we'll share it with Stray. "Would you like that?" I ask him. Stray thumps his tail, but he's not looking at me; his head is cocked, he's listening to something else. I listen too. A faint beat comes from the radio on the kitchen counter. Even before I turn it up I can tell it's a reggae beat, strong and sassy. I'm not sure I can catch it. Not sure I should try. Still, when Stray bows, I curtsy. And when the song starts, we dance.

ANTHONY WALTON

Divorce Education

This is the kind of stuff we used to fight about: whether to have the window up in the summer, or down in the fall; what color, black or red, to choose for our new Jeep Cherokee; where, if anywhere, to go on Thanksgiving; whether or not our son, Jack, Jr., should receive religious training, and if so, where; whether or not Bill Clinton was a once-in-a-lifetime visionary who had saved the Democratic Party or an asshole, or both; who was spending too much money on beer, fingernail polish, long-distance phone calls, gas; if I should put a zip on it; whether we would go to family therapy, which family members would go, when.

It's hard to believe she once loved me so much that she wanted to name our son Jack, Jr. Our biggest fight, and the end of it all, came over license plates. The state of Illinois started issuing vanity plates, and she kept nagging me about when I was going to let her get GRNTUAQT—eight characters, the maximum—before somebody else did. I said no, why did we have to give up the perfectly good and serviceable plates we had, BZD 1609? Not to mention paying the extra thirty bucks or whatever it was just so she could look silly. Like a teenager. Who in the hell did she have the need of informing of their "cutie" status while she was out on the freeway anyway? The breaking-the-camel's-back thing was that I had to drive her car sometimes, and I didn't want to look like an asshole driving around with plates like that. What if I got pulled over?

Then the state started issuing special "affinity" plates, a blue-and-orange FIGHTING ILLINI for alums and donors, one with a picture of corn on it, "amber waves of grain" or some such bullshit, and my favorite, a picture of a sunset and a prairie dog sticking his head up out of a hole with SAVE THE PRAIRIE stamped in huge letters. She wanted the blue-and-orange ones, being that she went to the U of I, but I was like, "ninety-five bucks for license plates?" Add the forty-two bucks for GRNTUAQT and we're over one hundred and thirty-five dollars *for license plates.* When all she had to do was go down to town hall, reregister, and put the new sticker on them every August. Then one day I come home from work and I see her car sitting there with new blue-and-orange one hundred and thirty-five dollar license plates reading GRNTUAQT. What can you do with a woman like that? I smashed her windshield with a golf club. That's how I ended up in Divorce Education.

Divorce Education is a series of seminars sponsored by the Du-Page County Court System in an effort to better prepare couples and families, especially couples, for the experience of divorce, the extremes of sadness and loss, and the anger and rage that will extend beyond those emotions. It's an attempt to get the couples a little ahead of the curve, so that the first time there's a conflict over who said what about Mommy taking Jesse and Winona to Disney World with her new boyfriend Jeff—it won't come as a surprise. It's an attempt to prepare people for what they're going to experience, the stuff that has to be thought out, then agreed to, then managed, in the hope that they'll behave when the showdown finally comes, which it will. The details.

I am not in theory opposed to any of this. If we couldn't agree on anything when we were sleeping in the same bed every night and blearily sharing a box of cereal in the morning—I like Shredded Wheat, she likes Frosted Flakes—how could we be trusted by the state of Illinois in the stern—I say humorless—personage of Judge

Susan Keslowski of the DuPage County Family Court System? Judge Keslowski is the judge who refused to give me any credit for allowing Dee Dee to cut back her hours as a paralegal and go to law school at night, when it was me who had given up everything and left my medical studies ten years before when her mother got sick. I was happy to make this sacrifice; there are things a man has to do for his family. One time Dee Dee—this was during the time when she was going to therapy on her own—came to me and said, "Jack, I forgive you for not becoming a doctor. Why can't you forgive yourself?" *She* forgives *me*. I couldn't take that kind of thing anymore.

I agreed to attend His House, Her House, Their Home seminars as a prerequisite to our final judgment. The judge said we had to go. The flyer read, "The purpose of these classes is to examine and instruct the family—and you are still a family, like it or not— on the impact of this tragedy on behavior and management strategies and to effect positive change. Anger and stress management, the differing cultures of the two parental homes, and the 'DMZ' feeling children often describe are all addressed in this short course." There was no charge.

My wife and I were placed in different sections, and in due time received our certification and divorce. I remember standing there after the hearing in the parking lot at the county complex in Wheaton—the same place where we had applied for the marriage license seven years before, with the same sort of sky, liquid blue and streaky cirrus clouds trailing off into vapor—and promising Dee Dee that I would be fair and open-minded, and that I would work with her on things and collaborate in the bringing up of Jack, Jr. I also said that I thought all of this could have been avoided if she hadn't been so profligate and promiscuous with our money and driven me to things I now regretted. She shook her head. As I watched her, her head moving from side to side as if in slow motion, my own head started to spin. I felt like I feel when I stand up too fast.

"You've got to learn to give a little bit, Jack," she said very quietly.

"Say what?" I couldn't hear her.

"I mean, you never could with me, but can't you just try, for the sake of our boy?" She spoke quite distinctly. "I'm asking you to not give up on him."

"I don't intend to."

"Don't give up on him."

"Are you saying I am somehow a quitter?" My voice was rising. "Are you implying somewhere that I am the one who quit?"

"I'm saying you have to try." She looked away for a second, then over my shoulder.

"You want to play hardball with me?" It was the only thing I could think of. "Is that what you're saying?"

She looked directly at me, narrowed her eyes behind her John Lennon shades, and smiled. "You've got a lot to learn, my friend."

I narrowed my eyes and smiled back. "That's why I'm taking Divorce Education."

This all happened in northern Illinois, out on the prairie, west of Chicago. Dee Dee moved farther west, to live with her older sister Judith in Louisville, Colorado, not long after that conversation. I don't know if it was part of the plan, but I lost touch with her and Jack, Jr., not more than a year and a half later. I was supposed to be able to call my son every Sunday at a mutually agreed-upon time, but they somehow always managed not to be there; I pictured her sitting there looking at the answering machine while I pleaded for my legal right to speak to my child. If I tried calling at any time other than the mutually agreed-upon and appointed one, she would have her lawyer fire off a letter to the supervising judge of the custody agreement—the Honorable Susan Keslowski—and she, the judge, would have her clerk write *me* a letter ordering me to remain within the terms of the agreement.

I was entitled to one weekend a month in Colorado, which was preposterous, and to have Jack, Jr., visit me for four weeks in

Chicago in the summer, but Dee Dee insisted on my paying for her to fly to O'Hare to escort the boy—she got some social worker, one of her cronies, to write up some smack about easing the disruptive transitions between respective parental environments—and also interpreted the clause in the divorce agreement that read that I would pay for all expenses surrounding the summer visits to her distinct advantage, to mean that she could fly to Chicago first-class and live it up in the Windy City for a week.

So I tried going out there on my vacation, but she wouldn't let Jack, Jr., stay with me in the motel, and anywhere I tried to take him, to a ballgame at Coors Field, to Six Flags Over the Rockies, to the movies, she insisted that she, or her sister, or her sister's idiot third husband, Marty—a six three, three-hundred-pound retired highway patrolman on disability—go with us.

How was I supposed to get to know my only son and namesake, who by now was going by his middle name, Jerome? I threatened to take her back before the judge and file a complaint concerning her breach of the custodial arrangement in Illinois—I had signed off on them leaving for Colorado; I thought the new life might do them both, all of us, good, but she just smiled at me again from behind her sunglasses (it seemed she never talked to me anymore without wearing shades)—and said, "Well, why don't you just do that, mister, as soon as you get back to Illinois. While you're out here you might look into getting yourself some local counsel." The smile evaporated. "That might be a good way to occupy your time. You can have your Colorado lawyer contact mine." With a rehearsed and orchestrated flourish she handed me a business card, smiling coldly from behind her sunglasses like a state trooper. I didn't even look at it. It was the last time I saw either her or my son.

But Divorce Education wasn't a complete washout. During intermission of the last His House, Her House seminar a young woman, kind of a sincere hippie chick—long black skirt down to her ankles,

Birkenstocks, tie-dyed T-shirt, page boy, rings on every finger, spacy, and with the softest smile—came up to me at the cookie table and said, "You know, I really liked what you said in there, about daddies being parents, too, and how everyone in the process should respect that. I really liked that."

I was caught off guard, scarfing a mouthful of Chips Ahoy while wrapping a bunch more up in a napkin for my midnight snack. "Beg pardon?"

"In the seminar. Your comments."

"Liked? How?" Stalling was giving me a chance to back up and check her out. I liked the rings.

"Oh, you know," she said.

"Really, I don't." I smiled as warmly as I could. She was the kind of girl who nodded when she was pleased, and she was nodding now. My friend Walt Rollins had said that counseling would be a great place to meet chicks, but I thought they'd all be like Dee Dee, sunglasses, hostile, and loaded for bear. It was looking like I owed Walt a bottle of scotch.

"I just think it's wrong to paint men as the villain. It takes two to get married, two to make a baby, two to mess it up."

I nodded vigorously, "Yes, yes," but before I could reply, much less ask her name or get her number, our facilitator, a gray-haired old Quaker named Trip MacLean, came by and put an avuncular hand on my shoulder. We trudged back into the multipurpose room with its ragged circle of folding chairs for another ninety minutes of sob stories and negotiation skills. I looked at her across the way a time or two, and returned her smiles. I was sure she would be waiting for me in the lobby or the parking lot afterward, but she was nowhere to be found.

I never thought much about divorce before it happened to me. It was like a car crash, a lightning strike, the very earth splitting into halves beneath my feet. It seemed to me to be life's most egregious failure, something that would cling to you like ivy, growing over and around everything until it defined your very being. I'd looked at people who were divorced as incompetents, if not losers. Then one day there I was, an all-star on that sorry team; it had happened to me.

It's funny how it works. I would come home from work and nobody would be there; I'd bang a chicken potpie into the oven and settle in with the six o'clock *Sportscenter,* and round about the time "Most Offensive Plays" came on, it would dawn on me that no one was coming home. I could listen for the click and slow drag of the electronic garage door opener as long as I wanted, till kingdom come. Never again, or at least never her. No more coming down from upstairs and singing, "Hey, baby!" in one of my old flannel shirts and her sweatpants from high school. This epiphany would dawn on me again and again, night after night, day after day after day. I started losing track of days, whether it was Tuesday or Thursday, Saturday or Sunday.

I never quite got used to it. I found myself getting an odd kind of pleasure-pain from thinking about all the good times, the times before Dee Dee became the terminator, like when you probe a fading bruise with your fingers: the long day and evening we spent nuzzling high up in the Indiana Dunes the first year we were married, the cold wind off the lake in our faces; or the bus trip we took—we were in college and didn't have any money—to meet her family. I'd think about the day I met her, when she walked into my mother's kitchen with my younger sister and I blinked and thought "This'll do." I remember the warm honey glaze I felt spreading all over my body, including and especially where it counted most, the way she smiled and I thought to myself, "Put the apple in my mouth and turn the spit, boys." I'd think, "There's two kinds of people in the world, the divorced and the not-divorced. How the hell did I get over here?"

———

Then again, there are times when fate seems to smile on you. Two months after the end of His House, Her House, almost to the day, who should I see, in capri pants, what I would come to know as the ever-present Birkenstocks, and a camisole, pushing a stroller down Washington Street in Naperville, stopped at the window of a candy shop? I crossed as elegantly as I could against afternoon traffic while angling behind her, and said in a low voice, "Turtles." She jumped and turned, falling backward on the stroller as if to protect the baby, then saw who it was. "Oh you," she said, covering her mouth with her hand in embarrassment. Then she smiled broadly.

Her name was Serena, Serena Haley nee McMahon, and in that first conversation in a Starbucks down the street, I learned not only her name but that she had grown up in Naperville, had gone to North High School, had gotten pregnant as a sophomore at Notre Dame, dropped out to marry James Haley, then a law student, moved with him to San Jose to establish a law practice where she never saw him and assumed he was doing quite well, which he was—but he was also doing quite well with some of the ladies in his office and at other firms, which led to a separation, her return to her parents' home for a few months, and, now, a new baby Beamer and a condo out in Waubonsie Valley, all financed by James Haley. She related all of this breathlessly, pausing only to look me in the eye and nod slowly and seriously from time to time. Then she trained a steady gaze on me and smiled, sadly—it seemed she always was just a little bit sad; some women, in my experience, are like that, always fighting the undertow—then said, "I've been pregnant out-of-wedlock and divorced by the age of twenty-five, two things my mother and sisters have sworn and promised will never happen to them in their entire lives." She took a deep breath and sighed.

Something happened to me. Something it was easier to go with than resist. I felt myself sighing with her, relaxing in a way I hadn't for ten or twenty years, if ever. She looked me in the eye—Serena was a girl who would look you in the eye—her pupils spreading like the deepest pool, and I felt myself spreading with them into her goodness and kindness and, most important, gentleness. A girl can be good and kind without being gentle, that's one thing you learn when you get to be my age. Serena Haley was gentle, just about the gentlest creature I had ever seen. It was a shock to me.

I've seen some things. I'm a pharmacist, and in that trade you see all kinds of things. You have to stand there behind the counter with your poker face and be compassionate yet professional with people at some of their worst moments. People who have to look me in the eye and chitchat about the weather as I give them Zovirax ointment for their herpes simplex, the AZT for their sister's AIDS, the Haloperidol for their child's schizophrenia. Strangest, and saddest of all, are the furtive and humiliated guys who try to wait until there's a lull in traffic at the counter so they can sprint up and hand over a scrip for ten 50mg tabs of Viagra, unaware that I'm going to have to tell them out loud that their insurance will only pay for six, and ask if they want to pay cash for the other four or just skip it. I think this must be what the priest feels like in the confessional. I don't know what they're so worried about. After Zovirax, AZT, and Haldol, Viagra seems like the simplest thing, a balm from heaven.

I've seen what assholes doctors are. More than once, I've averted what could have been disaster, a fatal drug interaction from prescriptions called in by doctors over at the Brave Eagle Country Club between rounds of golf and g&t's, doctors who couldn't be bothered to give a shit about their patients' lives or read the charts. And *they* look down at *me*.

I've seen some things. In my neighborhood, seven of the nine couples we started with have divorced; of the two remaining couples, one are Mormons, who don't exactly count. The other couple, Joe and Miranda Crawford, are lucky. But it happens: people have too much freedom and too much on their minds. On the other hand, even if the divorce rate goes to ninety percent, and who's to say that it won't, that means ten percent will make it. Ten percent, like Joe and Miranda, like the Mormons over on Trillium Place, will always rather stay home and make popcorn and retire early for a little fun than work every night until ten o'clock, stay on the road for weeks at a time, or fall into intrigues with the man or woman down the street.

In my neighborhood, one wife, the mother of four children, ran off with the landscaper in June, then came back in October. Her husband never said anything to any of us about it, and as far as I know, their marriage has continued as if nothing ever happened. Another couple, the Campbells, broke up when the husband decided that he was homosexual. The Eisleys never seemed for one second to be happy, not in the seven years I knew them since they moved here from New York, and the husband, Wally, who got to keep the house, now just stays inside all the time, keeping to himself. Every now and then I'll see him in the yard and he doesn't even wave, he's off in the sky somewhere.

The Leskowskis split after the wife, Judy, became the subdivision hot pants, contributing to a couple of other breakups, then ran off. My father, who had known her—he worked with her father— since she was a little girl, said ominously one night while we were watching the White Sox, "She's got some wrong ideas about life. She's been watching too many of them stories." By which he meant soap operas. I just rolled my eyes. This stuff, to me, has become so commonplace as to be undeserving of analysis. It's in the air. Like I said, it's more surprising when it doesn't happen.

Then there was Serena. Falling in love with some women, and having them fall in love with you, is like falling off a bicycle, or connecting the dots. It's too easy. And I mean that in the best of ways. My conversation at the Naperville Starbucks with Serena Haley lasted so long it turned into a date, little Miles stunned on chocolate and dozing agreeably in the stroller beside us. She gave me her number and said only, quite calmly, "I knew you would call" when we finally had the most conventional of first—official—dates. We went to dinner at the Chili's at Cantera, then we went to the movies and saw something about a hippie detective in Los Angeles who called every single person he met "Dude," and we laughed like children all the way through. Then we called each other "Dude" for the rest of the evening, "Dude, this" and "Did you see that, Dude," all the way from Cantera over to Waubonsie Valley until I dropped her off. She looked me dead in the eye as if we were going to kiss, and then said only, "Thanks for a great night, Dude."

As I watched her walk up the steps to her condo and turn to wave me good-night, I remember thinking about her sitting beside me and laughing in the dark: sweet, gentle Serena Haley, smiling and laughing and slapping her thigh, and leaning her head toward me like a teenager. Once, I laughed so hard I accidentally grabbed her hand and held on, just to see. She didn't let go.

Our second date was on a Sunday afternoon. We had some kind of plans I don't recall—we were going to look at Andrew Wyeth paintings over at the Cantigny museum or something—but while we were sitting in front of her house and she was putting on her seatbelt, out of nowhere I asked if she wanted to go for a ride and she looked at me and smiled that Serena smile, raised her eyebrows, one of them always a little higher than the other, and said, "Why not?"

I had surprised myself. Me and Dee Dee had hardly ever been spontaneous; it's hard to be when you're arguing all the time. We rode up 59 to Roosevelt Road, through Geneva over to 47, and ended up on U.S. 20, heading out toward Galena. I was doing something I had done all the time on Sundays when I was a teenager, by myself, heading into the sunset for the Mississippi River. I used to think of myself in those kinds of terms back then. I'd be listening to John Coltrane or Aaron Copeland, or something else profound, and contemplating what I was sure was my destiny.

My father never said anything about the mileage; I liked to get to the bluffs there just as it was getting dark, and park and watch the last bit of golden light slowly reflecting off the water. How a guy like that ended up a pharmacist in a Walgreen's on Eola Road I don't know; it is, in fact, the enduring burden and mystery of my life; but now I was doing that very thing with Serena Haley, running an easy sixty miles an hour up U.S. Highway 20 with the windows down, smelling the June corn and the spring breeze, both of us singing and bouncing to every song that came on the radio. I remember thinking that day that something significant was happening in my life.

I couldn't help but wonder why I hadn't ever done something like this with Dee Dee, let her in on some of my secrets. That thought was quickly followed by one, the honest one, that the woman I wanted to be there with me in Galena, Illinois, overlooking the Mississippi River and Dubuque, Iowa, in the gathering dusk, was not Dee Dee, hadn't ever been Dee Dee, certainly not after I found out what she was really like, but was Serena Haley. In fact, I was starting to think that wherever Serena Haley was, that's where I wanted to be, and it wasn't just the songs working on my subconscious.

Something about Dee Dee, after we'd been married a few years, made me want to be a tough guy; our thing was drama, always having these scenes, creating these scenes that felt like they were from the movies or from someone else's life. It wasn't me to smash up a lady's car, to be uncharitable, to be passive aggressive with lawyers and all that. Dee Dee brought that out in me. Something in her and something in me didn't fit, didn't work. It was like fire and water, or fire and gasoline. Or fire and fire. Or this: two rocks striking against each other and sparking up a flame.

Something about Serena, on the other hand—and I don't mean to compare them; I think Dee Dee, in the end, with her anchor girl haircut and her hard blue eyes, is a great gal and what happened to us is just life—something about Serena made me want to sit in the dark and talk all night, telling stories. We sat there a good long while after the sun set, and I decided to trust her and tell her a story I had never told anyone else, a story about a time when I was a real little kid, and there had been a blizzard, one so bad the roads were closed for several days. After a couple of days they opened the grocery stores, and people started walking and getting supplies; when my father started suiting up to go out, I insisted on going with him. My mother hadn't wanted to let me, but after a moment she smiled—I described to Serena how I remembered her smile, motherly and just to the edge of pity—and told me to "stop being so mannish" and laughed the way she did when I thought she was secretly pleased about something. She wrestled my long johns and snowsuit onto me and clipped the buckles on my rubber boots and kissed me three times, on the forehead and both cheeks. Then my Dad and me walked three-quarters of a mile and back through the wind and ice and snow down to the Buy-Rite to get milk and eggs, and I followed him, stepping in his footsteps both ways. I looked away from Serena, out the window over the dark river. "He broke the snow and told me to step in his footsteps."

By this time I was crying. Serena just held my hand and was very still. "How did that make you feel?"

"I don't know," I blurted. "I just wonder who's going to do that for Jack, Jr."

She pulled me to her chest and very gently stroked my head. "There'll be time, baby," she whispered. "There's plenty of time."

We drove back to Naperville, holding hands and in silence, except for Serena cooing and humming a song every now and then. I ran seventy and sometimes eighty down the two-lane highways, ignoring the blurry signs and slowing only for the towns: Stockton, Freeport, Rockford, Belvidere, as they loomed like scenes from bad dreams in the darkness, one by one. Only this was a good dream, my most secret secret, the one I wouldn't have dared to contemplate a year before. I did not feel ashamed. In fact, all I felt was lucky.

When we got back to her place she asked if I wanted to come in, and when I hesitated, she smiled and said, "Miles is with his grandparents." I thought it over, and not without some trouble, while she sat and waited in darkness, as nervous as I was, I imagine; I wasn't thinking about Miles. I didn't want to risk what we had apparently so easily achieved; I didn't want to overplay my hand. Then, sitting there looking at her looking at me so gently, I decided what a gentleman should always decide: to accept a lady's invitation, and to let her let me do whatever my heart felt I needed to do until morning.

One afternoon we were sitting in the milky sunlight of the atrium at the Fox Valley Mall, talking about the future. Serena took a long, final pull from her 32-ounce jumbo diet soda. "You know how you have those weeks when you're sleeping well every night, but you keep having the same dream? And it's a good dream, but you start falling asleep and wishing you could have a new dream? Well, that's me; I need some new dreams."

"What's the old dream?"

She looked at me carefully, as if deciding whether or not I was worthy of such intimate information. "The old dream is Miles and me sitting on a beach in very bright sunshine, the salt spray in our faces, until the sunset. It's very slow and peaceful, I must say. Almost like heaven. A very long dream."

"Beaches symbolize transition. It's where the ocean meets the land." I nodded firmly. "You're going through a big change. Most specifically, me."

"Thank you, Doctor. I didn't catch your name. Sigmund, was it? Or is it Carl?" Her sweet laugh ran into a cackle. I signaled for her to quiet down, please. Shoppers were taking notice.

"It's not rocket science. Miles is what is important to you, what you want to take into your new life. The sunset signals the ending of a phase and the beginning of a new one, again, *moi*. The fact that it's a long dream means that your mind is trying to comfort you, to tell you you're safe now. I don't know what the salt spray is."

"Are you making this up? I'm serious. Don't make fun." She gave me a look that told me she hadn't made up her mind.

"We sell something at the store called a dream encyclopedia. I read it sometimes when it's slow. That's all. Scout's honor." I put three fingers up in the air.

This seemed to placate her, a bit. "It better not be one of those things they sell up by the cash register, with the tabloids and the astrology and the lose-forty-pounds-in-two-weeks." Then she gave me her best move, and my favorite put-on in the multifacted Serena arsenal: a mock half-glare, half-pout. I just smiled, with that warm honey glaze spreading all over.

My father used to tell me that when you ended a relationship with one woman and took up with another, all you were doing was exchanging one set of problems for another. Serena Haley and I were in love, day after day, week after week, from the spring on into and through the summer. She told me the kind of stuff women tell you about things that happened to them when they were little girls, slights and small injuries; adults, including her parents and one of her sisters—she was the youngest, an "oops" baby, by ten years—who misunderstood her; and a betrayal by her one and only true friend. As silly as it sounds, it was like I was going back to some place, some dark room that I had closed off and locked up years ago. I felt like I was filling up with light.

It wasn't as if Serena didn't have her problems. She was young, absent-minded, and a single mother. She was used to being cared for, being taken care of. That's the kind of woman she was. The thing was, I was finally ready, in my mind, to care for somebody; there was something in Serena that set free something in me, set me free to do what I was supposed to do. I'll put it this way: I finally understood my father, how he worked and scraped at his construction company and killed himself doing it, but every night until he died, he came home to my mother. They bickered and fought every day for forty-three years, and went to sleep every night together in the same bed. Serena made me ready to do that. She made me want to. And it wasn't like she wasn't taking care of me; she used to say that she thought that was all there was of heaven: two people taking it a day at a time, taking care of each other.

I'm still not sure how it happened, how it came apart. All I can tell you is that I was sitting on the couch at Serena's house watching the eleven o'clock *Sportscenter* one Friday night—Miles was safely asleep in the next room and Serena was curled up on the couch with her head in my lap—when she said, "Jack?" This was in a tone of voice that I have concluded after years of hard-won experience can mean nothing but heartache.

I wasn't ready for heartache. I wanted to stay back in two people taking it a day at a time. "Yes?" I replied.

The long and the short of it is what you would expect. She had waited and waited and carried the burden, and now, she said, it felt like we were truly a couple and it was time for us "to come to a more full and complete understanding of ourselves and each other." She wanted me to know everything, which included facts, or the current version thereof, like that the truth was that in her view she was another well-off but spiritually lost suburban girl who couldn't find anything to grab onto in the smooth surfaces of DuPage County. She didn't have anyone to talk to in her family, her sisters were like several more mothers, and she slid into drugs and easy sex, that's how she put it.

Her parents freaked at her "malaise," and she ran away, became a serious addict—I didn't ask what exactly she meant by that—got pregnant, and came back home in defeat and shame. "I came home and my parents cleaned me up and got me going again. That's who your parents are, the people who are supposed to take care of you. Then I married James, who was this kind of straight-arrow boy from high school who was older and had always liked me; he said he wanted to take care of me and my baby, he said that was what he thought the Lord had put him on earth to do, and we moved to San Jose—he was just getting done with law school—and it was perfect at first. We had so much fun. Then I felt him moving away from me, inside himself. . . . I can't describe it, but I knew and felt he was slipping away.

"So I came back home again—that's where they have to open the door when you knock, right?—I remember that from a poem or a story or something, and my parents set me up. And I'm getting some money, a lot of money, from James. I think he feels guilty or something. Anyway, I'm supposed to start taking classes one of these days and get my degree, only I don't know what I want to take, and I'm liking this time with Miles, and then I met you. And there you go." I had been stroking her hair before all this began. I made myself keep going though my hand felt like something that had become detached from me. She sighed. "You know that fairy tale where the lady has this fantastic, unbelievable lover, and the only catch is that she can never see his face, she can never see who he really, truly is? Well, that's what I always feel like—felt like, until I found you. Like I was the fantastic, unbelievable lover, but that I could never let anybody see my true face, my true me. I could never let them see who I was. I had to be afraid that if they saw me they would run. So I made up those stories, true enough to make all the points line up, but never the whole truth, never the whole me . . ."

I stared at the television, muted, but with pictures of the highlights of the Arizona Diamondbacks and San Francisco Giants. "Why are you telling me now?" I hoped my voice was calm and even.

"Because I want you to see me. I want to be your lover, not just someone you sleep with. I want to be yours, for real, but I want you to see me. Can you understand that?"

I tried to be careful. "How can I see you if you lie to me?"

"Because I *liked* you. I didn't think you would like me if you knew. That's why I ran away that night we met. I couldn't tell you. I guess I thought I would give you a chance to love me before you knew, and then it wouldn't matter because we would be in love. Can you forgive me that? This one thing? Everything else is true. Everything I've said to you is true. I love you."

She told me all this with her head in my lap, facing up in the half-darkness and smiling. I didn't know what to say and I didn't have a lot of time to think. There were a lot of spaces in her story, spaces I needed to fill in, information and details that I needed fleshed out, facts I was fairly confident I couldn't have stood to hear filled in. Was she gone weeks or months or years? Who was the baby's father? Had she become pregnant in a drug-addled haze? Was the baby healthy? Had she been raped? I looked at gentle Serena Haley, and I couldn't help wondering if life, or some guy out in Haight Ashbury or Seattle or the East Village or who knows where, had beaten that gentleness into her.

By this time she was sitting up and facing me. I didn't know what exactly I should do, but I pulled her close to me. I kissed her on her forehead. I said, "It's okay, baby, it's okay." I noticed she was crying, and she said very softly, "I love you, Jack."

After a moment, she said, "You don't have to say anything; I know you love me. It used to bother me when I'd do something nice for you, or try to talk to you and tell you how I feel about you and you'd just shrug it off. At first I thought you didn't care, but then I realized you just didn't know how to say it. You walk around pretending you're this big old grizzly bear and growling and scaring people away from you, but really, you're just a great big old teddy bear, looking for a hug. Am I right?"

As I sat there holding her, I couldn't help thinking, but did not say, which I now regret—it is, perhaps, the only thing from that night that I truly regret—that this was why men couldn't trust women, because they put on a pretty face and let you believe in their innocence while they lied about everything until the past and the lie come crashing into the present like a freight train. I thought

I deserved better. Something very slowly went out of me, or maybe came back. Maybe I was waking up. Maybe Serena Haley had just been a dream. Or maybe I was just who I was. A bad guy. But I didn't think so. So I sat there, stroking her hair. We made love, careful and full of forgiveness, and just before she pulled away and fell asleep, she said in a gently groggy voice, "Jack, you know redemption isn't something you get, it's something you do." I just smiled at her. I thought to myself, Don't give me that twelve-step bullshit.

I slipped out of bed about 2 A.M. and went home, then went back out and drove to the late night McDonald's on Butterfield until they kicked me out, and then to the Denny's over at the Danada Shopping Plaza. I tried to sort out what I was feeling. Did my hurt—deep through my chest and down into my fingers—stem from the fact that she had lied and only that, or had all the rest bothered me? I started thinking that it was in the past and I should forgive her, that that was all I needed to do. Then I started thinking that it wasn't mine to forgive; she hadn't done anything to me—it was her life, her business, in the past—and if I was a man I could accept it, accept her, and live in the present. Had she ever questioned me about Dee Dee or anything else? Did I think she didn't have some questions about all of that, that my narratives didn't always quite add up?

I saw Serena for several months after that—she was a good girl and a blast to be with. But I gradually realized I was never going to get over it, whatever *it* was. The closest I got was that maybe I'd created a version of her in my head that I couldn't live without, however good the real thing was. And what else was out there? What was she not telling me now? She started slowly slipping away from me, a week, a day at a time, and then I let her go. I didn't want any more drama.

I next saw her about six months after all that, having breakfast with a friend of hers and their kids at a Poppin' Fresh over in Glen Ellyn. I was reading the Bears waiver list from the first cuts in train-ing camp, and tried to hide behind my *Tribune* sports section, but she caught my eye as I was turning the page, and came over and sat down in my booth. I played it as cool as I knew how, smiling and forking up another mouthful of my omelette to give me a little time to think. She beat me to the punch. "Small world, isn't it?"

I nodded. "Indeed."

"How have you been?"

She seemed to sincerely care. Same old Serena. I just smiled again. "Fine."

"Sure." She was nodding. Then she hardened, just a click. "Don't you wonder how I've been?"

"Of course I do. Give me that much."

"Then say something." She stared at me, fighting back tears. "We're trying to have a conversation here."

"I don't know what to say." I truly didn't. How could I say, *I'm sit-ting here eating my breakfast and minding my own business?*

She smiled again, and fought back a tear. "Well, I saw you over here, and I said to my sister, 'That's Jack, I'm going to go over and say hello.'" She stopped, and looked down, breaking eye contact. "And that's what I'm doing."

"Well, thank you. I'm touched." I almost reached to touch her hand, then thought better of it. She didn't notice.

She looked back up. "You don't have to be smart. We've been down a few too many roads for that."

"No. I truly am. You could have sat over there and pretended I was dead. Maybe you should have."

"No. I've never been any good at pretending, and certainly not pretending that. Never that. But I also wanted to tell you some-thing," she said, very evenly. I closed my eyes for a long blink. "There's something I wanted to say. You owe me that much. I think."

"Yes."

We both braced ourselves. It was like that moment in a play when the spotlight falls on the star-crossed lovers. I was definitely alone with her in that light. "You know, a woman falls in love with you, you let a woman fall in love, and she sleeps with you, and cleans your house, and gives herself to you. . . . You're not supposed to let them down. They're supposed to be able to believe in you."

"They?" I didn't know what else to say.

"I. Us. Me. I trusted you."

"I made a mistake."

"Promises were made."

"I don't think I made any promises."

She pursed her lips very tightly, reviewing the record, then nodded, this time as if something had just occurred to her. "You're right. You were very careful not to do that." She looked at me with eyes as clear, if shining, as they were that night in Galena. "Implied, then. Implied."

"I made a mistake."

"You said that." She cocked her head, but not in anger. More like she was inquiring. Asking me a question. "Are you saying you'd like to go back? That you'd do it differently if you could do it over? Is that what you mean by 'mistake'?" Looking back, it is easy to see that this was one of those moments, a time when you have to be careful, when you have to slow down and think and make the right decision as if your life depended upon it, because it does. I can see all that, now. But then I could only look at her, helplessly. We sat there, so quietly, while the restaurant clattered around us, looking at each other, until she reached in and pulled a tissue from her purse, wiped her eyes, blew her nose, smiled very mildly, and said, "Allergies."

Then she stood up, smiled at me again, and without saying anything walked back to her table. After a moment, she touched her sister's arm, stood and gathered up her son, walked to the front of the restaurant. She talked to the cashier for a moment, nodding, then paid their check and carried Miles through the double set of doors outside. She walked to the BMW, sat the boy on the trunk, opened the rear door, carefully locked him into the child's seat, then closed his door and opened her own. She got in, sat down, put on her seatbelt, started the car, pulled forward out of her space and through the parking lot, rolled the few feet over the sidewalk to the street, put on her blinker, and slowly turned right into the flow of traffic, going west on Roosevelt Road.

This all happened right in front of me, as if in slow motion, as if I were somebody else. As if I were watching a movie. And I play it over in my head, from time to time, as if it were a movie. As if I could rewind or re-edit or reshoot it and do it over again. Should I have gotten up and run after her, fallen to my knees in front of the car, asked her in the light rain to have mercy and pity and save my sorry life? I am not the fellow who could do that. I realize now I have never been the fellow who could do that. The events I am describing happened three years ago. I have not seen Serena Haley, nor do I expect to, again.

LUCIA NEVAI

Step Men

W e'd seen the body. Now we wanted to see the car.
The mortician's wife gave us directions. There are only
two stoplights in this town, she said. She said to go left at the second light—we'd see the car one block up.

We climbed into the big blue van—me; my son, Roddy; and his
stepfathers, two of my three exes. Within moments, we were barrelling east on the Arizona interstate, free of the town. Four lanes
of gleaming eighteen-wheelers surrounded us. The interstate felt
like a giant existential amusement park ride: We were all connected, our wheels were spinning, we were going nowhere. Straw-
colored scrub grass stretched for miles to the north, miles to the
south. A dry, sinister wind was blowing. Intermittently it gathered
steam and slammed the van, wrenching the steering wheel away
from Jacques, ex number two. Our son, Neil, was dead.

"We missed it." Roddy stated the obvious with a gentleness and
resignation that calmed all three of us. I was proud of Roddy. Gone
were the days of the angry shaved head, the endless scowl. Gone
was the hiss that passed for an answer to a yes or no question. At
twenty-four, Roddy looked and acted like a matinee idol from the
coming millennium, all groomed and glamorous with black finger-

nails and thrift-store seventies hoodlum polyester. His anger went into his music now, screaming free jazz that few people liked.

The van was a rental with plush velour seats. The armrests were adjustable, the backseats swiveled. There were drink holders here and there. Roddy and I flew out to Phoenix from New York and rented the van from Avis. I thought we might need a lot of room. I had called all the fathers, Jacques in Vermont, Howard in L.A., Sol in Nairobi, and left messages on their machines, telling them to meet us in Phoenix between twelve and one.

Howard, ex number three, was there waiting for us at the Avis lot. His jaw looked tan beneath his Armani sunglasses. His haircut made him look rich. He was doing well. When we split up, he changed his name from Howie to Howard and moved from New York to L.A. His movie was finally being made. He and Roddy shook hands, then Howard hugged me. His back was shivering. His back always shivered when he was upset.

Jacques showed up next, same wild mass of hair he'd had in the sixties, the same cocky, menacing air. Jacques was a brawling French Canadian Hells Angel still masquerading as a counter-culture type. He was now making a go of it as an exorcist.

Roddy was sitting in the driver's seat. Jacques told him to move over. "I want Roddy to drive," I said three times. Jacques had wrecks. He lost an eye in Mexico. He lost an ear in Maine. He felt hormonally obligated to terrorize his passengers with theatrical displays of traffic-related agility. I was prepared to wrestle Jacques for the keys, to walk the fifty miles to the mortuary in the scorching Arizona sun alone if Jacques won. "It's all right, Mom," Roddy said. "It's going to be fine." He got out, handing the keys to Jacques. I climbed into the back of the van to lie down. Roddy sat next to me. Howard rode shotgun, his back shivering madly.

"Don't wait for Sol," Roddy said wisely. His father, ex number one, was fanatical and obsessive, a man who was so busy saving the world he missed his son's birthday party ten years in a row. When he lived three blocks from us in Manhattan, he never showed up for family occasions. Why would he now that he lived in the Serengeti? Still, we called him. Roddy left urgent word with his guide, where to meet us, when, and why. That was Roddy's genius, always to give Sol the information but never to publicly allow himself to hope Sol would actually show.

Now Jacques was looking for a U-turn. He eased the van across three lanes and onto the shoulder. To do it safely took ten miles. Jacques had become a reasonable driver. We crept along the shoulder toward the U-turn, the van shuddering and jumping sideways with each passing tractor-trailer. Howard was petrified, but he didn't try to take over. He didn't even say a word. His tan jaw was flexing aerobically beneath his Armani sunglasses. Of the three, he had loved me the most.

Jacques came to a full stop on the median. It was calm, quiet, and strange there. The sound of the wind blended with the sound of the traffic in a serene New Age hum. I was glad we were all in shock. It was pleasant: death's free sedative. Here were four former big-time antagonists, neutered of agenda, purged of history, simplified and tranquilized, people who overshot a stoplight.

Jacques took a deep breath, gearing up to inch his way onto the westbound shoulder. Roddy crouched on the backseat facing out the rear window, watching hard for a break in traffic. Ahh. I felt sick with sorrow. He used to sit like that on car trips when he was ten. Neil used to poke him in the bottom. Roddy had lost his brother, his only sibling, the sole being who shared his childhood.

Slowly, Jacques brought the car up to speed on the shoulder. Roddy provided regular updates. "Not yet. Not yet." Howard closed his eyes. "Now!" Roddy said, and Jacques yanked the van hard into the fast lane, gunning the accelerator as he was born to do. We were caught up safely in the fleet again, tonnage roaring west, engines whining; truck drivers to our left and right, bald-eyed on uppers, pushing ninety.

"Well done," Howard said, opening his eyes.

So the step men knew how to behave after all. Why hadn't they all along? Why had they waited to cooperate until Neil was dead?

Back in town, we followed the directions backwards. We took a right at the first light. We went one block. On the left was a beauty parlor. Wanda's Hair World. No one wanted to get out of the car to ask Wanda anything.

Just in case the mortician's wife was off by a light, we drove to the second light and took a right. On the left, there was a gas station. We all felt better. At least a gas station had something to do with cars.

We rolled in and waited. A young man in a striped golf shirt and khaki pants came out. He had a very small nose. Jacques rolled down his window. "We're looking for the green Chevy that was in the accident with the bus," Jacques said.

"It used to be here," he said. He looked at us without curiosity as if there was no connection to be made between a blue van full of strangers from out of town and a dead boy who made headlines by setting fire to his motel room, then driving his car head-on into a Greyhound bus. "It's not here anymore," he said. "It's in the county yard." He gave us directions. None of us heard him very well.

"Did he say to pass a school?" Jacques asked.

"He said something about passing two motels," Howard said.

I felt totally confused. Everything in this town looked like a motel. The sheriff's office was in the Budget vein. The mortuary was more Ramada. How could we tell if we were passing actual motels?

Jacques crept forward. All four of us were watching hard out the windows on both sides of the van, eyes trained violently on the façades, façades with numbers missing, surfaces painted blank with Arizona light, blanker than seemed possible, like camouflage, taking information from us without giving any. I was afraid the town would soon be over and we would be barrelling west toward Las Vegas again in the unavoidable company of several hundred tractor-trailers.

"School," Roddy announced. We watched it go by, sunlight strobing hypnotically on windowpanes, paper tulips taped to the glass. "Motel," Roddy said. Then again, "Motel."

I saw it, I saw the car. Alone in knee-high grass behind chain-link twelve feet high. Neil's Chevy, a beautiful metallic color, the blue-green of the water in the Caribbean. I had expected a twisted, mangled mess, a stomach-turning dish of steel spaghetti splashed with glass and blood, a frozen 3-D interstate battle scream. True, the entire front half of the car was now in the backseat, but it seemed to me more whole than it should be given what happened, just as his body had seemed to me more whole than it should be. Given what happened.

We had gone in to see the body one at a time. I was elated. My darling, my darling. He wasn't shredded or disfigured. He wasn't charred or amputated. He was whole. His shoulders were cold to the touch, but they yielded pliantly when I hugged him—as if he were waiting for me to get there before he went into rigor mortis. I lifted the creepy cloth the mortician used to cover the body to look at his feet. I loved his feet. Our feet looked alike. Our big toes jut out where they connect to the bone at the ball of the foot. Neil, Neil, I said, do you have any message for me?

Be kind to Dad, I felt him say.

My hands were clutching the chain-link so hard my fingers and thumbs hurt. A tall, pot-bellied Hawaiian man in a cowboy hat came up to the gate with a key. His face looked a little like a wreck itself. He unlocked the padlock and dragged the gate open. "Take your time," he said, and he meant it. He leaned back against the gate to light a cigarette.

The car was loaded to the gills with Neil's stuff, things sweet and familiar to me: the red and black Navajo blanket, the subzero sleeping bag, the green nylon tent. He'd been driving across America for a year, camping out in conditions of extreme heat and cold. I had in my pocket the postcard he'd just sent from the Grand Canyon. It came in the mail yesterday, after I got the call from the Coconino

County Sheriff's Office. Detective Stu Lansberry told me what happened. He told me Neil or someone they believed was Neil had driven up and down the interstate shooting at the driver of a Greyhound bus—and missing. He said no one was hurt but Neil, and Neil was dead.

I took the postcard with me. On the plane, I kept reading and rereading it, looking for clues, but there was only one—Neil had signed it "love." Neil and I had been through a lot in the last two years. Like it or not, you have to respect someone who loses their mind. You can be sure they would have preferred not to. As with any out-of-control molecular process, it was surely packed with indescribable terror and required a great deal of bravery.

There were some unfamiliar things in the car, too. Guns. A gas mask. A night-vision scope. An unused U.S. Navy arctic weight jumpsuit, so new it still held the crease marks from being in the mail-order box. Neil was on the way to Alaska when he changed his mind and killed himself.

The wind picked up. "What's today?" I asked. Roddy put his arm around me. "It's Thursday, Mom," he said. The way he said it calmed me. I had asked him this before, perhaps five times. My throat was lurching toward a sob that would never end. Jacques saved me, handing me a smudge stick.

"Wild desert sage," he said, lighting the tip.

"Thank you," I said.

I had freaked out in the mortuary when the mortician asked us what were our "wishes." I said burial at sea. I said Neil had read a Chekhov story and told me burial at sea was the best kind of burial. Jacques had gently overruled me, recommending cremation. Then when I refused to leave the body, Jacques distracted me, gently again, saying we all had something important to do. We had to purge the car. And here we were, purging the car. How strange. When Neil was alive, Jacques had terrible ideas for family events. His ideas for how to spend birthdays, holidays, and Christmas always involved too much travel, too much waiting, and too many people along for the ride who he'd just met.

A silvery ribbon of soothing, pungent, herbal smoke curled off the tip of my sage stick.

"Eagle feathers," Jacques said, handing several long, strong, formidable feathers to Howard. "These are holy."

Howard accepted them as if they were.

To Roddy, Jacques presented a strange rattle made of skin and shells and hair. "For demons," he said. "The last time I tried to exorcize Neil, he had around eighteen demons."

Jacques himself was holding a large lavender quartz crystal on a sacred-looking pillow sewn of wine-colored velvet that looked suspiciously like a pillow I had sewn of wine-colored velvet for his mother twenty years ago.

"We're going to walk around the car—clockwise," Jacques announced. "Glenda will lead. We want to release the fragments of Neil's spirit, which are still attached to this site."

I walked the way we walked in choir in junior high school, a slightly labored, solemn, swaying processional. Roddy stepped into line behind me, shaking the rattle in 11/8 time.

"What do I do with the feathers?" Howard asked, with no hint of sarcasm.

"Raise them to the sky," Jacques said. "To give his spirit fragments wings." This I had to see, Howie raising eagle feathers to the sky. I looked over my shoulder, but before Howard could attempt it, Roddy stopped everything by yelling, "Dad!"

There he was, ex number one, climbing out of a yellow taxicab in African bush khakis, walking toward us with mild indignation, saying, "Where were you? I was there. At one. You said between twelve and one."

Sol gave me a quick, covetous once-over—apparently I looked better than his current lady friend—and said as if I'd only been away an hour instead of twenty-five years, "You cut your hair."

"Jacques," Roddy said, "do you have something for Sol?"

Jacques fished around in his backpack. "Aroma scent," he said, presenting Sol with a small, very blue bottle topped off with a Victorianesque atomizer. "It purifies negativity," Jacques said. Sol seemed to accept this along with the bottle.

I started up the processional again, clockwise around the car through the knee-high grass, my sage stick lacing the air with its heavy merciful scent, lacing my brain with the scent I would forever link with spiritual freedom. Howard clasped the quill ends in his hands and in an impressive abandonment of inhibition, raised the feathers high over his head, sweeping them across the sky to the beat of Roddy's rattle. Sol followed, spritzing the Chevy. Jacques fell in behind Sol.

We marched and swayed, marched and swayed. I assumed Jacques had some spiritually efficacious number of circuits in mind and that he would alert me when the number had been reached. Each time I looked at the Hawaiian man smoking at the gate, he had changed. He went from a scarred up, alcoholic gear-head to a gentle gatekeeper, neutral yet benign, a witness to our ceremony. The magic number of circuits turned out to be 81—nine times nine—we found out eventually when Jacques let us stop. Jacques often made the mistake of explaining too much about his magic. We were all happier. When we gave Jacques back his things, we took turns hugging. It was three o'clock. Neil was burning. We had a few more hours to kill before it was time to pick up his ashes and drive to the Grand Canyon to scatter them.

Jacques was wrapping our ritual objects in sacred silks and packing them carefully in his backpack. "What should we do now?" I asked, and I looked at Howard. It was his cue. He overcame his speechlessness and rose to the occasion as he had every time I'd been hungry in a crisis during the ten years of our marriage.

"Let's eat," he said, and raised his arms to include us all.

Lorrie Moore

Beautiful Grade

It's a chilly night, bitter inside and out. After a grisly month-long court proceeding, Bill's good friend Albert has become single again—and characteristically curatorial: Albert has invited his friends over to his sublet to celebrate New Year's Eve and watch his nuptial and postnuptial videos, which Albert has hauled down from the bookcase and proffered with ironic wonder and glee. At each of his three weddings, Albert's elderly mother had videotaped the ceremony, and at the crucial moment in the vows, each time, Albert's face turns impishly from his bride, looks straight into his mother's camera, and says, "I do. I swear I do." The divorce proceedings, by contrast, are mute, herky-jerky, and badly lit ("A clerk," says Albert): there are wan smiles, business suits, the waving of a pen.

At the end, Albert's guests clap. Bill puts his fingers in his mouth and whistles shrilly (not every man can do this; Bill himself didn't learn until college, though already that was thirty years ago; three decades of ear-piercing whistling—youth shall not be wasted on the young). Albert nods, snaps the tapes back into their plastic cases, turns on the lights, and sighs.

"No more weddings," Albert announces. "No more divorces. No more wasting time. From here on in, I'm just going to go out there, find a woman I really don't like very much, and give her a house."

Bill, divorced only once, is here tonight with Debbie, a woman who is too young for him: at least that is what he knows is said, though the next time it is said to his face, Bill will shout, "I beg your pardon!" Maybe not shout. Maybe squeak. Squeak with a dash of begging. Then he'll just hurl himself to the ground and plead for a quick stoning. For now, this second, however, he will pretend to be a braver, more evolved heart, explaining to anyone who might ask how much easier it would be to venture out still with his ex-wife, someone his own age, but no, not Bill, not big brave Bill: Bill has entered something complex, spiritually biracial, politically tricky, and, truth be told, physically demanding. Youth will not be wasted on the young.

Who the hell is that?

She looks fourteen!

You can't be serious!

Bill has had to drink more than usual. He has had to admit to himself that on his own, without any wine, he doesn't have a shred of the courage necessary for this romance.

("Not to pry, Bill, or ply you with feminist considerations, but, excuse me—you're dating a twenty-five-year-old?"

"Twenty-four," he says. "But you were close!")

His women friends have yelled at him—or sort of yelled. It's really been more of a cross between sighing and giggling. "Don't be cruel," Bill has had to say.

Albert has been kinder, more delicate, in tone if not in substance. "*Some* people might consider your involvement with this girl a misuse of your charm," he said slowly.

"But I've worked hard for this charm," said Bill. "Believe me, I started from scratch. Can't I do with it what I want?"

Albert sized up Bill's weight loss and slight tan, the sprinkle of freckles like berry seeds across Bill's arms, the summer whites worn way past Labor Day in the law school's cavernous, crowded lecture halls, and he said, "Well then, *some* people might think it a mishandling of your position." He paused, put his arm around Bill. "But hey, I think it has made you look very—tennisy."

Bill shoved his hands in his pockets. "You mean the whole kindness of strangers thing?"

Albert took his arm back. "What are you talking about?" he asked, and then his face fell in a kind of melting, concerned way. "Oh, you poor thing," he said. "You poor, poor thing."

Bill has protested, obfuscated, gone into hiding. But he is too tired to keep Debbie in the closet anymore. The body has only so many weeks of stage fright in it before it simply gives up and just goes out onstage. Moreover, this semester Debbie is no longer taking either of his Constitutional Law classes. She is no longer, between weekly lectures, at home in his bed, with a rented movie, saying things that are supposed to make him laugh, things like "Open up, doll. Is that drool?" and "Don't you dare think I'm doing this for a good grade. I'm doing this for a *beautiful* grade." Debbie no longer performs her remarks at him, which he misses a little, all that effort and desire. "If I'm just a passing fancy, then I want to pass fancy," she once said. Also, "Law school: It's the film school of the nineties."

Debbie is no longer a student of his in any way, so at last their appearance together is only unattractive and self-conscious-making but not illegal. Bill can show up with her for dinner. He can live in the present, his newly favorite tense.

But he must remember who is here at this party, people for whom history, acquired knowledge, the accumulation of days and years is everything—or is this simply the convenient shorthand of his own paranoia? There is Albert, with his videos; Albert's old friend Brigitte, a Berlin-born political scientist; Stanley Mix, off every other semester to fly to Japan and study the zoological effects of radiation at Hiroshima and Nagasaki; Stanley's wife, Roberta, a travel agent and obsessive tabulator of Stanley's frequent flyer miles (Bill has often admired her posters: STEP BACK IN TIME, COME TO

ARGENTINA says the one on her door); Lina, a pretty visiting Serb teaching in Slavic Studies; and Lina's doctor husband, Jack, a Texan who five years ago in Yugoslavia put Dallas dirt under the laboring Lina's hospital bed so that his son could be "born on Texan soil." ("But the boy is a total *sairb*," Lina says of her son, rolling her lovely *r*'s. "Just don't tell Jack.")

Lina.

Lina, Lina.

Bill is a little taken with Lina.

"You are with Debbie because somewhere in your pahst ease some pretty leetle girl who went away from you," Lina said to him once on the phone.

"Or, how about because everyone else I know is married."

"Ha!" she said. "You only believe they are married."

Which sounded, to Bill, like the late-night, adult version of *Peter Pan*—no Mary Martin, no songs, just a lot of wishing and thinking lovely thoughts; then afterward all the participants throw themselves out the window.

And never, never land?

Marriage, Bill thinks: *it*'s the film school of the nineties.

Truth be told, Bill is a little afraid of suicide. Taking one's life, he thinks, has too many glitzy things to offer: a real edge on the narrative (albeit retrospectively), a disproportionate philosophical advantage (though again, retrospectively), the last word, the final cut, the parting shot. Most importantly, it gets you the hell out of there, wherever it is you are, and he can see how such a thing might happen in a weak but brilliant moment, one you might just regret later while looking down from the depthless sky or up through two sandy anthills and some weeds.

Still, Lena is the one he finds himself thinking about, and carefully dressing for in the morning—removing all dry-cleaning tags and matching his socks.

————

Albert leads them all into the dining room and everyone drifts around the large teak table, studying the busily constructed salads at each place setting—salads, which, with their knobs of cheese, jutting chives, and little folios of frisée, resemble small Easter hats.

"Do we wear these or eat them?" asks Jack. In his mouth is a piece of gray chewing gum like a rat's brain.

"I admire gay people," Bill's voice booms. "To have the courage to love whom you want to love in the face of all bigotry."

"Relax," Debbie murmurs, nudging him. "It's only salad."

Albert indicates in a general way where they should sit, alternating male, female, like the names of hurricanes, though such seating leaves all the couples split and far apart, on New Year's Eve no less, as Bill suspects Albert wants it.

"Don't sit next to him—he bites," says Bill to Lina as she takes a place next to Albert.

"Six degrees of separation," says Debbie. "Do you believe that thing about how everyone is separated by only six people?"

"Oh, *we*'re separated by at least six, aren't we, darling?" says Lina to her husband.

"At least."

"No, I mean by *only* six," says Debbie. "I mean strangers." But no one is listening to her.

"This is a political New Year's Eve," says Albert. "We're here to protest the new year, protest the old; generally get a petition going to Father Time. But also eat: in China it's the Year of the Pig."

"Ah, one of those years of the Pig," says Stanley. "I love those."

Bill puts salt on his salad, then looks up apologetically. "I salt everything," he says, "so it can't get away."

Albert brings out salmon steaks and distributes them with Brigitte's help. Ever since Albert was denied promotion to full-professor rank, his articles on Flannery O'Connor ("A Good Man Really *Is* Hard to

Find," "Everything That Rises *Must Indeed* Converge," and "The Totemic South: The Vilent *Actually Do* Bear It Away!") failing to meet with collegial acclaim, he has become determined to serve others, passing out the notices and memoranda, arranging the punch and cookies at various receptions. He has not yet become very good at it, however, but the effort touches and endears. Now everyone sits with their hands in their laps, leaning back when plates are set before them. When Albert sits down, they begin to eat.

"You know, in Yugoslavia," says Jack, chewing, "a person goes to school for four years to become a waiter. Four years of waiter school."

"Typical Yugoslavians," adds Lina. "They have to go to school for four years to learn how to serve someone."

"I'll bet they do it well," Bill says stupidly. Everyone ignores him, for which he is grateful. His fish smells fishier than the others—he is sure of it. Perhaps he has been poisoned.

"Did you hear about that poor Japanese foreign student who stopped to ask directions and was shot because he was thought to be an intruder?" This is Debbie, dear Debbie. How did she land on this?

"Oh, God, I know. Wasn't that terrible?" says Brigitte.

"A shooting like that really makes a lot of sense, too," says Bill, "when you think about how the Japanese are particularly known for their street crime." Lina chortles and Bill pokes at his fish a little.

"I guess the man thought the student was going to come in and reprogram his computer," says Jack, and everyone laughs.

"Now is that racist?" asks Bill.

"Is it?"

"Maybe."

"I don't think so."

"Not in any real way."

"It's just us."

"What's that supposed to mean?"

"Would anyone like more food?"

"So Stanley," says Lina. "How is the research going?"

Is this absent querying or pointed interrogation? Bill can't tell. The last time they were all together, they got into a terrible discussion about World War II. World War II is not necessarily a good topic of conversation generally, and among the eight of them, it became a total hash. Stanley yelled, Lina threatened to leave, and Brigitte broke down over dessert: "I was a little girl; I was there," Brigitte said of Berlin.

Lina, whose three uncles, she'd once told Bill, had been bayoneted by Nazis, sighed and looked off at the wallpaper—wide pale stripes like pajamas. It was impossible to eat.

Brigitte looked accusingly at everyone, her face swelling like a baked apple. Tears leaked out of her eyes. "They did not have to bomb like that. Not like that. They did not have to bomb so much," and then she began to sob, then choke back sobs, and then just choke.

It had been a shock to Bill. For years, Brigitte had been the subject of his skeptical, private jokes with Albert. They would make up fake titles for her books on European history: *That Kooky Führer* and *Hitler: What a Nutroll!* But that evening, Brigitte's tears were so bitter and full, after so many years, that it haunted and startled him. What did it mean to cry like that—*at dinner?* He had never known a war in that way or ever, really. He had never even known a dinner in that way.

"Fine," says Stanley to Lina. "Great, really. I'm going back next month. The small-head-size data is the most interesting and conclusive thus far." He chews his fish. "If I got paid by the word, I'd be a rich man." He has the supple, overconfident voice of a panelist from the Texaco Opera Quiz.

"Jack here gets paid by the word," says Bill, "and that word is *Next?*" Perhaps Bill could adroitly switch the subject away from nuclear devastation and steer it toward national health plans. Would that be an improvement? He remembers once asking Lina what kind of medicine Jack practiced. "Oh, he's a gynecological surgeon," she said dismissively. "Something to do with things dropping into the vagina." She gave a shudder. "I don't like to think about it."

Things dropping into the vagina. The word *things* had for some reason made Bill think of tables and chairs, or, even more glamorously, pianos and chandeliers, and he has now come to see Jack as a kind of professional mover: the Allied Van Lines of the OB-GYN set.

"After all this time, Bill is still skeptical about doctors," Jack now says.

"I can see that," says Stanley.

"I once had the wrong tonsil removed," says Bill.

"Are you finding a difference between Hiroshima and Nagasaki?" persists Lina.

Stanley turns and looks at her. "That's interesting that you should ask that. You know, Hiroshima was a uranium bomb and Nagasaki a plutonium. And the fact is, we're finding more damaging results from the uranium."

Lina gasps and puts down her fork. She turns and looks in an alarmed way at Stanley, studying, it seems, the condition of his face, the green-brown shrapnel of his dried acne cysts, like lentils buried in the skin.

"They used two different kinds of bombs?" she says.

"That's right," says Stanley.

"You mean, all along, right from the start, this was just an experiment? They designed it explicitly right from the beginning, as *something to study*?" Blood has rushed to her face.

Stanley grows a little defensive. He is, after all, one of the studiers. He shifts in his chair. "There are some very good books written on the subject. If you don't understand what happened regarding Japan during World War Two, you would be well advised to read a couple of them."

"Oh, I see. Then we could have a better conversation," says Lina. She turns away from Stanley and looks at Albert.

"Children, children," murmurs Albert.

"World War Two," says Debbie. "Wasn't that the war to end all wars?"

"No, that was World War One," says Bill. "By World War Two, they weren't making any promises."

Stanley will not relent. He turns to Lina again. "I have to say, I'm surprised to see a Serbian, in a matter of foreign policy, attempting to take the moral high ground," he says.

"Stanley, I used to like you," says Lina. "Remember when you were a nice guy? I do."

"I do, too," says Bill. "There was that whole smiling, handing-out-money thing he used to do."

Bill feels inclined to rescue Lina. This year, she has been through a lot. Just last spring, the local radio station put her on a talk show and made her answer questions about Bosnia. In attempting to explain what was going on in the former Yugoslavia, she said, "You have to think about what it might mean for Europe to have a nationalist, Islamic state," and "Those fascist Croats," and "It's all very complicated." The next day, students boycotted her classes and picketed her office with signs that read GENOCIDE IS NOT "COMPLI-CATED" and REPENT, IMPERIALIST. Lina had phoned Bill at his office. "You're a lawyer. They're hounding me. Aren't these students breaking a law? Surely, Bill, they are breaking a law."

"Not really," said Bill. "And believe me, you wouldn't want to live in a country where they were."

"Can't I get a motion to strike? What is that? I like the way it sounds."

"That's used in pleadings or in court. That's not what you want."

"No, I guess not. From them, I just want no more motion. Plus, I want to strike them. There's nothing you can do?"

"They have their rights."

"They understand nothing," she said.

"Are you okay?"

"No. I banged up the fender parking my car, I was so upset. The headlight fell out, and even though I took it into the car place, they couldn't salvage it."

"You've gotta keep those things packed in ice, I think."

"These *cheeldren,* good God, have no conception of the world. I am well known as a pacifist and resister; I was the one last year in Belgrade, buying gasoline out of Coke bottles, hiding a boy from the draft, helping to organize the protests and the radio broadcasts and the rock concerts. Not them. I was the one standing there with the crowd, clapping and chanting beneath Milosevic's window: 'Don't count on us.'" Here Lina's voice fell into a deep Slavic singsong. "Don't count on us. Don't count on us." She paused dramatically. "We had T-shirts and posters. That was no small thing."

"'Don't count on us?'" said Bill. "I don't mean to sound skeptical, but as a political slogan, its seems, I don't know, a little . . ." Lame. It lacked even the pouty energy and determination of "Hell no, we won't go." Perhaps some obscenity would have helped. "Don't fucking count on us, motherfucker." That would have been better. Certainly a better T-shirt.

"It was all very successful," said Lina indignantly.

"But how exactly do you measure success?" asked Bill. "I mean, it took time, but, you'll forgive me, we *stopped* the war in Vietnam."

"Oh, you are all so obsessed with your Vietnam," said Lina.

The next time Bill saw her, it was on her birthday, and she'd had three and a half whiskeys. She exclaimed loudly about the beauty of the cake, and then, taking a deep breath, she dropped her head too close to the candles and set her hair spectacularly on fire.

What does time measure but itself? What can it assess but the mere deposit and registration of itself within a thing?

A large bowl of peas and onions is passed around the table.

They've already dispensed with the O. J. Simpson jokes—the knock-knock one and the one about the sunglasses. They've banned all the others, though Bill is now asked his opinion regarding search and seizure. Ever since he began living in the present tense, Bill sees the Constitution as a blessedly changing thing. He does not feel current behavior should be made necessarily to conform to old law. He feels personally, for instance, that he'd throw away a few First Amendment privileges—abortion protest, say, and all telemarketing, perhaps some pornography (though not Miss April 1965—never!)—in exchange for gutting the Second Amendment. The Founding Fathers were revolutionaries, after all. They would be with him on this, he feels. They would be for making the whole thing up as you go along, reacting to things as they happened, like a great, wild performance piece. "There's nothing sacred about the Constitution; it's just another figmentary contract: it's a palimpsest you can write and write and write on. But then whatever is there when you get pulled over are the rules for then. For now." Bill believes in free speech. He believes in expensive speech. He doesn't believe in shouting "Fire" in a crowded movie theater, but he does believe in shouting "Fie!" and has done it twice himself—both times at *Forrest Gump*. "I'm a big believer in the Rules for Now. Also, Promises for Now, Things to Do for Now, and the ever-handy This Will Do for Now."

Brigitte glares at him. "Such moral excellence," she says.

"Yes," agrees Roberta, who has been quiet all evening, probably figuring out airfare upgrades for Stanley. "How attractive."

"I'm talking theoretical," says Bill. "I believe in common sense. In theory. Theoretical common sense." He feels suddenly cornered and misunderstood. He wishes he weren't constantly asked to pronounce on real-life legal matters. He has never even tried an actual case except once, when he was just out of law school. He'd had a small practice then in the basement of an old sandstone schoolhouse in St. Paul, and the sign inside the building directory said WILLIAM D. BELMONT, ATTORNEY-AT-LAW: ONE LEVEL DOWN. It always broke his heart a little, that *one level down*. The only case he ever took to trial was an armed robbery and concealed weapon case, and he had panicked. He dressed in the exact same beiges and browns as the bailiffs—a subliminal strategy he felt would give him an edge, make him seem at least as much a part of the court "family" as the prosecutor. But by the close of the afternoon, his nerves were shot. He looked too desperately at the jury (who, once in the deliberation room, and in the time it took to order the pizza and wolf it down, voted unanimously to convict). He'd looked imploringly at all their little faces and said, "Ladies and gentlemen, if my client's not innocent, I'll eat my shorts."

At the end of his practice, he had taken to showing up at other people's office parties—not a good sign in life.

Now, equipped with a more advanced degree, like the other people here, Bill has a field of scholarly, hypothetical expertise, plus a small working knowledge of budgets and parking and E-mail. He doesn't mind the E-mail, has more or less gotten used to it, its vaguely smutty Etch A Sketch, though once he found himself lost in the Internet and before he knew it had written his name across some bulletin board on which the only other name was "Stud Boy." Mostly, however, his professional life has been safe and uneventful. Although he is bothered by faculty meetings and by the word *text*—every time he hears it, he feels he should just give up, go off and wear a powdered wig somewhere—it intrigues Bill to belong to academe, with its international hodgepodge and asexual attire, a place where to think and speak *as if* one has lived is always preferable to the alternatives. Such a value cuts down on regrets. And Bill is cutting down. He is determined to cut down. Once, he was called in by the head of the law school and admonished for skipping so many faculty meetings. "It's costing you about a thousand dollars in raises every year," said the dean.

"Really?" replied Bill. "Well, if that's all, it's worth every dime."

"Eat, eat," says Albert. He is bringing in the baked potatoes and dessert cheeses. Things are a little out of whack. *Is a dinner party a paradigm of society or a vicious pantomime of the family?* It is already 10:30. Brigitte has gotten up again to help him. They return with sour cream, chives, grappa and cognac. Debbie looks across the table at Bill and smiles warmly. Bill smiles back. At least he thinks he does.

This taboo regarding age is to make us believe that life is long and ac-tually improves us, that we are wiser, better, more knowledgeable later on than early. It is a myth concocted to keep the young from learning what we really are and despising and murdering us. We keep them sweet-breathed, unequipped, suggesting to them that there is something more than regret and decrepitude up ahead.

Bill is still writing an essay in his head, one of theoretical com-mon sense, though perhaps he is just drinking too much and it is not an essay at all but the simple metabolism of sugar. But this is what he knows right now, with dinner winding up and midnight looming like a death gong: life's embrace is quick and busy, and everywhere in it people are equally lacking and well-meaning and nuts. *Why not admit history's powers to divide and destroy? Why attach ourselves to the age-old stories in the belief that they are truer than the new ones? By living in the past, you always know what comes next, and that robs you of surprises. It exhausts and warps the mind. We are lucky simply to be alive together; why get differentiating and judgmental about who is here among us? Thank God there is anyone at all.*

"I believe in the present tense," Bill says now, to no one in par-ticular. "I believe in amnesty." He stops. People are looking but not speaking. "Or is that just fancy rhetoric?"

"It's not that fancy," says Jack.

"It's fancy," Albert says kindly, ever the host, "without being schmancy." He brings out more grappa. Everyone drinks it from the amber, green, and blue of Albert's Depression glass glasses.

"I mean—" Bill begins, but then he stops, says nothing. Chilean folk music is playing on the stereo, wistful and melancholy: "Bring me all your old lovers, so I can love you, too," a woman sings in Spanish.

"What does that mean?" Bill asks, but at this point he may not actually be speaking out loud. He cannot really tell. He sits back and listens to the song, translating the sad Spanish. Every song-writer in their smallest song seems to possess some monumental grief clarified and dignified by melody, Bill thinks. His own sadnesses, on the other hand, slosh about in his life in a low-key way, formless and self-consuming. *Modest* is how he sometimes likes to see it. No one is modest anymore. Everyone exalts their disappointments. They do ceremonious battle with everything; they demand receipts and take their presents back—all the unhappy things that life awkwardly, stupidly, without thinking, without bothering even to get to know them a little or to ask around! has given them. They bring it all back for an exchange.

As has he, hasn't he?

The young were sent to earth to amuse the old. Why not be amused?

Debbie comes over and sits next to him. "You're looking very rumpled and miffed," she says quietly. Bill only nods. What can he say? She adds, "Rumpled and miffed—doesn't that sound like a law firm?"

Bill nods again. "One in a Hans Christian Andersen story," he says. "Perhaps the one the Ugly Duckling hired to sue his parents."

"Or the one that the Little Mermaid retained to stick it to the Prince," says Debbie, a bit pointedly, Bill thinks—who can tell? Her girlish voice, out of sheer terror, perhaps, has lately adorned itself with dreamy and snippy mannerisms. Probably Bill has single-handedly aged her beyond her years.

Jack has stood and is heading for the foyer. Lina follows.

"Lina, you're leaving? asks Bill with too much feeling in his voice. He sees that Debbie, casting her eyes downward, has noted it.

"Yes, we have a little tradition at home, so we can't stay for midnight." Lina shrugs a bit nonchalantly, then picks up her red wool scarf and lassoes her neck with it, a loose noose. Jack holds her coat up behind her, and she slides her arms into the satin lining.

It's sex, Bill thinks. They make love at the stroke of midnight.

"A tradition?" asks Stanley.

"Uh, yes," Lina says dismissively. "Just a little contemplation of the upcoming year is all. I hope you all have a happy rest of the New Year Eve."

Lina always leaves the apostrophe *s* out of New Year's Eve, Bill notes, oddly enchanted. And why *should* New Year's Eve have an apostrophe *s*? It shouldn't. Christmas Eve doesn't. Logically—

"They have sex at the stroke of midnight," says Albert after they leave.

"I knew it!" shouts Bill.

"Sex at the stroke of midnight?" asks Roberta.

"I myself usually save that for Lincoln's Birthday," says Bill.

"It's a local New Year's tradition apparently," says Albert.

"I've lived here twenty years and I've never heard of it," says Stanley.

"Neither have I," says Roberta.

"Nor I," says Brigitte.

"Me, neither," says Bill.

"Well, we'll all have to do something equally compelling," says Debbie.

Bill's head spins to look at her. The bodice of her black velvet dress is snowy with napkin lint. Her face is flushed from drink. What does she mean? She means nothing at all.

"Black-eyed peas!" cries Albert. And he dashes into the kitchen and brings out an iron pot of warm, pasty, black-dotted beans and six spoons.

"Now this is a tradition I know," says Stanley, and he takes one of the spoons and digs in.

Albert moves around the room with his pot. "You can't eat until the stroke of midnight. The peas have to be the first thing you consume in the New Year and then you'll have good luck all year long."

Brigitte takes a spoon and looks at her watch. "We've got five minutes."

"What'll we do?" asks Stanley. He is holding his spoonful of peas like a lollipop, and they are starting to slide.

"We'll contemplate our fruitful work and great accomplishments." Albert sighs. "Though, of course, when you think about Gandhi, or Pasteur, or someone like Martin Luther King, Jr., dead at thirty-nine, it sure makes you wonder what you've done with your life."

"We've done some things," says Bill.

"Yes? Like what?" asks Albert.

"We've . . ." And here Bill stops for a moment. "We've . . . had some excellent meals. We've . . . bought some nice shirts. We've gotten a good trade-in or two on our cars—I think I'm going to go kill myself now."

"I'll join you," says Albert. "Knives are in the drawer by the sink."

"How about the vacuum cleaner?"

"Vacuum cleaner in the back closet."

"Vacuum cleaner?" hoots Roberta. But no one explains or goes anywhere. Everyone just sits.

"Peas poised!" Stanley suddenly shouts. They all get up and stand in a horseshoe around the hearth with its new birch logs and bright but smoky fire. They lift their mounded spoons and eye the mantel clock with its ancient minute hand jerking toward midnight.

"Happy New Year," says Albert finally, after some silence, and lifts his spoon in salute.

"Amen," says Stanley.

"Amen," says Roberta.

"Amen," say Debbie and Brigitte.

"Ditto," says Bill, his mouth full, but indicating with his spoon.

Then they all hug quickly—"Gotcha!" says Bill with each hug—and begin looking for their coats.

"You always seem more interested in other women than in me," Debbie says when they are back at his house after a silent ride home, Debbie driving. "Last month it was Lina. And the month before that it was . . . it was Lina again." She stops for a minute.

"I'm sorry to be so selfish and pathetic." She begins to cry, and as she does, something cracks open in her and Bill sees straight through to her heart. It is a good heart. It has had nice parents and good friends, lived only during peacetime, and been kind to animals. She looks up at him. "I mean, I'm romantic and passionate. I believe if you're in love, that's enough. I believe love conquers all."

Bill nods sympathetically, from a great distance.

"But I don't want to get into one of these feeble, one-sided, patched-together relationships—no matter how much I care for you."

"Whatever happened to love conquers all, just four seconds ago?"

Debbie pauses. "I'm older now," she says.

"You kids. You grow up so fast."

Then there is a long silence between them, the second in this new New Year. Finally, Debbie says, "Don't you know that Lina's having an affair with Albert? Can't you see they're in love?"

Something in Bill drops, squares off, makes a neat little knot. "No, I didn't see." He feels the sickened sensation he has sometimes felt after killing a housefly and finding blood in it.

"You yourself had suggested they might be lovers."

"I did? Not seriously. Really? I did?"

"But Bill, hadn't you heard? I mean, it's all over campus."

Actually, he had heard some rumors; he had even said, "Hope so" and once "May God bless their joyous union." But he hadn't meant or believed any of it. Such rumors seemed ham-handed, literal, unlikely. And yet wasn't reality always cheesy and unreliable just like that; wasn't fate literal in exactly that way? He thinks of the severed, crossed fingers found perfectly survived in the wreckage of a local plane crash last year. Such fate was contrary and dense, like a dumb secretary, failing to understand the overall gestalt and desire of the wish. He prefers a deeper, cleverer, even tardy fate, like that of a girl he knew once in law school who, years before, had been raped, shot, and left for dead but then had crawled ten hours out of the woods to the highway with a .22 bullet in her head and flagged a car. That's when you knew that life was making something up to you, that the narrative was apologizing. That's when you knew God had glanced up from his knitting, perhaps even risen from his freaking wicker rocker, and staggered at last to the window to look.

Debbie studies Bill, worried and sympathetic. "You're just not happy in this relationship, are you?" she says.

These terms! This talk! Bill is not good at this; she is better at it than he; she is probably better at everything than he: at least she has not used the word *text*.

"Just don't use the word *text*," he warns.

Debbie is quiet. "You're just not happy with your life," she says.

"I suppose I'm not." *Don't count on us. Don't count on us, motherfucker.*

"A small bit of happiness is not so hard, you know. You could manage it. It's pretty much open-book. It's basically a take-home."

Suddenly, sadness is devouring him. The black-eyed peas! Why aren't they working? Debbie's face flickers and tenses. All her eye makeup has washed away, her eyes bare and round as lightbulbs. "You were always a tough grader," she says. "Whatever happened to grading on a curve?"

"I don't know," he says. "Whatever happened to that?"

Her eyelids lower and she falls soundlessly across his lap, her hair in a golden pinwheel about her head. He can feel the firm watery press of her breasts against his thigh.

How can he assess his life so harshly and ungratefully, when he is here with her, when she is so deeply kind, and a whole new year is upon them like a long, cheap buffet? How could he be so strict and mean?

"I've changed my mind," he says. "I'm happy. I'm bursting."

"You are not," she says, but she turns her face upward and smiles hopefully, like something brief and floral and in need of heat.

"I am," he insists, but looks away, to think, to think of anything else at all, to think of his ex-wife—*Bring me all your old lovers, so I can love you, too*—still living in St. Paul with his daughter, who in five years will be Debbie's age. He believes that he was happy once then, for a long time, for a while. "We are this far from a divorce," his wife had said bitterly at the end. And if she had spread her arms wide, they might have been able to find a way back, the blinking, intermittent wit of her like a lighthouse to him, but no: she had held her index finger and her thumb up close to her face in a mean pinch of salt. Still, before he left, their marriage a spluttering but modest ruin, only two affairs and a dozen sharp words between them, they'd come home from the small humiliations they would endure at work, separately and alone, and they'd turn them some-how into desire. At the very end, they'd taken walks together in the cool wintry light that sometimes claimed those last days of Au-gust—the air chill, leaves already dropping in wind and scuttling along the sidewalk, the neighborhood planted with ocher mums, even the toughest weeds in bridal flower, the hydrangea blooms gone green and drunk with their own juice. Who would not try to be happy?

And just as he had then on those walks, he remembers now how, as a boy in Duluth, he'd once imagined a monster, a demon, chas-ing him home from school. It was one particular winter: Christmas was past, the snow was dirty and crusted, his father was overseas, and his young sister, Lily, home from the hospital's iron lung, lay dying of polio in her bed upstairs at home. His parents had al-ways—discreetly, they probably felt, though also recklessly and maybe guiltily, too—enjoyed their daughter more than their serious older boy. Perhaps it was a surprise even to themselves. But Bill, in studying their looks and words, had discerned it, though in re-sponse he had never known what to do. How could he make him-self more enjoyable? With his father away, he wrote long boring letters with everything spelled correctly. "Dear Dad, How are you? I am fine." But he didn't mail them. He saved them up, tied them in a string, and when his father came home, he gave him the packet. His father said, "Thank you," tucked the letters in his coat, and never mentioned them again. Instead, every day for a year, his father went upstairs and wept for Lily.

Once, when she'd still been pretty and well, Bill went through an entire day repeating everything Lily said, until she cried in torment and his mother slapped him hard against the eye.

Lily had been enjoyed. They enjoyed her. Who could blame them? Enjoyable girl! Enjoyable joy! But Bill could not attain such a thing, either side of it, for himself. He glimpsed it all from behind some atmosphere, from across some green and scalloped sea— "Dear Dad, How are you? I am fine"—as if it were a planet that sometimes sparkled into view, or a tropical island painted in hot, picture-book shades of orange.

But deep in his private January boyhood, he knew, there were colors that were true: the late-afternoon light was bluish and dark, the bruised tundra of the snowbanks scary and silver and cold. Stepping slowly at first, the hulking monster-man, the demon-man, red and giant, with a single wing growing out of its back, would begin to chase Bill. It chased him faster and faster, up and down every tiny hill to home, casting long shadows that would occasionally, briefly, fall upon them both like a net. While the church bells chimed their four o'clock hymn, the monster-man would fly in a loping, wonky way, lunging and leaping and skittering across the ice toward Bill's heels. Bill rounded a corner. The demon leapt over a bin of road salt. Bill cut across a path. The demon followed. And the terror of it all—as Bill flung himself onto his own front porch and into the unlocked and darkened house, slamming the door, sinking back against it, sliding down onto the doormat, safe at last among the clutter of boots and shoes but still gasping the wide lucky gasps of his great and narrow escape—was thrilling to him in a world that had already, and with such indifferent skill, forsaken all its charms.

COPYRIGHTS AND PERMISSIONS

"North Haven" from *Relations: New and Selected Poems* by Philip Booth. Copyright © 1986 by Philip Booth. Used by permission of Viking Penguin, a division of Penguin Putnam Inc.

"The Season of Divorce" from *The Stories of John Cheever* by John Cheever. Copyright © 1950 and renewed © 1978 by John Cheever. Reprinted by permission of Alfred A. Knopf, a Division of Random House, Inc.

"The Burning House" from *Park City* by Ann Beattie. Copyright © 1998 by Irony & Pity, Inc. Reprinted by permission of Alfred A. Knopf, a Division of Random House, Inc.

"A Temporary Matter" from *Interpreter of Maladies* by Jhumpa Lahiri. Copyright © 1999 by Jhumpa Lahiri. Reprinted by permission of Houghton Mifflin Co. All rights reserved.

"Separating" from *Problems and Other Stories* by John Updike. Copyright © 1979 by John Updike. Reprinted by permission of Alfred A. Knopf, a Division of Random House, Inc.

"The Children Stay" from *The Love of a Good Woman* by Alice Munro. Copyright © 1998 by Alice Munro. Reprinted by permission of Alfred A. Knopf, a Division of Random House, Inc.